THE

MANCHESTE

BY

MRS. G. LINNÆUS BANKS,

Author of "God's Providence House," "Bond Slaves," "Glory," "In His Own Hand,"

&c., &c.

Illustrated by Charles Green and Hedley Fitton.

Book originally published in 1896 by
Able Heywood & Sons, Manchester

This edition reprinted:
1991; 1992; 1996; 1997; 1998; 2001.

Reprint organised by

Cliff Hayes

ISBN: 1 899181 80 6

Printed and bound by MFP Design & Print,
Longford Trading Estate, Thomas Street, Stretford,
Manchester M32 0JT - Tel: 0161 864 4540

Front cover illustration: *The Rescue* by Charles Green

New Edition Introduction

Many years ago, just after moving to Manchester my wife gave me a book to read. Even though there were over 300 pages in small type, which made the book hard to read, I enjoyed 'The Manchester Man'.

This was my introduction to a book that has entertained and enriched its readers since it was first published in 1876.

Because second hand copies are hard to find, and because it has not been available as a new book for a few years, Printwise Publications decided to look into the possibility of reprinting this much sought after book.

After much searching of bookshops for an earlier edtion of this book I was offered a copy by Tony Gibb of Gibb's Bookshop – a rare illustrated copy printed in 1896 that he had just acquired. It was excellent, the large type and fine illustrations made this copy ideal for reproduction.

I hope readers will enjoy this classic book with its marvellous illustrations that bring to life the rich story that is 'The Manchester Man'.

Cliff Hayes

This edition is dedicated to
David Hayes (1973 - 88)

Mrs Linnaeus Banks

CONTENTS.

INDEX TO ILLUSTRATIONS.

PORTRAITS.

(DRAWN BY HEDLEY FITTON.)

FULL PAGE ILLUSTRATIONS.

INITIALS.

Index to Illustrations—*Continued.*

MAPS.

THE MANCHESTER MAN.

CHAPTER THE FIRST.

THE FLOOD.

AN ARK OF SAFETY.

WHEN Pliny lost his life, and Herculaneum was buried, Manchester was born. Whilst lava and ashes blotted from sight and memory fair and luxurious Roman cities close to the Capitol, the Roman soldiery of Titus, under their general Agricola, laid the foundations of a distant city which now competes with the great cities of the world. Where now rise forests of tall chimneys, and the hum of whirling spindles, spread the dense woods of Arden; and from the clearing in their midst rose the Roman castrum of Mamutium,* which has left its name of Castle Field as a memorial to us. But where their summer camp is said to have been pitched, on the airy rock at the confluence of the rivers Irk and Irwell, sacred church and peaceful college have stood for centuries, and only antiquaries can point to Roman possession, or even to the baronial hall which the Saxon lord perched there for security.

And only an antiquary or a very old inhabitant can recall Manchester as it was at the close of the last century; and shutting his eyes upon railway-arch, station, and esplanade, upon Palatine buildings, broad roadways, and river embankments, can see the Irk and the Irwell as they were when the Cathedral

* Prior to the close of the Fourteenth Century, Manchester was written Mamecester.

was the Collegiate Church, with a diminutive brick wall three parts round its ancient graveyard. Then the irregular-fronted rows of quaint old houses which still, under the name of Half Street, crowd upon two sides of the churchyard, with only an intervening strip of a flagged walk between, closed it up on a third side, and shut the river (lying low beneath) from the view, with a huddled mass of still older dwellings, some of which were thrust out of sight, and were only to be reached by flights of break-neck steps of rock or stone, and like their hoary fellows creeping down the narrow roadway of Hunt's Bank, overhung the Irwell, and threatened to topple into it some day.

The Chetham Hospital or College still looks solidly down on the Irk at the angle of the streams; the old Grammar School has been suffered to do the same; and—thanks to the honest workmen who built for our ancestors—the long lines of houses known as Long Millgate are for the most part standing, and on the river side have resisted the frequent floods of centuries.

In 1799 that line was almost unbroken, from the College (where it commenced at Hunt's Bank Bridge) to Red Bank. The short alley by the Town Mill, called Mill Brow, which led down to the wooden Mill Bridge, was little more of a gap than those narrow entries or passages which pierced the walls like slits here and there, and offered dark and perilous passage to courts and alleys, trending in steep incline to the very bed of the Irk. The houses themselves had been good originally, and were thus cramped together for defence in perilous times, when experience taught that a narrow gorge was easier held against warlike odds than an open roadway.

Ducie Bridge had then no existence, but Tanners' Bridge—no doubt a strong wooden structure like that at Mill Brow—accessible from the street only by one of those narrow steep passages, stood within a few yards of its site, and had a place on old maps so far back as 1650. Its name is expressive, and goes to prove that the tannery on the rocky banks of the Irk,

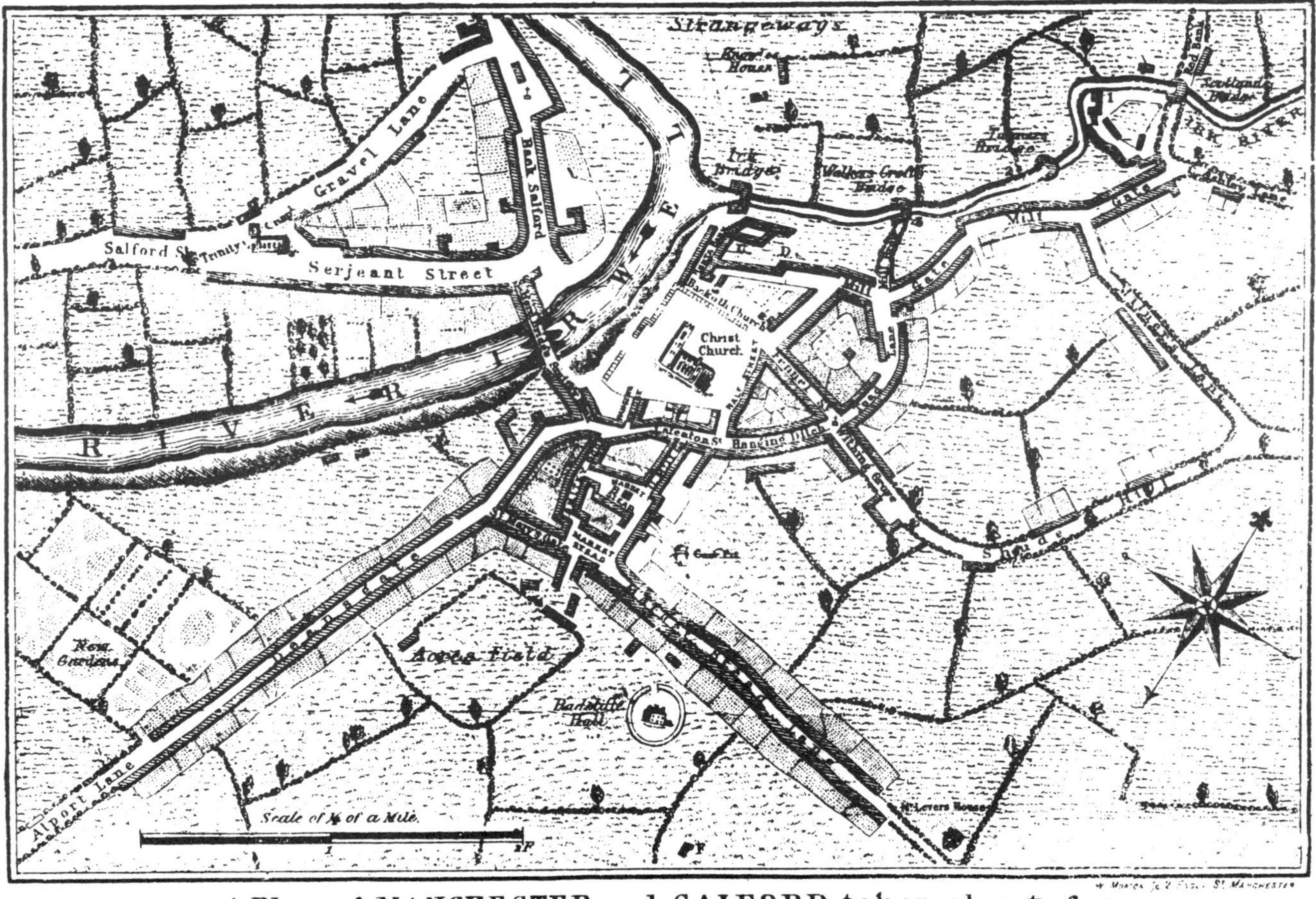

A Plan of **MANCHESTER** and **SALFORD** taken about 1650

behind the houses of Long Millgate, then opposite to the end of Miller's Lane, was a tannery at least a century and a half before old Simon Clegg worked amongst the tan-pits, and called William Clough master.

To this sinuous and picturesque line of houses, the streams, with their rocky and precipitous banks, will have served in olden times as a natural defensive moat (indeed, it is noticeable that old Manchester kept pretty much within the angle of its rivers), and in 1799, from one end of Millgate to the other, the dwellers by the waterside looked across the stream on green and undulating uplands, intersected by luxuriant hedgerows, a bleachery at Walker's Croft, and a short terrace of houses near Scotland Bridge, denominated Scotland, being the sole breaks in the verdure.

Between the tannery and Scotland Bridge the river makes a sharp bend; and here, at the elbow, another mill, with its corresponding dam, was situated. The current of the Irk, if not deep, is strong at all times, though kept by its high banks within narrow compass. But when, as is not unseldom the case, there is a sudden flushing of water from the hill-country, it rises, rises, rises, stealthily, though swiftly, till the stream overtops its banks, washes over low-lying bleach-crofts, fields, and gardens, mounts foot by foot over the fertile slopes, invades the houses, and, like a mountain-robber sweeping from his fastness on a peaceful vale, carries his spoil with him, and leaves desolation and wailing behind.

Such a flood as this, following a heavy thunder-storm, devastated the valley of the Irk, on the 17th of August, 1799.

Well was it then for the tannery and those houses on the bank of the Irk which had their foundations in the solid rock, for the waters surged and roared at their base and over pleasant meadows—a widespread turbulent sea, with here and there an island of refuge, which the day before had been a lofty mound.

The flood of the previous Autumn, when a coach and horses

had been swept down the Irwell, and men and women were drowned, was as nothing to this. The tannery yard, high as it was above the bed of the Irk, and solid as was its embankment, was threatened with invasion. The surging water roared and beat against its masonry, and licked its coping with frothy tongue and lip, like a hungry giant, greedy for fresh food. Men with thick clogs and hide-bound legs, leather gloves and aprons, were hurrying to and fro with barrows and bark-boxes for the reception of the valuable hides which their mates, armed with long-shafted hooks and tongs, were dragging from the pits pell-mell, ere the advancing waters should encroach upon their territory, and empty the tan-pits for them.

Already the insatiate flood bore testimony to its ruthless greed. Hanks of yarn, pieces of calico, hay, uptorn bushes, planks, chairs, boxes, dog-kennels, and hen-coops, a shattered chest of drawers, pots and pans, had swept past, swirling and eddying in the flood, which by this time spread like a vast lake over the opposite lands, and had risen within three feet of the arch of Scotland Bridge, and hardly left a trace where the mill-dam chafed it commonly.

Too busy were the tanners, under the eye of their master, to stretch out hand or hook to arrest the progress of either furniture or live stock, though bee-hives and hen-coops, and more than one squealing pig, went racing with the current, now rising towards the footway of Tanners' Bridge.

Every window of every house upon the lower banks was crowded with anxious heads, for flooded Scotland rose like an island from the watery waste, and their own cellars were fast filling. There had been voices calling to each other from window to window all the morning; but now from window to window, from house to house, rang one reduplicated shriek, which caused many of the busy tanners to quit their work, and rush to the water's edge. To their horror, a painted wooden cradle, which had crossed the deeply-submerged dam in safety, was floating foot-foremost down to destruction, with an infant calmly sleeping in its bed; the very motion of the waters having seemingly lulled it to sounder repose!

"Good Lord! It's a choilt!" exclaimed Simon Clegg, the eldest tanner in the yard. "Lend a hand here, fur the sake o' th' childer at whoam.'

Half a dozen hooks and plungers were outstretched, even while he spoke; but the longest was lamentably too short to arrest the approaching cradle in its course, and the unconscious babe seemed doomed. With frantic haste Simon Clegg rushed on to Tanners' Bridge, followed by a boy; and there, with hook and plunger, they met the cradle as it drifted towards them, afraid of over-balancing it even in their attempt to save. It swerved, and almost upset; but Simon dexterously caught his hook within the wooden hood, and drew the frail bark and its living freight close to the bridge. The boy, and a man named Cooper, lying flat on the bridge, then clutched at it with extended hands, raised it carefully from the turbid water, and drew it safely between the open rails to the footway, amidst the shouts and hurrahs of breathless and excited spectators.

The babe was screaming terribly. The shock when the first hook stopped the progress of the cradle had disturbed its dreams, and its little fat arms were stretched out piteously as strange faces looked down upon it instead of the mother's familiar countenance. Wrapping the patchwork quilt around it, to keep it from contact with his wet sleeves and apron, Simon, tenderly as a woman, lifted the infant in his rough arms, and strove to comfort it, but in vain. His beard of three days growth was as a rasp to its soft skin, and the closer he caressed, the more it screamed. The men from the tannery came crowding round him.

"What dost ta mean to do wi' th' babby?" asked the man Cooper of old Simon. "Aw'd tak' it whoam to my missis, but th' owd lass is nowt to be takken to, an' wur as cross as two sticks when oi only axed fur mi baggin* to bring to wark wi'

* Food for a meal, so called from the bag in which it was carried.

THE RESCUE.

mi this mornin'," added he, with rueful remembrance of the scolding wife on his hearth.

"Neay, lad, aw'l not trust th' poor choilt to thy Sally. It 'ud be loike chuckin' it out o' th' wayter into th' fire (Hush-a-by, babby). Aw'll just tak it to ar' Bess, and hoo'll cuddle it up and gi' it summat to sup, till we find its own mammy," answered Simon, leaving the bridge. "Bring the kayther† alung, Jack," (to the boy) "Bess'll want it. We'n noan o' that tackle at ar place. Hush-a-by, hush-a-by, babby."

But the little thing, missing its natural protector, and half stifled in the swathing quilt, only screamed the louder; and Simon, notwithstanding his kind heart, was truly glad when his daughter Bess, who had witnessed the rescue from their own window, met him at the tannery gate, and relieved him of his struggling charge.

"Si thi, Bess! here's a God-send fur thi—a poor little babby fur thee to tend an' be koind to, till them it belungs to come a-seekin' fur it," said he to the young woman; "but thah mun give it summat better than cowd wayter—it's had too mich o' that a'ready."

"That aw will, poor darlin'!" responded she, kissing the babe's velvet cheeks as, sensible of a change of nurses, it nestled to her breast. "Eh! but there'll be sore hearts for this blessed babby, somewheere." And she turned up the narrow passage which led at once from the tan-yard and the bridge, stilling and soothing the little castaway as adroitly as an experienced nurse.

"Neaw, luk thi, lad," Simon remarked to Cooper; "is na it fair wonderful heaw that babby taks to ar Bess? But it's just a way hoo has, an' theere is na a fractious choilt i' a' ar yard but'll be quiet wi' Bess."

Cooper looked after her, nodded an assent, and sighed, as if he wished some one in another yard had the same soothing way with her.

† Cradle.

But the voice of the raging water had not stilled like that of the rescued infant. Back went the two men to their task, and worked away with a will to carry hides, bark, and implements to places of security. And as they hurried to and fro with loads on back or barrow, up, up, inch by inch, foot by foot, the swelling flood rose still higher, till, lapping the foot-bridge, curling over the embankment, it drove the sturdy tanners back, flung itself into the pits, and, in many a swirling eddy, washed tan and hair and skins into the common current.

Not so much, however, went into its seething caldron as might have been, had the men worked with less vigour; and, quick to recognise the value of ready service, Mr. Clough led his drenched and weary workmen to the "Skinners' Arms," in Long Millgate, and ordered a supply of ale and bread and cheese to be served out to them.

At the door of the public-house, where he left the workmen to the enjoyment of this impromptu feast, he encountered Simon Clegg. The kind fellow had taken a hasty run to his own tenement, "just to see heaw ar Bess an' th' babby get on;" and he brought back the intelligence that it was "a lad, an' as good as goold."

"Oh, my man, I've been too much occupied to speak to you before," cried Mr. Clough. "I saw you foremost in the rescue of that unfortunate infant, and shall not forget it. Here is a crown for your share in the good deed. I suppose that was the child's mother you gave it to?"

Simon was a little man, but he drew back with considerable native dignity.

"Thenk yo', measter, all th' same, but aw connot tak' brass fur just doin' my duty. Aw'd never ha' slept i' my bed gin that little un had bin dreawned, an' me lookin' on loike a stump. Neay; that lass wur Bess, moi wench. We'n no notion wheere th' lad's mother is."

Mr. Clough would have pressed the money upon him, but he put it back with a motion of his hand.

"No, sir; aw'm a poor mon, a varry poor man, but aw

connot tak' money fur savin' a choilt's life. It's agen' ma conscience. I'll tak' mi' share o' the bread an' cheese, an' drink yo'r health i' a sup o' ale, but aw cudna' tak' that brass if aw wur deein'."

And Simon, giving a scrape with his clog, and a duck of his head, meant for a bow, passed his master respectfully, and went clattering up the steps of the "Skinners' Arms," leaving the gentleman standing there, and looking after him in mingled astonishment and admiration.

CHAPTER THE SECOND.

NO ONE KNOWS.

WHEN the scurrying water, thick with sand and mud, and discoloured with dye stuffs, which floated in brightly-tinted patches on its surface, filled the arch of Scotland Bridge, and left only the rails of Tanners' Bridge visible, the inundation reached its climax; but a couple of days elapsed before the flood subsided below the level of the unprotected tannery-yard, and until then neither Simon Clegg nor his mates could resume their occupations.

There was a good deal of lounging about Long Millgate and the doors of the "Queen Anne" and "Skinners' Arms" of heavily shod men, in rough garniture of thick hide—armoury against the tan and water in which their daily bread was steeped.

But in all those two days no anxious father, no white-faced mother, had run from street to street, and house to house, to seek and claim a rescued living child. No, not even when the week had passed, though the story of his "miraculous preservation" was the theme of conversation at the tea-tables of gentility and in the bar-parlours of taverns; was the gossip of courts and alleys, highways and byways; and though echo, in the guise of a "flying stationer," caught it up and spread it broadcast in catchpenny sheets, far beyond the confines of the inundation.

This was the more surprising as no dead bodies had been washed down the river, and no lives were reported "lost." Had the child no one to care for it?—no relative to whom its little life was precious? Had it been abandoned to its fate, a waif unloved, uncared for?

The house in which Simon Clegg lived was situated at the very end of Skinners' Yard, a *cul-de-sac*, to which the only approach was a dark, covered entry, not four feet wide. The pavement of the yard was natural rock, originally hewn into broad flat steps, but then worn with water from the skies, and from house-wifely pails, and the tramp of countless clogs, to a rugged steep incline, asking wary stepping from the stranger on exploration after nightfall. Gas was, of course, unknown, but not even an oil-lamp lit up the gloom.

In the sunken basement a tripe-boiler had a number of stone troughs or cisterns, for keeping his commodities cool for sale. The three rooms of Simon Clegg were situated immediately above these, two small bed-rooms overlooking the river and pleasant green fields beyond; the wide kitchen window having no broader range of prospect than the dreary and not too savoury yard. Even this view was shut out by a batting frame, resembling much a long, narrow French bedstead, all the more that on its canvas surface was laid a thick bed of raw (that is, undressed) cotton, freckled with seeds and fine bits of husky pod. Bess was a batter, and her business was to turn and beat the clotted mass with stout lithe arms and willow-wands, until the fibres loosened, the seeds and specks fell through, and a billowy mass of whitish down lay before her. It was not a healthy occupation: dust and flue released found their way into the lungs, as well as on to the floor and furniture; and a rosy-cheeked batter was a myth. Machinery does the work now—but this history deals with *then!*

During the week dust lay thick on everything; even Bessy's hair was fluffy as a bursting cotton pod, in spite of the kerchief tied across it; but on the Saturday, when she had carried her work to Simpson's factory in Miller's Lane, and came back with her wages, broom and duster cleared away the film; wax and brush polished up the old bureau, the pride and glory of their kitchen; the two slim iron candlesticks, fender and poker, were burnished bright as steel; the three-legged round deal table was scrubbed white; and then, mounted on tall pattens, she set about with mop and pail, and a long-handled stone, to cleanse the flag floor from the week's impurities.

She had had a good mother, and, to the best of her ability, Bess tried to follow in her footsteps, and fill the vacant place on her father's hearth, and in his heart. Her mother had been dead four years, and Bess, now close upon twenty, had since then lost two brothers, and lamented as lost one dearer than a brother—the two former by death, the other by the fierce demands of war. She had a pale, interesting face, with dark hair and thoughtful, deep grey eyes, and was, if anything, too quiet and staid for her years; but when her face lit up she had as pleasant a smile upon it as one would wish to see by one's fireside, and not even her dialect could make her voice otherwise than low and gentle.

Both her brothers had been considerably younger than herself; and possibly the fact of having stood *in loco parentis* to them for upwards of two years had imparted to her the air of motherliness she possessed. Certain it is that if a child in the yard scalded itself, or cut a finger, or knocked the bark off an angular limb, it went crying to Bessy Clegg in preference to its own mother; and she healed bruises and quarrels with the same balsam—loving sympathy. She was just the one to open her arms and heart to a poor motherless babe, and Simon Clegg knew it.

Old Simon, or old Clegg, he was called, probably because he was graver and more serious than his fellows, and had never changed his master since he grew to manhood; certainly not on account of his age, which trembled on the verge of fifty, only. He was a short, somewhat spare man, with a face deeply lined by sorrow for the loved ones he had lost. But he had a merry twinkling eye, and was not without a latent vein of humour. The atmosphere of the tannery might have shrivelled his skin, but it had not withered his heart; and when he handed the child he had saved to his daughter, he never stopped to calculate contingencies.

The boy, apparently between two and three months' old, was dressed in a long gown of printed linen, had a muslin cap, and an under one of flannel, all neatly made, but neither in make nor material beyond those of a respectable working-man's child; and there was not a mark upon anything which could give a clue to its parentage.

The painted wooden cradle, which had been to it an ark of safety, was placed in a corner by the fireplace; and an old bottle, filled with thin gruel, over the neck of which Bess had tied a loose cap of punctured wash-leather, was so adjusted that the little one, deprived of its mother, could lie within and feed itself whilst Bess industriously pursued her avocations.

These were not times for idleness. There had been bread riots the previous winter; food still was at famine prices; and it was all a poor man could do, with the strictest industry and economy, to obtain a bare subsistence. So Bess worked away all the harder, because there were times when babydom was imperative, and would be nursed.

She had put the last garnishing touches to her kitchen on Saturday night, had taken off her wrapper-brat,† put on a clean blue bedgown,* and substituted a white linen cap for the coloured kerchief, when her father, who had been to New Cross Market to make his bargains by himself on this occasion, came into the kitchen, followed by Cooper, who having helped to save the child, naturally felt an interest in him.

The iron porridge-pot was on the low fire, and Bess, sifting the oatmeal into the boiling water with the left hand, whilst with the other she beat it swiftly with her porridge-stick, was so intent on the preparation of their supper, she did not notice their entrance until her father, putting his coarse wicker market-basket down on her white table, bade Cooper "Coom in an' tak' a cheer."

Instead of taking a chair, the man walked as quietly as his clogs would let him to the cradle, and looked down on the infant sucking vigorously at the delusive bottle. Matt Cooper was the *un*happy father of eight, whose maintenance was a sore perplexity to him; and it may be supposed he spoke with authority when he exclaimed—

"Whoy, he tak's t' th' pap-bottle as nat'rally as if he'n ne'er had nowt else!"

* A short loose jacket. † A sort of close pinafore.

And the big man—quite a contrast to Simon—stooped and lifted the babe from the cradle with all the ease of long practice, and dandled it in his arms, saying as he did so,

"Let's hev a look at th' little chap. Aw've not seen the colour o' his eyen yet."

The eyes were grey, so dark they might have passed for black; and there was in them more than the ordinary inquiring gaze of babyhood.

"Well, thah'rt a pratty lad; but had thah bin th' fowest† i' o' Lankisheer, aw'd a-thowt thi mammy'd ha' speered‡ fur thi afore this," added he, sitting down, and nodding to the child, which crowed in his face.

"Ah! one would ha' reckoned so," assented Bess, without turning round.

"What ar' ta gooin' to do, Simon, toward fandin' th' choilt's kin?" next questioned their visitor.

Simon looked puzzled.

"Whoy, aw've hardly gi'en it a thowt."

But the question, once started, was discussed at some length. Meanwhile the porridge destined for two Bess poured into three bowls, placing three iron spoons beside them with no more ceremony than, "Ye'll tak' a sup wi' us, Mat."

Mat apologised, feeling quite assured there was no more than the two could have eaten; but Simon looked hurt, and the porridge was appetising to a hungry man; so he handed the baby to the young woman, took up his spoon, and the broken thread of conversation was renewed at intervals. What they said matters not so much as what they did.

The next morning being Sunday, Cooper called for Clegg just as the bells were ringing for church; and the two, arrayed in their best fustian breeches, long-tailed, deep-cuffed coats, knitted hose, three-cornered hats, and shoes, only kept for Sunday wear, set out to seek the parents of the unclaimed infant, nothing doubting that they were going to carry solace to

† Ugliest. ‡ Inquired.

sorrowing hearts.

Their course lay in the same track as the Irk, now pursuing its course as smilingly under the bright August sun as though its banks were not strewed with wreck, and foul with thick offensive mud, and the woeful devastations were none of its doing. There were fewer houses on their route than now, and they kept closely as possible to the course of the river, questioning the various inhabitants as they went along. They had gone through Collyhurst and Blakely without rousing anyone to a thought beyond self-sustained damage, or gaining a single item of intelligence, though they made many a detour in quest of it. At a roadside public-house close to Middleton they sat down parched with heat and thirst, called for a mug of ale each, drew from their pockets thick hunks of brown bread and cheese, wrapped in blue and white check handkerchiefs, and whilst satisfying their hunger came to the conclusion that no cradle could have drifted safely so far, crossing weirs and mill dams, amongst uprooted bushes, timber, and household chattels, and that it was best to turn back.

In Smedley Vale, where the flood seemed to have done its worst, and where a small cottage close to the river lay in ruins, a knot of people were gathered together talking and gesticulating as if in eager controversy. As they approached, they were spied by one of the group.

"Here are th' chaps as fund th' babby, an' want'n to know who it belungs to," cried he, a youth whom they had interrogated early in the day.

To tell in brief what Simon and his companion learned by slow degrees—the hapless child was alone in the world, orphaned by a succession of misfortunes. The dilapidated cottage had been for some fifteen months the home of its parents. The father, who was understood to have come from Crumpsall with his young wife and her aged mother, had been summoned to attend the death-bed of a brother in Liverpool, and had never been heard of since. The alarm and trouble consequent upon his prolonged absence prostrated the young wife, and caused not only the babe's premature birth, but the mother's death. The care of the child had devolved upon the stricken grandmother, who had brought him up by hand, as Matthew's sagacity had suggested. She was a woman far advanced in years, and feeble, but she asked no help from neighbours or parish, though her poverty was apparent. She kept poultry and knitted stockings, and managed to eke out a living somehow, but how, none of those scattered neighbours seemed to know—she had "held her yead so hoigh" (pursued her way so quietly).

She had been out in her garden feeding her fowls when the flood came upon them without warning, swept through the open doors of the cottage, and carried cradle and everything else before it, leaving hardly a wall standing. In endeavouring to save the child she herself got seriously hurt, and was with difficulty rescued. But between grief and fright, bruises and the drenching, the old dame succumbed, and died on the Thursday morning, and had been buried by the parish—from which in life she had proudly kept aloof—that very afternoon, and no one could tell other name she had borne than Nan.

Bess sobbed aloud when she heard her father's recital, which lost nothing of its pathos from the homely vernacular in which it was couched.

"An' what's to be done neaw?" asked Cooper, as he sat on one of the rush-bottomed chairs, sucking the knob of his walking stick, as if for an inspiration. "Yo canno' think o' keeping th' choilt, an' bread an' meal at sich a proice!"

"Connot oi? Then aw conno' think o' aught else. Wouldst ha' me chuck it i' th' river agen? What does thah say, Bess?" turning to his daughter, who had the child on her lap.

"Whoi, th' poor little lad's got noather feyther nor mother, an' thah's lost boath o' thi lads. Mebbe it's a Godsend, feyther, after o', as yo said'n to me," and she kissed it tenderly.

"Eh, wench!" interposed Matthew, but she went on without heeding him.

"There's babby clooas laid by i' lavender i' thoase drawers as hasna seen dayleet sin ar Joe wur a toddler, an' they'll just come handy. An' if bread's dear, an' meal's dear, we mun just ate less on it arsels, an' there'll be moore fur the choilt. He'll pay yo back, feyther, aw know, when yo're too owd to wark."

"An' aw con do 'bout 'bacca, lass. If the orphan's granny wur too preawd to ax help o' th' parish, aw'll be too preawd to send her pratty grandchoilt theer."

And so, to Matthew Cooper's amazement, it was settled. But the extra labour and self-denial it involved on the part of Bess, neither Matthew nor Simon could estimate.

In the midst of the rabid scepticism and Republicanism of the period, Simon Clegg was a staunch "Church and King" man, and, as a natural consequence, a stout upholder of their ordinances. Regularly as the bell tolled in for Sunday morning service, he might be seen walking reverently down the aisle of the old church, to his place in the free seats, with his neat, cheerful-looking daughter following him sometimes, but not always —so regularly that the stout beadle missed him from his seat the Sunday after the inundation, and meeting him in the churchyard a week later, sought to learn the why and wherefore.

The beadle of the parish church was an important personage in the eyes of Simon Clegg; and, somewhat proud of his notice, the little tanner related the incidents of that memorable flood-week to his querist, concluding with his adoption of the child.

The official h'md and ha'd, applauded the act, but shook his powdered head, and added, sagely, that it was a "greeat charge, a varry greeat charge."

"Dun yo' think th' little un's bin babtised?" interrogated the beadle.

"Aw conno' tell; nob'dy couldn't tell nowt abeawt th' choilt, 'ut wur ony use to onybody. Bess an' me han talked it ower, an' we wur thinkin' o' bringin' it to be kirsened, to be on th' safe soide loike. Aw reckon it wouldna do th' choilt ony harm

THE OLD CHURCH, FROM NORTH-EAST.

to be kirsened twoice ower; an' 'twoud be loike flingin' th' choilt's soul to Owd Scrat gin he wur no kirsened at o'. What dun yo' thinken'?"

The beadle thought pretty much the same as Simon, and it was finally arranged that Simon should present the young foundling for baptism in the course of the week.

CHAPTER THE THIRD.

HOW THE REV. JOSHUA BROOKES AND SIMON CLEGG INTERPRETED A SHAKESPERIAN TEXT.

MANCHESTER had at that date two eccentric clergymen attached to the Collegiate Church. The one, Parson Gatliffe, a fine man, a polished gentleman, an eloquent preacher, but a *bon vivant* of whom many odd stories are told. The other, the Reverend Joshua Brookes, a short, stumpy man (so like to the old knave of clubs in mourning that the sobriquet of the "Knave of Clubs" stuck to him), was a rough, crusted, unpolished black-diamond, hasty in temper, harsh in tone, blunt in speech and in the pulpit, but with a true heart beating under the angular external crystals; and he was a good liver of another sort than his colleague.

He was the son of a crippled and not too sober shoemaker, who, when the boy's intense desire for learning had attracted the attention and patronage of Parson Ainscough, went to the homes of several of the wealthy denizens of the town, to ask for pecuniary aid to send his son Joshua to college. The youth's scholarly attainments had already obtained him an exhibition at the Free Grammar School, which, coupled with the donations obtained by his father and the helping hand of Parson Ainscough, enabled him to keep his terms and to graduate at Brazenose, to become a master in the grammar school in which he had been taught, and a chaplain in the Collegiate Church.

So conscientious was he in the performance of his sacred duties that, albeit he was wont to exercise his calling after a peculiarly rough fashion of his own, he married, christened, buried more people during his ministry than all the other ecclesiastics put together.

It was to this Joshua Brookes (few ever thought of prefixing the "Reverend" in referring to him) that Simon Clegg brought "Nan's" orphan grandchild to be baptised on Tuesday, the 7th of September, just three weeks from the date of his involuntary voyage down the flooded Irk.

REV. JOSHUA BROOKES, M.A.

From a Woodbury-type Photograph by Brothers.

It had taken the tanner the whole of the week following his conversation with the beadle to determine the name he should give the child, and many had been his consultations with Bess on the subject. That very Sunday he had gone home from church full of the matter, and lifting his big old Bible from its post of honour on the top of the bureau (it was his whole library), he sat, after dinner, with his head in his hands and his elbows on the table, debating the momentous question.

"Yo' see, Bess," said he, "a neame as sticks to one all one's loife, is noan so sma' a matter as some folk reckon. An' yon's noan a common choilt. It is na every day, no, nor every year, that a choilt is weshed down a river in a kayther, and saved from th' very jaws of deeath. An' aw'd loike to gi'e un a neame as 'ud mak' it remember it, an' thenk God for his mercifu' preservation a' th' days o' his loife."

After a long pause, during which Bess took the baby from the cradle, tucked a napkin under its chin, and began to feed it with a spoon, he resumed—

"Yo' see, Bess, hadna aw bin kirsened Simon, aw moight ha' bin a cobbler, or a whitster,† or a wayver, or owt else. But feyther could read tho' he couldna wroite; an' as he wur a reed-makker, he towt mi moi A B C wi' crookin' up th' bits o' wires he couldna use into th' shaps o' th' letters; an' when aw could spell sma' words gradely*, he towt me to read out o' this varry book; an aw read o' Simon, a tanner, an' nowt 'ud sarve mi but aw mun be a tanner too; so tha sees theer's summat i' a neame after o'."

Bess suggested that he should be called Noah, because Noah was saved in the ark; but he objected that Noah was an old greybeard, with a family, and that he knew the flood was coming, and built the ark himself; he was "not takken unawares in his helplessness loike that poor babby."

Moses was her next proposition—Bess had learned something of Biblical lore at the first Sunday school Manchester could

† Bleacher. * Properly.

boast, the one in Gun Street, founded by Simeon Newton in 1788—but Simon was not satisfied even with Moses.

"Yo' see, Moses wur put in' th' ark o' bulrushes o' purpose, an' noather thee nor mi's a Pharaoh's dowter, an' th' little chap's not loike to be browt oop i' a pallis."

Towards the end of the week he burst into the room; "Oi hev it, lass, oi hev it! We'n co' the lad 'Irk'; nob'dy'll hev a neame loike that, an' it'll tell its own story; an' fur th' afterneame, aw reckon he mun tak' ours."

Marriages were solemnized in the richly-carved choir of the venerable old Church, but churchings and baptisms in a large adjoining chapel; and thither Bess, who carried the baby, was ushered, followed by Simon and Matt Cooper, who were to act as its other sponsors.

At the door they made way for the entrance of a party of ladies, whom they had seen alight from sedan-chairs at the upper gate, where a couple of gentlemen joined them. A nurse followed, with a baby, whose christening robe, nearly two yards long, was a mass of rich embroidery. The mother herself,—a slight, lovely creature, additionally pale and delicate from her late ordeal—wore a long, plain-skirted dress of vari-coloured brocaded silk. A lustrous silk scarf, trimmed with costly lace, enveloped her shoulders. Her head-dress, a bonnet with a bag-crown and Quakerish poke-brim, was of the newest fashion, as were the long kid gloves which covered her arms to the elbows.

The party stepped forward as though precedence was theirs of right even at the church door, heeding not Simon's mannerly withdrawal to let them pass; and the very nurse looked disdainfully at the calico gown of the baby in the round arms of Bess, a woman in a grey duffle cloak and old-fashioned flat, broad-brimmed hat, tied down over the ears.

Is there any thrill, sympathetic or antagonistic, in baby-veins, as they thus meet there for the first time on their entrance into the church and the broad path of life? For the first time—but scarcely for the last.

Already a goodly crowd of mothers, babies, godfathers and godmothers had assembled—a crowd of all grades, judging from their exteriors, for dress had not then ceased to be a criterion; and all ceremonies of this kind were performed in shoals—not singly.

The Rev. Joshua Brookes, followed by his clerk, came through the door in the carven screen, between the choir and baptismal chapel, and took his place behind the altar rails. And now ensued a scene which some of my readers may think incredible, but which was common enough then, and there, and is notoriously true. The width of the altar could scarcely accommodate the number of women waiting to be churched; and the impatient Joshua assisted the apparitors to marshal them to their places, with a sharp "You come here! You kneel there! Yon woman's not paid!" accompanied by pulls and pushes, until the semi-circle was filled.

But still the shrinking lady, and another, unused to jostle with rough crowds, were left standing outside the pale.

Impetuous Joshua had begun the service before all were settled. "Forasmuch as it hath pleased——"

His quick eye caught the outstanding figures. Abruptly stopping his exordium, he exclaimed, in his harsh tones, which seemed to intimidate the lady,

"What are you standing there for? Can't you find a place? Make room here!" (pushing two women apart by the shoulder), "thrutch up closer there! Make haste, and kneel here!" (to the lady, pulling her forward). "You come here; make room, will you?" and having pulled and pushed them into place, he resumed the service.

Presently there was another outburst. There had been a hushing of whimpering babies, and a maternal smothering of infantile cries, as a chorus throughout; but one fractious little one screamed right out, and refused to be comforted. The nervous tremor on that kneeling lady's countenance might have told to whom it belonged, had Joshua been a skilful reader of hearts and faces. His irritable temper got the better of him.

He broke off in the midst of the psalm to call out, "Stop that crying child!" The crying child did not stop. In the midst of another verse he bawled, "Give that screaming babby the breast!" He went on. The clerk had pronounced the "Amen" at the end of the psalm; the chaplain followed, "Let us pray;" but before he began the prayer, he again shouted, "Take that squalling babby out!"—an order the indignant nurse precipitately obeyed; and the service ended without further interruption.

Then followed the christenings, and another marshalling (this time of godfathers and godmothers, with the infants they presented), in which the hasty chaplain did his part with hands and voice until all were arranged to his satisfaction.

It so happened that the tanner's group and the lady's group were ranked side by side. The latter was Mrs. Aspinall, the wife of a wealthy cotton merchant, who, with two other gentlemen and a lady, stood behind her, and this time gave her their much-needed support. Indeed, what with the damp and chillness of the church, and the agitation, the delicate lady appeared ready to faint.

"Hath this child been already baptized or no?" asked Joshua Brookes, and was passing on, when Simon's unexpected response arrested him.

"Aw dunnot know."

"Don't know? How's that? What are you here for?" were questions huddled one on the other, in a broader vernacular than I have thought well to put in the mouth of a man so deeply learned.

"Whoi, yo' see, this is the choilt as wur weshed deawn th' river wi' th' flood in a kayther; an' o' belungin' th' lad are deead, an' aw mun kirsen him to mak' o' sure."

Joshua listened with more patience than might have been expected from him, and passed on with a mere "Humph!" to ask the same question from each in succession before proceeding with the general service. At length he came to the naming of several infants.

"Henrietta Burdelia Fitzbourne" was given as the proposed

name of a girl of middle-class parents.

"*Mary*, I baptise thee," &c., he calmly proceeded, handed the baby back to the astonished godmother, and passed to the next, regardless of appeal.

Mrs. Aspinall's boy took his name of Laurence with a noisy protest against the sprinkling. Nor was the foundling silent when, having been duly informed that the boy's name was to be "*Irk*," self-willed Joshua deliberately, and with scarcely a visible pause, went on—

"*Jabez*, I baptise thee in the name," &c., and so overturned, at one fell swoop, all Simon's carefully-constructed castle.

Simon attempted to remonstrate, but Joshua Brookes had another infant in his arms, and was deaf to all but his own business. Such a substitution of names was too common a practice of his to disturb him in the least. But Simon had a brave spirit, and stood no more in awe of Joshua Brookes—"Jotty" as he was called—than of another man. When the others had gone in a crowd to the vestry to register the baptisms, he stopped to confront the parson as he left the altar.

"What roight had yo' to change the neame aw chuse to gi'e that choilt?"

"What right had yo' to saddle the poor lad with an *Irksome* name like that?" was the quick rejoinder.

"Roight! why, aw wanted to gi'e th' lad a neame as should mak' him thankful for bein' saved from dreawndin' to the last deays o' his loife."

"An *Irksome* name like that would have made him the butt of every little imp in the gutters, until he'd have been ready to drown himself to get rid of it. Jabez is an honourable name, man. You go home, and look through your Bible till you find it."

Simon was open to conviction; his bright eyes twinkled as a new light dawned upon them.

The gruff chaplain had brushed past him on his way to the robing-room; but he turned back, with his right hand in his breeches pocket, and put a seven-shilling piece in the palm of the tanner, saying:

"Here's something towards the christening feast of th' little chap I've stood godfather to. And don't you forget to look in 'Chronicles' for Jabez; and, above all, see that the lad doesn't disgrace his name."

Joshua Brookes had the character, among those who knew him *least*, of loving money overmuch, and this unwonted exhibition of generosity took Simon's breath.

The chaplain was gone before he recovered from his amazement—gone, with a tender heart softened towards the fatherless child thrown upon the world, his cynicism rebuked by the true charity of the poor tanner, who had taken the foundling to his home in a season of woeful dearth.

And, to his credit be it said, the Rev. Joshua Brookes never lost sight of either Simon or little Jabez. He was wont to throw out words which he meant to be in season, but his harsh, abrupt manner, as a rule, neutralized the effect of his impromptu teachings. Now, however, the seed was thrown in other ground; and, as he intended, Simon's curiosity was excited. The Bible was reverently lifted from the bureau as soon as they reached home, and after some seeking, the passage was found.

Simon's reading was nothing to boast of, but Cooper could not read at all; and in the eyes of his unlettered comrades Clegg shone as a learned man. He could decipher "black print," and that, in his days, amongst his class, was a distinction. Slowly he traced his fingers along the lines for his own information, and then still more slowly, with a sort of rest after every word, read out to his auditors—Bess, Matthew, and Matthew's wife (there in her best gown and best temper)—with slight dialectal peculiarities which need not be reproduced—

And Jabez was more honourable than his brethren: and his mother called his name Jabez, because she bare him with sorrow. And Jabez called on the God of Israel, saying, O that Thou wouldst bless me indeed, and enlarge my coast, and that Thine hand might be with me, and that Thou wouldst keep me from evil, that it may not grieve me! And God granted him that which he requested.*

* 1 Chron. iv. 9, 10.

"Eh, Simon, mon, owd Jotty wur woiser nor thee. Theer's a neame for a lad to stand by! It's as good as a leeapin'-pow'* that it is, t' help him ower th' brucks† and rucks‡ o' th' warld."

Simon sat lost in thought. At length he raised his head, and remarked soberly—

"Parson Brookes moight ha' bin a prophet; th' choilt's mother did bear him wi' sorrow. The neame fits th' lad as if it had bin meade for him."

"Then aw hope he's a prophet o' eawt, feyther, an' o' th' rest'll come true in toime," briskly interjected Bess; adding—"Coom, tay's ready;" further appending for the information of their visitors—"Madam Clough sent the tay an' sugar, an' th' big curran'-loaf, when hoo heeard as feyther had axed for a holiday fur the kirsenin'; an' Mester Clough's sent some yale [ale], an' a thumpin' piece o' beef."

"Ay, lass; an' as we'en a'ready a foine kirsenin' feast, we'en no change parson's seven-shillin' piece, but lay it oop fur th' lad hissen."

But the christening feast did not proceed without sundry noisy demonstrations from Master Jabez. If, as Simon had once hinted, he was an angel in the house, he flapped his wings and blew his trumpet pretty noisily at times.

"Eh, lass, aw wish Tum wur here neaw, to enjoy hisself wi' us. Aw wonder what he'd say to yo' nursin' a babby so bonnily?"

Simon was munching a huge piece of currant-cake as he uttered this, after a meditative pause. A look of pain passed over Bess's face. She rarely mentioned the absent Tom, though he was seldom out of her thoughts.

"Yea, an' *aw* wish he wur here!" she echoed with a sigh, the fountain of which was deep in her own breast. "Aw wonder where he is neaw."

"Feightin,' mebbe!" suggested her father.

"Killed, mebbe!" was the fearful suggestion of her own heart,

* Leaping-pole. † Brooks. ‡ Heaps—impediments.

and she was silent for some time afterwards.

But the feast proceeded merrily for all that, and no wonder where Charity was president. And there was quite as happy a party under that humble roof in Skinners' Yard as that assembled in the grand house at Ardwick, where Master Laurence Aspinall was handed about in his embroidered robes for the inspection of guests who cared very little about him, although they did present him with silver mugs, and spoons, and corals, and protest to his pale and exhausted mamma that he was the finest infant in Manchester.

CHAPTER THE FOURTH.

MISCHIEF.

'SEVEN STARS'—INTERIOR.

IT was a time of distress at home and war abroad. Glory's scarlet fever was as rife an epidemic in Manchester as elsewhere. The town bristled with bayonets; corps of volunteers in showy uniforms, on parade or exercise, with banners flying, dotted it like spots on a peacock's tail; the music of drum and fife drowned the murmurs of discontented men, the groans of poverty-stricken women, and the cries of famishing children. All nostrums were prescribed for the evils of famine except a stoppage of the war. The rich made sacrifices for the poor; pastry was banished by common consent from the tables of the wealthy in order to cheapen flour; soup-kitchens were established for the poor, and in the midst of the general dearth the nineteenth century struggled into existence.

It was this war-fever which had carried off Bessy Clegg's sweetheart, Thomas Hulme, to Ireland, in Lord Wilton's Regiment of Lancashire Volunteers, three years before. The honest, true-hearted fellow could not write for himself, postage was expensive and uncertain, and in all those three years only two letters, written by a comrade, had reached the girl. To her simple, uninformed mind, Ireland was as foreign and distant a country as Australia is to us in these days. And to be stationed there with his regiment amongst those "wild Irishmen," conveyed only the idea of battles and bloodshed. Yet she kept a brave heart on the matter, and hid her anxieties from her father as well as she was able. In some respects little Jabez *was* a Godsend to her. The frequent attention he required, combined with her labours at the batting-frame and her household duties, tended to distract her mind from the dark picture over which she was so much inclined to brood, and to make her, if anything, more cheerful. Once more the voice which had been silent tuned up in song, for the gratification of the youngster, and in amusing him she insensibly cheered and refreshed herself.

Yet, as she trilled her quaint ballads, or Sabbath-school hymns, she little thought her vocalization was to furnish an envious mind with a shaft to wound herself, and the one of all others dearer than herself.

Soon after the memorable christening feast, Matthew Cooper and his family had removed—or "flitted," as they called it—from Barlow's Yard to Skinners' Yard; and Sally, that peaceable man's termagant wife, was not the most desirable of neighbours. The tea, and the currant-cake, and the beef, on that unusually well-spread board, had filled her with pleasure for the time, but turned to gall and bitterness ere they were digested. Why should the Cleggs be so high in the favour of Mr. and Madam Clough, and her Matt get nothing better than half-a-crown-piece? He'd quite as much to do in saving the brat's life as Simon had, and, with such a family, wanted it a fine sight more. So she argued and argued with herself, quite ignoring, or blind to the fact that it was not the mere impulse which saved, but the humanity which *kept* the babe, that Mr. Clough recognized, and never lost sight of.

As Simon grew in favour at the tannery, the more excited grew Sally Cooper, until nothing would do but a removal to the opposite yard, where she could see for herself the "gooin's on o' them Cleggs;" and once there, she contrived to harass Bess by numberless little spiteful acts, as well as by her vituperative tongue.

Nor did little Jabez himself escape. Parson Brookes, grumbling loudly at every downward step, found his way to Bess o' Sim's, guided by the quick-swishing, regular beat of the batting-wands.

Mrs. Clough having, by ocular demonstration, satisfied herself that Bess was a sufficiently notable house-wife and a kindly nurse, had replaced the worn out long-clothes which Jabez inherited from "brother Joe," by a set of more serviceable and suitable short ones; had, moreover, sent an embrocation to allay Simon's rheumatic pains, and to crown the whole, supplied a go-cart for the boy, to help him to walk, and yet leave the hands of industrious Bess at liberty.

As Miss Jewsbury has said, in her exquisite story of "The Rivals," that go-cart "was the drop added to the brimming cup, the touch given to the falling column."

Matt's worse-half—an inveterately clean woman, be it said—was occupied with her Saturday's "redding up," when she saw the wood-turner carry it in; and she thereupon trundled her mop at the door so vigorously and viciously, that the children instinctively shrank into corners, or ran out of the yard altogether, beyond reach of her weighty arm. And as, one by one, they ventured back, after what they thought a safe interval, creeping stealthily over the freshly-sanded floor, and mayhap leaving the impression of wet clogs thereon, jerks, cuffs, and slaps were administered with a freedom born of her supposed wrongs.

When Mat came home, to offer his wages upon the household altar, the storm had not subsided, and he was fain to retreat to the quiet fireside of Simon to smoke his pipe in peace, and escape its pitiless peltings. He could not have selected a worse haven. It was a flagrant going over to the enemy. Thither she followed him in her wrath, and in her blind fury assailed not only him, but Bess, Simon, Mr. Clough, and Joshua Brookes, whom she mingled in indiscriminate confusion, casting aspersions on the girl, which wounded nobody more than her own husband.

In the midst and in spite of all this, Jabez grew apace. Life was not altogether sweetened for him by Mrs. Clough's kindness, only made a little less bitter, and certainly not less hard; since almost his first experience with the go-cart was to tilt at the open doorway, and pitch head-foremost down a flight of three steps into the stony yard, whence frightened Bess raised him, with a bleeding nose and a great lump on his forehead, amidst the mocking laughter of Sal Cooper.

A chair was overturned across the doorway as a barrier, until Simon could place a sliding foot-board there. But Jabez had still many a knock against chair or table until Bess made a padded roll for his forehead, as a protective coronal. Then every tooth cost him a convulsion, and any one less patient and tender hearted than Bess would have abandoned her self-imposed charge in despair, his accidents and ailments made such inroads on her rest and on her time.

But even patience has its limits, and Sally Cooper strained the cable until it snapped. At a war of words Bess was no match for her antagonist: and, rather than endure a second contest, the Cleggs left the fiery serpent behind, and quitted the yard.

Not willingly, for Simon, contrary to the roving habits of ordinary weekly tenants, had not changed his abode since his wedding-day, and the river was as a friend to him. He declared he "could na sleep o' neets without wayter singin' to him." However, he contrived to find a very similar tenement, in just such another *cul-de-sac*, with just such another tripe-dresser's cellar underneath, and that, too, without quitting Long Millgate. Midway between the College and the tannery this court was situated, its narrow mouth opening to the breezes wafting down Hanover Street; they could still look out on the verdure of Walker's Croft, and the Irk laved its stony base as at that same Skinners' Yard, which Simon lived to see demolished.

It was May; bright, sunny, perfumed May. The hawthorn hedges on the ridge of the croft were white with scented blossoms, and the Irk—not the muddled stream which improvement (?) is fast shutting out of remembrance—went on its dimpled way, smiling at the promise of the season. The echoes of the May-day milkcart bells, and the flutter of their decorative ribbons, were dying out of all but infantile remembrance—the month was more than a fortnight old.

It was 1802, and Jabez was almost three years old. He was running, or rather scrambling, about the uneven court, gathering strength of limb and lung from their free use, albeit at the cost of dirt on frock and face, and the trouble of washing for Bess.

She was singing at her batting-frame—not an unusual thing now, for rumour had whispered in her ear that the Lancashire Volunteers were on their homeward march. Even as she sang, a stout young fellow in uniform stopped at the narrow entrance of the court, and questioned two or three gossiping women, who, with arms akimbo, blocked up the passage, if they knew the whereabouts of Simon Clegg, the tanner, and his daughter Bess.

"What! th' wench as has the love-choilt?" answered one of the women.

"The girl I mean had no child when I saw her last," responded he, between his set teeth.

"Happen that's some toime sin', mester, or it's not th' same lass. That's her singin' like a throstle o'er her wark at the oppen winder."

"And that's her choilt," said another, ending by a lusty call, "Jabez, lad, coom hither."

Jabez, taught to obey his elders, came at a trot in answer to the woman's call. The volunteer looked down upon him. The child had neither Bess's eyes nor Bess's features; but he heard the voice of Bess, and over the woman's shoulder he caught a glimpse of her face at the distant window. It *was* Bess, sure enough!

Sick at heart, Tom Hulme, for it was he, leaned for support against the side of the dark entry. These women but confirmed what he had heard in Skinners' Yard from Matt Cooper's vindictive wife. The deep shadow of the entry hid his change of countenance. Without a condemnatory word, without a step forward towards the girl whose heart was full of him, he steadied

SEVEN STARS INN.

himself and his voice, and mustering courage to say, "No, that is not the lass I want," strode resolutely out of the entry; and, bending his steps to the right, turned up Toad Lane, and so on to the "Seven Stars," in Withy Grove, where he was billeted.

He had come back from Ireland full of hope, and *this* was the end of it! He had been constant, and she was frail! She whom he had left so pure had sunk so low that, though she bore the brand of shame, she could sing blithely at her work, unconscious or reckless of her degradation! Tom had only been a hand-loom weaver, and was but a private in his regiment, but he had a soul as constant in love, as sensitive to disgrace, as the proudest officer in the corps. He might have doubted Sally Cooper's artful insinuations, but for the unconscious confirmation of the other women, and the personal testimony of poor little Jabez; the innocent child, borne with sorrow by his own dead mother, bringing sorrow to his living maiden-foster-mother.

The little lispings of the child conveyed no impression to Bess's understanding, but one of the women bawled out to her from the open court——

"Aw say, theer's bin a volunteer chap axin' fur a lass neamed Bess Clegg, but he saw thee from th' entry, and said yo're not th' lass he wanted!"

Her heart gave a great leap, and the blood flushed up to her pale face. Could it be possible that there was another Bess Clegg of whom a volunteer could be in search? Yet, had that been *her* Tom, he would have known his Bess again, even after five—ay, or twenty years. She would know *him* anywhere! And so all that day, and the next, her heart kept in a flutter of expectation and perplexity. She wondered he did not come. The regiment was in town; he surely had not been misled in his inquiries because they had "flitted." Yet in all her thoughts the grim reality had no place. Her perfect innocence and singleness of heart had never suggested such a possibility to her.

The days went by from the 13th to the 22nd, yet he came not. After working hours Simon tried to hunt him up; but the billeting system and ill-lighted streets, set his simple tactics at defiance. On the latter day, Lord Wilton gave a dinner in the quadrangle of the College, to the non-commissioned officers and privates in his regiment, to celebrate their return, and the peace and plenty then restored to the land.

At the first sound of fife and drum, Bess snatched up Jabez, and leaving house and batting-frame to take care of themselves, rushed along the street to the "Sun Inn" corner, where Long Millgate turns at a sharp angle, the old Grammar School and the Chetham College gate standing at the outer bend of the elbow. The better to see, she mounted the steps of the house next to the "Sun"—a house kept by a leather-breeches maker,—and strained her eyes as the gay procession wound from the apple-market, passed the handsome black-and-white frame-house of the Grammar School's head-master, and, with banners flying, and drums beating, marched under the ancient arched gateway between a double row of blue-coat boys.

She held Jabez high up in her arms to let him see, and his little arms clasped her neck, as she scanned every passing soldier's features. Two-thirds of the corps had passed—she saw the loved and looked-for face, and, radiant with delight, stretched forward, and in eager tones called—"Tom!"

There was a mutual start at recognition; two faces crimsoned to the brow; then one white as ashes, a keen meaning glance at the child, teeth clenched, and eyes set with stern resolution; and, without another look, without a word, Tom Hulme went on under the Whale's-jawbone gateway; and Bess, with brain bewildered, hands and limbs relaxed, sank on to the breeches-maker's steps in a dead faint.

A lady (Mrs. Chadwick), who had a little girl by the hand, caught Jabez as they fell, and putting his hand in her daughter's, bade her take care of him—she was perhaps a year or two older than he—whilst she raised the poor young woman's head, and applied a smelling-bottle to her nose.

Strange parting, strange meeting! How close the founts of sweet and bitter waters lie! How often separate streams of life meet and part again; some to meet and blend in after years, some to meet never more!

Another week, and Lord Wilton's Lancashire volunteer regiment had a man the less, the line had a man the more. Private Thomas Hulme had exchanged.

CHAPTER THE FIFTH.

ELLEN CHADWICK.

THE song of the human throstle was heard no more floating across the batting frame out of the window of its cage, in the dreary yard on the banks of the Irk. The swish of the wands might be heard when other sounds were low, but no more snatches of melody flowed in between.

Kind-hearted Mrs. Chadwick had not been content to leave poor Bessy at the breeches-maker's when her swoon was over; but, seeing that the girl continued in a dazed kind of stupor, sent to the adjoining "Sun Inn" for cold brandy-and-water, to stimulate the dormant mind. Bess drank, half unconsciously, and Mrs. Chadwick, leaving her little daughter Ellen to amuse astonished Jabez, waited patiently until the young woman could collect her ideas, and not only tell where she lived, but prepare to walk home.

By that time the road was tolerably clear. Mrs. Chadwick thanked the breeches-maker, and bidding Miss Ellen march in advance with little Jabez, herself helped Bessy Clegg homeward.

She never asked herself why or wherefore the girl had fainted, or whose the child she carried in her arms. She merely saw a modest-looking young woman stricken down by illness or distress, and put out a Christian hand to help her.

It was past Simon's dinner-hour, and they found him on the look-out for the absentees. He was more bewildered than Bess when he saw her brought home pale and trembling by a stranger, whose dress and manner bespoke her superior station. Mrs. Chadwick explained, seeing that Bess was incapable.

"The poor girl fainted almost opposite to the College gate, as she watched Earl Wilton's regiment march past. She recovered so slowly, I was afraid to let her come through the streets unprotected, especially as she had so young a child in her charge."

Simon thanked her, as well he might. Benevolence will relieve distress with money, or passing words of sympathy, but it is not often silken skirt and satin bonnet walk through a crowded thoroughfare in close conjunction with bonnetless cotton and linsey.

Yet Simon was utterly at a loss to account for her swoon. He could only conjecture that she had missed her sweetheart from the corps, and that the enquiring volunteer had been a comrade sent to announce Tom Hulme's death. Observing how much he was confounded, the good lady thought it best to retire, and leave them to themselves.

"Come, Ellen, it is time we went home.'

But Ellen, seated on a low stool in the corner, had her lap full of broken toys, which had found their way hither from the Clough nursery, and which Jabez displayed to all comers."

"My daughter appears wonderfully attracted to your little grandson."

"He's noa gran'son o' moine, Missis, though aw think aw love th' little lad as much as if he did belung to us. Aw just picked him eawt o' th' wayter, i' th' greet flood abeawt two year an' hauve back. Aw dunnot know reetly who th' young un belungs to."

"And you have kept him ever since—through all the trying time of scarcity?"

"Yoi; aw could do no other, an' a little chap like Jabez couldna ate much."

"It does you credit," said the lady.

"Mebbe. Aw dunnot know. Aw dunnot see mich credit i' doin' one's clear duty. But aw think theer'd ha' bin *dis*credit an' aw hadna done it."

"I wish everyone shared your sentiments," replied she.

By this time the little girl had relinquished the toys, kissed the little boy patronisingly, and was by her mother's side, ready to depart. A word of sympathy and encouragement from Mrs. Chadwick, and father and daughter were left alone with their

ELLEN CHADWICK WANTS PRINCE WILLIAM.

new sorrow.

Sorely puzzled was Simon to account for Tom Hulme's strange conduct. He could only come to the conclusion that he had picked up a fresh sweetheart in Ireland, and was ashamed to show his face.

"An' if so, lass, yo're best off without him," said he.

The stern, troubled look on the young volunteer's face, which Bess had seen and her father had not, he could not understand, and therefore could not credit.

One day the girl said, as if struck by a sudden thought—

"Feyther, aw saw Tum look hard at Jabez. D'un yo' think as heaw he fancied aw wur wed?"

"He moight, lass, he moight," said he, knocking the ashes out of his pipe; "but dunnot thee fret, aw'll look Tum up, and set it o' reet, if that's o'."

But there was no setting it right, for by that time Tom had left the corps and the town, and thenceforth Bess's musical pipe was out of tune, and stopped utterly. She worked, it is true, but she had no heart in her work; and though before her father she kept up a show of cheerfulness, in his absence she shed many and bitter tears.

Smiles and tears are among a child's earliest perceptions and experiences. Of the mother's smile in its full sense Jabez knew nothing. With all her winning ways, Bess could never supply that want, if want it could be, where it was never missed, having so good a substitute. But of the change which came over her when she knew that Tom was indeed lost to her, even the three years' child could be sensible. He had been early taught to show a brave front when he hurt himself, and the starting tears would subdue to a whimper; but, for all that, tears to him meant pain or disappointment, and as they fell and wetted the (not always clean) little cheek laid lovingly against hers, a tender chord was struck; he would press his small arm tighter round her neck, and with a sympathetic "Don't ky, Beth!" nestle closer, and try to kiss away the drops, which only fell the faster.

Low-spirited nurses do not make lively children, and Jabez, after a stout tussle with the whooping-cough, began to droop as much as Bess; so clear-eyed Simon instituted a series of Sunday rambles for the three, in search of plants and posies, to brighten their dull home, and of bloom to brighten the fading cheeks. Sometimes Matt Cooper, with one or two of his youngsters, would join them, but not often, Sal was so jealous of his friendship with the Cleggs, and the pleasant day was so certain to be marred by an unpleasant reception in the evening at home.

These summer walks seldom extended beyond Collyhurst Clough and quarries, or Smedley Vale, or through the fields to Cheetham Hill, stopping at the "Cow and Calf" to refresh, and rest the little ones, before they came back laden with wild flowers down Red Bank and over Scotland Bridge, to their respective "yards" in Long Millgate.

At first, whenever they took the pleasant lower road through Angel Meadow, they did their best to ferret out the parentage and connections of Jabez, hoping by their inquiries even to keep alive the memory of his marvellous deliverance, so that in case the missing father should return, there might be a mutual restoration.

These Sunday excursions did not drop with the sere autumnal leaves. A crisp clear day called them forth surely as sunshine had done, Jabez mounting pick-a-back on the shoulders of Simon or Matt when his little feet could no longer keep up their trot beside the bigger Cooper boys. Frames were invigorated, cheerfulness came back to face and home, and Simon, who had a deep-seated love of Nature in his soul, finding her so good a physician, kept up the acquaintance through rounding seasons and years. And from Nature he drew lessons which he dropped as seed into the boy's heart, as unconscious of the great work he was doing as was Jabez himself.

The boy throve and grew hardy. Companionship with older

and rougher lads, sturdy fellows with wills of their own, made him sturdy too ; a làd who would take a blow and give one on occasion ; who would run a race and lose, and a second, and third, until he could win. But Bess's gentle training was something very different from Sal's, and Jabez grew up tender as well as strong and bold.

A persecuted kitten had taken refuge under Bess's batting-frame in the foundling's go-cart days, and in care for that kitten, and for a wounded brown linnet brought home one Sunday, he learned humanity. Matthew's lads were given to bird-nesting, and Matt himself saw no harm in it; but when that young linnet's wing was broken in a scuffle for the nest stolen from a clump of brushwood, Simon read the robbers such a homily they had never heard in their young lives, and as a corollary he took the bird home to be fed and nursed by Bess and Jabez till it could fly, an event which never came about.

In hot weather the lads pulled off clogs and stockings (there were no trousers to turn up—they wore breeches), and waded into pools and brooks, and Jabez would be no whit behind. On one of these occasions, either the current was too strong for the venturesome child, or the gravel slipped from under his feet, or his companions pushed him—no matter which,—but in he went, and, but for the presence of Simon, would have been drowned. Simon had been born on the river banks, and could swim like a fish. At once he resolved that Jabez should learn to do the same, and begin at once.

"Yo' see, Bess, if aw hadna bin theer he'd a bin dreawnded, sure as wayter's wet, an' th' third toime pays off fur o'; so he mun larn to tak' care on himsel' th' next toime he marlocks [gambols] among th' Jack-sharps."

Jabez was not six years old when Simon Clegg gave him and the young Coopers their first lesson in swimming, in a delightful and sequestered part of Smedley Vale, where the Irk was clear and bright. He had shown them, nearer home, how a frog used its limbs, and then, after a few preliminary evolutions, to show how a man used his, took the lad on his back, and, after swimming with him awhile, shook him off into the water to flounder about for himself.

Bess was often left at home on Sundays after that; and Jabez was not merely the better for his bath, but by the time he was eight years old was a fearless swimmer.

Yet, although these country rambles had become an institution, Simon Clegg never neglected his Sabbath duties. Sunday morning was sure to see him, clean-shaven, in his best suit, with Jabez by the hand, and mild-eyed Bess beside, on the free seats of the Old Church, under the eye of parsons and churchwardens; and Jabez, if he could understand little of the service, could gather in a sense of the beautiful from the grand old architecture, from the swell of the solemn organ, the harmonious voices of the choristers—of the Blue-coat boys in the Chetham gallery over the churchwardens' pew, and of the Green-coat children farther on. Then the silver mace carried before the parson was a thing to wonder at, and fill him with awe; and no one could tell how the clerical robes, and choristers' surplices, transfigured common mortals in his admiring eyes.

Those years of Jabez Clegg's young life had been full of history for Manchester and Europe. The town had grown as well as the foundling. Invention had been busy. Volunteer regiments had been one by one disbanded, a daily newspaper was started, and peaceful arts flourished. Then, ere another year expired, Napoleon declared the British Isles in a state of blockade; British subjects on French soil, whether civil or military, to be prisoners of war; British commodities lawful spoil; and so War—red-handed War—broke loose once more. Again Manchester rose up in arms to defend country and commerce. A "Loyalty Fund" of £22,000 was raised for the support of Government. No fewer than nine separate volunteer corps sprang from the ashes of the old ones, and the town was one huge garrison. The commander of one regiment—the Loyal Masonic Rifle Volunteer Corps—Colonel Hanson—a remarkable man in many ways—was distinguished by a command from George III. to appear at Court in full regimentals, and with his hat on.

Messrs. Pickford offered to place at the disposal of Government four hundred horses, fifty waggons, and twenty-eight boats. Loyal townsmen, with more money than courage of their own, sought to stimulate that of others by sending gold medals flying amongst the officers of the volunteer corps. "The British Volunteer" came from the press of Harrop in the Market Place, and once more the music of drum and trumpet was in the ascendant.

To crown the whole, Manchester, which had never been called upon to entertain British Royalty since Henry VII. looked in upon the infant town, was visited in 1804 by Prince William, Duke of Gloucester, commander of the North-west District, and his son, to review this Lancashire volunteer army; and the whole town was consequently in a ferment of excitement. Nothing was thought of, or talked of, but the visit of the Duke and Prince, and the coming review, the more so as reports differed respecting the appointed site.

Market Street, Manchester, which George Augustus Sala has commemorated as one of the "Streets of the World," was then Market Street Lane, a confused medley of shops and private houses, varying from the low and rickety black-and-white tenement of no pretensions to the fine mansion with an imposing frontage, and ample space before. But the thoroughfare was in places so very narrow that two vehicles could not pass, and pedestrians on the footpath were compelled to take refuge in the doorways from the muddy wheels which threatened damage to dainty garments, while the whole was ill-paved and worse lighted.

At the corner where it opens a vent for the warehouse traffic of High Street, *then* stood a handsome new hotel, the Bridgewater Arms, in front of which a semi-circular area was railed off with wooden posts and suspended chains. Within this area, on the bright morning of April the 12th, two sentinels were placed, who, marching backwards and forwards, crossed and recrossed each other in front of the hotel door; tokens that the Royal Duke and his suite had taken up their quarters within.

Beyond the semi-circle of chained posts, mounted horsemen kept back the concourse of spectators which pressed closely on the horses' heels. Among the crowd was Simon Clegg, with Jabez mounted on his shoulders, albeit he was a somewhat heavy load. Simon was a man of peace, but he was a staunch believer in Royalty, and that, quite as much as the spectacle, had drawn him thither.

It was a mild and cheery April morn; the windows of the upper room in which sat the Prince, the centre of a brilliant circle, were open, and the loyal multitude feasted their unaccustomed eyes with the sight. As Jabez looked on in a child's ravishment, a little dark-haired, dark-eyed girl, some six or seven years old, turned sharply round the narrow street by the side of the hotel on the flags where there was no chain to bar; passing unquestioned the sentinel on guard, who, seeing only a well-dressed solitary child in white muslin, with a sash and hat-ribbons of pink satin, concluded that she belonged to the hotel. Once there, she asked fearlessly—

"Where is Prince William? I want Prince William!"

Then the sentinel began to question; but the little maid had but one reply—

"I want Prince William!"

The soldier would have turned her back, but the disputation had attracted attention in the room above.

An officer's head was thrust out.

"What's the matter?" asked he.

"I want to see the Prince. I want to know——"

'Bid the little lady come up hither."

And the little lady went up, all unconscious of state etiquette or ceremonial.

An officer in rich uniform, with jewels on his breast, took her on his knee, and asked what she wanted with Prince William.

"Oh, mamma and my aunts are wanting ever so to know if

the review is going to be on Camp Field or on Sale Moor; and Aunt Ellen says it's to be in one place, and mamma thinks it's the other; and so, as I was dressed first, I just slipped out at the back door and ran here to ask Prince William himself, for I thought *he* would be sure to know.

The gentleman laughed heartily, and the others followed suit.

"And who is your mamma, my dear?"

"My mamma is Mrs. Chadwick, and I'm Ellen Chadwick; and we live in Oldham Street."

"Oh, indeed! And why are the ladies so anxious to know where the Prince holds the review?" asked the officer on whose knee she sat.

"Ah—that's just it. If he reviews at Sale Moor he will go past our house; and then we shall see all the soldiers from our own windows. Won't it be fine?"

Another gentleman asked what the ladies were doing when she left; and I'm afraid Ellen made more revelations anent their toilettes than were strictly necessary, for the laughter was prolonged.

She did not, however, lose sight of her self-imposed mission. Struggling from her seat, she said—

"Oh, please do tell me where is Prince William; I must go home, and I do so want to know."

"Tell your mamma, Miss Ellen," said he, smiling, "that the Prince will review at Sale Moor; and take this, my dear, for yourself," putting a shilling (shillings at that time were perfectly plain from over-long use) in her hand.

"Oh, thank you! But are you sure—quite sure it is Sale Moor?"

"Quite sure."

The little damsel set off, as much elated with her news as with her shilling. As she ran briskly down the broad steps, and beyond the barrier, she came in contact with Simon, who made way for her exit; and, as she looked up smiling to thank him, her glance rested for a moment on the boy he carried; but no spark of recognition flashed into the eyes of either, and no one in all that crowd saw any connection between that dainty, white-frocked, pink-slippered, pink-sashed miss, and the rough lad in the patched suit (a Clough's cast-off) and wooden clogs.

CHAPTER THE SIXTH.

TO MARTIAL MUSIC.

PRINCELY RECOGNITION.

A SECOND time Jabez and Ellen saw each other ere the day was out.

She had rushed home with eager feet and eyes, through back streets, to startle Mrs. Chadwick, her newly-married sister, Mrs. Ashton, and a bevy of friends, with the confident assurance that the review would be at Sale, and to confirm it by a display of the plain shilling, which "an osifer had given her."

New Cross, where the volunteers assembled, was not then a misnomer. A market cross occupied the centre space between the four wide thoroughfares, of which Oldham Street is one; and the open area was considerable.

The trumpets' bray, the tramp of troops, were heard long before the brilliant cavalcade was set in motion; and every window—every house in Oldham Street (all good private residences of the Gower Street stamp) held its quota of heads and eyes and costumes as brilliant as the eyes.

The house of Mr. Chadwick was situated near the lower end, and commanded a good view of the Infirmary, its gardens, and pond in Piccadilly. To-day, however, the royal party and the volunteers, many of whom had friends looking out for them, were the only prospect worth a thought; and as they marched proudly on, to the gayest of gay tunes, kerchiefs waved, heads nodded, and eyes sparkled with delight and pleasure.

As the Duke of Gloucester and his suite rode by, their charges prancing to the music, Ellen, mounted on a chair by the window, between Mrs. Ashton and her mother, suddenly pointed to an officer in their midst, resplendent with stars and orders, and in an ecstasy of delight screamed out—

"Mamma, mamma! that's the gentleman that gave me the shilling!"

The little treble voice pierced even through the clamorous music. A noble head was bowed, a plumed hat was raised, and lowered until it swept the charger's mane.

"Why, child, that is Prince William!" was the simultaneous exclamation, as all the eyes from all the houses across the street were turned in wonderment to see the Chadwicks so distinguished; and Simon, who, still carrying Jabez, was trying to keep pace with the troops, wondered too. Moreover, he recognised the lady and the little girl, though seen but once; for he earned his own living, such as it was, and had been too proud to call on the Chadwicks to say how his daughter fared, lest they should think he sought charity.

"Jabez, lad, si thi; yon's th' lady and little lass as browt yo' whoam, when yo' went seein' the sodgers afore!"

And Jabez, from his shoulder-perch, looked up at the little bright-eyed brunette, to remember the white frock and pink ribbons he had seen at the Bridgewater, but nothing beyond.

The man's exclamation and attitude had at the same time attracted Mrs. Chadwick, who, smiling down on him and Jabez, spoke to Ellen; and she, reminded of the little baby who had been saved from drowning in a cradle, looked down and, in the fulness of her new importance, nodded too.

The momentary stoppage called forth a loud objurgation, as a reminder, from Sally Cooper, who was in advance with Matthew and such of her bigger lads as could step out; and Simon, equally anxious not to lose sight of the royal party, hurried on. But Sale Moor is beyond the confines of Lancashire, and Simon found the five miles stiff walking, with a child nearly six years old on his shoulders, and Master Jabez had to descend from his seat, and trudge on his own feet. This caused them to lag behind their friends, Sally insisting on Matt's keeping up with the soldiers, in order that they might get a good place on the Moor, and they were thus separated. Bess had remained at home. Never again could she look on marching troops without a pang.

Sale Moor was alive with expectant sightseers. Stands and platforms had been erected for the accommodation of those who could afford and cared to pay; there was a sprinkling of heavy carriages, and a crowd of carts, but the mass of spectators were on foot, vehicular locomotion being of very limited capacity.

Of these latter were the Coopers and Cleggs, of course. Sally, with the elders of her turbulent brood, had reached the ground in time to be deafened by the score of cannon Lord Wilton's artillery fired as a salute to princedom. She had planted herself firmly against one of the supports of an elevated platform, where the crowd of hero-worshippers was densest. She was tightly jammed and crushed against the woodwork; but what matter? she had a fine sight of the field, and as she watched the evolutions of the volunteers, congratulated herself and Matthew on having left "that crawling Clegg an' the brat so far behint."

Almost as she spoke, there was a faint crackle, then another, and a yielding of the post against which she leaned—a loud crash, a chorus of shrieks, half drowned by music and musketry, and the whole platform was down, with the living freight it had borne; and she was down with it.

The fashion, wealth, and beauty of Cheshire and South Lancashire had their representatives amongst that struggling swooning, writhing, shrieking, groaning mass of humanity, heaped and huddled in indiscriminate confusion, with up-torn seats, posts, and draperies. Strange to say, only one person was killed outright—that is, on the spot—for in its downfall the stand bore with it many of the throng beneath. But of the injured and the shaken, those who went to hospital and home to linger long and die at last, history has kept no record.

Amongst these, this story tells of two—two differing in all

but sex. Mrs. Aspinall, ever frail and delicate, was borne to her carriage with whole limbs, but insensible, her husband and their son Laurence both uninjured by her side. Physicians were in attendance, and never left her until she was safely lodged in her own luxurious chamber, overlooking Ardwick Green, and could be pronounced out of immediate danger. Sally Cooper, with a sprained ancle, a dislocated shoulder, and many internal bruises, was placed in a light cart on a bed of straw procured from a neighbouring farm, with another of the injured, and carried to the Manchester Infirmary, to try the skill and the patience of the doctors and nurses.

Neither recovered. The unwounded lady, sorely shaken, succumbed to the shock her nervous system had received; and Master Laurence, already petted and wilful, was left to be still further spoiled by his widowed father and Kitty, his mother's old nurse. Sally, strong of frame and will, impatient of pain and of restraint, was restive under the surgeons' hands, and defeated their efforts to ascertain her injuries. She exhausted herself with shrieks and cries, tossed about and disturbed bandages, rejected physic, which she called "poison," and soon put her case beyond the cure of physicians. Too late she became sensible of her own folly. Then, when recovery was impossible, she repented of many misdeeds, and of none more than her slander of poor Bess.

And thus it was. When the mother was taken from the head of Cooper's home, Bess's kind heart yearned to help the disconsolate man and his troop of children. Fortunately, the eldest was a girl of sixteen, and there was a younger girl of ten. Both of these had gone out to work, but now Molly had to stay at home and try to keep all right and tight there. And here Bess came to her aid. Without scolding or brawling, she put the girl into the way of doing things quickly and quietly. She encouraged her to persevere, so that her cleanly mother should detect no eyesores when she came home restored. She tried to persuade the boys to be less refractory—to help, not to irritate, their sister; and somehow Cooper's home began to miss Sall, much as one misses a whirlwind.

The kindness of Bess o' Sim's was duly reported to the Infirmary patient, and at first chafed her sorely. She "hated to be under obligations, and to that lass o' a' others." But Bess, leaving her own work—and the loss of an hour meant the loss of an hour's earnings—herself went to see Sally; and such was the influence of her gentle voice and touch, that Sally's chagrin imperceptibly wore away.

Towards the last she grew delirious, raved of Bess and Tom Hulme and forgiveness, and in the short calm preceding dissolution, confessed to Matt Cooper and the attendant nurse that she had cast a slur on Bess Clegg's good name. Had made Tom Hulme believe that Simon had taken the lass from Skinners' Yard to hide her shame. That everybody in the yard knew that Bess had a child. And that she had bade him inquire for himself. And almost her last word was a hope that Bess would forgive her.

Matthew Cooper himself hardly forgave his dead wife. How, therefore, should he carry this confession to Bess, and ask her to forgive? He took a medium course; and after a few days' consideration, while they and the rest of the tanners were eating their "baggin" (a workman's luncheon, so called from the bag it is, or was, usually carried in), sat down beside Simon on a bundle of thick leather, and told him as well as he was able.

Simon was troubled; but he was not vindictive. He would have been less than a man had he not been bitter against the cruel woman who had causelessly wrecked his good daughter's life. But he was sorry for Matt, and broke out into no revilings. The woman was dead. The ill she had done had been fearfully punished, and neither curses nor reproaches could affect her or undo the mischief.

He left his cheese and jannock on the hides untasted, drew his hand across his forehead, and went down to the river-side and across the wooden bridge for a breath of fresh air and a waft of

THE INFIRMARY, FROM OLDHAM STREET.

fresh thought. He was only a rugged tanner, but he had a heart within his breast; he had a daughter on his hearth with a great wound in *her* heart, a blast on her good name, and he was called upon to forgive the author of this mischief!

Simon had long been used to commune with his own heart. He had built up a wall round it with the leaves of that one book on his bureau; and whenever he was in doubt or difficulty, he read the precepts inscribed upon that wall. He went back to Cooper, whose appetite had been no better than his own.

"Aw mun think this ower, Matt. Aw connot say aw furgive yo'r Sall o' at a dash. Hoo's done that as may niver be undone whoile thee an' me's alive; an' aw connot frame to say as aw furgive her loike o' on a sudden. An' aw mun think it ower before eawt be said to eawr Bess, poor wench!"

A week elapsed before the subject was broached again. Then Simon spoke to Matthew as they were leaving the tannery-yard.

"Coom into th' 'Queen Anne'" (he called it quëan), "Matt, and have a gill; aw've summat t' say to thee."

There was nobody in the taproom. They sat down to their half-pint horns of ale—times were too hard to afford deeper draughts—and Simon said:

"Aw've bin thinkin' o' this week, an' as aw connot furgive yo'r Sall, gradely loike, aw'll no put th' same temptation i' th' way of eawr Bess. Hoo'd better think Tum's takken oop wi' some other wench, than ha' th' shame o' knowin' th' lad's toorned her up i' disgrace. Hoo's getten ower th' worst o' her trouble, an' awm not gooin to break her heart outreet, and mebbe set her agen little Jabez into th' bargain."

Matthew could but assent to Simon's proposition. But Simon had not said all his say.

"But aw'm not gooin' to sit deawn wi' my honds i' mi' lap, an' that grëat lump o' dirty slutch stickin' to moi lass. Yo' mun help me t' find eawt wheer Tom Hulme's getten to, an' help to set o' straight afore aw forgive yo'r Sall, tho' hoo be dead an' gone."

"Wi' o' my heart!" responded Matt; and he gave his huge hand to Simon in token thereof.

When the Duke of Gloucester inspected the volunteers at Ardwick on the 30th of September that same year, not one of the people I have linked together witnessed the show.

The blinds were down at Mr. Aspinall's to shut out a sight the like of which had made him a widower; and within the darkened nursery, wilful, obstreperous Laurence fought and kicked and bit at old Kitty, because she kept him within doors and from the windows at his father's command.

There was a christening party in Mosley Street, at the Ashtons', at which not only the Chadwicks, but the Rev. Joshua Brookes—who had that day named the infant Augusta—were present. They had selected a public occasion for their private festival. It was a grand affair. Mr. Ashton was a small-ware manufacturer in an extensive way of business, his house and warehouse occupying a large block of buildings at the corner of York Street. And the baby Augusta, born the previous month, was a first child, his wife being younger than himself considerably. Miss Ellen, too, was there, her wonderful shilling, through which a hole had been drilled, suspended from her neck like an amulet.

Simon and Matt had given up their holiday to fruitless inquiries after Tom Hulme; and Jabez, after a stand-up fight with a boy in the yard in defence of his kitten, had come to have his bleeding nose and bruised forehead doctored by Bess, who shed over him the tears long gathering in their fountains for Tom Hulme's defection And somehow at that stylish christening feast, where the baby Augusta was a personage of importance almost as great as the celebrated Miss Kilmansegg, the orphan Jabez and his fosterers came on the table for discussion along with the dessert; Mrs. Chadwick, Mr. Clough, and Joshua Brookes concurring in the opinion mooted by the lady that something should be done to relieve the worthy tanner and his daughter of the cost and trouble of maintaining the boy as he grew older and would want educating. That they should talk of the cost of maintenance when bread was a shilling a loaf, was no marvel; but that "education" should be named as a necessity for one of "nobody's children," can only be cited as a proof that either the boy's strange introduction to Manchester, or Simon's strange generosity, had excited an interest in both beyond the common run.

Yet that something was vague. The only definite and practicable view of the subject was held by Joshua Brookes, and he kept his opinion to himself.

CHAPTER THE SEVENTH.

THE REVEREND JOSHUA BROOKES.

COLLEGE OUTLET TO THE RIVER.

JOSHUA BROOKES had a child's love for toffy and other sweetmeats. These he purchased—or obtained without purchase—from an old woman as odd and eccentric as himself, a Mrs. Clowes, who occupied a bow-windowed shop in Half Street, which literally overlooked the churchyard, three or four steps having to be mounted by her customers.

And how numerous were her customers, and how great the demand for her toffy, lozenges, and "humbugs" may be judged from the fact that her workmen and apprentices used up eight or nine tons of sugar every week. Yet she was apparently only a shop-keeper, and had begun business in a very humble way; but she was persevering and industrious, and success followed. She was active and energetic, and expected those around her to be the same. Yet she was kind to them, as may be supposed, for she gave every Sunday a good dinner to fourteen old men and women on whom fortune had looked unkindly, waiting upon them herself, and never tasting her own dinner until her pensioners had dined.

Regular in her own attendance at the old Church, she required her household to be regular too, though she left them little enough time to dress—possibly because her own toilette was so scant. The dress in which she presented herself at church was certainly unique for a woman of wealth. Her gown of sober stuff was well worn; a mob-cap (a fashion which came in with the French Revolution) adorned her head, over which, by way of bonnet, a brown silk handkerchief was tied. On rare—very rare—occasions, an old black silk bonnet covered all.

Joshua Brookes, at odds with his clerical brethren, with his pupils, and half the world besides, was on good terms with Mrs. Clowes. Rough, prompt, and uncompromising was she; rough, irritable and unmannerly was he; both unpromising hard-husked nuts, with sweet and tender kernels. So rough, few ever suspected the soft heart; yet the woman who fed the poor before herself, and the learned clergyman who had a fancy for pigeons, and who cherished the drunken and abusive old crippled shoemaker, his father, to the last, must have intuitively known the inner life of each other.

The day following Augusta Ashton's christening, it fell within the round of the Reverend Joshua's duty to read the burial service over a dead townswoman in the churchyard. And now occurred one of those incidents in which the ludicrous and the profane blended, and brought impulsive Joshua into disfavour. As was not unfrequently the case, he broke off in the midst of the service, left the mourners and the coffin beside the open grave, threw his legs over the low wall, and, mounting the steps into the confectioner's shop, said:

"Here, quick, dame? Give me some horehound drops for my cough."

On his entrance Mrs. Clowes broke off a narrative over which she and her shopwoman were laughing heartily, in order to reach the required drops, which went into a paper without weighing, and for which no payment was tendered. Back he strode over the churchyard wall to resume the interrupted ceremonial.

It must here be observed that Joshua had remarkably shaggy eyebrows, overhanging his quick eyes. like pent-houses, and that it was the wont of the schoolboys and others to annoy him by drawing their fingers significantly over their own. A young sweep sat upon the churchyard wall to witness the funeral, and—young imp of Satan that he was!—he could not forbear drawing a thumb and forefinger over each brow, full in Joshua's sight, just as he reached the passage—"I heard a voice from heaven saying——"

The shaggy eyebrows contracted; he roared out—

"Knock that little black rascal off the church wall!"

The mischievous little blackamoor was off, with a beadle after him; and the eccentric chaplain, whom no sense of irreverence seemed to strike, concluded the ceremony with no further interruption.

At its close, Mr. Aspinall and another mourner took the clergyman to task for his disrespect to the remains of the deceased Mrs. Aspinall, whose obsequies had been so irregularly performed. They said nothing of disrespect to the Divinity profaned; their own feelings and importance had been outraged, and they forgot all else even by the dust and ashes in the gaping grave; and little Laurence, cloaked and hooded, forgot his grief in watching the chase after the sweep.

"How dare you, sir, give way to these indecencies at the funeral of my wife? It has been most indecorous and insulting, both to the dead and her afflicted relatives."

"She's had Christian burial, hasn't she?" gruffly interrogated Joshua.

"Hardly," was the hesitating answer.

"She's been laid in consecrated ground, and I've read the burial service over her; what more would you have? Some folk are never satisfied."

Emptying half his horehound drops into the hand of Master Laurence, Joshua turned on his heel, went to the chapter-house to disrobe, and then back over the wall to Mrs. Clowes.

"I say, dame, you were not at church on Sunday."

"No, Parson Brookes; I was in Liverpool."

"Oh!" grunted he, "in Liverpool. Sugar-buying, I suppose?"

"Yea; an' a fine joke I've had."

"Joshua pricked up his ears; he did not object to a little fun.

"You mun know I thought I'd give Branker, the new sugar-broker, a trial, an' I went there an' asked to see samples; but the young whipper-snapper of a salesman looked at me from top to toe, an', I suppose, reckoned up the value of my old black bonnet, my kerchief an' mutch, an' my old stuff dress, and fancied my pockets must match my gown, for he was barely civil, and didn't seem to care for the trouble o' showin' th' samples. So I bade my young man good day, an' said I'd call again."

"And didn't, I suppose. Just like a woman," put in Joshua.

"Oh, yea, I did. I borrowed my landlady's silk gown and fine satin bonnet, and put on my lady's manners; and then Mr. Whipper-snapper could show his samples, and *his* best manners, too. But when I gave my orders by tons, and not hundred-weights, he looked at me, and looked again, as if he thought I'd escaped from a madhouse; an' at last he began to h'm an' ah, an' talk of large orders, an' cash payment, an' references; an' I told him to make out th' invoice and bring it. An' when I pulled out this old leather pocket-book, and counted the bank-notes to pay him down on the nail, good gracious! how the fellow stared! I reckon I'll not need to borrow a silk dress when I give my next order. It was as good as a play."

"Um! You women-folk think yourselves wonderfully clever. But come, I can't waste my time here. (Joshua had heard all he went for.) Give me quarter-a-pound of humbugs; I threw half the other things away," said he.

"I don't think it's much you'll throw away, Jotty," replied the old confectioner, with independent familiarity, as she weighed and parcelled the sweets, for which this time he put down the money.

"It's much you know about it, Mother Clowes," he jerked out, as if throwing the words at her over his shoulder, as he turned to leave the shop, putting the package in one of the large pockets of his long flap waistcoat as he went.

His own house, not more than three hundred yards away,

adjoined the Grammar School, a red brick building, with stone quoins, now darkened by time and smoke, one gable of which overhung the Irk; the other, pierced for four small-paned windows, almost confronting the antique Sun Inn, at the acute angle of Long Millgate, and quite overlooking an open space, flanked by the main entrance to the College. From this, the east wing of the College, it is separated by a plain iron gateway and palisades on the Millgate side, and by a low wall which serves as a screen from the river on the other side; the enclosed space between rails, wall, College, and the front of the school serving as a playground for such scholars as were willing to keep within bounds. It was divided into upper, middle, and lower schools, the last being in the basement, and designed for elementary instruction. The high and middle schools together occupied the same long room above this. Joshua Brookes, as second master, presided over the middle school, and surely never M.A. had so thankless an office. He was placed at a terrible disadvantage in the school, not altogether because he had risen from its lowest ranks—not altogether because a drunken, foul-mouthed cripple interfered with their sports, or went reeling to his son's domicile next door—not because he was unduly severe; other masters were that—but because his own eager thirst for knowledge as a boy had made him intolerant towards indolence, incredulous of incapacity; and his constitutional impatience and irritability made his harsh voice seem harsher when he reproved a dullard. He lost his self-command, and with that went his command over others. Meaning to be affable to the poor, from whose ranks he sprang, he became familiar; and they reciprocated the familiarity so fully as to draw down the contempt of his *confreres.* He was a man to be respected, and they slighted him; a man to be honoured, and they snubbed him. What wonder, then, that eccentricities grew like barnacles on a ship's keel, or that the boys failed in obedience and respect to a master when their elders set them the example?

This defence of a misunderstood man has not taken up a

tithe of the time he gave to his refractory class, to whom he went straightway from the confectioner's, whose "humbugs" had melted considerably, not wholly down his own throat, before the hour when the boys closed their Latin Grammars and Greek Lexicons, and poured as if they were mad down the steps, and through the gate, to the road. Yet even the sweets he gave to the attentive did not conciliate; they only made the intractable more defiant; and the recipients felt they were bribed.

Warned by the uproar of a large school in motion, as well as by the long-cased clock, Tabitha, his one servant, had her master's tea ready for him the instant he came in from the school, as he generally did, fagged and jaded, with the growl of a baited bear.

That day he simply put his head into the house, and bawled, "Tea ready, Tab?" and without waiting for an answer, went on, "Keep it hot till I get back;" then, closing the door, took his way eastwards down Long Millgate. His journey was not a long one. It ended at the bottom of a yard where a sad, pale-faced young woman was switching monotonously at a mass of downy cotton, and listening at the same time to the equally monotonous drawl of a youngster in the throes of monosyllabic reading.

"Get larning, lad!—get larning! Larning's a great thing. Yo' shan read i' this big picture-book when you can spell gradely,' had been Simon's precept and inducement; and Jabez, to whom that big pictorial Bible was a mysterious, unexplored crypt, did try with all his little might.

"J-a-c-k—Jack, w-a-s—was, a g-o-o-d—good, b-o——"

"And I hope you're a good boy, as well as Jack," said Joshua Brookes abruptly, as he put his head into the room, and put a stop to the lesson at the same time. "But, hey-day" (observing the swollen nose and bruised forehead), "You've been in the wars. Good boys don't fight."

"Then what did Bill Barnes throw stones at ar pussy for? Good boys dunnot hurt kittlins," said Jabez, nothing daunted.

Bess explained.

"Um!" quoth Joshua, when she had finished, "he's fond of his kitten, is he?" and drawing Jabez towards him by the shoulder, with one finger uplifted as a caution, he looked down on the shrinking child, and said, impressively—

"Never fight if you can help it, Jabez; but if you fight to save a poor dumb animal from ill-usage, or to protect the weak against the strong, Jotty Brucks is not the man to blame you. Here, lad," and into the pinafore of Jabez went the remainder of the "humbugs."

He patted the boy on the head, bade him get on with his reading, he did not know what good fortune might come of it, told him to come regularly to church, to love God and God's creatures, and went away, leaving Bess to prepare her father's porridge (tea was from twelve to sixteen shillings a pound, and beyond their reach).

Almost on the threshold he encountered Simon.

"Can't you keep that young sprig out of mischief? If he begins fighting and quarrelling at six years old, what will he do when he is sixteen?" he cried, gruffly, as he brushed past the tanner, and was far up the yard before the man could think of a reply.

A couple of young pigeons were sent for Jabez about a week after, with a large bag of stale cakes and bread to feed them with. The name of the sender was unknown, but anyone acquainted with the habits of Joshua Brookes (who contracted for Mrs. Clowes' waste pastry, to fill the crops of his own feathered colony) would not have been troubled to guess.

Simon stroked his raspy chin, and seemed dubious, cost of keep being a question; but Jabez looked so wistful, his foster-father borrowed tools and answered the appeal by making a triangular cote for them, and Jabez found fresh occupation in their care. Yet occupation was not lacking, young as he was. He could fetch and carry, run short errands, and help Bess to clean. Their living-room no longer waited a week to be swept and dusted, Jabez did it every day, standing on a chair to reach the top of the bureau, where lay the cynosure of his young eyes. He still took his Sunday lessons in field or stream with Simon, and through the week clambered up from monosyllables to dissyllables with Bess.

CHAPTER THE EIGHTH.

THE BLUE COAT SCHOOL.

EXIT FROM COLLEGE YARD.

THE children of the poor begin early to earn their bread. Legislature has stepped in to regulate the age and hours for labour in manufacturing districts, and to provide education for the humblest. Jabez Clegg was not born in these blissful times, and he only narrowly escaped the common lot.

He was not eight years old, yet Simon, on whom war-prices pressed as heavily as on his neighbours, began to discuss with Bess the necessity for sending the lad to Simpson's factory (where Arkwright's machinery was first set in motion).

"He mun goo as sune as the new year taks a fair grip," decided Simon, and 1805 was at its last gasp as he said it.

But the new year brought Jabez a reprieve by the uncourtly hands of Joshua Brookes. Meeting Simon and Jabez at a stall in the Apple Market, where, the better to bargain, he had laid down a pile of old classical school-books (Joshua was a collector of these, which he retailed again to the boys at prices varying with his mood, or his estimate of the purchaser's pocket), he accosted the former.

"Well, old Leathershanks, what are you going to make of young Cheat-the-fishes there? I suppose he's to follow your own trade, he began to *tan hides* so early?" And the glance which shot from under his shaggy brows caused the boy to blush, and shrink behind his protector.

Simon's eyes twinkled, but he shook his head as he answered:

"Nay, Parson Brucks, we'n thowt o' sendin' him t' th' cotton fac'try; but it fair goos agen th' grain to send th' little chap through th' streets to wark Winter an' Summer, weet or dry, afore th' sun's oop an' abeawt *his* wark. But we conno' keep him bout it—toimes are so bad."

"H'm! Then what a stupid old leather-head you must be not to think of the College, where he'd be kept and fed and clothed and educated!—*educated*, man, do you hear?"

Simon heard, and his eyes again twinkled and winked at the new idea presented to him.

"And 'prenticed!" he echoed, with a long-drawn, gasping breath.

"Ay, and apprenticed."

The parson, cramming his pockets with apples, for which he had higgled with much persistence, handed one to Jabez with the question—

"How would you like to be a College boy, Jabez, and wear a long blue coat, like that fellow yonder" (pointing to a boy then crossing the market on an errand), "and learn to write and cypher, as well as to read?"

"If you please'n, aw'd loike it moore nor eawt." His animated face was a clearer answer than his words.

Joshua then read the lad a brief homily to the effect that only good and honourable boys could find admission, winding up with—

"If you're a *very* good lad, I'll see what can be done for you."

He interrupted thanks with—

"Easter's very near, Sim, so you'll have to stir your stumps to prove that our *honourable* young friend came honourably into the world. I'll get the forms and fill them up for you, and his baptismal register too."

He snatched up his books and was off, the tassel of his collegiate cap and the cassock he wore flying loose as he hurried away muttering to himself—

"What an old fool I am to bother about the lad! I daresay he'll turn round and sting me in the end, like the rest of the snakes I have warmed. As great an idiot as old Dame Clowes!"

Chetham's College, or Hospital, is a long, low, ancient stone edifice, built on the rock above the mouth of the Irk, with two arms of unequal length, stretching towards church and town, and embracing a large quadrangle used as a playground, which has for its fourth and southern boundary a good useful garden.

It is needless to grope upward from the time when the Saxon Theyn built a fortified residence on its site; sufficient for us that Thomas de la Warr, youngest son of the feudal baron of Manchester, was brought up to the Church, and in the fourteenth century inducted into the Rectory of Manchester, his father being patron. His elder brother dying at the close of the century, the rector (a pious Churchman) became baron. And then he put his power and wealth to sacerdotal uses. He petitioned the king, obtained a grant to collegiate Christ Church, erected the College, endowed it with lands; and here at his death the Warden of the Collegiate Church had his residence. Of these wardens, the celebrated Dr. Dee, whose explorations into alchemy and other occult sciences brought him into trouble with Queen Elizabeth, was one; and Dr. Dee's room is still extant—in occupation of the governor.

In 1580, at Crumpsall Hall, Humphrey Chetham was born; and he, a prosperous dealer in fustians, never marrying, at his own expense fed and clothed a number of poor boys; and, by his will, not only bequeathed a large sum of money to be expended in the foundation and endowment of a hospital for the maintenance, education, and apprenticing of forty poor boys for ever, but one thousand pounds to be expended in a library, free to the public—*the first free library in Britain.*

The estate was vested in feoffees, and with them lay the power alike to elect boys and officials. From the townships of Manchester, Droylsden, Crumpsall, Bolton-le-Moors, and Turton, the boys were to be elected between the ages of six and ten, and were required to be of honest, industrious parents, and neither illegitimate nor diseased; and baptismal registers had to be produced. They had to be well maintained, well trained, and carefully apprenticed at fourteen, a fee of four pounds (a large sum in Humphrey Chetham's time) being given with them. The churchwardens and overseers were to prepare lists of boys, doubling the number of vacancies, stating their respective claims, which lists they had to sign.

Easter Monday was the period for election, after which the feoffees dined together in Dr. Dee's quaintly-carved room.

Joshua Brookes was as good as his word. He procured a blank form from the governor, and, Simon being no great scholar, filled it in for him. He found him the baptismal register without charging the regulation shilling, got the name of Jabez inserted in the churchwardens' list, and such influence as he had with feoffees he exerted to the utmost, for the case was one involving doubt and difficulty.

Nor had Simon Clegg been idle. He and his crony, Matthew, scoured Smedley and Crumpsall, and more successful than in their quest for Tom Hulme, discovered the nurse who presided at the birth of Jabez. Her testimony, so far as it went, was important. He had interested both Mr. and Mrs. Clough in the election of the foundling, and where the influence of the gentleman failed, that of the lady prevailed; so that when the important Easter Monday arrived, two-thirds of the feoffees were fully acquainted with his peculiar case, and more or less impressed in his favour.

It was on the 18th of April, bright, sunny, joyous. Compared with its present proportions, Manchester then was but as a cameo brooch on a mantle of green; and that green was already starred with daisies, buttercups, primroses, and cowslips. By wells and brooks, daffodil and jonquil hung their heads and breathed out perfume. Bush and tree put out pale buds and fans of promise. The tit-lark sang, the cuckoo—to use a village phrase—had "eaten up the mud;" and the town was alive with holiday-

CRUMPSALL HALL, HUMPHREY CHETHAM'S BIRTHPLACE.

makers from all the country round about.

It was the great College anniversary, not only election day, but one set apart for friends to visit Blue-coat boys already on the foundation, and for the curious public to inspect the Chetham Museum.

The main entrance in Millgate (said to be arched with the jaw-bone of a whale) and the smaller gate on Hunt's Bank, were both thrown open. A stream of people of all grades, in festival array, poured in and out, and College cap and gown seemed to be ubiquitous.

The pale, sad widow or widower, holding an orphan boy by the trembling hand, the uncle or next of kin to the doubly-orphaned candidate, were there, standing in a long line ranged against the building, and representing hopes and fears and eventualities little heeded by the shifting stream of gazers.

For the previous week Mrs. Clowes and her assistants had been working night and day; her shop was in a state of siege. Every boy, and every boy's friend, seemed to have pocket-money to spend, and to want to spend it over her counter. Then it was the great wedding-day of the year, and the churchyard swarmed like a hive; from every one of the many public-houses round College and Church, music and mirth, clattering feet, and loud-voiced laughter issued. "The Apple Tree," "The Pack Horse," "The Ring o' Bells," "The Blackamoor's Head," were filled to repletion with wedding guests; whilst "The College Inn" and the old "Sun Inn" held a less boisterous quota of the Collegians' friends and relatives.

On those wet days when outdoor play was impossible, the boys, besides darning their stockings, occupied their spare hours in carving spoons and apple-scrapers out of bone, in working balls and pincushions in fanciful devices with coloured worsted, and a stitch locally known as "colleging;" and with these, on Easter Monday and at Whitsuntide, they reaped a harvest of pocket-money, having liberty to offer them for sale. And when it is remembered that our notable female ancestors, poor and rich, wore indoors a pincushion and sheathed scissors suspended at their sides, it is not to be

READING ROOM, CHETHAM LIBRARY.

wondered that these found ready purchasers as memorials of the visit.

But in that College Yard were anxious and expectant as well as buoyant faces. And there in that line, waiting to be called when their turn came, stood Jabez between Simon Clegg and Bess, with Matthew and the nurse on either hand. And ever and anon their eyes went up to the oriel window which faced the main entrance, for in the room it lighted the arbiters of the boy's destiny sat in judgment on some other orphan's claim. At length the summons came for "Jabez Clegg."

With palpitating hearts—for any body of men with irresponsible powers is an awful tribunal—they passed under the arched portal at the western angle of the building, following their guide past the doors of the great kitchen on the right hand, and the boys' refectory and Dr. Dee's room on the left, up the wide stone staircase, with its massive carved oak balusters, along the gallery, at once library and museum, where gaping holiday-folk followed a Blue-coat cicerone past shelves and glass cases, and compartments separated for readers' quiet study by carven book-shelf screens, hearing, but heeding little of the parrot-roll the boys checked off: "Here's Oliver Crummle's sword; theer's a loadstone; theer's a hairy mon; theer's the skeleton of a mon;" and so forth, but following their own guide to the nail-studded oaken door of the feoffees' room—that door which might open to hope, only to close on disappointment.

The feoffees' room—now the reading-room of the library—deserves more than a passing notice. It is a large, square, antique chamber, with a deeply-recessed oriel window, opposite the door, containing a table and seats for readers. There are carved oak buffets of ancient date, ponderous chairs, and still more ponderous tables, one of which is said to contain as many pieces as there are days in the year. Dingy-looking portraits of eminent Lancashire divines stare at you from the walls; but the left-hand wall contains alone the benevolent presentment of Humphrey Chetham, the large-hearted, clear-headed founder. Its place is over the wide chimneypiece, which holds an ample grate; and on either hand it is flanked by the carved effigy of a bird, the one a pelican feeding its young brood with its own blood, the other a cock, which is said (and truly) to crow when it smells roast beef.

But we smell the feoffees' dinner, and must not delay the progress of Jabez and his friends. A large body of feoffees were present, many in the uniforms of their special volunteer regiments.

"So this is the little fellow who was picked up asleep in a cradle during the flood of August, 1799," observed rather than inquired one of the gentlemen, who appeared as spokesman.

"Yoi, yo'r honours," answered Simon, making a sort of bow.

"Who can bear witness to that?"

"Aw con"—"An' aw con," responded Simon and Matt Cooper in a breath. "It wur uz as got him eawt o' th' wayter."

"Anyone else?"

Bess stepped forward modestly.

"He wur put i' moi arms on Tanners' Bridge, an' aw've browt him oop ivver sin'."

"Have you never sought for his parents?"

"Ay, mony a toime. Matt an' me have spent mony a day i' seekin' 'em," said Simon promptly, an' we could fand no moore than that papper tells"—referring to a sheet in the questioning feoffee's hand.

"Then how do you date the boy's age with such precision?"

The nurse now sidled confidently to the front.

"If it please your honour's worship, aw wur called to stiff-backed Nan's dowter in the last pinch, when hoo wur loike to die, an' that little chap wur born afore aw left, an' that wur o' th' fifth o' May, seventeen hunderd and nointy-noine. Aw know it, fur aw broke mi arm th' varry next day."

"And the mother died?"

"Yea!—afore the week wur eawt."

"And you think she was lawfully married? Where was her

husband?"

"Ay! that's it! Hoo had a guinea-goold weddin'-ring on; an' owd Nan said it wur a sad thing th' lass had ever got wedded, an' moore o' the same soort. An' aw geet eawt o' her that they'n bin wedded at Crumpsall, an' a' th' neebors knew as th' husbant had had a letter to fatch him to Liverpool, an' had niver come back. Onybody i' Smedley knows that!"

"And you think they were honest, industrious people?"

"Ay! that they were, but raything stiff i' th' joints, yo' know —seemed to think theirsel's too good to talk to folk like; or, mebbe we'd ha' known th' lad's neäme an' o' belongin' to him. They owed nobbody nowt, an' aw wur paid fur moi job."

Jabez was called forward and examined, and he came pretty well out of the fire. They found that he could read a little, knew part of his catechism, and they saw that he was a well-behaved, intelligent boy, with truthful dark grey eyes and a reflective brow.

There was a long and animated discussion, during which the boy and his friends were bidden to retire. It was contended that the marriage of the boy's parents was not proven—that his very name was dubious,—and that the founder's will was specific on that head.

Then one of Mrs. Clough's friends rose and grew eloquent. He asked if they were to interpret the will of the great and benevolent man, whose portrait looked down upon them, by the spirit or by the letter? If they themselves did not *feel* that the boy was eligible, as the nurse's testimony went to prove? That this was a case peculiarly marked out for their charitable construction. And he wound up by inquiring if they thought Humphrey Chetham would expect his representatives to be less humane, less charitable, less conscientious in dealing with a bounty not their own, than that poor struggling, hard-working tanner and his daughter, who had maintained and cherished the orphan in spite of cruelly hard times, and still more cruel slander. And then he told, as an episode, what Sally Cooper had confessed, and how and why Bess had lost her lover.

This turned the quivering scale. "Jabez Clegg and his friends" were called in; the verdict which changed the current of his life was pronounced—Jabez Clegg was a Blue-coat boy!

Before the night was out, while the flood-gates of all their hearts were open, Matthew Cooper, though nearly twenty years her senior, asked Bess to be his wife!

CHAPTER THE NINTH.

THE SNAKE.

HOWEVER ambitious either Jabez or his kind fosterers had been to see him a Blue-coat boy, the parting between them was a terrible wrench. They were to him all the friends or parents he had ever known. Then there were his playmates in the yard, with liberty to run in and out at will; and lastly, there were his dumb pets—his kitten (grown to a cat), his pigeons, and the lame linnet, hopping from perch to finger, and paying him for his love with the sweetest of songs.

He was not more stunned by the noise and Easter Monday bustle in the College Yard, or more awed by the imposing presence of Governor Terry and the feoffees, than by the magnitude, order, and antique grandeur of the building henceforth to be his home. Nevertheless, wide open as the gates were for the day, he felt that they would close, and shut him in among the cold strong walls and strangers, never to see his pets or his loving friends again until Whitsuntide should bring another holiday.

They older, more experienced, with a better knowledge of all the boy would gain—all the privation and premature labour he would escape—felt only how dull their humble home would be without the willing feet and hands, the smiling face, and the cheerful voice of the sturdy little fellow who for more than seven years had been as their own child.

He had given his last charge respecting his furry and feathered brood, exchanged the last clinging embrace under the dark arch, then tore away in quest of a deserted corner, where he could hide the tears he could not wholly restrain.

At first the new dress of which he was so proud, the yellow stockings and clasped shoes in place of clogs, the yellow baize petticoat, the long-skirted blue overcoat or gown, the blue muffin-cap, the white clerical band at the throat (all neat, and fresh, and unpatched as they were), felt awkward and uncomfortable—the long petticoat especially incommoded him.

But in a few days this wore off. There were other lads equally strange and unaccustomed to robes and rules. Fellow-feeling drew them towards each other, and with the wonderful adaptability of childhood, they fell into the regular grooves, and were as much at home as the eldest there in less than a fortnight. And from the Chetham Gallery in the Old Church he could see and be seen by Simon and Bess on Sabbath mornings from the free seats in the aisle, and that contented them.

The training and education of the Chetham College boys was, and is, conducted on principles best adapted for boys expected to fight their way upwards in the world. They were not encumbered with a number of "ologies" and "isms" (the highest education did not stand on a par then with the moderate ones of this day); their range of books and studies was limited. Reading, writing, and arithmetic, sound and practical information alone were imparted, so much as was needed to fit the dullest for an ordinary tradesman, and supply the persevering and intelligent with a fulcrum and a lever. Nor did their education end with their lessons in the schoolroom, nor was it drawn from books and slates alone.

Their meals were regular, their diet pure and ample, but plain. They rose at six, began the day with prayer, and retired to rest at eight. Besides their duties in the schoolroom, they darned their own stockings, made their own beds, helped the servants to keep their rooms clean, and six of the elder boys were set apart to run errands and carry messages beyond the precincts of the College.

Strength of muscle and limb were gained in the open courtyard in such games as trap and football; patience and ingenuity had scope in the bead purses, the carved apple-scoops and marrow-spoons, the worsted balls and pincushions they made to fill their leisure hours indoors. There was no idleness. Their very play had its purpose.

Let us set Jabez Clegg under the kind guardianship of Christopher Terry, the Governor, and under the direct supervision of the Reverend John Gresswell, the schoolmaster, to con his Mavor, and make pothooks-and-ladles, on a form in the large schoolroom at the east end of the College, and to rise, step by step, up the first difficult rungs of that long ladder of learning which may indeed rest on our common earth, but which reaches far above the clouds and human ken.

Christmas and Midsummer vacations came and went, so did those red-letter days of his College life, Easter and Whitsuntide, when he was free to rush to the old yard, so near at hand, and after hugging Bess and Simon, whom he astonished with his learning, could assure himself his dumb family had been well-cared for.

And if those passing seasons traced deeper lines on Simon's brow, gave more womanly solidity to Bess's form and character, they brought no change the foundling could mark. Tom Hulme's whereabouts was still undiscovered. Matt Cooper was still a widower. But they and his masters could note the steady progress *he* made, and his chivalrous love of truth and sense of honour shown in many ways in little things. Yet there was one event a grief to him. His little brown linnet pined for its young friend, and died before the first Whitsunday came.

He was not much over ten years old when he was proved to possess courage, as well as truth and honour.

For some time Nancy, the cook, had observed that the cream was skimmed surreptitiously from the milk-pans in the dairy, that the milk itself was regularly abstracted, and she was loud in complaint. She could scarcely find cream enough to set on the governor's table, and servants and schoolboys were in turn accused of being the depredators.

Complaints were made to Mr. Terry, servants and boys were alike interrogated and watched, and punished on suspicion, but nothing could be proved, and no precautions could save the milk. The lofty and spacious kitchen had its entrance almost under the porch, and close beside it was a flight of stone steps leading to the dairy, a cellar below the kitchen, lit by a small window high up

SNAKE CELLAR, CHETHAM HOSPITAL.

on the side towards the river, and of course opposite to the steps.

Stone tables occupied the two other sides, on which were ranged a number of wide, shallow pans of good milk. In the extreme corner, at right angles with the door at the head of the stairs, was another entrance, a small oaken door in a Gothic frame, which opened on another and shorter flight of steps, cut in the rock and washed by the river, which sometimes rose and beat against the cellar-door for admission, beat so oft and importunately as to wear away the oak where it met the floor.

It was nearly breakfast time. Long rows of wooden bowls and trenchers were ranged on the white kitchen-table. The oatmeal porridge was ready to pour out. The cook ran short of milk. Through a window overlooking the yard she espied Jabez, whip in hand, driving a biped team of play-horses.

"Jabez, Jabez Clegg!" she called out at the pitch of her voice, "come hither."

Down went the reins, and the prancing steeds proceeded without a driver.

"Fetch a can of milk from the cellar, Jabez; an' look sharp. An' see as yo' dunna drink none!"

"I never do," said Jabez, not overpleased at the imputation.

"Well, see as yo' don't, for some on yo' do."

Jabez took the bright tin can, without putting down the whip, and descended the unguarded cellar-stairs, whistling as he went. He gave a jump down the last few steps, and to his utter surprise, I cannot say dismay, saw that he had disturbed a great greenish-brown snake, spotted with black and having a yellowish ring round its neck. It lay coiled on the stone table opposite to him, and with its head elevated above the rim of a milk-pan, was taking its morning draught, and in so doing reckoning without its host.

"Oh! you're the thief, are you, Mr. Snake? It's you've robbed us of our milk, and got us boys thrashed for it!" cried Jabez, without a thought of danger, planting himself between the culprit and the small postern door, as the snake, gliding from the slab, turned thither for exit, putting out its forked tongue and hissing at him as it came.

Without thought or consideration—without a cry of alarm to those above, he struck at the threatening foe with his whip; and as the resentful snake darted at him, jumped nimbly aside, and struck and struck again; and as the angry snake writhed and twisted, and again and again darted its frightful head at him with distended jaws, he whipped and whipped away as though a top and not a formidable reptile had been before him.

Cook, out of patience, called "Jabez Clegg!" more than once, in anything but satisfactory tones; and then, patience exhausted, came to the top of the dairy stairs. Then she heard Jabez, as if addressing some one, say: "Oh! you would, would you?" and the commotion having drawn her so far down the steps that she could peer into the cellar and see what was going on, she set up a prolonged scream. This was just as Jabez, shifting the position of his whip, brought the butt-end down on the head of the snake with all the force of his stout young arm, and his exhausted foe dropped, literally whipped to death.

The woman's screams brought not only the governor and the school-master, but Dr. Stone, the librarian, to the spot. And there stood Jabez, all his prowess gone, with his back towards them, his head down on his arms, which rested on the stone slab, sobbing violently for the very life he had just destroyed.

"Oh, he's bin bitten—he's bin bitten! The vemonous thing's bitten the lad! He'll die after it!" cried the cook in an ecstasy of terror.

"Stand aside, Nancy," said Dr. Stone; "that snake is not venomous. If I mistake not, the brave boy's heart is wounded, not his skin."

And, coming down, the kind, discerning librarian lifted the snake with the one hand, and took hold of Jabez with the other, simply saying to him—

"Come into the governor's room, Jabez, and tell us all about it."

And Jabez, drying his red eyes on the cuff of his coat, was ushered before the Doctor up the stairs, and into the governor's room, where breakfast was laid for the three gentlemen. There he briefly told how he had found the snake drinking the milk; and having intercepted the reptile's retreat, had been obliged, in self-defence, to fight with it until he had whipped it to death—a consummation as unlooked for as regretted.

He had not, as at first surmised, escaped unwounded in the contest; but, as Dr. Stone had said, and the surgeon who dressed the bites confirmed, the terrible-looking reptile was but the common ringed-snake, which takes freely to the water; and its bite was harmless. From the dais in the refectory both snake and whip were exhibited to the boys after breakfast.

"My lads," said the governor, "I daresay you will all be glad to know that the thief who stole the milk has been taken."

There was a general shout of assent, with here and there a wondering glance at the vacant seat of Jabez, who, having his wounds washed and bound up, had not sat down with them, but had a sort of complimentary breakfast with the servants in the kitchen.

"And I daresay you would like to see the thief, and know how he was caught."

There was another general "Ay, ay, sir!"

"Well, here he is" (and he held the snake aloft); "but I don't think any of you will be thrashed on his account again. Jabez Clegg, here" (and he pulled the reluctant boy forward by the shoulder), "caught the sly robber drinking the milk, and, with nothing but this whip and a fearless, resolute arm, put a stop to his depredations, and restored the lost character of the school."

There was a loud hurrah for Jabez Clegg, who for the time being was a hero. Then, the snake being carried to the schoolroom, the Rev. John Gresswell improved the occasion by a lesson on snakes in general, and that one in particular. But when he dissipated the popular belief that all snakes were venomous, and assured the boys that the bite of this was innocuous, more than one of the Blue-coated lads thought Jabez was not such a hero after all.

The heads of the College thought otherwise. The snake, and whip also, were placed high up against a wall in the College museum, close beside the "woman's clog which was split by a thunderbolt, and hoo wasn't hurt." They made part of the catalogue of the Blue-coat guides—nay, even Jabez may have run the rapid chronicle from the reel himself; but the pain and shock of having wilfully killed a living creature neutralised and prevented the harm which might have followed self-glorification.

The long unknown secret spoiler of the dairy had been such a blemish on the spotless character of the Chetham Hospital—such a scandal in its little world—that its capture became of sufficient importance for Dr. Thomas Stone to communicate to the Reverend Joshua Brookes on his next visit to the library, Jabez being considered a sort of *protégé* of his.

Before the day was out the parson found his cough troublesome, and, of course, went to Mrs. Clowes for horehound-drops.

"Well, what do you think of young Cheat-the-fishes now?" came raspily from his lips, as he leaned on the counter, evidently prepared for a gossip, shop-chairs being unheard-of superfluities in those days.

Mrs. Clowes knew perfectly well whom the parson meant by "young Cheat-the-fishes"; indeed, the boy, on his rare holidays, had been a customer, as were the boys of College and Grammar School generally.

"Now? Why, what's th' lad been doing? Naught wrong, I reckon?"

You see she had faith in the boy's open countenance.

"Humph! that's as folk think," he growled, keeping his own opinion to himself. "I don't suppose I need to tell you the hubbub there's been over there" (jerking his finger in the direction of the College) "about the stolen milk? That tale's old enough."

Mrs. Clowes nodded her mob-cap in assent.

"Well, that lad Jabez found a snake, four feet long, with its head in the milk pans the other morning. The sly thief turned spiteful, and the two had a battle-royal all to themselves in the cellar. The pugnacious rapscallion had a whip in his hand, and he—lashed the snake to death!"

Mrs. Clowes echoed his last words, and uplifted her hands in amazement. A snake was a terrible reptile to her.

"Ah! and then blubbered like a cry-a-babby because he had killed it! What do you think of that, Dame Clowes?"

"Eh! I think he was a brave little chap to face a sarpent, but I think a fine sight more of his blubbering, as you call it," said she, taking a tin canister from a shelf, and putting it on the counter with an emphatic bounce.

"Ah! I thought I could match the young fool with an old one," said he derisively, to hide his own satisfaction, as he took his short legs to the door.

But Mrs. Clowes called him back, put a large paper parcel in his hand, and said—

"Here, Jotty, see you give these sweetmeats to your cry-a-babby, and tell him an old woman says there's no harm in fighting in self-defence with any kind of a snake, or for his own good name, or to protect the helpless; but, if he fights just to show off his own bravery, he's a coward. And you tell him from me never to be ashamed of tears he has shed in repentance for injury he may have done to any living thing. Now see you tell him, parson; and maybe my preachment may be worth more to him than my cakes or toffy, or your sarmons." And she nodded her head till her cap-border flapped like a bird's wings.

"Ugh! dame, you'll be for wagging that tongue and mutch of yours in my pulpit next," said he, gruffly.

But he delivered the parcel and the "preachment" both faithfully, and, moreover, turned over his stores of old school books for a Latin grammar, which he put into the hand of Jabez, with a promise to instruct the boy in the language, if he would like to learn.

Forthwith Jabez, not caring to seem ungracious, though without any special liking for the task, had to encroach upon his play hours for a new study, under-rated by the pupil, over-rated by the teacher.

Could Joshua Brookes have put mathematical instruments within his reach, or given him pencils and colours, the boy's eyes would have sparkled, and study been a pleasure.

CHAPTER THE TENTH.

FIRST ANTAGONISM.

COLLEGE GATE AND GRAMMAR SCHOOL.

THE extensive oblong enclosure known as Ardwick Green, situated at the south-eastern extremity of the town, on the left-hand side of the highway to Stockport and London, was, in 1809, part of a suburban village, and from Piccadilly to a blacksmith's forge a little beyond Ardwick Bridge, fields and hedges were interspersed with the newly-erected houses along Bank Top.

The Green, studded here and there with tall poplars and other trees, was fenced round with quite an army of stumpy wooden posts some six feet apart, connected by squared iron rods, a barrier against cattle only. A long, slightly serpentine lake spread its shining waters from end to end within the soft circlet of green; and this grassy belt served as a promenade for the fashionable inhabitants. And there must have been such in that village of Ardwick early in the century, as now, for the one bell in the tiny turret of St. Thomas's small, plain, red-brick chapel rang a fashionable congregation into its neat pews, to listen to the well-toned organ and the devoutly-toned voice of the perpetual curate, the Reverend R. Tweddle, if we may credit an historian of the time.

Red-brick church, red-brick houses, hard and cold outside, solid and roomy and comfortable within, as Georgian architecture ever was, overlooked green and pond, but, luckily, overlooked them from a reasonable distance, and, moreover, did not elbow each other too closely, but were individually set in masses of foliage, which toned down the staring brickwork. Time and

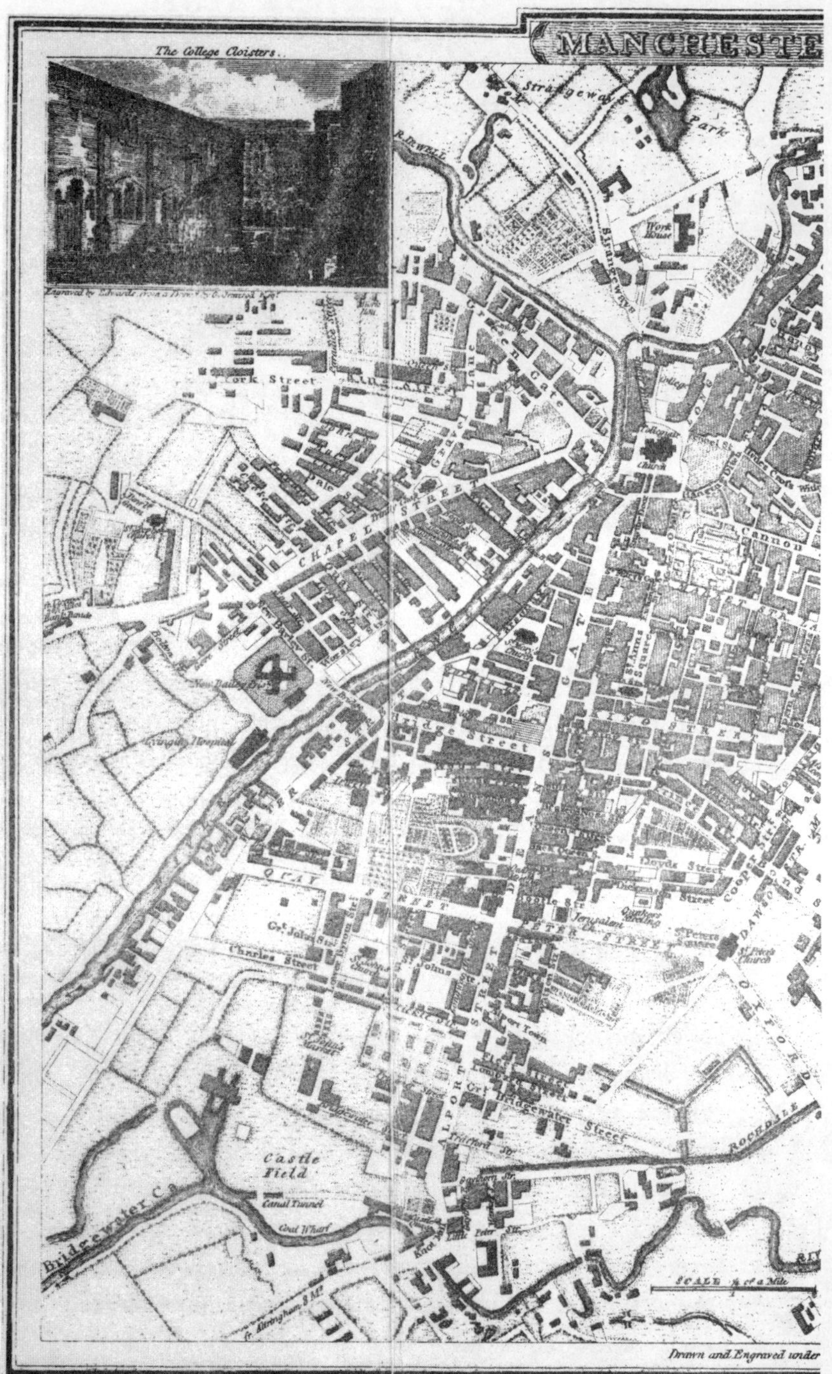
MANCHESTE
The College Cloisters.
Strangeways Park
R. IRWELL
Work House
York Street
Chapel Street
Bridge Street
Quay Street
Gt. John St.
Charles Street
St. Johns Church
St. Peters Church
Lloyds Street
Cannon
Castle Field
Canal Tunnel
Coal Wharf
Bridgewater Ca.
Bridgewater Street
Rochdale
Oxford
SCALE ¼ of a Mile
Drawn and Engraved under
Engraved by J Roper from a Survey by Thornton
London Published for the Proprietors, by

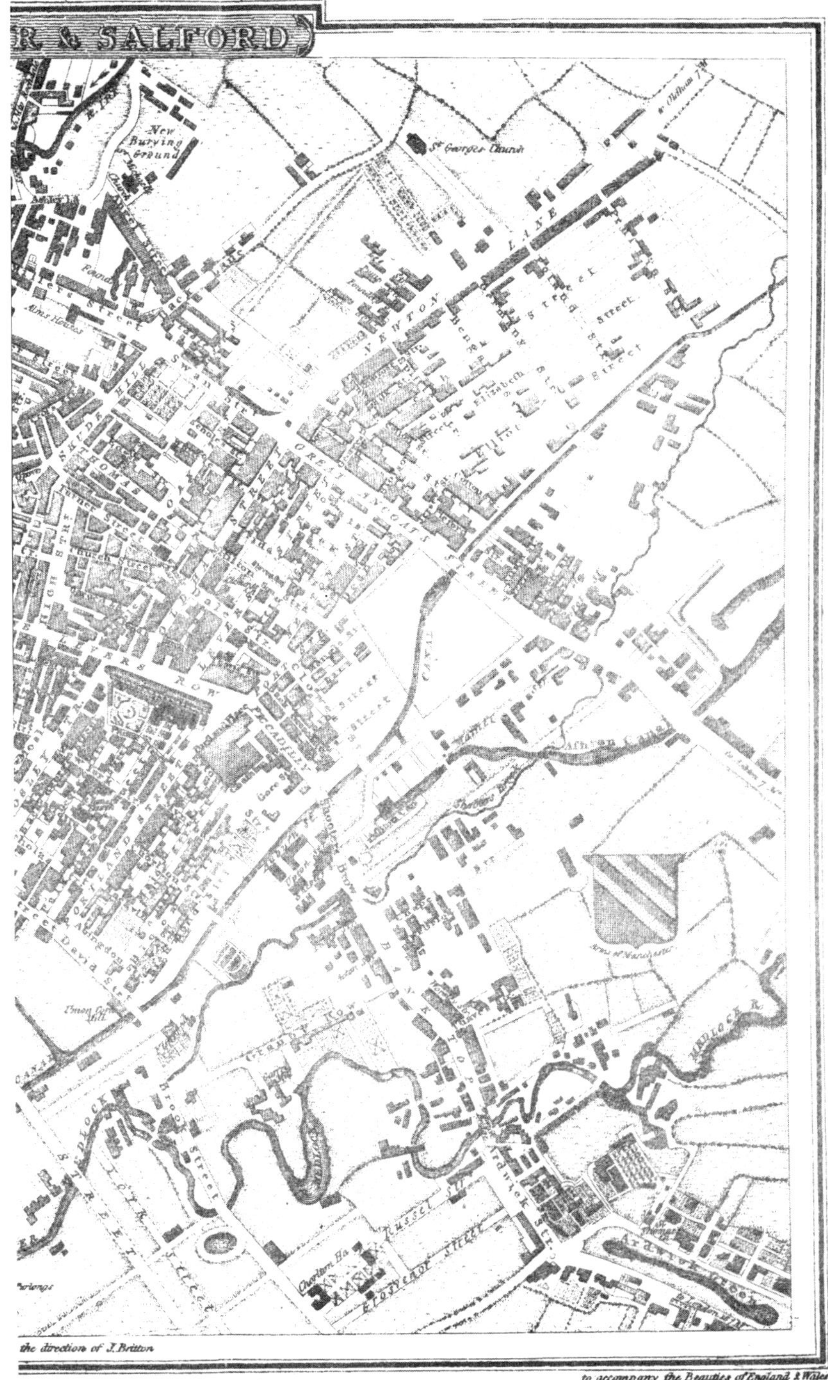

to accompany the Beauties of England & Wales.

Vernor, Hood & Sharpe, Poultry. Apr. 1st 1807.

smoke have done so more effectually since.

One of the best, and best-looking of these houses, near the church, was the one in which the delicate Mrs. Aspinall had presided for a few brief years. An iron palisade, enclosing a few shrubs and evergreens, separated it from the wide roadway, but behind the screen of brick ran a formal but extensive garden and orchard, well-kept and well-stocked, with a fish-pond as formal in the midst.

Fish-ponds encourage damp, and damp encourages frogs, efts, and their kin. Here they abounded, and Master Laurence had a sort of instinctive belief that they were created solely for his sport and amusement. Mr. Aspinall, his father, immersed in business during the day, and occupied with friends at home or abroad until late hours at night, saw very little of his son, who was thus consigned to servants during those hours not spent, or supposed to be spent, at a preparatory school close at hand.

The boy was quick and intelligent, had his mother's amber curls and azure eyes, her delicate skin and brilliant colour, but the handsome face had more of the father therein, and was too unformed to brook description here.

What he might have been with other training is not to be told, but under the supposition that he inherited his mother's fragile constitution, he had been woefully spoiled and pampered. Opposition to his will was forbidden.

"Bear with him, Kitty, for my sake, and do not thwart him, or you will break his fine spirit," had been Mrs. Aspinall's dying charge to her old nurse; and as every demonstration of temper was ascribed by both parents to this same "fine spirit," what wonder that he grew up masterful—and worse?

His imperious disposition early ingratiated him into the favour of Bob, his father's groom; and this man, thinking no evil, ignorantly sowed the seeds of cruelty in his young heart.

When the horses were singed, the boy was allowed to be a spectator; if a whelp had his ears cropped, or the end of its tail bitten of, he was treated to a sight. If a brood of kittens or a litter of puppies had to be drowned, Master Laurence was sure to be in at the death. He was taken to surreptitious cock-fights and rat hunts; and though, when too late, Mr. Aspinall turned the man away for inclining his son to "low pursuits," nothing was said or done to counteract these lessons of cruelty! No wonder, then, that to him the sight of pain inflicted brought pleasure, or that inhumanity went hand-in-hand with self-will.

One incident—a real one—will suffice to show what Laurence Aspinall was, when Jabez Clegg shed tears over the snake he had killed perforce.

Kitty was in the kitchen alone. The maids were in other parts of the house. She was sitting close to a blazing fire on account of her "rheumatics," and was in a dose. The evening was drawing in. Master Laurence, coming direct from the garden and the fish-pond, burst open the kitchen door with a whoop which made Kitty start from her nap in a fright. Thereupon he set up a loud laugh as the poor old woman held her hand to her side, and panted for breath. In his hand was his pocket-handkerchief, tied like a bundle, in which something living seemed to move and palpitate. They were young frogs in various stages of development. "Now, Kitty," said he, "I'll show you some rare sport" and taking one of the live frogs out of the handkerchief, deliberately threw it into the midst of the glowing fire.

"There, Kitty; did you hear that?" cried he in rapture, as the poor animal uttered a cry of agony almost human, whilst he danced on the hearth like a frantic savage round a sacrificial fire.

"Oh, Master Laurence! Master Laurence! don't do that—don't be so cruel!" appealed Kitty, piteously.

But he had drawn another forth, and crying, "Cruel! It's fun, Kitty—fun!" tore it limb from limb, and threw it piecemeal into the blaze.

"There's another! and there's another!" he shouted in glee, as the rest followed in swift succession; and Kitty, shrieking in pain and horror, ran from the kitchen, bringing the cook and housemaid downstairs with her cries.

For the first time in his life Mr. Aspinall administered a sound castigation to his son, regretting that he had not done it earlier.

No more was said of his son's fine spirit; but, prompt to act, he lost no time in seeking his admission into the Free Grammar School; and either to spare him the long daily walk, in tenderness for his health (Ardwick was more than a mile away), or to place him under strict supervision, boarded Laurence with one of the masters.

Yet he gave that master no clue to his son's besetting sin; so he was left free to tantalise and torment every weaker creature within his orbit, from the schoolmaster's cat, which he shod with walnut-shells, to the youngest school-boy, whose books he tore and hid, whose hair he pulled, whose cap and frills he soused in the mud.

It was a misfortune for himself and others that his pocket money was more abundant than that of his fellows. Never had the apple-woman or Mrs. Clowes a more lavish customer, or one who distributed his purchases more freely. Boys incapable of discriminating between generosity and profusion dubbed him generous; and that, coupled with his handsome face and spirited bearing, which they mistook for courage, brought him partizans.

Thus, long before his first year expired, and he was drafted from the lower school to the room above, where he came under the keen eye and heavy ferule of Joshua Brookes, he had a body of lads at his beck (many older than himself), ready for any mischief he might propose.

As well may be supposed, there was a natural antagonism between the boys of the Grammar School and of Chetham's Hospital. As at the confluence of two streams the waters chafe and foam and fret each other, so it is scarcely possible for two separate communities, similar, yet differing in their constitutions, to have their gateways close together at right angles without frequent collision between the rival bodies.

In the great gate of the College, only open on special occasions, was a small door or wicket, for ordinary use; and some of the Grammar School boys, under pretence of shortening their route homeward, finding it open, would make free to cross the College Yard at a noisy canter, and let themselves out at the far gate on Hunt's Bank. It was a clear trespass. They were frequently admonished by one official or another; their passage was disputed by the Blue-coat boys; but they persisted in setting up a right of road, and opposition only gave piquancy to their bravado.

That which began with individual assumption soon attained the character of boldly-asserted party aggression, and, as the Blue-coat boys were as determined to preserve their rights as the others were to invade them, many and well-contested were the consequent fights and struggles. And thus the two boys, Jabez Clegg and Laurence Aspinall, brought together first at the church door and the baptismal font, came into collision again. But now there was no deferential stepping aside of the humble foundling to make way for the merchant's son. They stood upon neutral ground, strangers to each other, equal in their respective participation in the benefits of a charitable foundation. Nay, if anything, Jabez had the higher standpoint. His orphanhood and poverty had given him a right to his position in Humphrey Chetham's Hospital; the very wealth of the gentleman's son made Laurence little better than a usurper in Hugh Oldham's Grammar School.

But it is no part of the novelist's province to prate of the use or abuse of charitable institutions, or to set class in opposition against class. It is only individual character and action as they bear upon one another with which we have to deal.

On more than one occasion Jabez—since his conquest of the snake, the recognised champion of his form—had stopped Laurence Aspinall at the head of a file of boys, and had done his best to bar their passage through the quadrangle.

Success depended on which school was first released.

If in time, Jabez planted himself by the little wicket with one or two companions, and, like Leonidas at Thermopylæ, fought bravely for possession of the pass, and generally contrived to beat off the intruders. Sometimes the Blue-coat boys made a sortie from the yard, and, falling upon the others pell-mell, left and bore away marks of the contest in swollen lips and black eyes.

At length matters were brought to a crisis. Thrice had Laurence and his clique been repulsed, and the shame of their defeat heightened by derisive shouts from a tribe of Millgate urchins—"Yer's the Grammar Skoo' lads beat by th' yaller petticoats agen!" "Yaller petticoats fur iver!" "College boys agen Skoo'! Hoorray!"

Master Laurence might have ground his teeth, and harangued his followers, without obtaining an additional recruit, or spurring them to a fresh attempt, but for the taunts of the rabble. But the ignominy of defeat by petticoated College boys was too much for the blood of the Grammar School, and youngsters threw themselves into the party quarrel who had hitherto stood aloof.

Laurence Aspinall was superseded. A big, raw-boned fellow named Travis took the lead, and rallied round him not only the lads from the lower school, but the bulk of the juniors in the upper room. It is only fair to add that the senior students were in no wise cognisant of the league, or, being so, carefully shut their eyes and ears.

As the result of this organism, on a set day, towards the close of October, when the dusk gathered as the school dispersed, the boys who ran down the wide steps from the upper, and the juveniles who ran up from the lower room, instead of darting forward with a "Whoop!" and "Halloo!" through the iron gate, on their homeward way, clustered together within the school-yard, and made way for seniors and masters to pass out before them.

"Get off home with you, and don't loiter there!" cried Joshua Brookes, as he turned in at his own gate, and saw the crowd massing together in the outer playground.

"Get home yourself, St. Crispin!" shouted Laurence, but not before the house door had closed upon the irascible master.

All books and slates not purposely left in school were consigned to three or four of the smallest boys, duly instructed to carry them to Hunt's Bank in readiness for their owners.

For a week or more the College boys had been unmolested; not a forbidden foot had stepped within the wicket. The schoolmaster had remarked to the governor, in the presence of his pupils, that he thought Dr. Smith must have prohibited further intrusion.

All the greater was the surprise that dusky October afternoon when a troop of young ruffians, who had stolen quietly one by one through the wicket, and kept under the cavernous shade of the deep gateway until all were within, rushed, with vociferous shouts, from under cover, and tore across the large yard in the direction of the other gate, daring anyone to check them.

The College boys, just emerging from their school-room door in the corner, were, for the moment, taken aback. Then, from the mouth of Joshua Brookes' new Latin scholar, rang, clear and distinct, Humphrey Chetham's motto—"Quod tuum tene!" (What you have, hold!) and the Blue-coat boys, with one George Pilkington for their leader, threw themselves, at that rallying cry, like a great wave, headlong upon the intruders.

They met the shock as a rock meets a wave, and down went many a gallant Blue-coat in the dust. Up they were in an instant, face to face with the besiegers; and then, each singling out an opponent, fought or wrestled for the mastery with all the courage and animosity, if not the skill, of practised combatants. Ben Travis and George Pilkington fought hand to hand, and Jabez —not for the first time—measured his strength with Laurence.

Heavier, stronger, older by a few months, Jabez might have overmatched his antagonist; but Laurence had profited by the lessons of Bob, the discarded groom, and every blow was planted skilfully, and told. Then Bob's teaching had been none of the most chivalrous, and Laurence took unfair advantage. He "struck below the belt," and then tripping Jabez up, like the coward that he was, kicked him, as he lay prostrate, with the fury of a savage.

Governor, schoolmaster, librarian, and porter had hastened to the scene; but the assailants nearly doubled the number of the College boys, and set lawful authority at defiance, hurling at

THE FIGHT IN THE COLLEGE YARD.

them epithets such as only schoolboys could devise.

Fortunately, their own Blue-coat boys were amenable to discipline, and, called off, one by one retreated to the house, often with pursuers close at their heels. Then the Grammar School tribe set up a scornful, triumphant shout, and, with Ben Travis and Laurence Aspinall at their head, marched out of the College Yard at the Hunt's Bank gate, exulting in their victory, even though they left one of their bravest little antagonists insensible behind them

CHAPTER THE ELEVENTH.

THE BLUE-COAT BOY.

A BLUE-COAT BOY.

THOSE were rough days, when an occasional brawl was supposed essential to test the mettle of man or boy, so that bruises and black eyes (the result of an encounter for the honour of the school) were passed over with much lighter penalties than would be dealt out now-a-days if young gentlemen in a public academy descended to blackguardism.

At that time, too, the pupils of the Grammar School assembled at seven in the morning, and sure punishment awaited the laggard who failed to present himself for prayers. There were few loiterers on that drear October morning. Conscience, and perhaps a dread of consequences, had kept the preceding day's war-party sufficiently awake, even where sore limbs did not. But, with the exception of a few smart raps with the ferule, to warm cold fingers, and a general admonition—little heeded—the early hours of the morning passed quietly enough, more congratulatory than prophetic.

That day went by, and the next. Laurence Aspinall, whose "science" had saved his head from more damage than a cut lip, was especially boastful; and, after his own underhand fashion, strove to stir big Ben Travis to fresh demonstrations.

Then a cloud loomed in the horizon and darkened every master's brow. Another whisper was in circulation that Governor Terry had been seen to enter the head-master's ancient black and white old house, and had been closeted with Dr. Smith for

THE REV. JEREMIAH SMITH, D.D.

From an Engraving.

more than an hour. Still the quiet was unbroken, and, to the wise, the very calm was ominous.

The second of November brought a revelation. On the slightly-raised floor of the high school, at the Millgate end of the room, sat, not only Dr. Jeremiah Smith, but the trustees of the school, the Reverend Joshua Brookes, and the assistant masters; and with them was Governor Terry, of the Chetham Hospital—all grave and stern. Dr. Smith's mild face was unusually severe, and Joshua's shaggy brows loured menacingly over his angry eyes. The senior pupils, chiefly young men preparing for college, were ranged on either side.

As the last of these awful personages filed in through the two-leaved door, and took his place, the palpitating hearts of the delinquents beat audibly, and courage oozed from many a clammy palm.

The boys were summoned from the lower school, and one by one, name by name, Ben Travis and his followers were called to take their stand before this formidable tribunal, Laurence Aspinall shrinking edgeways, as if to screen himself from observation.

There was little need for Dr. Smith to strike his ferule on the table to command attention, silence was so profound. Even nervous feet forgot to shuffle. Dr. Smith's commanding eye swept the trembling rank from end to end, as he stood with impressive dignity to address them.

After a brief exordium, in which he recounted the several charges brought against the boys by Governor Terry, he proceeded to say that the good character of the Manchester Grammar School was imperilled by lawless conduct such as the boys before him had exhibited the previous Tuesday, in forcibly entering, and then rioting within, the College Yard.

One of the youths—most likely Ben Travis—blurted forth that they had a right to go through the College Yard, and that the College boys stopped them.

"You mistake," said the doctor, sternly; "there is no public right of road through the College Yard. Permission is courteously granted, but there is no *right.* There is a right for the public to pass to and from the College and its library on business, within the hours the gates are open; but even that must be in order and decency. Your conduct was that of barbarians, not gentlemen."

At this point of the proceedings Jabez Clegg came into the school-room, leaning on the arm of George Pilkington. The face of the latter was bruised and swollen, but Jabez looked deplorable. His long blue overcoat was rent in more than one place; he walked with a limp; a white bandage round his head made his white face whiter still, showing more distinctly the livid and discoloured patches under the half-closed eyes. In obedience to a nod from Governor Terry, George Pilkington led his Blue-coat brother to a seat beside him; but Dr. Smith, drawing the boy gently to his side, removed the bandage, and showed Jabez to the school with one deeply-cut eyebrow plaistered up.

"What boy among you has been guilty of this outrage?" he asked, sternly.

There was no answer. Some of the little ones took out their handkerchiefs and began to whimper, fearing condign punishment. The doctor repeated his question. The boys looked from one to another, but there was still no reply. Laurence Aspinall edged farther behind his coadjutor, but he had not the manliness either to confess or regret. His only fear was detection, or betrayal by a traitor. There was little fear of that; grammar-school boys have a detestation of a "sneak."

"Boys, we cannot permit the perpetrator of such an outrage to remain in your midst; he must be expelled!"

Still no one spoke.

"Do you think you could recognise your assailant—the boy who kicked you after you were down?" (a murmur ran round the school as the classes were ordered to defile slowly past Dr. Smith's desk).

Ben Travis walked with head erect—he would have scorned such a deed—and Laurence tried to do the same, but his cruel blue eyes could not meet those of his possible accuser.

There was a struggle going on in the heart of Jabez. It was in his power to revenge himself for many taunts and sarcasms, and much previous abuse. He called to mind—for thought is swift—that Shrove Tuesday when Laurence and his friends caught him as he descended Mrs. Clowes' steps with a pennyworth of humbugs in his hand, and snatching his cap from his head, kicked it about Half Street and the churchyard as a football. And he seemed to feel again the twitch at his dark hair and the dreadful pain in his spine and loins, as they bent him backwards over the coping of the low wall, in order to wrest his sweets from him, and held him there perforce till stout Mrs. Clowes, armed with a rolling-pin, came to his rescue, laying about her vigorously, and kept him in her back parlour until he revived.

"Forgive and forget" are words for the angels, and Jabez was not an angel, but a boy with quick-beating pulses, and a vivid memory. There was a fight going on in his breast fiercer than either that in Half Street or that in the College Yard. His sore, stiff limbs, and smarting brow, urged him like voices to "pay him off for all," and revenge began to have a sweet savour in his mouth.

As he hesitated, watching the slow approach of his foe among his nobler mates, a harsh voice behind him called out, "*Jabez*, why do you not answer Dr. Smith?"

The emphasis Joshua Brookes had laid upon the "Jabez" recalled the boy's better self. The oft-repeated text flashed across his mind, "Jabez was an honourable man," and it shaped his reply.

"Well, sir, it was almost dark, and—and"—he was going to add too dark to distinguish features, but he recollected that that would be a falsehood, and lying was no more honourable than malice.

"And you could not recognise him, you mean?" suggested Dr. Smith.

His lip quivered.

"No, sir, I do not mean that. It was very dark, but I think I should know him again. But, oh! if you please, sir, I should not like to turn him out of school. You see, we were all fighting together, and we were all in a passion, and—and—it would be very mean of me to turn him out of school because he hurt me in a fight" (Jabez did not say a fair fight).

"Ah!" said Dr. Smith, and, turning to Mr. Terry, asked, "Are all the Chetham lads reared on the same principle?"

Then there was a low-voiced discussion amongst trustees and masters. Finally, Dr. Smith turned round. His clear eye had detected the culprit as he winced beneath the gaze of Jabez. But the injured boy had forgiven, and it was not for him to condemn.

Again he spoke—proclaimed how Jabez had magnanimously declined to single out his cowardly antagonist; and that the boy, whoever he might be, had to thank his most honourable victim that he was not ignominiously expelled. Then quietly, but emphatically, he pronounced the decision of the trustees that instant expulsion should follow any or every repetition of the offence which had called them together—not only the expulsion of the ringleaders, but of all concerned; and that even a fair fight between a Grammar School and a Blue-coat boy should be visited with suspension pending enquiry, the offender to be expelled, whether from School or College.

"Good lad, Jabez—good lad!" said Joshua Brookes to him, as George Pilkington helped his limping steps from the room.

On the broad flat step outside the door they encountered big Ben Travis, who caught the hand of Jabez in a rough grip, with the exclamation, "Give us your fist, my young buck! You've more pluck in your finger than that carroty Aspinall has in his whole carcase, the mean cur! An' look you, my lad, if any of them set on you again, I'll stand by and see fair play; or I'll fight for you if it's a big chap, or my name's not Ben Travis."

"Who talks of fighting? Haven't you had enough for one while, you great raw-boned brute? You'd better keep your ready fists in your pockets, Travis, if you don't want to be kicked out of school!" After which gruff reminder Joshua left them, and Jabez went back to the College with one more friend in the world; but that friend was not Laurence Aspinall.

He, smarting under a sense of obligation, shrunk away to bite his nails and vent his spleen in private, conscious that he was shunned by his classmates, and despised by honest Ben Travis.

As months and seasons sped onwards, they plucked the hairs from Simon Clegg's crown, and left a bald patch to tell of care or coming age; they stole the roundness from Bess's figure, the hope from her heart and eyes. There was less vigour in the beat of her batting-wand, less elasticity in her step. The periodical holidays and cheering visits of Jabez were the only pleasant breaks in the monotonous life of the Cleggs. Beyond the knowledge obtained at the billeting office in King Street that Tom Hulme had entered the army and gone abroad with his regiment, no tidings of the self-exiled soldier had come to them. In the great vortex of war his name had been swallowed up and lost. But she never said "Ay" to Matthew Cooper, though he waited and waited, smoking his Sunday pipe by the fireside even till his own Molly was old enough to have a sweetheart, and to want to leave her father's crowded hearth for a quieter one of her own.

Those same months and years added alike to the stature and attainments of Jabez Clegg and Laurence Aspinall, though in very unequal ratio. The former, though he had long since astonished Simon with his fluent rendering of the big Bible, was but a plodding scholar of average ability, the range of whose studies was limited, notwithstanding Parson Joshua's voluntary Latin lessons. The latter had an aptitude for learning, which made his masters press him forward; and Joshua Brookes forgave the tricks he played, his translations were so clear and so correct. Yet, when he wrote stinging couplets or "St. Crispin" on the Parson's door, or put cobblers'-wax on the pedagogue's chair, the covert reference to his parentage stung the irascible man more than the damage to kerseymere, and in his wrath he birched his pupil into penitence.

His penitence took a peculiar form. A discovery was made that a general dance in the school-room would shake the pewter platters and crockery down from dresser and corner-cupboard in Joshua's house adjoining. Whenever the dominie had growled over bad lessons with least cause, Laurence was sure to propose a grand hornpipe after school hours. Back would rush Joshua fast as his short legs would carry him, spluttering with passion; but the nimbler lads disappeared when they heard the crash, and, as a rule, Joshua's temper cooled before morning.

Laurence Aspinall's chief source of amusement from his first entrance into the Grammar School had been the crippled father of Joshua Brookes. As the old fellow staggered home drunk, the street boys would hoot at him, pull him about, pelt him with mud, and mock at him, till his impotent fury found vent in a storm of vile and opprobrious language. Laurence was sure to enjoy a scene of this kind, but he was generally sly enough to act as prompter, not as principal.

The old man was a great angler; and that he might enjoy unmolested his favourite pastime, his son had obtained from Colonel Hansom permission for him to fish in Strangeways Park ponds. Thither he had an empty hogshead conveyed, and the crippled old cobbler, with a flask of rum for company, sat within it, often the night through, to catch fish. The Irk had not then lost its repute for fine eels, and old Brookes—who, by the way, wore his hair in a pigtail—was likewise wont to plant himself, with rod and line, on what was the Waterworth Field, on the Irwell side of Irk Bridge, to catch eels.

Returning one afternoon (Joshua was busied with clerical duties), Laurence Aspinall and his fellows met the old man staggering along with his rod over his shoulder and a basket of eels in one hand.

He had called at the "Packhorse" for a dram, and went on, as was his wont, talking noisily to himself. He had steered round the corner in safety; but hearing one lively voice call out, "Here's Old Fishtail;" and another, "Here's St. Crispin's Cripple;" and a third, "Make way for Diogenes," as he was passing the high-master's ancient house he gave a lurch, meaning to reprove them solemnly—the top of his rod caught in the prominent pillar of the doorway, and was torn from his insecure grasp. Striving to recover it, he pitched forward. and in falling dropped his basket in the mud, and set the writhing, long-lived fish at liberty to swim in the gutter swollen with recent rain.

The lounging lads at once set up a shout; but Laurence, with a timely recollection that the front of Dr. Smith's was scarcely the most convenient place for his purpose, winked at his companions, and, with an aspect of mock commiseration, politely assisted the old man to rise, begged the others to capture the eels and carry the basket for him, and, under pretence of putting the angler's rod in order, contrived to fasten the hook to the end of his old-fashioned pigtail.

Then he helped his unsteady steps until they were fairly out of Dr. Smith's sight and hearing; but they did not suffer him to reach his son's house before they showed their true colours. Loosing his hold, Laurence snatched at the rod, and, darting with it towards the College gate, cried out in high glee, "I've been fishing; look at the fine snig (eel) I've caught!" And, as he capered about, he dragged the poor old cripple hither and thither backwards by his pigtail, to which hook and line were attached.

Old Brookes screamed in impotent rage and pain; the boys laughed and shouted the louder. The one with his basket set it on his head, and paraded about, crying, "Who'll buy my snigs? Fine fresh snigs!" with the nasal drawl of a genuine fish-seller.

Once or twice the old man fell down, uttering awful threats and imprecations; but Laurence only laughed the more, and jerked him up again with a smart twitch of the line, which was a strong one, and the other three or four young ruffians put up their shoulders, and limped about singing—

"The fishes drink water,
Old Crispin drinks gin;
But the fishes come out
When the hook he throws in.
Tol de rol."

It may be wondered that none of the neighbours interfered. But it must be remembered that they were accustomed, not only to the uproar of a boyish multitude, but to the drunken ravings of old Brookes, who was an intolerable nuisance. Public traffic then was not as now, and policemen were unborn.

The satisfaction of Laurence was at its height. He kept hold of the line; one of his comrades, named Barret, lashed the persecuted man with an eel for a whip, and their mirth was boisterous, when Jabez (now thirteen) came quietly through the wicket on an errand from the governor.

He took in the scene at a glance. He could not stand by and see injustice done. His dark eyes flashed with indignation as he dashed forward, pulling the line from the hand of Laurence, and tried to disentangle the cruel hook from the unfortunate pigtail.

"Who asked you to interfere? you petticoated jackanapes!" bawled Laurence, darting forward, his face as red as his hair, at the same time dealing Jabez a heavy blow on the chest.

"My duty!" answered Jabez, stoutly, taking no notice of the sneer at himself. "How could you gentlemen torment a poor old cripple like that?"

"He's a drunken old sot!" cried Barret.

"It's downright cruel!" continued Jabez, as he stood between the jabbering drunkard and his tormentors.

"We're no more cruel than he is! He's been catching fishes all day. We've only given him a taste of his own hook; and we'll have none of your meddling!" and out went the pugilistic arm of Laurence straight from the shoulder to deal another blow, when it was caught from behind by the bony hand of Ben Travis, bigger and stronger by two years' growth, whilst the other hand gripped his jacket collar.

"So you're at your cowardly tricks again, Aspinall?" exclaimed he, holding the other as if in a vice. But if I see you lay another finger on that lad, I'll report you to Dr. Smith."

"Oh! you'd turn sneak, would you?" sneered Laurence, striving to twist himself loose, and disordering his broad white frill in the endeavour.

"I'd think I did the Grammar School a service to turn either you or Barret out of it, I would! Think of you setting on that noble chap who wouldn't turn tell-tale, though he'll carry the mark of your boot to his grave with him!"

Pointing with outstretched hand to Jabez, who, by this time, was handing old Brookes over to the grumbling care of Tabitha, and whose right eyebrow yet showed a red seam, Travis relaxed his hold of Laurence, and he shook himself free.

Some warm altercation followed. There was a scowl of sullen defiance on Aspinall's face, and an evil glance towards Jabez, which Travis observing, with a significant nod he linked his arm in that of the Blue-coat boy, and never left him till he reached his destination, Mr. Hyde's ancient and picturesque tea-shop, in Market-street Lane. Yet it meant a détour by Cateaton Street, to leave an important note from Dr. Stone at the shop of Ford, the dealer in rare books, and a stretch up Smithy Door to the Market Place, where the office of Harrop the printer confronted them, and the trusty messenger had to wait.

SMITHY-DOOR AND CATEATON STREET

CHAPTER THE TWELFTH.

THE GENTLEMAN.

THAT afternoon a gentleman who had witnessed part of the foregoing scene from the breeches-maker's window, whither he had gone for a pair of buckskin riding-gloves—struck by the dauntless manner of Jabez, related what he had seen to his wife, Mrs. Ashton, the stately sister of Mrs. Chadwick; whilst Augusta, their eight-year-old daughter, sat on a footstool by her side, hemming a bandana handkerchief for her father, an inveterate snuff-taker—occasionally putting in a word, as only spoiled daughters did in those days.

"Mamma, I daresay that's the little boy Cousin Ellen told me about."

"Pooh, pooh! Augusta," said Mr. Ashton, tapping the lid of his snuff-box, and then, from force of habit, handing it to his wife, the wave of whose hand put it back—"pooh, pooh! child. Do you think there's only one Blue-coat boy in the town? Besides, he was not such a little boy. I know I thought something of myself when I was his size," said Mr. Ashton, dusting the snuff from his ruffles as he spoke.

"But he would be a little boy when Ellen knew him first. She says it was before I was born."

"He could not be a Blue-coat boy then, my dear," observed Mrs. Ashton; "he was too young."

"But Ellen showed him to me when we went to the College at Easter; and she says he has killed a snake—a real live snake, papa. And Aunt Chadwick bought Ellen such a pretty pincushion he had worked, and, oh! such a handsome bead purse!"

Mr. Ashton smiled at his daughter's enthusiasm.

"Ah! I think I have heard of him before; he is a sort of *protégé* of Parson Brookes."

"He is a very honest boy," appended Mrs. Ashton, as she examined Augusta's hemming by the light of the nearest wax candle. "Ellen lost Prince William's shilling that same day.

You know she always wears it dangling from her neck, absurd as it is for a great girl of fifteen."

"Well?" said Augusta, looking up inquiringly.

"Well, my dear, the very next afternoon, the boy Jabez Clegg knocked at the door in Oldham Street, bearing the shilling, which he said he had found in sweeping the library, and remembered seeing it on Miss Chadwick's neck. Many a boy, at Easter, would have spent it in cakes or toffy."

"I suppose, to use one of your favourite maxims, he must have thought 'honesty the best policy,'" remarked her husband.

"Yes; and 'duty its own reward'—for he refused the half-crown that Sarah offered him."

Mr. Ashton took another pinch of snuff, with grave consideration, then put the box, after some deliberation, into his deep waistcoat pocket, and again flapped the snuff off ruffles and neck-cloth ends.

"Wouldn't take the money, you say?"

"Would not take it," his wife repeated, folding up the finished handkerchief.

After a pause, Mr. Ashton said, with his head on one side,—

"I think I shall look after that younker. What is he like?"

"Oh! that I cannot tell; I was not with them. But I think Sarah said he had got an ugly scar on one of his eyebrows."

Mr. Ashton brought down his hand with a clap on that of Augusta, resting on his knee.

"Then, my little Lancashire witch, the poor cripple's champion and Ellen's hero of romance *will* be one and the same. I must certainly look after that lad."

But even as Mr. Ashton came to that conclusion Jabez was in mortal peril, and his romance and theirs threatened to end at the beginning.

Laurence Aspinall was not of a temper to brook interference with his sport, or to be treated as the inferior of a "common charity boy." Since the hour that Jabez had declined to single him out for punishment, he had resented the sense of his own inferiority, which conscience pressed upon him. In refusing to tender either thanks or apology at Ben Travis's instigation, he lost caste in the school, and the knowledge rankled in his breast. Against the debt of gratitude he owed to Jabez he laid up a fund of envy and spite, out of which he meant to pay him in full the first opportunity. That opportunity had arrived. There were some birds of his own feather, who stuck by him, of whom Ned Barret was one.

Old Brookes had been too drunk to swear positively who had molested him, or to obtain credence if he did; but the inopportune arrival of Jabez and Ben Travis had made detection certain, and nothing was Joshua Brookes so sure to punish with severity as an attack on the father who made his life a burden to him.

On the principle that they might "as well be hanged for a sheep as a lamb," the noble five resolved to waylay the Blue-coat boy on his return, and either extract from him a promise of secrecy, or give him a sound drubbing for his pains.

They were too like-minded for long conference. To put the old breeches-maker off the scent, all dispersed but one, Kit Townley, who pulled a top from his pocket and whipped away at it with as much energy as ever did his Anglo-Saxon ancestors. Perhaps he thought he had a meddlesome College boy under his lash.

After a time, the others sauntered back one by one, from contrary directions; there was more top-whipping, and some of the whips and tops were new. Then when they saw they were unobserved, they adjourned to the school-yard, and laying a cap on the broad step, two or three of them sat down to a game at cob-nut, so that if any unlikely straggler did come that way there might be an apparent reason for their presence.

It was late in the year. The breeches-maker was seated at early tea, and so were most of his neighbours. The twilight was coming gently down, and the boys, tired of waiting, were about to go home to their own—Aspinall expecting a reprimand for being late. Jabez, who had been delayed at the office of Harrop the printer in the Market Place, came briskly up with a parcel in his hand just as they reached the gate. One of them snatched the parcel from him and ran with it into the school-yard. As a natural consequence Jabez followed to regain his property.

That was just what they wanted. The light iron gate was pushed-to, and there they were, shut in and screened from observation, between the deserted Grammar School on the one hand, and the College School-room on the other, which with the dormitory above, was equally sure to be empty at that hour. They were free to torment him as they pleased. The parcel was tossed from hand to hand with subdued glee, and their whip-lashes and strung cob-nuts cut at his arms and shoulders, as Jabez sprang forward and darted hither and thither, perplexed and baffled in his efforts to recover it. Once or twice it went down on the damp ground, and gained in grime what it lost in shape.

"Oh! dear, dear! do give me my parcel!" cried Jabez, in perplexity. "Our governor will think I've been loitering."

"And so you have, you canting yellow-skirt. You stopped to put your long finger in our pie!" was the swift retort of Laurence, as he interposed his body between Jabez and the boy who held his lost charge.

"Eh! and you went off with Travis, wasting your time!" added Kit Townley.

"I never waste my time on an errand."

"Oh! Miss Nancy never wastes time on an errand," mimicked Ned Barret; and still they kept the boy on the run, until he leaned, out of breath, against the wall which served as a parapet above the river.

Then, the disputed prize being kept by Kit Townley at a respectable distance, Laurence advanced to parley with him, offering to restore his parcel and let him go if he would take a solemn oath, which he dictated, to maintain silence on all

MARKET PLACE AND EXCHANGE

which had transpired that afternoon.

"I cannot; I must account for my time," firmly answered Jabez, "and I must account for that dirty parcel."

"Tell them you tumbled down and hurt yourself," suggested Aspinall.

"I cannot; it would be untrue!"

At this the lads set up a loud guffaw, as if truth were somewhat out of fashion; but the one who stood nearest the gate with the parcel looked restless, as if beginning to be tired of the whole business. Just then Laurence went blustering up to the College boy, and, thrusting his face forward, said—

"If you don't go down on your marrow-bones this instant, and swear to tell no tales, we'll pitch you over the wall."

"You dare not!" boldly retorted Jabez, with a set face.

"Oh! daren't we? We'll see that! Lend a hand."

"No, you dare not!" repeated he, planting himself firmly against the wall.

There was a sudden rush; they closed round him, more in bravado than with any intent to do him bodily harm; sliding him up against the smooth-worn brickwork, they hoisted him above their shoulders, meaning to hold him there. But in their eagerness they had thrust him too far, and crowding on each other, one, being jostled, let go, and Jabez toppled over the precipice!

There was a scream; a splash in the water. Tabitha, taking clothes from a line in the back-yard, cried out, "What is that?" Parson Brookes' startled pigeons flew from their dove-cote, and wheeling round in widening circles, cooed affrightedly.

The white-faced boys stood aghast. Unless his fall had been seen from the opposite croft, their victim would be drowned before any aid they could bring was available; a wide circuit must be taken before a bridge could be reached. Buildings blocked up that side of the river. They looked at each other and spoke in whispers; then, with an animal instinct of self-preservation, sneaked off in silence and terror, leaving him to his fate.

Not all. Kit Townley, who held the parcel, had drawn near to remonstrate. With a shriek he threw down the paper, and, hardly conscious what he did, tore wildly through the gates, and across the College Yard, to startle the first he met with the alarm that a College boy was drowning in the Irk!

CHAPTER THE THIRTEENTH.

SIMON'S PUPIL.

JABEZ ON CELLAR STEPS.

IT was fortunate for Jabez that the late rains had raised the level of the Irk; otherwise, that being the shallowest part of the stream, there would not have been sufficient depth of water to buoy him up when he was pitched over the wall; and had his head come in contact with rock or stone, falling from such an elevation, his history would have closed with the last chapter. It was doubly fortunate that sensible Simon had taught him that without which no boy's education—nor, indeed, any girl's either—is complete, and that Jabez, from very love of the water, had kept himself in practice whenever a holiday had given him opportunity.

He had gone over the wall backwards, turning a somersault as he fell, and so clearing the rock, but not altogether unprepared; and to him head first, heels first, forward or backward, were all as one. Like a cork he rose, and struck out across the river. The slimy stone embankment seemed to slip from his touch; there was no hold for his hand; it was too steep and smooth to climb; and he felt that the river, swift in its fulness, was bent on bearing him to the Irwell, so dangerously near.

He raised his voice for "Help!" Tabitha, listening, answered with a scream and a shout, and, bolting into the house, disturbed the Parson and his besotted father "at their tea" by the outcry she made, as she rushed on into the street with the alarm of "A lad dreawndin!" just as the conscious culprits slunk past to their own quarters.

Doctor Stone, the first recipient of terrified Kit Townley's incoherent intelligence, was simultaneously racing at full speed, with a troop of College boys at his heels, down towards Hunt's Bank and the outlet of the Irk, with the swift consciousness that the only hope of saving life was in the chance of reaching the confluence of the rivers first. He thought the dusk never came down so rapidly. A lamplighter, with ladder and flaring long-spouted oil-can light, was going his rounds.

"Turn back, my man, with ladder and light," he called out, without stopping; and the man, seeing something unusual was astir or amiss, followed at a canter without question.

At Irk Bridge the librarian took the light from the man, and swung it to cast its reflection over the Irwell; but nothing was to be seen or heard but the full river, and the wash of its waters. To cross the bridge, in fear that the boy was beyond help, was but the work of a moment.

Slower, along the wooden railing of the Irk embankment, he held the lamp low. There was neither eddy or bubble on the water to tell where a drowning mortal had gone down.

"Jabez! Jabez Clegg!" he cried, but there was no response. Again and again he raised his voice—"Jabez! Jabez!" The only answer was from an advancing crowd, with Parson Brookes and Tabitha in their midst, who had rushed to the rescue with ropes and poles down the bridge at Mill Brow.

"I fear it's no use, Parson Brookes," said the librarian sadly; "the river's high, and poor Jabez may have been drifting past Stannyhurst before we were out of the College Yard."

"Jabez?" exclaimed Joshua aghast, "you cannot mean that Jabez Clegg is the boy drowned!" and he staggered as if some one had struck him.

"Indeed, Parson, if this boy speaks truth, I fear it is so," and he turned to question his informant; but Kit Townley, seeing his impulsive schoolmaster approach, had edged away, and was gone.

IRK BRIDGE AND HUNT'S BANK.

Gruff Joshua drew the back of his hand across his shaggy brows.

"And so the greedy river has swallowed the bright lad at last! He was a boy of promise, Dr. Stone, and his untimely fate is a—a—trouble to me;" and the rough Parson's harsh voice shook with emotion. "I baptised him, Doctor, and I hoped to see him grow up a credit to us all."

They, and the dispersing crowd, seeing the uselessness of longer stay, were moving on towards Mill Brow as he spoke.

"Who's this?" he cried, as they neared the bridge, and a working woman, her hair flying loose from the kerchief on her head, rushed across it with an impetus gained in the steep descent.

It was Bess, with Simon at her heels, close as his stiff rheumatic limbs would carry him. She wrung her hands bitterly.

"Is it true?" she cried in anguish, "is it true? Oh, Parson Brucks, is it true that ar Jabez is dreawnded?"

There was the same choking in his voice as he answered—

"I'm afraid so, Bess."

Simon's voice now broke in.

"But are yo' sartain, Parson? Ar Jabez couldn swim loike a duck. An' how cam' he i' th' wayther, aw shouldn loike to know?"

"Swim, did you say?" interrogated Dr. Stone. "Then there may be hope yet. If the eddies would not let him land at Waterworth Field, he might swim ashore at Stannyhurst."

"Pray God it be so!" ejaculated Bess, from a full heart.

Dr. Stone, hurrying forward, continued—

"Follow me to the College for lanterns to renew the search." And no second invitation was needed.

And where was Jabez? He heard Tabitha's cry, but it came from the wrong side, and he had sense to know was useless to save, unless he could withstand the current till help came round. But the strong stream was bearing him on against his will. Suddenly he bethought him of the dairy steps, and, with a stroke of his left arm, swerved towards the hoary building looming through the twilight. One moment later, and the steps had been passed, not to be recovered, for the current was stronger than he; but that providentially abrupt turn, and a few skilful strokes brought him upon them. Literally upon them, for the water was within a few steps of the door. With difficulty he obtained a footing, they were so slippery. Once above the water, he hammered at the door and called, but his voice was weakened by exertion and the shivering consequent on cold, wet, clinging garments. Again and again he knocked and called, but everyone was out in the quadrangle, or away in search of him, and no one heard.

He had been excited and over-heated in his prolonged struggle with his persecutors, and, short as was the distance he swam, his efforts to stem the overmastering current had exhausted him. Cold and exposure did the rest. He sank on the topmost step with his head against the door, in the angle it formed with the wall, his feet in the water; and there he lay, too faint to respond when Dr. Stone's voice fell on his ear as on that of a dreamer. His dark robe, his position, the jutting wall—all contributed to hide him from the poor rays of the one oil-lamp which was flashed along the stream to find him.

And there he might have lain and died had not Nancy, for lack of a boy at hand to wait on her, gone down to the cellar for milk for the boys' supper. As she filled the wooden piggin she had taken with her, she fancied she heard a moan, and, listening breathless, heard another, and another, from the outside of a door which was (to her thought) inaccessible to mortal.

Down went the piggin and the milk (she was not a strong-minded woman, and it was a superstitious age), up the steps she stumbled in her fright, crying—

"Oh, theer's a boggart in th' dairy!—theer's a boggart!"

Dr. Stone and his companions came in at the porch as she fled upwards towards the kitchen. The firelight gleaming on her

KITCHEN, CHETHAM HOSPITAL.

frightened face caught his attention. Half-fainting she repeated her exclamation, adding—

"It moaned like summut wick."

"Moaned, did you say? Goodness! If it should be——"

Not stopping to finish his sentence, he snatched a light from the table, and was unbolting the cellar-door before the governor or anyone else could comprehend his movements. They understood well enough when he came back into their midst, burdened with the limp, dripping form of Jabez, white and insensible, and depositing him on a settle near the kitchen fire, cried out for restoratives.

That was a terrible next morning, when the young miscreants, as much afraid to play truant as to face possibilities at school, sneaked to their places and set to their studies with industry out of the common. Laurence Aspinall, boarding with a master, had no choice in the matter.

How Jabez got into the water was not clear; he was too ill to be questioned over-night, and was in a fever and delirious by noon the next day. But he had never been known to loiter or go astray when sent on an errand. Kit Townley's impulsive cry of alarm had suggested foul play, and neither Joshua Brookes nor Governor Terry had let the night pass without an effort to dive into the truth.

Dr. Stone had conjectured Kit Townley to be a Grammar School boy, although personally unknown to him; and that conjecture recalled to Joshua his father's ravings of ill-usage, which he had at the time regarded as drunken maudling. It was ascertained that the boy had been at Ford's and at Harrop's. Inquiry, and the search for the missing parcel, resulted in the discovery of a trampled playground, broken whiplashes, a string of cobnuts, and, neatly marked in red cotton with his initials, one of Laurence Aspinall's cambric ruffles, torn and muddy as the parcel.

There was a conference with Dr. Jeremiah Smith before the night was out. A messenger was sent to Mr. Aspinall in Cannon

Street the next morning, as well as to the trustees of the school.

The following day saw such another conclave as before in the Grammar School. Dr. Stone, who was present, picked out the boy who had given the alarm; and Kit Townley, trembling for himself, told all he knew. Ben Travis, at the outset, in his indignation, proffered his evidence, which went to prove *malice prepense.*

The boys, asked what they had to say for themselves, simply answered they had done it for "sport"—that they did not mean to throw him over, but only to frighten him to "hold his tongue," and excused their running home on the plea that they were "afraid." Laurence Aspinall boldly said that he knew the boy could swim and did not think a ducking would do him much harm, and offered to jump off the wall and swim down the river himself. Liar as well as boaster, he received a summary check from Dr. Smith, apart from the reprimand administered to him as the proven ring-leader.

In these days such a case of outrage would have been brought before a magistrate, and the offenders' names sent flying through newspaper paragraphs. Then, whether to spare the parental feelings of such influential men as Mr. Aspinall, or to save from tarnish the fair fame of the school, or to avert the further debasement of the boys from prison contact, and give them a chance to amend, the school tribunal was allowed to be all-sufficient.

Ignominious expulsion was dealt out not only to Laurence Aspinall and to Ned Barret, but to each of the conspirators—Kit Townley, honourably acquitted by them of participation in the final attack, alone escaping with a caution, a severe reprimand, and as severe a flogging; which special immunity he had purchased by running white-faced to give the alarm. It is possible he scarcely estimated the value of that immunity at the time.

But the loud hurrahs which hailed this sentence testified how the Grammar School boys valued their honour as a school, and how proud they were to be purged of such offenders.

Mr. Aspinall, too much agitated to witness his son's public disgrace, waited the result of the inquiry in the head-master's house; and if ever Laurence Aspinall felt ashamed of his own misconduct, it was when his father refused to take his unworthy hand as they left the door-step, and he heard Dr. Smith's closing words of reproof mingled with compassion for the father, in whose eyes were signs of tears a bad son had drawn.

Long before Jabez was able to resume his own place in the school, Laurence Aspinall had been removed to an expensive boarding-school at Everton, near Liverpool; and this time the merchant laid stress on his tendency "for vicious and low pursuits," and begged that no efforts or expense might be spared to make him a gentleman in all respects. Still he tampered with the truth, lest the school-master (he would be called a Principal in these factitious days) should refuse to admit a pupil with such antecedents, and decline the task of eradicating cruelty and ingratitude.

Here Laurence certainly mixed only with boys of his own class, from whom money could buy neither flattery nor favour, and where only his own merits could procure either. And here we must leave him, to pursue the fortunes of the boy whose life he had wantonly imperilled.

Had anything been wanting to bespeak Joshua Brookes's good-will, Jabez supplied it when he interfered to protect the elder Brookes from the derisive indignities of others. Not only to Mrs. Clowes did he rehearse in his own peculiar manner the story, as told by Ben Travis, with its supplementary drama which had so nearly proved a tragedy, but at such tables as he frequented—Mr. Chadwick's among the rest.

Mr. Ashton, who was present, spoke of being himself a witness to the former scene, and, whilst presenting his inevitable snuff-box to the eccentric chaplain, repeated his previous observation—"I must look after that boy—I must indeed!"

If the parson had been commonly observant he would have noticed a pair of black eyes fixed in eager attention on his, as he, who rarely uttered a commendation, held forth in praise of his father's champion, the Blue-coat boy; the said black eyes being matched by the black hair, and somewhat dark skin, of the plain but intelligent daughter of his host.

But girls of fifteen were then counted in the category of children, and were taught only to "speak when spoken to," so Ellen Chadwick passed no other commentary on the actions of Jabez than was expressed by her glowing cheeks and eloquent eyes.

CHAPTER THE FOURTEENTH.

JABEZ GOES INTO THE WORLD.

KITCHEN DOOR.

A SHARP illness followed the precipitation of Jabez into the Irk; but he was young, had a strong constitution, and, to the satisfaction of all in the College, and many out of it, was able to take his place in the refectory, and clear the beef or the potato-pie from his wooden trencher before the month expired. Prior to this, he was allowed an afternoon, ere he was well enough to resume fully his routine duties, to show himself to the kind friends who had exhibited most anxiety for his recovery.

Mrs. Clowes was one of these. Jam, jelly, and cakes, never concocted within the area of the College, had found their way to his bedside. Grateful for kindness from so unlikely a quarter, Jabez paid his first visit to the shop in Half Street, to thank the queer old lady. But not one word of thanks would she hear.

"Eh, lad, say naught about it; you did your duty, and I did mine, and so we're quits;" and shook her open hand a few inches in advance of her face, as if she were shaking a disclaimer out of it. "And where are you taking your white face to now?" she asked quickly, the better to turn the tide of his stammering thanks.

"To Aunt Bess's."

"Why, lad, Bess Clegg'll have naught to give thee fit for sick folk to eat. It's much to me if she'll have either a potato or a drop of milk. If she's a bit of jannock, or oat-cake, it's as much as the bargain. War may be glorious for kings and generals, but it's awful for poor folk; Mesters can't sell their goods, and can't pay wages bout money; and I've heard that, since th' potato riots in Shudehill last spring, the folk have been so clemmed that some on them couldna be known by their friends who hadna seen them for awhile; they were naught but skin and bone, poor things!"

Whilst indulging in this tirade against war and its concomitants, to distract his attention, she bustled about, often with her back to him; then dived into her parlour, and returned with a basket, which she was handing to him with a charge to "take that to Bess, and be sure to bring the basket back safe," when she found that Joshua Brookes was standing behind Jabez, amongst waiting customers, with a sharp eye on her proceedings.

"I say, young Cheat-the-fishes, what have you got to say for yourself? A nice young ragamuffin you are, to go a-bathing without leave, spoiling your clothes, and giving yourself cold! I hope they gave you plenty of physic, to teach you better," said Joshua roughly, taking the boy by the shoulder, and turning him sharply round to confront him.

"Yes, sir—they gave me plenty of physic," said Jabez, doffing his cap respectfully. "But I did not go bathing; I got into the water by accident."

"By what? Do you call that an accident?" growled the parson, to get at the boy's meaning.

"An accident done a-purpose," chimed in Mrs. Clowes, whilst her scales jingled, and she and her helper weighed out her commodities for the people at the counter.

"Yes, sir," answered Jabez, composedly: "it must have been an accident. I don't think they really could mean to push me over. I think they only meant to frighten me——"

"Well?" queried Joshua, seeing that he hesitated.

"I think one of them slipped, and let go, and then I slipped too, sir," he replied, modestly.

"Slipped, indeed! You'd very nearly slipped into the next world!" exclaimed the parson "I suppose you'll say next that my poor old father was dragged about by the young wretches by accident, too?"

The colour of Jabez rose.

"No, sir; that was very cruel."

"Oh! you do call some things by their right names (here, let that woman pass out). I suppose you're glad enough the rascals have got their deserts?"

A dubious change came over the boy's face. He did not answer at once; he hardly knew his own feelings on the subject. The question was repeated.

"Well, sir, I'm glad they won't be there to torment me any more, but it must be a very dreadful thing for a young gentleman to be turned out of school in disgrace, and I don't think I *ought* to be glad of that. I should never get over it, if it was me."

"Here, take your basket, and be off with you!" said Joshua Brookes, hurrying him out of the shop, that he might stay and rate the old woman for "spoiling young Cheat-the-fishes," conscious all the while that he had been doing *his* best to get the lad a good home in the future.

Bess and Simon received him with open arms, glad not only to see him well again, but thankful he had been placed where he was secure from the bitter want which pinched both their stomachs and their faces. To them Mrs. Clowes' basket brought what they had not seen for months—a white loaf and a good lump of cold meat, to say nothing of a tiny paper of tea, and some sugar—those luxuries of the rich—and half-a-crown in another paper.

How those half-famishing hard-workers, whose home had been denuded of their goods to keep life within them, thanked old Mrs. Clowes! She had made it a festival to them indeed, and all for the sake of the boy they had kept.

There were no pigeons—these had been sold long ago, to pay for provisions, though much against Simon's will. The cat was there, lean and gaunt; it managed to pick up a subsistence somehow; and the big bible was there—Simon had not parted with that, though the bright bureau was gone, ay, and the cradle which had been an ark to the orphan.

The change touched Jabez sorely. Snugly housed and fed within the College, rumours of outer poverty made no lasting impression; but here he saw its grim reality, and sitting down on the three-legged stool, he covered his face with his hands to hide the tears called up by that insight into their impoverished condition. Yet they had some alleviation of their pain. Poverty appeared to have lost half its bitterness for Bess. She had had a letter from her long-mourned Tom, and the joyful news served to brighten up the visit for Jabez and all.

It was a long and deeply repentant letter, of course, written by a comrade. It was dated from Badajoz, and had been a weary while in reaching them. He had been wounded in that brilliant assault, and while in hospital had fallen in with another Lancashire lad, also wounded—no other than the boy who had lent a hand to rescue the infant Jabez, and who had been driven to enlist by the sharp pangs of hunger, only two years before. From this young fellow, Private John Smith (Tom was himself a Corporal), he had learned how grievously his Bess had been slandered; but with that knowledge had come the conviction that he had condemned her hastily and harshly on mere hearsay, and the letter was incoherent in its remorseful contrition. In his soldier-life he had been tossed hither and thither—known pain, and thirst, and famine; and said he owed it all to his own jealous credulity, when he ought to have known so much better. He told of marchings and counter-marchings, battles and bloodshed; but of never one wound to himself, though he had not "cared a cast of the shuttle" for his life until that bayonet-thrust which had laid him side by side with John Smith, who had lost an eye. But he wound up with a prayer for Bess and himself, and a hope for their re-union, if the war should ever end. He "was sick of it."

All that letter was to Bess and Simon, Jabez could not comprehend; but he took Mrs. Clowes her empty basket, and went back to the College satisfied that one ray of sunshine lit up the poor home of his friends.

And Matthew Cooper's last chance was gone.

* * * * *

Mr. Ashton was what is known in trade as a small-ware manufacturer—that is, he was a weaver of tapes, inkles, filletings ; silk, cotton, and worsted laces (for furniture) ; carpet bindings, brace-webs, and fringes. Moreover, he manufactured braces and umbrellas, for which latter his brother-in-law supplied the ginghams. He had at work, both in Manchester and at Whaley-Bridge, a number of swivel-engines, the design of which came from those unrivalled tape-weavers, the Dutch, and which would weave twenty-four lengths of tape or bed-lace at one time. Otherwise, the bulk of his workpeople—winders, warpers, brace, fringe, and umbrella-makers—carried away materials to their own homes, and brought back their work in a finished state.

Mr. Chadwick, as we have mentioned, was a manufacturer of ginghams—this included checks and fustians ; but much of his trade being foreign, the war had locked up his resources, and his anxieties preyed on his health.

Mr. Ashton had suffered less in this particular, not having disdained to take his sensible wife's advice—"Never put too many eggs in one basket." Mrs. Ashton, be it said, had a leaning towards "proverbial philosophy" more homely and terse than Tupper's, which, vulgar as it is accounted now, was in esteem when our century was young ; and, had it been otherwise, would have been equally impressive from her deliberately modulated utterance. This same lady had, moreover, an aptitude for business. Mr. Ashton employed a number of young women, and Mrs. Ashton might be found most days in the warehouse, either "putting out" or inspecting the work brought in by them, with a gingham wrapper over her "silken sheen." If the footman announced visitors, the wrapper was thrown aside in a moment, and she stepped into her drawing-room as though fresh from her toilette, and with no atmosphere of dozens, grosses, or great-grosses about her.

She was wont to say, "The eye of a master does more work than both his hands;" accordingly in house or warehouse her active supervision kept other hands from idling, and she certainly dignified whatever duties she undertook, whether she used hands or eyes only.

In those days a seven-years' apprenticeship to any trade or business was deemed essential; apprentices were part and parcel of commercial economy, and when Mr. Ashton spoke of "looking after that boy," it was that he thought Jabez Clegg bade fair to be a fitter inmate and a more reliable servant than others whose terms were about to expire.

Through his friend the Rev. Joshua Brookes he ascertained the boy's age and other particulars, and sought the House-Governor, Mr. Terry, and laid before him a proposition to take Jabez Clegg as his apprentice, on very fair terms. He then learned that Mr. Shaw, the saddler at the bottom of Market-street Lane, was also desirous to obtain the same Blue-coat boy as an apprentice, his friend the leather-breeches maker having named the lad to him.

At the Easter meeting of feoffees both proposals were laid before them—Simon Clegg, as standing *in loco parentis* to Jabez, being present. After some little discussion Mr. Ashton's proposal was accepted, to the great satisfaction of the tanner, and in a few days Jabez was transferred to his new master for mutual trial until Ascension Day, when, if all parties were satisfied, his indentures would be signed. As the Governor said, it had "been but the toss of a button" whether he had gone to Mr. Shaw or Mr. Ashton, yet upon that toss of a button the whole future of Jabez depended.

The boy entered on his new career under good auspices—that is, he bore with him a good character for steadiness and probity, though nothing was said of brilliant parts, or any special talent which he possessed. Indeed, his schoolmaster had said that only his indomitable perseverance had enabled him to keep pace with others. If he had any latent genius—any particular vocation, no one had discovered it; his faculty for disfiguring doors and walls with devices in coloured chalks, picked up amongst the gravel, had been matter for punishment, not praise, and none but the College-boys themselves cared to know where the fresh patterns for purses and pincushions came from. Steadiness, perseverance, probity—they were good materials out of which to manufacture a tradesman (so Mr. Ashton thought), and congratulations were mutual.

Jabez Clegg went, with his new outfit, to his new home under good auspices, inasmuch as both master and mistress were prepossessed in his favour, and they stood in the foremost rank of those who began to recognise that English apprentices were not bondslaves in heathendom. Instead of being crammed to sleep like dogs in holes under counters; left to wash at a pump and wipe themselves where they could; obliged to sit at a table in a back kitchen, and dip their spoons into one common dish of porridge, or potatoes and buttermilk; to eat such scraps and refuse as sordid employers, or ill-disposed cooks, chose to set before their primitive Adamite forks—instead of a system like this, from which apprentices (of whatever grade) only emerged at the beginning of this century, the Ashtons' apprentices had a comfortable dormitory in the attic, there was a coarse jack-towel by the scullery-sink for their use, they had their meals with the servants in the kitchen, where was an oak settle by the fire for them when work was over.

But work did not end with the close of the warehouse. They were expected to keep their attic clean and in order, to cleanse the wooden or pewter platters, or porringers, from which they had dined or supped; to rinse the horns which had held their table-beer; to fetch and carry wood, coals, and water, for servants too lazy to do their own work; and it was not much rest any apprentice had from five or six in a morning until eight or nine at night, when he went to his bed.

As the youngest apprentice, the roughest of this work fell on

Jabez, but, luckily, his training had made him equal to the occasion; though Kezia, the red-faced cook, set herself steadfastly to dislike him, because Mr. Ashton had bespoken her favour for him. In the warehouse, too, the evident goodwill of principals roused the jealousy of underlings, so that "good auspices" had their corresponding drawbacks.

It was not much of a pleasure to Jabez to find Kit Townley also seated as an apprentice on the kitchen settle; but the youth seemed disposed to be friendly, and Jabez forbore to create a grievance by recalling unpleasant reminiscences. With Kit Townley, who was his senior by a year, a heavy premium had been paid, and on this he was inclined to presume. But neither Mr. nor Mrs. Ashton made any social distinction between the twain, and Jabez was strong enough to hold his own.

During the few weeks' probation, Jabez was transferred from department to department, alike to test his capacity and his own liking for the business. Both proved satisfactory.

On Ascension Day, 1813, there was another appearance in that ancient room before the College magnates, many of whom, as officers in volunteer regiments, were in full-dress uniform (a dinner pending). The indentures had to be signed, the premium of £4 (returnable to the boy when his term expired) had to be paid.

Simon Clegg's best clothes had long been lost in the pawnbroker's bottomless pit; but some one unknown (mayhap Mrs. Clowes or Mrs. Clough) had sent him overnight a suit of fresh ones, pronounced by him and Bess "welly as good as new;" and he presented himself for the important ceremony (overlooked by the painted face of the orphan's benevolent friend, Humphrey Chetham) as proud almost of his own restored respectability as of the part he was about to perform. When it came to his turn to sign the document, the little man took the pen with a flourish, as if he were a hero about to perform some mighty action. He stooped to the heavy oaken table, bent his head low, alternately to the right and left, and with

HUMPHREY CHETHAM.

From an Engraving.

his fingers in an unaccountable crump, imprinted his self-taught signature in Roman capitals thereon, then handed back the quill, as if to say "The deed is done!"

Governor, schoolmaster, and feoffees congratulated Mr. Ashton and Jabez both. Simon, with moist eyes, shook Jabez by the hand, and holding the boy's shoulder with his left to look the better in his clear, dark eyes, said, with deliberate emphasis—

"Jabez, lad, aw'm preawd on yo' this day. But moind—thah's an honourable neame; do nowt to disgrace it, an' yo'r fortin's made!"

Jabez was too abashed to make reply at the time; but at the supper given in the Mosley Street kitchen to mark his installation at Mr. Ashton's—to which Bess and Simon were both invited—Jabez contrived to whisper,

"You needn't clem any more, Bess; I'll give you all my wages."

CHAPTER THE FIFTEENTH.

APPRENTICESHIP.

JABEZ now began his work in earnest, in the packing-room—the very lowest rung of the ladder. Not long did he remain there. The bright colours in the rooms for brace-webs and upholsterers' trimmings had an attraction for him, and he argued with himself that the better he did the rough work assigned him the sooner he should mount above it. And Jabez, the plodding Blue-coat boy, was ambitious. That ambition had a threefold stimulus.

Manchester people were then, as a rule, steady church and chapel-goers. Mr. Ashton had two pews at the Old Church: one for his family, the other for servants and apprentices, the attendance of the latter being imperative. Jabez thus came in frequent contact with his old-time friends, from the Blue-coat boys in the Chetham Gallery to the Cleggs, to whom went every penny of his earnings; their distress, like that of others, having deepened with the continuation of the Napoleonic war.

Sometimes old Mrs. Clowes, meeting him in the churchyard, would grasp him by the hand, and leave something in it, as, in her old black stuff dress and a coloured kerchief tied over her mob-cap, she hurried home to scold dilatory handmaids, and put her Christianity in practice amongst her pensioners.

Now and then Joshua Brookes crossed his path, and if he did not put his hand in his breeches' pocket for Jabez—now a well-grown youth—he gave him more than sterling coin in sterling advice, though, unfortunately, in so abrupt and grotesque a manner its effect was frequently lost. Yet one day when the Blue-coat boy had been barely two years at the Mosley Street manufacturer's, he put a spur into the sides of his ambition.

"Young Cheat-the-fishes, were you ever in Mrs. Chadwick's green parlour?"

"Yes, sir—I was there once for half-an-hour." (The day he took back Miss Ellen's shilling.)

"Well, did you read the sermons on the walls?"

Jabez answered respectfully—

"I did not see any sermons, sir. I saw some pictures in black frames with gilt roses at the corners."

"And didn't look at them, I suppose?" in a harsh grunt.

"Yes, sir, I did! I was waiting till Mrs. Chadwick had done dinner. They were about two boys—a good and a bad apprentice."

"Oh, then, you did use your eyes? The next time they let you inside that room, just use your understanding, too. William Hogarth, the artist, from his grave preaches a sermon to you and your fellows as good as Parson Gatliffe preached from the pulpit this morning, mark that!" and he turned on his heel with an emphasising nod to fix *his* sermon on the boy's mind.

The opportunity came before long. It was customary when an apprentice went with a message to leave him in the hall, or send him into the kitchen; but Jabez, being sent by Mrs. Ashton with several samples of furniture-binding and fringes for her sister's use, he was shown with his parcel into the parlour, where Mrs. Chadwick, neatly attired in a brown stuff dress, with a French cambric kerchief lying in folds under the square bodice, sat at work with an upholsteress, in the midst of a mass of chintz and moreen, preparing for the new home of Ellen's elder sister Charlotte; for, in spite of war, distress, or famine, people will marry and give in marriage. And had not a glorious peace just been concluded?

Ellen, a comely but not pretty girl, about seventeen, whose black eyes and hair were her chief attractions, sat there in a purple bombazine dress, with her sheathed scissors and College pincushion suspended by a chain from her girdle, plying her needle most industriously. He was not accustomed to parlours, and no doubt his bow was as awkward as his blush; but he had a message to deliver, and he did that in a business-like manner. He had to wait until pattern after pattern was tried against the chintz, and calculations made. Mrs. Chadwick, seeing his eyes wander wistfully from picture to picture, courteously gave him permission to examine them.

At once Ellen, who was sitting close under one, rose to act as interpreter. She was recalled by the mild voice of her mother. "Sit down, Ellen. Jabez Clegg does not require a young lady's help to understand those pictures—they explain themselves."

Ellen went back to her seat and her sewing with a raised colour, and a private impression that the rebuke was uncalled for, though she spoke never a word. Perhaps Mrs. Chadwick thought condescension should have its limits, and did not believe in a lady's impulsive civility to an apprentice Blue-coat boy. Yet that was not like Mrs. Chadwick.

Miss Augusta had been staying with her aunt. Part of his commission was to convoy her home; she was an only child, and too precious to be trusted out alone, though she was in her eleventh year, and the distance was nothing. But so many desperadoes had been let loose by the termination of the war, that crime and violence was rampant, footpads infested highways and byways, and Cicily, Augusta's maid—ex-nurse—was no longer deemed a protection.

He stood before the last engraving when Augusta—in no awe of her father's apprentice—came dancing into the room in a nankeen dress and tippet, a hat with blue ribbons, long washing-gloves which left the elbows bare, and blue shoes tied with a bunch of ribbons.

Bright, beautiful, buoyant—she was a picture in herself; and Jabez turned from the dingy engraving to think so. She often came tripping into the warehouse or the kitchen, and exchanged a bright word with one or other, and away again; but Jabez had thought of her only as a pretty playful child until that afternoon. Joshua Brookes pointing Hogarth's lessons had given the one spur; that lovely brown-eyed, brown-haired maiden, with her simple, "Come, Jabez—I'm ready," had given another.

She put her little gloved hand in his, after bidding her aunt and cousin good-bye, and went dancing, skipping, and chattering by his side down Oldham Street, and let him lift her over the muddy crossing to Mosley Street, unconscious of the chimerical dreams floating through his apprentice brain all the while. His original ambition to make a home for Simon and Bess, where neither penury nor care should trouble them, dwarfed before the new ideas crowding upon his mind. He had read the sermon on the wall, but the old "Knave of Clubs," as Joshua was called, little thought how that pretty, piquant little fairy, the "master's daughter," would point it with something higher than ambition.

There were at that period in Manchester two schools for young ladies, which, being celebrated at the time, deserve to be mentioned. The one was situated at the extreme end of Bradshaw Street, looking through its vista across Shudehill to the gaps in brickwork called Thomas Street and Nicholas Croft, where, in highly genteel state Mrs. (or Madame, as she insisted on being called) Broadbent superintended the education of a large and very select circle.

Education must have been at a low ebb when the chief manufacturers of the town consigned their daughters to this pompous, pretentious woman, who could not speak correctly the language she professed to teach. In her attempt to appear the print and pattern of a lady, she "clipped the King's English," and made almost as glaring errors as Mrs. Malaprop. Yet, strange to say, she turned out first-class pupils (for the period). The fact is, she was shrewd enough to know her own deficiencies, and relegated her duties to others who were in all respects efficient.

Then she was a wonderful trumpeter of her own fame; made frequent visitations at houses where she was well-entertained, and her bombast was listened to for the sake of her young charges; held half-yearly recitations, and also exhibitions of the plain sewing, embroidery, knitting, knotting, filigree, tambour, and lace work of her pupils; and matrons, proud of their own daughters' achievements, seldom paused to reckon up the tears, the headaches, the heartaches, the sore fingers which those minutely-stitched shirts, those fine lace aprons and ruffles, those pictures and samplers, had cost. For Madame Broadbent, besides being a martinet rigid in her rule—having a numbered rack for pattens and slippers, numbered pegs for cloaks and hats, book-bags and work-bags, safe-guards (receptacles for sewing, &c., like a huckster's pocket) and slates, all numbered likewise—was not of too mild a temper, and had a *penchant* for pinching her pupils' ears until the blood tinged her nails; while stocks for the feet, backboards for the shoulders, and dry bread diet were her prescriptions for the cure of such delinquencies as an unauthorised word, an omitted curtsey, a bag or garment on the wrong hook, a dropped stitch in knitting, a blotted copy, a puckered seam; and work had to be done and undone until stitches were almost invisible, and little eyes almost blind. She had other peculiarities, had Madame Broadbent—but my portrait is growing too large for its frame, and she was not a large personage at all.

It was to this delectable individual's school ("establishments" had not been invented then, or her's would have been one) that Miss Augusta Ashton was consigned for conversion into a well-behaved, well-informed, useful, and accomplished young lady.

Her cousins, the Misses Chadwick, had in their turns escaped from this penitentiary for the manufacture of ladyhood. But in Piccadilly was a school of a very different description, where young ladies of talent and fortune went to qualify for *wifehood;* and here at this time Ellen Chadwick was finishing her education, with many others, in learning *the culinary art* in all its branches.

How came it that Madame Broadbent's school flourished and survived the decay of its neighbourhood, being in existence when the writer of this was a child, and the other had died and been forgotten, save by the antiquary, before she was born?

To fetch Miss Ashton home from Madame Broadbent's on dark or stormy afternoons, was the understood duty of one or other of the apprentices; but Kit Townley, having no more liking for wet weather than a cat, generally contrived to be out of earshot when his services were required. It devolved on Jabez, therefore, to carry the grey duffel hooded-cloak with which to cover the dainty one of scarlet kerseymere, to tie the pattens on the tiny feet, to carry the school-bag, and hold the brilliant blue gingham umbrella over the head elevated by the pattens so much nearer to his shoulder, and to be thanked by one of the sweetest voices in the world.

It was dangerous work, though no one knew it, least of all Jabez. True, she was only a child, but she was tall for her age. And was he much more than a boy? A boy let out from the seclusion of an almost monastic institution, to whom her little airs and graces, her pretty vanities, her very waywardness and caprice, only made her beauty more piquant.

Madame Broadbent's infallibility being taken for granted, all attempts to make known school troubles and grievances were met with "Never tell tales out of school," from Mrs. Ashton, but they were poured fresh and warm into the ear of Jabez, as she trotted by his side; and he, his school-days unforgotten, listened with ready sympathy. And this went on as months and years went by, adding to her stature, narrowing the space between them; and he still did duty as her humble escort, unless when Kit Townley was especially told off for the service, and went reluctantly, grumbling at being made "lackey to a school miss."

Yet Kit Townley did not think it any degradation to play practical jokes on Jabez, or on Kezia, leaving the younger apprentice to bear the blame. Billets of wood, scuttles of coal, pails of water brought in for her use by Jabez, were dexterously removed to doorways and other unsuspected places, where "cook" was sure to stumble over them, and then cuff Jabez for his carelessness or wilfulness, all protestations on his part being disregarded. Creeping behind the settle where Jabez sat watching, and perhaps basting the roast for the master's table for late dinners on company days, he would steal his sly arm round the corner, himself unseen, and lifting the wheel of the spit out of the smoke-jack chain, bring spit and all thereon into the dripper, with a splash which brought the irate Kezia down on astounded Jabez with whatsoever weapon of offence came nearest to her hand, from the paste-pin to the basting-ladle, or even a saucepan lid—it was all one to Kezia.

From Kezia, however, these frequent chances and mischances went to Kezia's mistress; and, appearances being against him, the very steadiness of denial, unaccompanied with any accusation of another (other waggeries of Kit Townley in the warehouse being also laid on his shoulder), Mrs. Ashton's faith in the youth was somewhat shaken, and he was conscious of being under a cloud. But he still kept on his way, and looked to the end

The cloud dispersed after a while. Kit Townley was something of a glutton, with a very boy's love of pastry and sweets. It so happened that on a special occasion (rejoicing for peace or something) Kezia had set aside in her roomy pantry, the door of which fastened only with a button, a tray of tartlets, custards, a trifle, moulds of jelly and blanc-mange, and other dainties for a large party. Kit's mouth watered to get at these things. Often and often had he stolen the fruit from under a pie-crust, and sat silent while Jabez bore the blame, but now he meditated a more sweeping raid. There was a fine young retriever in the yard. Watching Kezia out of the way, he crammed mouth and pockets with the pastry, and made an inroad into the trifle. Then he whistled to Nelson, raised the dog on his hind feet, and printed the forepaws on the pantry-shelf, dishes, and tart-tray, and round the button of the door.

But he was compelled to wait until bedtime to fairly enjoy his spoil, and then could not manage it unknown to his companion. Hoping to close the other's mouth literally and figuratively, he offered him a share, but Jabez told him he was not a receiver of stolen goods, and left him to digest that with his feast. It was a harder morsel than even Jabez knew.

The next morning before breakfast they were in the warehouse, when there was heard a terrible commotion in the yard. From the back windows Kezia was seen belabouring Nelson with a broomstick, her face redder than ordinary, whilst the poor beast whined piteously.

Jabez ran down to interpose, and the infuriated woman turned on him, then ran in her rage to fetch her mistress to witness the damage done, and the footprints of the depredator, and to own that punishment was just.

But as Mrs. Ashton ascended the warehouse stairs that afternoon, she heard Jabez and Kit loud in altercation, and before they were aware she possessed a clue to much that had gone before.

Something Jabez had said was answered by a loud guffaw from Kit, and the words—

"Let them laugh that win. I call it a deuced good joke."

"And I call it cowardly and dishonourable to let the poor beast suffer for your greediness," Jabez answered, indignantly.

"Now don't you put in your oar, young yellow-skirt. I'll let no charity-boy hector over me," blustered Kit.

Jabez put down a bundle of umbrella whalebones he had on his shoulder, to confront the other, then counting ferules into dozens. Umbrellas used to have brass ferules, like elongated thimbles, on the sticks.

"Look you, Kit, I've borne many a scurvy trick of yours without saying a word, but I will not even give the sanction of silence to dishonesty, and will not see a noble animal ill-used to screen a coward."

"Won't you?" sneered Kit, "then we'll see whose word weighs heaviest."

Mrs. Ashton came into the room.

"Townley," said she, "your word will not weigh down a feather henceforth," adding in the same dignified tone, "Are those ferules counted? Jackson is waiting for them."

No further notice was taken, but Jabez soon found he stood on a firmer footing in house and warehouse. Mrs. Ashton remarked to her husband, as she finished dressing for their dinner party—

"It was a slight circumstance, William, but straws show which way the wind blows."

And he tapped his silver snuff-box, and said, "Just so;" then courteously offering his hand to his fine-looking wife, led her from the room, her purple velvet robe trailing after her, the plumes on her head nodding as they went.

CHAPTER THE SIXTEENTH.

IN WAR AND PEACE.

SHAW'S SHOP, MARKET STREET.

A CLAP of thunder burst over Europe, and the great war-eagle flapped his monstrous wings again. Napoleon had escaped from Elba ere crops had had time to grow on his trampled battle-fields; yet crops of men rose ripe for the sickle, and home expectations were dashed to the ground.

How many an anxious parent, how many a longing, love-sick maiden, looked for her warrior back from Canada or the Continent, if only on furlough or sick-leave! How many a weary soldier, sated with blood, looked for discharge with pension or reward, and thirsted for the fountain of home joys!

And from how many lips was the cup of delight dashed when the cry "To arms!" rang out from mount to vale, from peak to peak, from town to town, and the sheathed sword flashed forth to light, and forges belched forth flame through day and night, preparing for fresh holocausts in the new carnival of blood!

Trade centres at all such times are most convulsed, as being also centres of humanity—depôts whence fresh relays are drafted from the ranks of men whose peaceful work is at a sudden standstill. But that war-blast came like a fiery flash, and commerce, only then a feeble convalescent, sank crushed and hopeless.

Mr. Chadwick felt it keenly, and, but that his more cautious and wealthy brother-in-law came to his help with hand as open as his snuff-box, his credit must have gone. His two eldest sons had gone from him, drawn away by the phantom, "Glory." One, Richard, was a midshipman upon Collingwood's ship; the other, Herbert, a lieutenant in the 72nd, or Manchester Volunteers, had departed with his regiment to fight in the Peninsula. A third son, John, had been left to do his quiet duty in the counting-house, but Death had laid its clutches upon him soon after his sister Charlotte's marriage, and Ellen alone kept the house from utter desolation.

She was a girl of strong feelings and quick impulses, but pursued her way with so little show or pretence, she was hardly accredited with all the comfort she brought to the hearth; and scarcely her mother even suspected how that hidden heart of hers could throb—how intense were her emotions.

Her love for every member of the family was deep, but when her brother John died, after the first terrible outburst of grief she dried her tears, and by mere force of will set herself to soothe those who had lost a son. The prolonged absence of the others had been fruitful of pain, and the blighted prospect of Herbert' return came to her, as to father and mother, with a shock like a stab.

There was another hearth we have ere-while visited—a hearth which, thanks to Jabez and a few months' regular employment for the batting-rods and the tanner's plunger, was less poverty-stricken than it had been—and where Hope had held out delusive banners to herald a soldier's return, only to furl them again for another march, before eye could meet eye, or lip meet lip.

Thirteen years had come and gone since last Tom Hulme and Bessy Clegg had looked woefully upon each other—thirteen years of unrecorded trial and suffering—yet still they were apart. The home in which he had known her first, Tanner's Bridge, on which he had first made love to her, had been swept away to make room for Ducie Bridge and a new high-road; and the best years of her womanhood were passing too. Would he ever come back whilst grey-haired Simon could bless their union?

MARKET STREET LANE.

Would he ever come back again? Tears fell on Bess's batting; and Simon had not one word of comfort to give her. Even Matt Cooper, who had long since resigned himself to his widowhood, was magnanimous enough to be sorry.

The new war between the "Corsican Vampire" and allied Europe was fortunately of short duration; but how much of carnage and misery was compressed into that campaign which had its brilliant close at Waterloo!

In the onset of that terrible conflict, Herbert Chadwick and a cousin, fighting side by side, fell in a storm of grape-shot like green corn under an untimely shower of hail, and their blood went to fertilise the Belgian farmer's future crops of wheat.

Herbert was his father's favourite son. Not a mail-morning passed but the old man made one of the crowd hurrying down the narrow way called Market-street Lane to the Exchange, to catch a sight of whatever bulletins might be posted up; and, his own mind relieved, sent an apprentice from the Fountain Street warehouse with the words, "All's well!" to cheer up those at home. That dreadful morning when his fearful eye ran down the black list of the killed at Waterloo, and rested on Lieutenant Chadwick's name, the letters seemed to turn blood-red; he shrivelled up like a maple-leaf in a blighting wind his face and limbs began to twitch, and he fell forward into the arms of a bystander, in a fit

He was carried by compassionate hands to the nearest house, that of John Shaw, the saddler. A merchant on 'Change (Mr. Aspinall) undertook to break the doubly-calamitous intelligence to Mrs. Chadwick. Dr. Hardie, whom the general excitement had drawn to the spot, was with him in an instant, his white neckcloth was loosened, and, whipping out a lancet, the doctor bled him in the arm without delay. He rallied sufficiently to bear lifting into a carriage, kindly placed at the doctor's disposal to convey him home.

Dr. Hull was already in waiting. All that their united skill could suggest was tried. His recovery was slow and imperfect;

he dragged his right leg after him; he was paralysed for life. He was not a young man, and the supreme shock, coming as it did above a pressure of commercial difficulties, had been too much for him.

It was an overwhelming disaster; but in anxiety and active care for the stricken one, whose life was in imminent peril, the sharp edge of the keener stroke was blunted for Ellen and her mother.

The Ashtons were, as ever, kind and thoughtful.

"William," said Mrs. Ashton, meditatively, to her husband over the tea-urn, the day after Mr. Chadwick's attack, "we must not forget that if John is not related to us, Sarah [Mrs. Chadwick] and Ellen are. 'Blood is thicker than water,' and it will not do, for their sakes, to let John's business go to rack and ruin for want of supervision."

"Just so, just so," he replied, reflectively, taking his snuff-box out of his pocket mechanically, and putting it back again unopened, as contrary to tea-table propriety; "I have been thinking the same myself. I will go round to the warehouse to-morrow, and see how matters stand; we must keep things ship-shape somehow till John is himself again."

And he was as good as his word, though he had really never thought about it until prompted by his clear-headed wife. He had a habit of thus falling in with her suggestions, though had anyone hinted that he followed the lead of a woman, so much younger than himself, too, he would have rejected the imputation with scorn.

With returning peace came joyful restorations to many homes, humble as well as lofty.

Before the time of their extreme privation, before even Simon was out of work, he had taken one of the smallest of the garden plots on the higher ground on the opposite side of the Irk, and cultivated it in what little leisure he had, Bess giving him a helping hand occasionally, and by the sale of penny posies to Sunday ramblers from the town, and herbs and salad

ENTRY TO CLEGG'S YARD, MILLGATE.

to the market women in Smithy-door, he did his best to beat back the gaunt wolf when the wolf came.

Bess had laid by her batting-wands, put a turf in the grate to kindle up a handful of cinders and slack to boil their supper-porridge, for, though autumn was striding on, they could not waste fuel on a mid-day fire; Simon was away working in his garden whilst the daylight held, and she sat, as she frequently did now, on a low stool in front of the grate, her elbows on her knees, and her head on her hands, watching, in a kind of hazy dream, the red glow creeping through the heart of the turf, when a footstep on the threshold caused her to turn round.

Like a picture framed by the doorway, stood the tall figure of a bronzed soldier, with his left arm in a sling. Before the sharp cry of joy had well parted her lips, his other arm was around her—both hers around his neck; their lips met in a long kiss, which told of pain and trouble past, and love through all; and then her head fell on his shoulder in a fit of convulsive sobbing such as had not shaken her frame for years.

Sorrow and joy have alike their baptism of tears!

It was a glad sight for Simon to see them sitting with their hands locked in each other's, side by side on an old box, which served them for a seat—all Simon's lost furniture had not come back—silent from excess of happiness, yet radiant as though the glow of youth were returning in the Midsummer of their lives.

In the roughest war-time the common requirements of life have to be satisfied, and peaceful trades and arts are of necessity carried on, albeit they flourish not. And the farther from the seat of war, and the less private interest is involved, the less business and household routine is infringed on.

Thus Mr. Ashton, whose large capital had enabled him to bide the issues of the Continental and American stoppage of trade, and who had no nearer relatives in danger than his wife's nephews, pursued his way in comparative quiet. Indeed, he was an easy-going man, with much less vigour of character than his wife; and she bore little resemblance to her own sister.

So we may carry our readers away from the poorly-furnished room in a dreary Long-Millgate yard, leaving the re-united lovers to the enjoyment of the present and their reminiscences of the past, and look in upon the Ashtons in their cosy tea-room *before* Waterloo cast a black shadow over the family.

It was a spacious apartment (as were most of the rooms in that habitation), the walls above the surbase (a wooden moulding some two feet above the skirting-board) were painted a warm dove colour, the surbase and all below in two shades of light blue. The window-tax—a result of war—laid an embargo on light, by restricting size and number, so the house, like most in the neighbourhood, having been built subsequently to "Billy Pitt's" obnoxious impost, there were only two windows, and those were narrow. They were draped with heavy curtains, and festooned valances of dove-coloured moreen, trimmed with blue orris-lace, and worsted-bullion fringe, with spiral silken droplets here and there to shimmer in the rays of sun or chandelier. For there was a chandelier, of fanciful device, pendent from the wonderfully moulded ceiling, a septenary of lacquered serpents, whose interlaced and twisted tails met upwards, separated below in graceful coils, and branching out their seven heads, turned up their gaping jaws to close them on wax-lights. The chandelier was no misnomer; but the fiery serpents kept their flames for state occasions, when the serpent branches on each side the long Venetian looking-glass, between the windows, were on duty likewise. There was another Venetian glass above the high, painted chimney-piece, so elaborately carved, but here the serpent candelabra lit the room for common use, and were supplemented with lights in tall silver candlesticks upon the centre table.

Spanish mahogany alike were chairs and tables, and Miss Augusta's grand piano—ranged against the wall from the door, so that the window light should fall upon the keys—and chairs and tables were alike club-footed, massive, and plain; there were two

"WHAT WOULD MRS. BROADBENT SAY?"

folded card tables, a cellaret, and a work-table, all with tapering legs and club-feet; and there was a ponderous sofa on the flower-besprent Brussels carpet, which, without the adventitious aid of artificial steel springs, was elastic and soft, and wooed the weary to rest aching limbs or aching head upon its cushions. There were no antimacassars—hair-seating did not soil readily.

The air was odorous with rose, lavender, and jessamine, for the windows were both open, and what little air there was stirring swept over a large summer nosegay in a china vase between the windows. The mahogany teaboard was set with miniature unhandled cups and saucers of china, more precious than the fragrant decoction they were designed to hold; the brass tea-urn hissed and spluttered; Mrs. Ashton, in a rich dress, sat at the table to infuse the tea; Mr. Ashton had drawn his softly-cushioned easy-chair nearer; it was past five by the tall clock in the hall, and Miss Augusta had not presented herself.

As a thorough business woman, Mrs. Ashton was punctuality itself. She expected her family to be punctual also. Five o'clock, the Manchester hour for tea, and no Augusta!

"James!" (to the footman), "inquire for Miss Ashton; she is not kept in at school—it is a holiday."

As the man retired, Augusta, in a white cambric frock heavy with tambour-work, tripped in at the door, her diaper pinafore not so clean as it might have been, her hands full of something which she set down on a side table.

"It is past five o'clock, Augusta; where have you been until now? And how came Cicily to send you in to tea with a soiled pinafore?" asked Mrs. Ashton, with the quiet dignity which seldom relaxed.

"Is it? I did not hear the clock strike, I was so busy; and Cicily has not seen my pinafore," was Augusta's light, consecutive reply.

"So busy!—Cicily not seen you!" her mother exclaimed in surprise. "Let me look at your hands. I am shocked, Augusta!

What would Mrs. Broadbent say?" (The hands were worse than the pinafore.) "Have I not told you repeatedly that 'cleanliness is next to godliness?' Go to Cicily and be washed immediately, or you can have no tea."

Augusta pouted.

"Must I, papa?"

The management of this child was the only point on which Mr. and Mrs. Ashton differed.

"Well, my dear, your mamma says so; but I think for this once it may be overlooked, if you will be more careful another time," said he, willing to excuse and temporise.

"'Only this once,' William, 'is the parent of thrice,'" responded Mrs. Ashton, gravely, as she poured out the tea, giving something like milk-and-water to Miss Augusta. "You will spoil that child; and if you spoil her to-day, she will spoil herself to-morrow. However, as *you* are inclined to tolerate that which I think disrespectful to us, and wanting in self-respect on the child's part, I can say no more."

Thus Mrs. Ashton yielded against her judgment; Mr. Ashton took out his snuff-box, to put it back like a culprit; and Miss Augusta sat down to the table, not knowing whether to be more pleased or sorry that she had got her own way.

To turn the subject, Mr. Ashton asked—

"What is that you put on the card-table, my dear?"

"Oh! I'll show you," and away the young lady was running, only to be recalled by her mother's decided—

"After tea, Augusta."

So after tea it was that Miss Augusta brought her treasure to her father—sundry sheets of paper, on which scraps of variously-coloured leather had been arranged and pasted in ornamental patterns, floral and geometrical, aided by the stamps employed in piercing brace-ends for the embroiderers, and in cutting stars to cover the umbrella-wheels inside.

"Who did those?" asked mother and father in a breath.

"Jabez Clegg, in the warehouse. Aren't they pretty?" was

Augusta's ready reply, as she looked admiringly on her curious pictures.

"Oh! then that accounts for your being late, and in that condition at the tea-table," said Mrs. Ashton, as she glanced from the rich designs before her to the sullied hands and pinafore.

"And so Jabez Clegg has been wasting our leather to make playthings for you?" remarked Mr. Ashton interrogatively, in a not unkindly tone of voice.

"No, he hasn't!" answered little miss, briskly. "He only used the waste tiny bits. I wanted to take a big piece to make a housewife" (a case for thread and needles), "and he would not let me have it. He said he had no right to give it, and I had no right to take it. Was he right, mamma?"

[Along with many other vain fashions, "papa" and "mamma" had come over from France to supersede our more sterling "father" and "mother," as refugees from the Revolution.]

"Yes, my dear, quite right; but I wish my little daughter would not run so much into the kitchen and warehouse among the apprentices," said the mother, kindly, smoothing down the light brown hair, in which the sunbeams seemed to weave golden threads. "It is not becoming in a young lady."

Mr. Ashton, who had been all the while examining the glowing devices before him, interrupted her with—

"I think I have discovered a new faculty in our apprentice. I shall buy Jabez Clegg a box of colours to-morrow. We are sadly in want of fresh patterns, and I think he can make them." Mr. Ashton took a large pinch of snuff on the strength of his discovery.

And Jabez, for the first time in his life the possessor of paints and brushes, became valuable to his master.

CHAPTER THE SEVENTEENTH.

IN THE WAREHOUSE.

JABEZ TEACHING TOM HULME.

MUTABILITY is the epitaph of worlds. Change alone is changeless. People drop out of the history of a life as of a land, though their work or their influence remains. A passing word may suffice to dismiss such from our pages.

The Reverend John Gresswell had been taken by Death from the Chetham College schoolroom before more than half the term of Jabez Clegg's pupilage had run. Dr. Stone's resignation of his librarianship followed closely on his discovery of the half-drowned boy on the dairy steps. After a long engagement with a young lady who refused many eligible offers, and withstood much parental persuasion for his sake, he—the curate of St. John's Church—accepted the first vacant living in the gift of the College whereof he was Fellow. A bridal closed their almost Jacob's courtship, and the constant couple retired to the seclusion of Wooton Rivers, where his learning and eloquence had seldom more appreciative auditory than smock-frocked Wiltshire rustics and their families.

About the same time, or not long after, old Brookes was missed from the Packhorse, and the Ring-o'-Bells, and the Apple Tree, and the Sun Inn—the breeches-maker and his neighbours ceased to hear his foul and offensive maunderings and imprecations as he staggered past to his son's home, there to test *his* endurance. He had gone home to his mother-earth, sober and silent for evermore. And Parson Brookes, left to his books and his pigeons, sent in his resignation, and the Grammar

GRAMMAR SCHOOL AND COLLEGE GATE.

School knew him no more as a master. So the boys felt themselves free to take greater liberties with him than ever and kept his hot blood for ever on the simmer.

As all these changes preceded the change which converted Jabez from a Blue-coat boy into Mr. Ashton's apprentice, so were they anterior to the changes wrought by war in the homes of the Chadwicks and the Cleggs—changes differing even more widely than did the two homes.

Poverty had made sad havoc amongst Simon Clegg's household goods; but Tom Hulme had not come home empty-handed, and soon their furniture came back, or was replaced, and the three rooms brightened up wonderfully. Though Simon's flowers brought pence to his pocket as well as the other produce of his garden, he had always a spare posy for the broken jug on window-sill or mantel-shelf; and Bess, full-hearted, if not full of work, sent her voice quivering through that unmusical yard in songs of gladness and rejoicing.

Very little fresh wooing was necessary. To people who had been so stinted as they had been, in common with others, Tom's pension seemed more than it was; and no sooner was he able to discard his sling than he talked of immediate marriage, and was wonderfully sanguine about obtaining work as soon as his left arm regained its old power—which it never did. It was no use setting up a loom; he could no longer throw the shuttle back. He would have to seek some other employment. But thousands of other men were seeking employment too—men with the full use of all their limbs—men who had not disqualified themselves for peaceful arts by "going soldiering," and Tom Hulme stood little chance. Mr. Clough would have taken him on as a timekeeper, but lack of penmanship was a barrier in the way.

Lamenting this in the presence of Jabez, the youth offered to be his instructor; and with the permission of Mr. Ashton, who granted leave of absence, set him copies and gave him lessons on Sunday afternoons, at first on an old slate, to save the cost of paper, which was dear. And then, at Mr. Ashton's suggestion,

Jabez superadded arithmetic, thus keeping himself in practice, besides helping one dear to those who had helped him.

Of course, a weekly or fortnightly lesson was not much; but the disabled soldier was a persevering pupil, and brought a clear head and an eager desire to his task. The maintenance of a better home for Bess depended on it.

About this time a matter occurred at the Ashtons' which had a material influence on the fortunes of the Cleggs. Though the house of Mr. Ashton was in Mosley Street, the premises extended as far as Back Mosley Street, where was the warehouse door. The workpeople entered at a side door under a gateway which led to the stable, gighouse, and courtyard between house and warehouse, guarded by the black retriever, Nelson.

You may look in vain for house and warehouse now. A magnificent block of stone warehouses, having threefold frontage, occupies the site.

More than once Jabez Clegg, frequently entrusted with outdoor business requiring promptitude and accuracy, came upon Kit Townley, and one or other of the tassel-makers or fringe weavers, in close conference under the dim gateway at closing-time on Saturdays, or in the still darker doorway at the stairfoot of the workmen's entrance. The first time they moved aside to let him pass, afterwards they separated hastily; but not before Jabez, who had quick ears, caught the chink of money as it passed from one to the other.

On the first of these occasions his attention was barely arrested; it was the repetition and the avoidance which struck him with its air of secrecy, and set him pondering what business his fellow-apprentice could have with the hands out of proper place and time. He knew him to be not over-scrupulous. He had seen him at Knott Mill Fair and Dirt Fair (so called from its being held in muddy November), or at Kersal Moor Races, with more money to spend in pop, nuts, and gingerbread, shows and merry-go-rounds, flying boats and flying boxes, fighting cocks and fighting men, than he could possibly have saved out of the sum his father allowed him for pocket-money, even if he had been of the saving kind; and, coupling all these things together, Jabez was far from satisfied. He was aware that of late years stock-taking had been productive of much uneasiness to both Mr. and Mrs. Ashton. There were deficiencies of raw material in more than one department, for which it was impossible to account, save that the quantity accredited to "waste" was far out of reasonable proportion.

Mr. Ashton, suspecting systematic peculation or embezzlement (of which many masters were complaining) had privately communicated with Joseph Nadin, the deputy constable, a gnarled graft from Bow Street, who bore the official character of extraordinary vigilance and smartness. He was supposed to set a watch on workpeople and others, but nothing came to light. Perhaps he was too busy manufacturing political offences, or hunting down political offenders, to look after the interests of private manufacturers. Sure it is that silk, worsted, webs, and gingham once gone were not to be traced. Jabez was also aware that a shade rested on the establishment of which he was an item, and felt that it behoved him to clear it away for his own sake, if possible.

Since the discovery of his faculty for design, much of his time had been occupied at a desk with pencils and colours, making patterns for the wood-turner, the mould-coverer, the tassel-maker, the fringe-weaver; for bell-ropes, brace-webs, carpet and furniture bindings; and although some of those things admitted but of little variety, there was plenty found for him to do.

This was well-pleasing enough to Jabez, but the College officials, who never lose sight of the boys they apprentice, demurred. His indentures provided that he should learn small-ware manufacturing in all its branches; and pattern-designing, if part and parcel, was only one branch. Mr. Ashton was too just not to assent, and Jabez went to his active employment again. But he had a love for his new art, and an interest in his master's interest, which prompted him to say—

"If it would be all the same to you, sir, I could draw patterns before breakfast, or in the dinner-hour, or in an evening, if Kezia had someone else to wait on her."

The inevitable snuff-box came out, Mr. Ashton's head went first on one side, then on the other, as he took a long pinch before he answered.

"No, my lad, it won't be all the same to me, nor to you either," he said, at length, and Jabez began to look rueful. "You're a lad of uncommon parts, and I'm willing enough to find them employment. But if you work extra hours, apprentice or no apprentice, you must have extra pay. So you see, Jabez, it won't be the same to either of us You shall have the little room at the end of the lobby to yourself, and there you may earn all you can for your own friends and for me."

"Oh, thank you, master!" interjected Jabez, his thoughts flying at once to the old yard in Long Millgate.

"And let Kezia wait upon herself if there are no other idle folk about;" concluded Mr. Ashton, and the business was settled.

This was about the time Jabez first began to suspect Kit Townley of unfair dealing; and being once more in frequent contact with him in the warehouse, he could not shut his eyes or his ears.

Kit was then assistant putter-out in the fringe and tassel department, counted out the moulds, weighed out silk and worsted, and called out the quantities each hand took away, for a young booking-clerk to enter.

Jabez was still in the brace and umbrella room, but there was a wide door of communication between the two, and he had frequently to pass through the former with finished goods for the ware and show-rooms on the lower floors, and had to go cautiously past the large scale, lest he should tilt the beam with his ungainly burdens. Now and then it occurred to him that the bulk of silk or worsted in the scale was large in proportion to the weight, as called out by Kit Townley, and once he was moved to say—

"Is that balance true? or have you made a mistake, Townley?"

"Mind your own business, Clegg, and don't hinder mine. Naught ails the scales, and I know better than make mistakes."

"Well, I only thought," persisted Jabez.

"I wish you'd think and keep those umbrellas clear of the beam. You're always thrutching past with great loads on your shoulder when I am weighing out," interrupted Kit, testily, and Jabez held his peace.

But if he went on his way quietly, he was equally observant, and saw the same thing happen again too often to be the result of accident. Moreover, from the window of the little room where he had a broad desk for designing, he saw Kit meet the same men and women stealthily after hours under the opposite gateway.

"Kit," said he, one night, when they went to their attic, "what do you meet Jackson, Bradley, and Mary Taylor under the gateway for so often?"

Kit, arrested with his warehouse jacket half on and half of asked sharply—

"Who says I meet them under the gateway?"

"I say so. I have seen you myself."

"And what if you have?" Kit retorted, snappishly. "There's no harm in saying a civil word to poor folk that I know off."

"No harm, if that were all," returned Jabez, seriously, sitting down on the edge of his truckle-bed to take off his blue worsted stockings (knitted by himself), "but I have seen them give you money."

"And what of that, you Blue-coat spy? If they're kind enough to call at old mother Clowes' shop for toffy and humbugs for me, and give me the change back, what's that to you?" he blustered, coming up to Jabez with a defiant air.

"I know you've a sweet tooth, Townley," replied Jabez, unmoved, "but I fear nothing half so good as Mrs. Clowes' toffy takes you there so stealthily."

"Perhaps, Mr. Wiseacre, you know my business better than I do myself?" returned Kit, bold as brass, though he did begin to feel qualmish.

"Perhaps I do, for I suspect you of double-dealing, and I know what the end of that must be; and I warn you that I cannot stand by and see our good master robbed. I should be as bad as you if I did."

Townley, enraged, struck at him, and there was a scuffle in the dark, the bit of candle in their horn lantern having burnt out.

Kezia, who slept in the adjoining attic, rated them soundly the next morning for the disturbance they had made, threatening to tell Mrs. Ashton. Had she done so, inquiry would have followed.

Jabez, troubled and perplexed, the very next Sunday consulted old Simon Clegg as to the course he should pursue, being alike unwilling to tell tales on suspicion, or to see his kind master wronged.

"Eh, lad," quoth Simon, rubbing down his knees as he sat, "aw've manny a time bin i' just sich a 'strait atween two;' but aw allus steered moi coorse by yon big book, and tha' mun do t' seame. Thah munnot think what thah loikes, or what thah dunnot loike; but thah mun do *reet*, chuse what comes or goes. It is na reet to steeal; and to look on an' consent to a thief is to be a thief. Thi first duty's to thi God, an' thi next to thi payrents (if tha' had anny), an' thi next to thi measter. Thah's gi'en the chap fair warnin', an' if he wunnot tak it th' faut's noan thoine."

It so happened that the "putter-out" in the brace and umbrella-room was an old man named Christopher, who had been in the employment of the Ashtons (father and son) for thirty years. He professed to be very pious and very conscientious, but lamented that increasing years brought with it many ailments and infirmities, such, for instance, as headaches, dizziness, sudden weakness of the limbs, and attacks of spasms—for the cure of which he kept a bottle of peppermint in a corner cupboard.

It was into this room Augusta used to come dancing, to coax old Christopher out of bits of waste leather, and other odds and ends, for which only a child could find use. She was fond of cutting and snipping, and, with an eye to his own advantage, the cunning old fellow had taught her how to use the stamps, so that she might *amuse* herself by helping him. Then he bespoke her compassion for his aches and pains, and often, on holiday afternoons, was troubled with one or other ailment, which a pull at the bottle and a nap on the bundles of leather, or gingham, alone could relieve—"if Miss Augusta would be so obleeging an' so koind as to stamp out a few tabs or straps for him, or count out umbrella ferules, or wheels, or handles," for him.

And she, full of the superabundant energy of youth, did it, nothing loth; though as her own years increased, and with them her ability to help, came a sharp sense that old Christopher was a hypocrite—knowledge she confided to Jabez one day, when the sanctimonious putter-out was resting his aching head and uncertain legs, as usual; and in order to convince him, she drew a bottle of gin, *not* peppermint, from under a pile of white kid.

Jabez, too, had been sorry for the old fellow, and often added a good part of Christopher's work to his own, to relieve him. It was this fact which brought both Christophers to book. The old cant was so grievously afflicted on the Monday afternoon, that Jabez, seeing him quite incapable of doing his work properly (he was putting out umbrellas), undertook to do it for him, though it was no business of his—and so Mrs. Ashton would have told him, had she been there.

He measured off what he knew to be sufficient gingham for two dozen umbrellas (a workwoman standing by in waiting), and was about to cut off the length when the woman arrested his hand.

"Yo're furgettin' th' weaste, mi lad; Mester Christopher allus alleaws fur weaste."

He looked at the woman, aware there could be no waste in

cutting umbrella-gores. She winked at him.

"Oh!" said Jabez, conscious he was learning something not down in his indentures. "And how much does he allow?"

"Abeawt a yard an' a hauve th' dozen," she replied.

"And how do you contrive to waste it?" Jabez asked.

She winked again.

"Eh, but yo're a young yorney. Yo'd best ax Mester Christopher that."

"I think I'd best ask Mrs. Ashton that, if she's in the warehouse," rejoined he, sending his scissors through the gingham at the proper place.

"Yo'd better not, or yo'n cut off yo'r nose to spite yo'r own feace;" and the woman nodded her head knowingly. "T'other 'prentice knows whatn weaste means, if thah dunnot; an' manny's th' breet shillin' it's put in his breeches pocket, my lad."

"Oh, that's it, is it?" said Jabez, whilst he was counting over the already bundled up whalebone, sticks, &c., to complete the umbrella fittings. "As our mistress would say, 'We may live and learn.'"

He found the whalebone, ferrules, handles, leathers, wheels, were all in excess. An extra umbrella might be made from the superabundant materials. Thereupon he wakened Christopher to do his own work, simply remarking that he thought the bundles of sticks, &c., had been miscounted.

"Oh, no, Clegg, they're a' reet; we're obleeged to put in moore fur fear some on 'em shouldn' split in makkin' oop," said old Christopher, cunningly, as if for his information.

Jabez took no further notice then, but shouldering a great bundle of large umbrellas, carried them through the fringe room, and there noticed that, despite the caution he had given, his fellow-apprentice was dexteriously manipulating silk and scales to falsify the weights he called out.

CHAPTER THE EIGHTEENTH.

EASTER MONDAY.

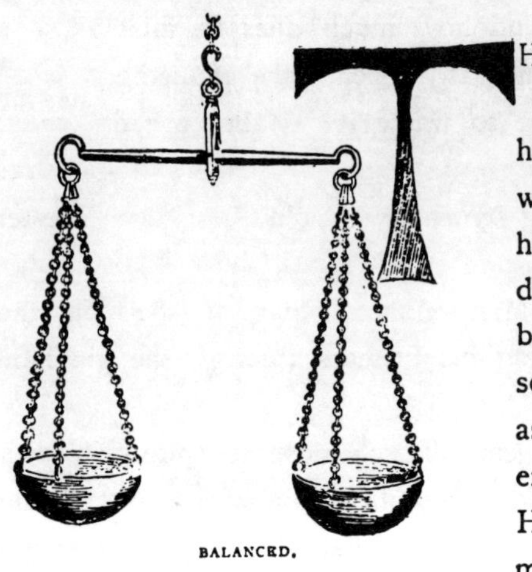

BALANCED.

THAT evening Jabez, a clear-eyed, open-browed youth in his seventeenth year, upright, well-knit, and firmly built for his age, knocked at the parlour-door after Miss Augusta had been sent to bed. There was some trouble on his countenance, as though he was bent on an errand utterly repugnant to him. He was truly sorry to be the means, however remotely, of bringing disgrace on both an old man and a young one; but Simon had led him to the conclusion that if there was little honour in turning informer, there would be absolute dishonesty in keeping silence whilst he saw his master robbed.

Yet he hesitated, and lingered with his hand on the handle of the door, after the clear voice of Mr. Ashton had twice invited him to "come in."

Mr. Ashton therefore opened the door, and saw Jabez with a design for a bell-rope tassel in his hand.

"Well, Jabez, what is it? Something special you have to show us?"

"No, sir; I only brought this lest any of the servants should be curious about my errand here."

Mrs. Ashton, who was reading a romance from Mrs. Edge's circulating library in King Street, lifted up her head at this; and Jabez came in, closing the door.

"Then what is the errand which needs such precaution?" asked Mr. Ashton, resuming his seat and looking up at the clear face of Jabez.

"I *think*, sir,"—and he laid an emphasis on the "think"—

"I have found out how you are being robbed, and who it is that robs you."

"You—what?" exclaimed Mr. Ashton, placing his hand on the elbows of his chair, and bending forward inquiringly.

Jabez repeated his statement, adding, "I think, sir, some of your putters-out and workpeople are in league to defraud you."

Out came Mr. Ashton's snuff-box, down went Mrs. Ashton's romance, whilst Jabez told succinctly how his suspicions had been first aroused, and how they had been confirmed that day.

"I did not tell my suspicions to Christopher, sir, thinking I had best not interfere, or put the—the—them on their guard until I had spoken to you. I feared lest I should defeat your plans," said Jabez, modestly.

"Just so, Jabez, just so; you were quite right, Jabez," said his master, whilst a shower of snuff fell on neckcloth ends and shirt frills.

"Yes, quite right!" assented Mrs. Ashton, with customary dignity. "'A still tongue shows a wise head;' but we seldom see an old head on such young shoulders."

No active steps were taken for a few days, but Mrs. Ashton was in the warehouse, and doubly observant; and Mr. Ashton was also on the alert. They saw enough to convince them that Jabez was correct, and, acting on first impulses, Nadin was again communicated with.

From the window of Jabez Clegg's little room, Kit Townley was seen to receive payment from a fringe-weaver for his share of the spoil; and then Nadin, who knew all about it quite well enough before, followed up the clue to a waste dealer's who bought at his own price workpeople's "waste" (*i.e.*, warp, weft, silk, &c., remaining after work was completed), and found trades-people willing enough to re-purchase, well knowing that commodities so varied, and so far below market value, were not honestly come by.

Nadin, big and blustering when there was nothing to be gained by silence, was for hauling the whole lot off to prison—the two Kits, the waste dealer, and sundry workpeople—and the criminal code was a very terrible dispensation then.

But Mr. Ashton was more merciful; he was for milder measures. Besides, Mr. Townley was an old friend of his, and for the sake of the father he forbore to drag the son into a court of justice; and unless he prosecuted all, he could not prosecute any.

The sight of Nadin and his rough men, in their red-cuffed, red-collared brown coats, with their staves and handcuffs ready for use, was sufficiently terrifying. The distress of old Mr. Townley was painful to witness. As for Kit himself, he seemed less conscious of his guilt than ashamed of being found out, openly declaring that he "*did no more than was customary*," and no more than old Christopher, who had led him into it, had done for years.

That old hypocrite went down on his knees with many whining protestations of his innocence; but, finding proof too strong, he made a clean breast of it, and on learning that, through the generosity of his employer, he was about to escape prosecution, which would have led to transportation, he begged piteously to be allowed to retain the situation he had held for so many years.

"No, Kit," said Mrs. Ashton; "'there is no rogue like an old rogue;' you have not only robbed us yourself, but taught others the trick. Think well you have escaped the New Bailey," (the Manchester and Salford prison).

At that period the constable who apprehended a criminal received a bonus on each conviction, called "blood-money," so large a proportion of felons were executed; and Nadin, gruff and uncourteous even to his superiors, was disposed to resist Mr. Ashton's amiable "interference with the course of justice." A liberal douceur from the elder Mr. Townley's well-stocked purse was potent to allay his zeal. His runners were dismissed,

JOSEPH NADIN

From a Print in the Chetham Library.

and his friend the waste-dealer had a longer lease.

The clearance of rogues paved the way for honest men, besides suggesting measures to prevent like embezzlement in future. The Ashtons rightly thought that the best way to reward Jabez was to serve his friends. A situation as putter-out to the weavers was offered to Tom Hulme, Mr. Ashton having had his eye on him for some time, and old Simon, being sent for, went home delighted with commendations of Jabez, and the consciousness that the only barrier to Bess's marriage was now removed, and that through the foundling's instrumentality.

The only bar, that is, save the double fees of Lent, and the "ill-luck" supposed to follow a couple united during the penitential forty days. Tom put up the banns, however, and Easter Monday was chosen as the day of days for the ceremony. Tom Hulme's parents had been married on an Easter Monday, Simon had been tied to his wife on an Easter Monday, Jabez had been made a Blue-coat boy on an Easter Monday, and apprenticed on an Easter Monday; it was consequently an anniversary to be observed and respected.

Early marriages prevail amongst the class made early self-dependent by earning their own living. Matt Cooper had long been a grandfather, Molly and his three eldest boys having been married and settled. A brisk young butcher coming to the tannery with hides had met Martha, the other girl, bearing her father's dinner, and been so taken with her sharp, active gait, and saucy answers, that he proposed to transfer her to his shop beyond Ancoats Lane canal bridge, and to make his offer more palatable, suggested an amalgamation of the two households, and to take the youngest lad—Matthew, aged fourteen—as his apprentice.

So ardent and promising a lover was not to be despised. Martha did not say "No," and Matt, beginning to stoop in the shoulders, rejoiced at the prospective haven for his declining years.

It was arranged that they should be married along with Bess

and Tom Hulme; and so Matthew Cooper went with the Cleggs to church, not as a gallant bridegroom, but, more suitably, to give away a bride.

And now, how shall I describe the scene at the Old Church on Easter Monday, to convey anything like an idea to modern readers, unacquainted with the locality, the period, and the habits of the people?

It must be borne in mind that registrars' offices did not exist; that there was no marrying at dissenting chapels; that few, if any, churches were licensed for the solemnisation of matrimony; and that the collegiate parish church of Manchester was the nucleus towards which the marriageable inhabitants of all the surrounding townships and villages turned at the most important epoch of their lives.

The venerable pile (now being doctored by restorers) was set, as it were, in a ring-fence of old houses, with an inner ring of low wall encircling the churchyard, which, as grave-stones testified, had once extended to the very house steps. As I have elsewhere said, the path between this wall and the houses was known as Half Street, a portion of which, containing Mrs. Clowes' old shop, still remains; and did I enumerate all the public-houses in this ring-fence which offered accommodation to wedding and christening parties, only a future generation of antiquaries would thank me; and even they might doubt the facts set down in a work of fiction.

Nevertheless, on Easter Monday not one of these hostelries had a spare foot of room. Every window and every door stood wide open. Men and women, gaily dressed as their own means or friendly wardrobes would allow, went in and out, filled rooms and passages, leaned from the windows with ribbons flying loose, or with pipes and ale-pots in their hands, calling to their friends below, whilst rival fiddlers (almost every party having its own) scraped away in anything but harmony. Horses and carts blocked up every avenue, and the churchyard itself was thronged with an excited crowd.

Only the parties immediately interested were admitted into the sacred edifice, but to reach the doors they had to force their way, and could only return in couples through a dense avenue of humanity, amid a shower of jests, many not the most seemly.

Bess wore only a white cambric gown, and a straw bonnet crossed with white ribbon, both of which Mrs. Ashton had provided; but somewhere in Tom's Peninsular campaigns he had picked up a bright-coloured scarf, which made her glorious to behold, and the envy of many a country bride. His old uniform had been kept for the occasion, and they looked grand together; but the quiet content on Bess's face was better than the grandeur.

Nat Bradshaw, the butcher-bridegroom, was of a jovial turn, and nothing would do but the whole double wedding-party, Jabez included, should turn into the Ring-o'-Bells to drink health and happiness to the brides, and give them spirit to go through the ceremony befittingly. Bess and Martha hung back blushing like peonies; but Nathaniel was not to be gainsaid, and in they went; and whilst the brides sipped, he quaffed, and pressed the others to do likewise.

At length Jabez, who had been brought up temperately, cried out they would be too late—Parson Brookes had been gone into the church half-an-hour.

There was a general rush from the room, and in the scramble to get first the party got separated; Matthew pulling his daughter along and leaving the bridegroom to follow. They elbowed their way into the church, and reached the choir just as Joshua pronounced the benediction over some twenty couples closely packed around the altar. Then there was a jostle and a scramble for "first kisses," amidst which rose the rough voice of the chaplain.

"Now clear out, clear out! Do your kissing outside. There are other folks waiting to be wed. Do you think I want to be kept here all day tying up fools?"

That instalment of the married having been hustled away to sign the church books, with their attendant witnesses, Joshua called out impatiently to the waiting couples, amongst which were Bess and Tom—

"Come, come! How long do you mean to keep me standing here? Do you intend to be married or not? Oh! it's thee, is it? [to Bess.] Well, thah's waited long enough. See that you make her a good husband [to Tom.] Kneel down here," and he placed them, not roughly, almost in the centre of the altar, pulling others to their knees beside them, with scant ceremony.

"What do *you* want here?" in his harshest tones he asked a very youthful-looking couple.

"To be wed," was the prompt answer of the young man.

"Ugh!" grunted the Parson, "what's the world coming to? I used to marry men and women—now I marry children! Here, you silly babies, take your places."

Another file of candidates for matrimony being ranged (after some pushing and pulling) in pairs round the altar, Joshua took his book, and the service began.

So long as it was general, all went tolerably smoothly—women and men alike were too bashful and confused to know much what was said, or what they responded, and certainly they rarely looked in each other's faces. At length there was a slight stir and a whispering from the quarter where Matt Cooper stood beside his daughter.

"Silence there!" roared Joshua, in a voice which set a row of hearts in a flutter, and there *was* silence.

But he had come to the troth-plight, and again the same commotion was apparent as he approached the Coopers.

"What's wrong here?" he demanded, pausing before Martha, who was all in a tremble.

"Moi lass is waitin' fur her mon," answered Matthew from behind.

"Ugh! I can't wait for laggards. Here, you [addressing Tom Hulme], answer for him. What's his name?" [to Martha.]

"Nathaniel," she faltered.

"I, Nathaniel, take thee, Martha, to be my——" he went on,

insisting on the response of Tom, who looked aghast at the prospect of marrying the wrong woman, and being told "to pair as they went out," as Joshua had summarily adjusted a like mistake heretofore; or, what was worse, of being saddled with two wives.

On imperturable Joshua went with the ceremony, bent on a marriage by proxy. His experience having taught him that women of the working class, as a rule, took charge of their wedding-rings, he asked Martha for hers, which was duly produced, and without further ado he directed Tom Hulme to place it on Martha's finger, as he had previously put one on Bess's, and with the same formula.

They had got as far as "With this ring I thee wed," when the missing bridegroom came in hot haste through the side door into the chancel, closely followed by Jabez, who had been in quest of him.

He was flushed with ale and excitement, but was clear-headed enough to perceive what was going forward, and to the chaplain's chagrin, plucked the young woman back from the altar and his proxy, and the ring rolled to the ground.

Then ensued an altercation between the butcher and Joshua Brookes, the latter insisting that what was good enough for princes might be good enough for him, and refusing to go over the ceremony again. But an apparitor drew the tardy bridegroom aside, and whispered to him a few mollifying words, whilst Joshua concluded the ceremonial, and then hurried from the altar with hardly a look at either Jabez or Simon as he passed out of the chancel, chafed and angry. Another clergyman took his place, and in the next group Nat Bradshaw and the half-married Martha took theirs. The lost ring had a substitute provided by the clerk for such emergencies; and this time they were as surely married as Bess and Tom had been.

Jabez had found the truant bridegroom at the "Ring-o'-Bells," oblivious of the flight of time, or of his party. The story having got wind, there was a general rush in their direction.

"Here's th' mon wur too late to be wed!"—"Tak' care thi woife hasna two husbants!"—"Hoo's getten two husbants o'ready!'—"See thah's tied up gradely, lass!"—"Thah'rt a pratty fellow!" and much more which might have provoked a man less good-humoured in his cups.

As it was the new brides clung to their husbands, half afraid of those noisy demonstrations, and were not sorry to get clear of the crowd, and thread their way to Ancoats Lane, where the thriving butcher, assisted by Mrs. Ashton, Mrs. Clowes, and Mrs. Clough, had prepared a dinner which bore no proportion to the "short commons" of every-day fare.

CHAPTER THE NINETEENTH.

PETERLOO.

SAM BAMFORD'S COTTAGE.

PEOPLE had been naturally sanguine that the conclusion of peace would inaugurate prosperity, that commerce would flourish with the flourish of pens on the parchments of a treaty. But the war had been of too long continuance, too universal, too destructive of life and property and crops. When grounds lie untilled for years; when swords reap harvests that should have been left for the sickle; when cattle are slaughtered wholesale for unproductive soldiery, or for lack of provender; when orchards and vineyards which have taken years to mature are given to the flames, there can be no sudden re-adjustment of commercial matters. Food products are the staple of trade, which is only a system of exchange facilitated by coin and paper.

What could a food-producing continent, down-trod by the iron hoof of war, have to offer in exchange for our textile fabrics and hardware?

Trade could not revive until there was food to sustain it. Yet the mass of the people in 1816, still further impoverished by a deficient home harvest, imputed the evil to defective legislation, and the exclusion of foreign corn, save at famine prices, and discontent became universal.

Strangely enough, the agricultural districts which the Corn Laws were supposed to protect, were the first to cry out against them, and to break out into riot—not Manchester, Oldham, Nottingham, and the manufacturing centres.

Swan Electric Engraving Co

TO HENRY HUNT, ESQ.[R]

As CHAIRMAN of the Meeting assembled on St. Peter's Field, Manchester on the 16TH OF AUGUST, 1819.

and to the Female Reformers of MANCHESTER and the adjacent TOWNS who were exposed to and suffered from

THE WANTON AND FURIOUS ATTACK MADE ON THEM BY THAT BRUTAL ARMED FORCE THE MANCHESTER AND CHESHIRE YEOMANRY CAVALRY,

this Plate is dedicated by their Fellow Labourer. RICHARD CARLILE.

This year closed on a popular demand for Parliamentary reform, but not a riotous one. Sunday schools had created readers on humble hearths, and William Cobbett supplied them with books and pamphlets bearing on their own rights and wrongs. They were read with avidity, and he became a power. He counselled peaceful persistence, not armed resistance. Hampden Clubs were formed all over the country, in which the political questions of the day were discussed with as much freedom as stringent law permitted. Public speakers and poets, of whom Samuel Bamford was one, arose from the ranks of the working classes; and the men banded together under such leadership called themselves Radical Reformers, a title which soon degenerated into Radicals.

The members of these rapidly-spreading clubs subscribed a penny a week each. Delegates were sent to meet and debate together; and on the 4th November, 1816, a large meeting was held in St. Peter's Field, Manchester (strangely enough, the site of the present Free Trade Hall), "to take into consideration the distressed state of the country."

Other meetings were held by the Reformers and their delegates; and on the 13th January, 1817, their political opponents held a counter-meeting, to consider the "necessity of adopting measures for the maintenance of the public peace;" for certainly the meeting of large masses of disaffected people, however peacefully disposed in the outset, and individually, becomes threatening in the aggregate. No one cares much for a grain of gunpowder; but mass the grains into pounds, and the pounds into tons, and there is certainly need of precaution in dealing with it.

Amongst the precautionary measures deemed necessary for the protection of the peace, and the suppression of seditious meetings, were the suspension of the Habeas Corpus Act, and the enrolment of the Manchester and Cheshire Yeomanry Cavalry, under the command of Sir T. J. Trafford; Laurence Aspinall, Ben Travis, and John Walmsley joining the corps.

On the 24th of March—since known as Blanket Monday—a

large number of men assembled in St. Peter's Field, with blankets upon their shoulders, with the openly-expressed design of walking to London, to lay their grievances before George, the Prince Regent, in person. The blankets were intended for coverlets on the wayside beds Mother Earth alone would spread for them. The meeting was dispersed by military, the newly-formed Yeomanry distinguishing themselves by trapping a number of the Blanketeers who had prematurely set out, and who had not got farther than Stockport.

This was the signal for widespread alarm, and for Joseph Nadin to prove his discrimination and vigilance by scenting out imaginary plots, and arresting suspected plotters, whom he tied together, handcuffed, ill-used, and hauled to prison, or before magistrates (whether for acquittal or conviction), for little other reason than the dangerous power given by the suspension of the Habeas Corpus Act. He was a big, blustering, overbearing fellow, with a large grizzled head, closely set on strong, broad shoulders, with overhanging brows drawn close, and a sallow skin; and his officious zeal in arresting such persons as Samuel Bamford, the weaver-poet, Thomas Walker, and the amateur actors he had earlier laid hands on at a public-house in Ancoats Lane, laying to their charge plots which had their origin in his own brain, did more to embitter the people against their rulers than those dust-blinded rulers suspected.

The Radical agitation reached its climax in 1819, when our friend Jabez was a well-formed, well-favoured young man of twenty, high in the estimation of his master and mistress. Popular rights had found a fresh champion in Henry Hunt, the son of a well-descended Wiltshire yeoman, a man of gentlemanlike bearing and attire, agreeable features, mobile in expression, and dull grey eyes which lit like fiery stars when in the fervour of his speech his soul shone out of them.

"Orator Hunt," as he was ironically dubbed by those who loved him not, was the very man to move the people as he himself was moved; his energy and fervid eloquence carried his hearers with him, and as he was wont to lash himself to a fury which streaked his pale eyes with blood, and forced them forward in their sockets, no wonder the Manchester magnates were afraid of his influence on the multitude, or that the Prince Regent should issue a proclamation against seditious meetings and writings, or the military drilling of the populace, then carried on with so fervid an orator to inflame them.

When Henry Hunt made a public entry into Manchester, and attended the theatre the same evening, a disturbance ensued; he was expelled, and the next evening the theatre was closed to preserve peace. Then a Watch-and-Ward, composed of the chief inhabitants, was established; a meeting called by the Radicals was prohibited; but that did not deter the calling of another on St. Peter's Field, on the 16th of August, when a couple of large waggons were boarded over to serve as temporary hustings, whence Orator Hunt from the midst of his friends might address the assembled multitude.

Augusta Ashton had just passed her fifteenth birthday. She was slim, graceful, and tall beyond her age, and was surpassing lovely. She was still under Mrs. Broadbent's care, and went to school that morning as usual, other meetings having passed off quietly, and no apprehension of disorder being entertained until long after nine oclock.

About that hour the people began to assemble from all quarters on the open ground near St. Peter's Church—not blood-thirsty roughs, but men, women, and children, drawn thither for a sight of a holiday spectacle. True, of the collective eighty thousand, though there were many thousands of earnest, thinking men who went to grapple with important questions, yet no such mighty gathering could be without its leaven of savagery and mischief.

But those who went from the mills and the workshops, the hills and the valleys around Manchester, walking in procession, with bugles playing and gay banners flying, though they might look haggard, pinched and careworn, made no attempt to look deplorable, or excite compassion. They wore their Sunday suits and clean neckties ; and by the side of fustian and corduroy walked the coloured prints and stuffs of wives and sweethearts, who went as for a gala-day, to break the dull monotomy of their lives, and to serve as a guarantee of peaceable intention.

Such at least was the main body, marshalled in Middleton by stalwart, stout-hearted Samuel Bamford, which passed in marching order, five abreast, down Newton Lane, through Oldham Street, skirted the Infirmary Gardens, and proceeded along Mosley Street, each leader with a sprig of peaceful laurel in his hat. Women and little ones preceded them, or ran on the footway, singing, dancing, shouting gleefully in the bright sunshine, as at any other pageant to which the music of the bugle gave life and spirit, and waving flags gave colour.

Such, too, were the bands which, with banners and music, fell in with them on their route, and together parted the dense multitude as a wedge, on their way to the decorated platform. Thence Samuel Bamford observed that other leaders had been less temperate. There were to be seen black banners and placards inscribed with seditious mottoes and emblems: caps of liberty, skull and crossbones "Bread or Blood," "Liberty or Death," "Equal Representation or Death;" this last with an obverse of clasped hands and heart, and the one word "Love," but all of the same funereal black and white.

But ere he could well note or deplore this, the scattered bands struck up "God Save the King," and "Rule, Britannia," deafening shouts rent the air, and Henry Hunt, drawn in an open barouche by white horses, made his way slowly to the hustings amidst the enthusiastic cheering of the multitude. A Mrs. Fildes, arrayed in white, with a cap of liberty on her head, and a red cap borne on a pole before her, sat on the box-seat. It is said she had been hoisted there from the crowd. Be this as it may, she paid dearly for her temerity before the day was out.

Barely had Henry Hunt ascended the platform, taken off his

SAMUEL BAMFORD.
From a Photograph.

white hat, and begun to address his attentive auditory, when there was a startling cry, "The soldiers are upon us!" and the 15th Hussars, galloping round a corner, came with their spare jackets flying loose, their sabres drawn, and threw themselves, men and horse, upon the closely-packed mass, without a note of warning. All had been preconcerted, pre-arranged.

From the early morning, magistrates had been sitting in conclave at the "Star Inn," and there Hugh Birley, a cotton-spinner, was said to have regaled too freely the officers and men of his yeomanry corps, so soon to be let loose on the "swinish multitude," as they called them.

A cordon of military and yeomanry had been drawn round St. Peter's Field, like a horde of wolves round a flock of sheep. The boroughreeve and other magistrates issued their orders from a house at the corner of Mount Street, which overlooked the scene; and thence (not from a central position, where he could be properly seen and heard) a clerical magistrate read the Riot Act from a window in an inaudible voice.

Then Nadin, the cowardly bully, having a warrant to apprehend the ringleaders—although he had a line of constables thence to the hustings,—declared he *dared* not serve it without the support of the military.

His plea was heard; and thus through the blindness, the incapacity, the cowardice, or the self-importance of this one man, soldiery hardened in the battle-field, yeomanry fired with drink, were let loose like barbarians on a closely-wedged mass of unarmed people, and one of the most atrocious massacres in history was the result.

Amid the shouts and shrieks of men and women, cries of "Shame! shame!" "Break! break!" "They are killing them in front!" "Break! break!" Hussars, infantry, yeomanry rushed on the defenceless people. They were sabred, stabbed, shot, pressed down, trampled down by horse and infantry; and in less than ten minutes, the actual field was cleared of all but mounds of dead and dying, severed limbs, torn garments, pools of blood, pawing steeds and panting heroes (?). Men and maidens, mothers and babes, had been butchered by their own countrymen for no crime.

Hunt had been taken, Bamford had escaped—to be arrested afterwards—and Mrs. Fildes, hanging suspended by a nail in the platform which had caught her white dress, was slashed across her exposed body by one of the brave cavalry.

But the butchery and the panic had spread from the deserted Aceldama over the whole town, and ere long the roar of cannon began to add its thunder to the terrors of the day. As the first shrieking fugitives rushed for their lives down Mosley Street, with the Manchester and Cheshire Yeomanry in swift pursuit, Mrs. Ashton, for the first time alarmed for the safety of Augusta, hurried through the warehouse in search of Mr Ashton, who was nowhere to be found. On the stairs she met Jabez, in a state of equal excitement.

"Miss Augusta! Is she at school? Had I not better——"

"Oh, yes! Run! run!" cried the mother, anticipating him. "Go through the back streets, and take her to her aunt's. It is not safe to bring her home."

He was gone before she concluded. (His master's daughter was the very light of his young eyes.) From Back Mosley Street he tore down Rook Street and Meal Street, into Fountain Street, across Market Street—already in a ferment—and onward down High Street without a pause.

By good fortune he met the young girl and a schoolfellow on their usual homeward route, at the Corner of Church Street, almost afraid to proceed, the distant firing had so scared them.

"This way, this way, Miss Ashton!" was his impetuous cry, as he hurried them from the main thoroughfare (into which a stream of terror-stricken people was flowing), through by-streets, and a private entry to the back door of Mr. Chadwick's house, which they found unfastened; and then he thanked God in his heart of hearts that she at least was safe.

Upstairs rushed Augusta, followed by her young friend, in search of her aunt and cousin, whom she found in the drawing-room in a state of the greatest trepidation and alarm.

Dolly, a stout woman-servant, had gone to Fountain Street, as was her custom, to assist her paralysed master home to dinner. From the windows, meanwhile, they had seen men, women, and children flying along, hatless, bonnetless, shoeless, their clothes rent, their faces livid and ghastly, cut and bleeding, shrieking in pain and terror as they ran or dropped in the path of pursuing troopers; and their hearts throbbed wildly with affright as they pictured the helpless old man caught in that whirlpool of horror and destruction, with only a woman's arm to protect him.

"Jabez will go and meet them," cried Augusta; "he is below!"

"Jabez!" exclaimed Ellen, starting to her feet, her white face flushed for a brief moment. "Oh, no! no!"

But without waiting to hear her cousin's exclamation, or to note her change of colour, Augusta had run downstairs to Jabez, waiting in the long kitchen, and communicated her aunt's fears to him.

Personal danger was unthought of when Augusta Ashton pointed to needful service. The lobby door closed after him with a bang before she had well explained her wishes; and when Augusta re-appeared in the drawing-room, Ellen Chadwick's head was stretched from the window, watching the sturdy young man stem the on-rushing tide of humanity—the only one in all that crowd with his face turned towards the danger from which the rest fled in desperation.

The sights and sounds that met her eyes and ears were terrible; gashed faces and maimed limbs; appeals and imprecations mingled with the roar of a surging crowd; the dropping fire of musketry; the coarse shouts of the yeomanry, drunk with wine and blood!

As her fearful eyes followed Jabez, a man rushed past whose hand had been chopped off at the wrist. With the remaining hand he held his hat to catch the vital stream which gushed

A PETERLOO INCIDENT.

from the bleeding stump; and as he ran, he cried "Blood for blood! blood for blood!" in a tone which made her shudder.

Faint and sick she drew back her head; but open apprehension for her dear father, and secret fear for the apprentice who had gone so readily to pilot him through that surging human sea, caused her to look forth once more. Augusta and her friend, with blanched cheeks and lips, were also at the window, fascinated as it were with that which chilled them.

Jabez turned the corner into Piccadilly, where one or two good brick houses had been converted into shops without lowering the floors or removing the original palisades, which enclosed bold flights of steps leading to doors with respectable shop-windows on each side. A confectioner of some standing named Mabbott occupied the second of these. He and his neighbour were hurriedly putting up their shutters as Jabez, crushing his way through the thickening crowd, saw Molly and Mr. Chadwick jammed up against the palisades, a young mounted yeomanry officer, in all his pride of blue and silver, brandishing his sabre, urging his unwilling steed upon them, and shouting—

"Move on, you rebels, move on! or I'll cut you down!"

Strong of nerve and will, Jabez thrust the impending throng aside, and grasped the horse's reins to force it back, crying as he did so—

"Shame, you coward! to attack a woman and a paralysed man!"

"Come in here, quick, Mr. Chadwick!" cried Mr. Mabbott at that instant, opening his closed gate and drawing the feeble gentleman and his attendant within, as the sabre, raised either to terrify or strike the old man, came down on the outstretched arm of Jabez, gashing it frightfully.

Another of the corps riding past, with his eyes full upon them, stopped his horse at the gallop, as if to interpose, but he was too late.

"My God! Aspinall, what have you done?" he exclaimed, and

throwing his own reins over the palisades, he dismounted hastily, caught at Jabez, who had staggered back, and drew him too within the iron screen, and helped him also into the confectioner's, as the other, with a derisive laugh which ill-became his handsome face, turned at a hand-gallop up Oldham Street, where he overtook a *confrere,* and with him sneered at "that soft-hearted Ben Travis."

Ellen and Augusta had not lost sight of Jabez many minutes when two of the Manchester Yeomanry, their dripping sabres flashing in the August sun, wheeled their panting charges round, and rode (heedless of the shrinking wretches beneath their hoofs) across the footway, and made the brute beasts rear and plunge against the area-rails.

"Shut your windows, or we'll fire upon you!" they shouted.

Nothing daunted, Ellen called back indignantly—

"John Walmsley, I'm ashamed of you!"

Not sober enough to distinguish friends from foes, again the pair launched their threat, "Shut the window, or we fire!" and Ellen, seeing pistols advanced, drew the window down, Mrs. Chadwick, in much trepidation, closing the other.

"Who was that handsome officer with John?" asked Augusta, as they drew back; "he's a perfect Adonis." (Augusta dipped surreptitiously into Mrs. Edge's novels at times, and a handsome man in uniform was, of course, a hero in her eyes.)

"Oh, Augusta, how can you talk of handsome officers at such a fearful time?" remonstrated Ellen. "I think them hideous, every one!"

"But who is he? Do you know him?" she asked, even through the tears drawn by the scenes she beheld.

"Oh, yes; know him? yes. He's a friend of John Walmsley. He's too wild to please either Charlotte or me!—Oh, mother! I do wish father had come home!" and Ellen turned a worried look towards Mrs. Chadwick, whose rigid face and clasped hands betrayed the anxiety which kept her silent.

Augusta, though not naturally void of feeling, longed to know more of the handsome yeomanry officer who had so captivated her young fancy; but that was not the season for such inquiries, and she was conscious of it.

"Hark! what is that?" burst from Mrs. Chadwick, some half-hour later, as the sound of feet was heard from below; and Ellen, rushing to the stairs, came back followed by her father leaning on the arm of a big muscular man, in the blue and silver uniform of the yeomanry cavalry, a red cord down his pantaloons, hessian boots, and, to make assurance sure, M.Y.C. upon the shako which his height compelled him to doff ere he entered the doorway.

"Where is Jabez Clegg?" faltered Ellen, as she pressed to her father's side, led him to his chair, and placed his cushions to his liking, Augusta bringing a buffet on which to rest his foot.

The stalwart young fellow's eyes followed the attentive daughter, as he answered—

"We have left Jabez Clegg at Mr. Mabbott's, Miss Chadwick," with an inclination of his head. "He was afraid you would be anxious for your father's safety, and I offered to see Mr. Chadwick home in his stead."

Ellen's black eyes expanded questioning, and Mrs. Chadwick's mild voice, in accents indicative of some fear, asked—

"I hope not of necessity, sir?"

"Well, yes, madam; and I must hasten back; he has received a sabre-cut on——Eh, dear!"

Ben Travis, for he it was, darted forward to catch Ellen Chadwick, just as he had previously caught Jabez at Mabbott's gate:—Aspinall's sabre had wounded two instead of one—Ellen Chadwick, who that day had seen what sabre-cuts meant, had fainted. Ben Travis bore her to the sofa, Mr. Chadwick pulled the bell-rope, Augusta ran for water, Mrs. Chadwick called for vinegar and burnt feathers, and in the midst of the commotion Mr. Ashton burst into the room in a state of excitement very foreign to his nature, which was tolerably easy-going.

"Thank God, Augusta, you are here!" he exclaimed. "Your

mother is almost distracted about you—Why, what is the matter with Ellen? The whole world seems gone mad to day—or hell has set its demons loose. I've just seen our friend Captain Hindley's horse take fright in Mosley Street at the firing, and dash with him against those half-built houses at the corner of Stable Street. He was pitched off amongst the bricks and scaffolding, and the horse dropped. Old Simon Clegg happened to be there, and he helped me and another to raise Hindley, who had fared better than his horse, for it was stone-dead, and he is only badly hurt."

He had gone on talking, though hardly anyone had listened to him. Ellen's fainting fit engrossed feminine attention, and the yeoman, seeing her revive, was saying to Mr. Chadwick, "You will excuse me now, sir. I must look after our poor friend Jabez."

"Eh! what! Jabez? You don't mean to say anything has happened to Jabez Clegg?" exclaimed Mr. Ashton, pausing in the act of drawing forth his snuff-box.

Travis was gone, but Mr. Chadwick, whose tongue now was none of the readiest, stammered out—

"Yes, William, w-we le-ft him at Mab-bott the confectioner's. In try-ying to-o save me he got b-badly wounded. I'm v-very s-sorry, for he is a n-noble y-young man."

"The wretches! I'd almost as soon they'd wounded me! Stay here, Augusta;" and with that Mr. Ashton was off after Ben Travis. The main streets were unsafe, so he also took the back way, and across Back-Piccadilly to Mr. Mabbott's, with a celerity scarcely to have been expected, for he was not a young man. But his apprentice had won upon him not only by his integrity and business qualifications, but by his manifest interest in the family he served, especially the daughter. Let me not be misunderstood. Augusta was the cynosure of Mr. Ashton's eyes; the homage of the apprentice to the school-girl, he estimated as the homage of an apprentice merely, and was gratified thereby, but his imagination never travelled beyond.

He found Jabez on a chintz-covered couch in Mr. Mabbott's sitting-room, his arm bound tightly with a towel, through which the blood would force its way. He was pale and exhausted from excessive hæmorrhage, but seemed more concerned about the fate of the multitude outside than for his own.

Ben Travis, discovering that no one had dared to venture in quest of a doctor, threw himself across his horse, which he found where he had left it, and was off up Mosley Street and thence back to Piccadilly, intent on bringing either Dr. Hull or Dr. Hardie. His uniform was a protection, and so the doctors told him; Dr. Hardie plainly saying that black cloth was not plate-armour, and that his friend, whosoever he might be, must wait until the tumult had somewhat subsided.

But Jabez was only a couple of hours without attention. There were hundreds wounded that day, who had to skulk into holes and corners to hide themselves and their agony as best they might, afraid of seeking surgical aid, lest Nadin and his myrmidons should pounce upon them, and haul them to prison as rebels.

CHAPTER THE TWENTIETH.

ACTION AND RE-ACTION.

SHOT DOWN.

THE August sun had looked down in its noontide splendour when the events I have attempted to describe took place, but the tide of terror and destruction swept beyond the limits I have covered, and after the fierce onslaught, as if the carnage had been insufficient, artillery went rattling and thundering through the streets, to awe the peaceful and terrified inhabitants. As the flying crowd, dispersing, left bare St. Peter's Field, pressing outward and onwards through all accessible ramifications, the main thoroughfares thinned, and the scene of action took a wider radius.

Still the gallant hussars and yeomanry went prancing through these thoroughfares, dashing hither and thither, slashing at stragglers, shouting to the rebels, and to each other, to "clear the way"; driving curious and anxious spectators from doors and windows, and firing at refractory outstretched heads.

To clear the streets more effectually, cannon were planted at the entrances of the leading outlets from the town, and, as if that were not enough, the artillery had orders to fire.

At New Cross two of these guns (which went rattling up Oldham Street, to the dismay of Augusta and the Chadwicks, as well as their neighbours) were posted, one with its hard iron mouth directed up Newton Lane, the other set to sweep Ancoats Lane, not then so wide as at present.

Nathaniel Bradshaw's butcher's shop was situated at the narrowest part of Ancoats Lane, a little beyond the canal bridge.

The shutters had been closed precipitately on the first alarm, but Martha Bradshaw and her young brother Matthew opened the window of the room above, and had their heads stretched out to watch and question the white-faced people scurrying past in disorder, when Matt Cooper, who lived with his genial son-in-law, came hurriedly home for dinner. His route from the tannery lay in a straight line up Miller's Lane, past Shude Hill Pits, and the New Cross, into Ancoats Lane, where he crossed only just before the cannon lumbered up.

His clogs had rattled as swiftly over the pavement as his stiffening, hide-bound, long legs would carry them, and observing the heads of Martha and Matthew advanced from the window, he waved his hand in gesticulation for them to withdraw from a post so fraught with peril. But youth is wilful, and woman curious. They either did not understand, or did not heed his warning. They did not know all he had seen at New Cross, or how narrow an escape he had had from Aspinall's flashing sabre.

"Do goo in, childer!" he cried, as he drew near, "if yo' wantn to kep the yeads on yo'r shoulders. Wenches and lads shouldna look on such soights."

"Han yo' seen Nat?" the wife asked, anxiously.

"Nawe."

"He's gone t' see what o' th' mob and feightin's abeawt. Aw wish he wur whoam!"

Matt wished the same, but went in at the unfastened door, and passed on to the room beyond, where he found the untended lobscouse boiling over into the fire. He took the lid off the pot; then went to the stair-foot, and called "Martha!"

There being no answer, he strode back through the shop, saying as he went—

"Dang it, hoo'll not be content till hoo's hurt!"

He stepped out on the rough pavement, and, looking up, called out—

"Do put yo'r yeads in; yo'll——"

A musket-shot, splintering a corner of the stone window-sill on which they leaned, was more effective than his adjuration. The cannon boomed simultaneously—a shriek recalled the hastily-withdrawn heads; and there, on the rough, sun-baked ground before their eyes, lay weltering in blood, a doubled-up form, which a minute before had been their father, Matt Cooper the tanner, the preserver of Jabez, the friend of Simon and Bess.

This harrowing event was the last of the painful incidents of that fatal day coming within the scope of this history, which, isolated as they are, the writer knows to be true, even though they may not be chronicled elsewhere.

The streets grew silent and deserted, save by the military and medical men, as the day and the night advanced; but within the houses of poor and rich there were loud complaints and groans, and murmurings, which did not sink to silence with the day that called them forth.

The town was, as it were, in a state of siege; and men of business, whether Tories or Radicals, alike felt the stoppage of trade and commerce in their pockets, whether they felt the cruelty and injustice to the injured in their hearts or not.

But chiefly those who had friends wounded by design or accident in the *melee* were loud in their denunciation of the whole proceedings; and of these neither Mr. Chadwick nor Mr. Ashton was the least prominent, even though the one was paralysed, and they were of contrary shades of politics, the former being what he himself called "a staunch and true out-and-out Tory," the latter having a leaning towards Liberal—not to say Radical—opinions, and at county elections voting with the Whigs.

The stiff "Church and King" man, whose sons had distinguished themselves in the Army and Navy, and whose son-in-law, Walmsley, might also be said to have distinguished himself in the loyal Manchester Yeomanry—he who had been a member of John Shaw's Club in the Market Place, and called for his P. or his Q. bowl of punch even before the aroma of Jacobitism ceased to flavour the delectable compound, and while yet John Shaw himself lived to draw his silver spoon from its particular pocket to concoct the same, and (inexorable autocract that he was) could crack his whip in his poky bar-parlour in the ears of even noble customers who lingered after his imperative "Eight o'clock, gentlemen; eight o'clock!" or summon his sturdy factotum Molly, with mop and pail, to drive thence with wetted feet those whom the whip had failed to influence—he who had stuck to the club even after John Shaw, Molly, and the punch-house itself had gone to the dust—he, Charles Chadwick, whose Toryism had grown with his growth, was foremost in condemning the proceedings of Peterloo.

In his own person he had witnessed how the actual breakers of the peace were those commissioned to preserve it. In the wanton attack on himself, an unarmed, defenceless, disabled old man, he recognised the general characteristics of the whole affair, and entered his protest against so lawless an exposition of the law. He was himself a peaceable man, a loyal subject, going quietly about his own business when Jabez intercepted, to his own hurt, the sabre destined for his grey head; Matthew Cooper, his tenant's father-in-law, was as peaceable and well-disposed; and, if so, might not the bulk of the so-called rebels have been the same? In his gratitude to Jabez he denounced the mounted yeoman who had sabred him as "a drunken, blood-thirsty miscreant," though in the hurry, excitement, and agitation attending his own withdrawal from the press by Mr. Mabbott, he had failed to identify his pursuer with John Walmsley's dashing friend, and the exclamation of Ben Travis had not reached his ear in the confusion.

Easy-going Mr. Ashton also seemed transformed by the event. He had certainly lost the valuable services of his apprentice for some time to come; but that was the very least ingredient in the cup of his wrath. By faithful, intelligent service; by persevering industry, by a thousand little actions which had shown his interest in his employers, and his devotion to his old friends,

STAR INN.

Jabez had won a place in his master's esteem and affection no other apprentice of any grade had ever attained.

And now that Jabez had risked the dangers of the soldier-ridden streets to bear his beloved daughter to a place of safety, and had braved the storm of foot and horse, and fire and steel, to rescue his brother-in-law by endangering his own life or limbs, his admiration and gratitude rose to their highest, and in proportion his denunciation of an outrage which called for such a sacrifice was strong and vehement—all the more that he sympathised with the objects of the meeting.

When he and Simon Clegg (who had been drawn to the scene in his dinner-hour with others, like moths to a candle) picked up his cavalry friend, Robert Hindley, from amongst the building materials, and disengaged him from his dead horse, he could not refrain from telling the disabled warrior, with all a friend's frankness, that "it served him right!"

Open expression of private opinion on the conduct of rulers was dangerous at that period, as may be supposed; but private opinion became public opinion, too strong and too universal to be put in fetters.

Mr. Tyas, the *Times* reporter, had been taken prisoner on the hustings, and it was imagined that only a one-sided account—forwarded by the magistracy in justification of their conduct—would reach London. But other intelligent reporters were at large, the garbled statements sent to the Government press were confuted by the truth-telling narratives of Messrs. Archibald Prentice and John Edward Taylor, which appeared the following day, and roused the indignation of the realm. These statements being more than substantiated by the *Times* reporter on his liberation, national indignation rose to a ferment.

This alarmed the Manchester magistrates; a meeting was hurriedly arranged to take place on Thursday, the 19th (the third day from Peterloo), at the Police Station; thence adjourned to the "Star Inn" in Deansgate; and, as though the meeting had been a public one, resolutions were passed thanking magistrates and soldiers for their services on the previous Monday.

Then Manchester rose, as it were, *en masse*, to vindicate its own honour, and reject participation in a disgraceful deed.

"A declaration," says one historian, "was issued, protesting against the 'Star Inn' resolutions, which, in the course of two or three days, received close upon five thousand signatures," in obtaining which none were more active than Mr. Ashton and (despite his paralysis) Mr. Chadwick. Old Mrs. Clowes talked her customers into signing, and Parson Brookes was not idle. Mr. William Clough, whose old servant Matthew Cooper had been shot down at his own door, gave the tanners a holiday, that they might influence their fellows; and Simon Clegg, Tom Hulme, and Nathaniel Bradshaw seemed ubiquitous, they went to work with such determined zeal. *They* did not feel "thankful" to the magistrates for the blood shed on Peterloo Monday.

Neither did the bulk of the inhabitants; and an energetic protest against the proceedings and representations of the magistracy was the result.

To counteract this, the Prince Regent, through his mouthpiece, Lord Sidmouth, sent his thanks to the magistrates and the military leaders for "their prompt, decisive, and efficient measures." But this, instead of calming, lashed the public mind to frenzy. Meetings to remonstrate with the Regent and to petition for inquiry were held in all the large towns, Sir Francis Burdett presiding at one held in Westminster.

Subscriptions were also got up for the relief of such wounded and disabled persons as had crept into holes and corners to hide themselves and their wounds from Nadin and his constabulary; and here, too, William Ashton and William Clough worked hand-in-hand to bring relief to sufferers not in the Infirmary; and Parson Brookes, to the disgust of some of his clerical brethren, lent his aid in ferreting out the miserables, if he did not ostentatiously flourish his subscription in their service; and I rather think a certain "J. S." in the subscription list represented the mite of the Grammar School head-master, but I could not take an affidavit on the subject. But when the wounded, as far as ascertained, amounted to six hundred, irrespective of the killed, subscriptions had need to be many and ample.

Another token of the change in public sentiment was shown in the satires and pasquinades which appeared on the walls, or were distributed from hand to hand. Previously to Peterloo a set of anonymous verses in ridicule of the popular leader had been distributed. They began and were headed as follows :—

ORATOR HUNT.

I.

Blithe Harry Hunt was an orator bold—
    Talked away bravely and blunt ;
And Rome in her glory, and Athens of old,
With all their loud talkers, of whom we are told,
    Couldn't match Orator Hunt !

II.

Blithe Harry Hunt was a sightly man—
    Something 'twixt giant and runt ;
His paunch was a large one, his visage was wan,
And to hear his long speeches vast multitudes ran,
    O rare Orator Hunt !

. . . . . .

VI.

Orator Hunt was the man for a riot—
    Bully in language and front—
And thought when a nation had troubles to sigh at,
'Twas quite unbecoming to sit cool and quiet,
    O rare Orator Hunt !

. . . . . .

VIII.

How Orator Hunt's many speeches will close—
    Tedious, bombastic, and blunt—
In a *halter* or *diadem*, God only knows :
The sequel might well an arch-conjurer pose.
    O rare Orator Hunt !

Sufficient has been given to show the nature of the lampoon

without repeating its scurrility. The following, of which we only quote the first two stanzas, is of pretty much the same order, though emanating from the other side, and after terrible provocation had been given:—

THE RENOWNED ATCHIEVEMENTS OF PETERLOO,

ON THE GLORIOUS 16TH OF AUGUST, 1819.

BY SIR HUGO BURLO FURIOSO DI MULO SPINNISSIMO, Bart., M.Y.C. AND A.S.S.

The music by the celebrated DR. HORSEFOOD; *to be had at the "Cat and Bagpipes," St. Mary's Gate, Manchester.*

RECITATIVE.

When fell sedition's stalking through the land,
It then behoves each patriotic band
Of NOBLE-MINDED YEOMAN CAVALIERS
To sally forth and rush upon the mob,
And execute the MAGISTERIAL JOB
Of cutting off the ragamuffins' ears.

ARIA BRAVURA.

Forte. How valiantly we met that crew
Of infants, men, and women too,
Upon the plain of Peterloo:.
And gloriously did hack and hew
The d——d reforming gang.
Our swords were sharp, you may suppose,
Some lost their ears—some lost a nose;
Our horses trod upon their toes
Ere they could run t' escape our blows:
With shouts the welkin rang.
Andante. So keen were we to rout these swine,
Whole shoals of constables in line
We galloped o'er in style so fine,
By orders of the SAPIENT NINE—
First friends, then foes, laid flat.
By Richardson's best grinding skill
Our blades were set with right good will,
That we these rogues might bleed or kill,
And "give them of Reform their fill!"
And what d'ye think of that?

And so on the satire ran, in mock-bravura style, through the whole course of *piano*, *sotto voce*, *pianissima-mento*, and *con baldanza*, with foot-notes to strengthen or elucidate the text. And that the writer remained undiscovered and unprosecuted spoke loudly for the re-action which had taken place in men's minds.

CHAPTER THE TWENTY-FIRST.

WOUNDED.

AT the extreme end of Mr. Mabbott's long double-countered shop was an expansive archway, closed in general by folding doors, through which entrance was afforded to a narrow sitting-room, the length of which was just by so much less than the width of the shop as was required for a passage and staircase. Once a year the open archway revealed a shimmering mass of snowy sugar-work, the towers and turrets of a castle on a rock, or the illuminated windows of a magnificent palace, fit for any princess of fairyland, with pleasure-gardens and lake, or fountain and pond, wherein stately swans floated, and were overlooked by dames and cavaliers created by the confectioner and his satellites.

For the fifty other weeks it was simply a snug parlour, comfortably furnished according to the fashion of the time.

And it was in this room we left Jabez, whilst good-natured Ben Travis, leaving his more patriotic comrades to "hack and hew" at their pleasure, galloped hither and thither in search of a surgeon to dress the wounded arm.

Every doctor in the Infirmary had his hands full; Dr. Hull, from his windows in Mosley Street, and Dr. Hardie from his in Piccadilly, had been satisfied that if they ventured forth they might soon need doctoring themselves—and they both pleaded "medical etiquette" in excuse for their lukewarmness. They were "physicians, not surgeons." He bethought himself of Mr. Huertley, in Oldham Street, but even he had more than one wounded patient in his surgery, and was loth to encounter the danger outside. Ben Travis, however, would take no denial. He waited until sundry gaping wounds were closed, cuts plaistered and bandaged, a broken limb set, and a bullet extracted, even lending a hand himself where unskilled help could be available, being less bemused with liquor than many of his cavalry corps. Then, although they were almost within a stone's throw of their destination—as Oldham Street was not safe for a civilian to cross on foot, with loaded cannon in such close proximity—Travis mounted the surgeon behind him, the latter not sorry to have the yeoman's capacious body in its conspicuous uniform for a shield, as they dashed across into Back-Piccadilly to Mabbott's back door.

Ere they rode off the younger man cast a sharp glance of scrutiny at Chadwick's drawing-room windows, and bowed low in recognition of the face for which he was looking—the face he had seen so pale and pitiful, bending over an afflicted father, and so shocked to hear of even an apprentice wounded in that father's behalf.

Ben Travis had a big body and a big heart, but he had little knowledge of the hearts of womankind, or he might have found another solution for Ellen Chadwick's fainting fit. He did not know how she had trembled for another on seeing him dismount at Mr. Huertley's door, nor how she had watched, too sick and sad to descend to the dining-room, when the spoiled dinner was at length set on the table—watched eagerly and anxiously, her heart's pulsations counting each second a minute, as hours elapsed before she saw them mount and ride away, and noted the direction they took. And she saw no admiration in the low bow of the fine soldierly young gentleman—only the polite salutation of a stranger introduced casually by the untoward events of the day, albeit, having rendered her father a service, and professed himself the friend of Jabez, she was bound to recognise him as he passed.

To Jabez himself, lying faint and exhausted with loss of blood on kind Mr. Mabbott's chintz-covered squab-sofa, everything was a haze, and the people around him little more than voices. He was perfectly conscious when Mr. Mabbott hastily cut away the sleeve of his jacket, and bound the wounded arm as tightly as towels could bind. When Mr. Ashton put his troubled face into the confectioner's small parlour, Mr. Mabbott was in the act of reaching from a corner-cupboard a small square spirit decanter, and an engraved wine-glass, in order to administer a dose of brandy to the young man, then rapidly sinking into unconsciousness.

Under its influence he revived for awhile; but, as the blood gradually soaked through the towelling, he grew fainter, in spite of brandy, and by the time Ben Travis (who had surely kept the promise made in school-boy days) brought Dr. Huertley to his aid, he had lapsed into a stupor from which the manipulations of the surgeon barely aroused him.

"You should have tied a ligature tightly as possible round the arm above the wound, first thing," said the surgeon, addressing those around him—"a bit of tape, a strip of linen, a garter—anything narrow to stop the hæmorrhage. Had this been done, there would have been less effusion of blood, and our patient would not have been so utterly prostrated."

"Just so, just so," assented Mr. Ashton, adding, "but Mr. Mabbott had——"

"Done his best—no doubt," interrupted the surgeon, "or our young friend might have bled to death. But the tight, narrow ligature would have been better; and many a valuable life may have been saved or lost this day through that bit of knowledge or—the want of it."

Mr. Ashton's "Just so, just so; I daresay you are right," was followed up by "Shall we be able to remove him to-night, Mr. Huertley? He is my apprentice, and has been injured whilst bravely protecting your opposite neighbour, Mr. Chadwick, my brother-in-law. I should like to get him home, to be under Mrs. Ashton's care, as well as to relieve Mr. Mabbott, to whom, I am sure, we all feel greatly indebted."

"Don't name it, I beg; at fearful times like this," said Mr. Mabbott, with a shudder, "it does not do to think of trouble or of ceremony. But I do not imagine the doctor would counsel the young man's removal to-night, even if the road were clear and safe."

"Certainly not," replied Mr. Huertley, as he packed up his lint and instruments. "And in my opinion, if you remove him to-morrow you must do it carefully on every account, and will have to smuggle him away in a hackney-coach, lest he should be pounced upon as a wounded rebel."

Two days, however, elapsed before Mr. Mabbott's sofa lost its occupant, and even then the strong arm of Tom Hulme and the loving care of Bess were needed to help Jabez, feeble and wan, to the hackney-carriage brought up to the back door, which bore him slowly away, avoiding the main streets until they passed under the arched gateway in Back Mosley Street, whence he had last emerged at a headlong pace to prevent Miss Augusta getting into danger.

Some remembrance of this flashed through the brain of Jabez as the coach stopped in the courtyard, and on the house doorsteps he beheld Mrs. Ashton, Augusta, and Ellen Chadwick, all three waiting to receive him as if had been a wounded relative returning from far-off victories to his own hearth. Nay, the very servants hovered in the background, even cross Kezia pressing to have a first look at him.

Mrs. Ashton herself, with the graceful dignity which sat so well upon her, went down the steps to lead him up and into the house, and, as she touched his left hand and unwounded arm, she said impressively,

"Jabez Clegg, I understand we owe our brother's life to your self-abnegation, if not that of our daughter also. I regret that your noble intervention should have cost you so dear; but I thank you most truly, and *shall not forget it.*"

The stately lady's eyes were humid as she led Jabez into their common parlour (the room in which Augusta had displayed his specimens of incipient artistry), and there placed him on the large soft sofa, already prepared with pillows for his reception. The attention touched him to the heart; the humble apprentice, feeling himself honoured, raised the lady's hand to his lips as gracefully and reverently as ever did knight of old romance.

And then he would have closed his eyes for very weariness; but a little soft, warm hand stole into his feeble one, and, thrilling through him, a faint tinge chased the deathly pallor from his face as Augusta's voice, full of commiseration, said apologetically,

"I had no idea, Jabez, that I was sending you into danger when I asked you to look for Uncle Chadwick; I am so sorry you have been hurt."

He held the little hand of his master's daughter for one or two delicious minutes, while he answered feebly, "Never mind, Miss Ashton; I was only too glad to be there in time;" and lapsed into so ethereal a dream as he released it, that the low, broken, grateful thanks of Ellen Chadwick left but the impression on his mind that she was very much in earnest, and had called him *Mr. Clegg.*

Mr. Clegg! When had the College-boy—the Blue-coat apprentice—been anything but Jabez Clegg? *Mr.* Clegg! It was from such lips social recognition, and so blent strangely with his dream. Ah! could he but have known how much of latent tenderness was embodied in those incoherent expressions of a daughter's gràtitude, or that the speaker dared not trust her faltering tongue with his Christian name!

Mrs. Ashton called the young ladies away.

"My dears, you had better resume your occupations, and leave Jabez to repose; it is not well to crowd about an invalid on so sultry a day as this."

So Miss Chadwick went, with her tatting-shuttle, back to her seat by the one window where the friendly shade of the dove-coloured curtains screened from observation any glances which might chance to stray from the tatting to the sofa; and Miss Ashton went back to her music-stool, where the sunbeams, falling through the other window, lit up her lovely profile, shot a glint of gold through her hair, and showed the dimples in her white shoulder to the half-shut, dreaming eyes of Jabez, who listened, entranced, as she practised scales and battle-pieces, waltzes and quadrilles, totally unconscious that she was feeding a fever in the soul of the apprentice more to be feared than the stroke of Aspinall's sabre, though it had cut into the bone.

Not that she was a simple school-girl, and ignorant of the power of beauty. She was pretty well as romantic as any girl of that romantic age who, being fifteen, looked a year older, and learned the art of fascination from the four-volume novels of the period. Mrs. Ashton herself subscribed to the fashionable circulating library of the town, but she was somewhat choice in her reading, and had Miss Augusta stopped where her mother did she would have done well. But it so happened that, after feasting on the wholesome peas her mother provided, she fell with avidity on husks obtained surreptitiously elsewhere. Kisses from Augusta could always coax coins from papa, and as a Miss Bohanna kept open a well-known, well-stocked circulating library in Shudehill, albeit in a cellar, its contiguity to Bradshaw Street and Mrs. Broadbent's enabled Miss Ashton (or Cicely for her) to smuggle in amongst her school-books other fictions, such as Elizabeth Helme and Anna Maria Roche used to concoct, and Samuel Richardson provided, to delight our grandmothers with.

So Miss Ashton was quite prepared to be admired and play the heroine prematurely; but she had been reared in the same house with Jabez, had been caressed and waited upon by him as a child, and anything so absurd as her father's apprentice falling in love with her had never dawned upon her apprehension. Then not even his wounded arm could make him handsome enough for a hero, so she plunged through the "Battle of Prague," and "Lodoiska," and glided into the "Copenhagen Waltz," with no suspicion of a listener more than ordinary.

Mrs. Ashton, who was back-stitching a shirt-wristband (family linen was then made at home), imagined that Jabez was dozing, and, unwilling to disturb him, only spoke when a false note, or a passage out of time, called for a low-voiced hint to her daughter, or when she found occasion to make some slight observation to the equally silent Ellen.

Presently the clock in the hall proclaimed "five." Miss Ashton closed music-books and piano; Miss Chadwick completed a loop, then put her tatting away in a small, oblong, red morocco reticule; Mrs. Ashton laid the wristband in her work-basket, which she put out of sight in a panelled cupboard within the wall, sheathed the scissors hanging from her girdle, and folded up the leather housewife containing her cut skeins of thread, &c. James brought in the tea-board, with its genuine China tea-service, plates with cake and bread-and-butter, and whilst he went back to Kezia for the tea-urn, in walked Mr. Ashton, and with him the Reverend Joshua Brookes.

One might have supposed his first salutation would have been to the lady of the house. Nothing of the kind! With a passing nod to Mrs. Ashton, who had extended her hand, he marched straight to the sofa, and greeted its occupant with——

"Well, young Cheat-the-fishes, so you've been in the wars again?"

"Yes, sir," said Jabez, attempting to rise.

"Lie still, lad! And so you thought a velveteen jacket defensive armour against sharpened steel?"

"I never thought about it, sir."

"Ugh! Then I suppose you reckoned a young man's arm worth less than an old man's head! Eh?"

Jabez smiled.

"Certainly, sir."

"Humph! I thought as much!" Then darting a keen inquisitive glance from under his shaggy eyebrows at the prostrate young fellow, he added, in his very raspiest tones, "And I daresay you've no notion whose sabre carved the wing of the goose so cleverly?"

What little blood was left in his body seemed to mount to the face of Jabez, the old scar on his brow—which every year made less conspicuous—purpled and grew livid. Old Joshua needed no more.

"Ah, I see you do! Well, are you inclined to forgive the fellow this time?"

All ears were on the alert. Jabez caught the quick turn of his kind master's head. He hesitated, paled, and flushed again.

Joshua Brookes waited. There was some indecision in the reply when it did come.

"I am not sure, sir. But he was very drunk. I don't think he would have done it if he had been sober."

"Just so, Jabez—just so!" assented Mr. Ashton with evident satisfaction, and a tap on his snuff-box lid.

Ben Travis had revealed the name of Mr. Chadwick's assailant to the manufacturer, and he to the chaplain.

"Oh! that's your opinion, is it?" cried the latter, crustily, wheeling sharply round to disguise a smile. "Here, madam, let's have a cup of sober tea after that!"

"I think, Mr. Brookes," said Mrs. Ashton, as she seated herself, "with all due deference to you—I think you ask too much from Jabez. I do not consider drunkenness any excuse for brutality."

"No excuse for the brute, madam, certainly; but a reason why a reasoning man should forgive the brute incapable of reason."

"Just so, Parson!" chimed in Mr. Ashton, laying his Barcelona handkerchief across his knee.

"I don't see it, sir," argued Mrs. Ashton, handing a willow-patterned cup and saucer, with his tea, to her interlocutor; "a man who is a brute when intoxicated should keep sober. For my own part, I should be loth to let the same stick beat me twice. Our apprentice has borne quite too much from that fellow" (she waxed indignant), "and there is a limit to forgiveness."

"Yes, madam," answered the Parson snappishly, "there *is* a limit to forgiveness; but the limit is 'not seven times, but seventy times seven!'"

There was no more to be said. The rough chaplain spoke with authority, and from experience, and Jabez knew it.

CHAPTER THE TWENTY-SECOND.

MR. CLEGG!

HOUSE OF JOSHUA BROOKES.

HOWEVER grateful Mrs. Ashton might be she never lost sight of her personal dignity, and had no idea of admitting Jabez on terms of equality after that first reception.

In his helpless condition he required attention, which she could not condescend to render personally; yet she was as little inclined to delegate the duty to Kezia, who was never over well-disposed towards him, and might have resented the call to "wait on a 'prentice lad," or to Cicily, who was too young to have the run of a young man's chamber. It was like herself to hit on a happy mean, and invite Bess Hulme at once to satisfy her own longings, and meet the requirements of the case, by waiting on her foster-child in his helplessness, bringing with her her own boy, now two years old, to be committed to willing Cicily's care when the mother was herself engaged.

Yet the apprentice never again sank into the old ruts. His bed in the attic was turned over to his successor. From that parlour where he had lain and listened to Augusta's music, and Parson Brookes' dictum; where Mrs. Ashton had placed his pillows, and Ellen Chadwick had supplied his wants with such intuitive perception at tea-time; from that room he went to a chamber on an upper floor, furnished neatly but plainly, with due regard to comfort.

There was a mahogany camp-bedstead, draped with chintz of most extraordinary device. The bed was of feathers—not flock. An oak chest of drawers, which did duty for a dressing-table, stood by the window, which itself overlooked the yard, and on the top stood a small oval swing looking-glass. There were small strips of carpet along the two sides of the bed which did not touch the wall; an almost triangular washstand in one corner, and near the middle of the room a rush-bottomed chair and a small tripod table. There was also a cushioned easy-chair, which had a suggestiveness of being there for that special occasion only; and Jabez, who, on his first glance around, began to speculate whether the whole would not vanish with his convalescence, was reassured when he saw that his wooden box had been brought from the attic and stood against the wall.

The six-foot, bronzed, bearded man of forty remains a child to the mother who bore him, or the woman who nursed him. And as she had laid him in his cradle when a baby, Bess helped Jabez to his new bed, fed him with the beef-tea which Kezia had prepared (for a wonder, without a grumble), gave him the cooling draught Mr. Huertley had sent in, smoothed his pillows for repose, and kissed his brow, with a "God bless thee!" much as she had done when he was an ailing child, but with all the access of motherliness her own maternity had given.

Nevertheless he did not sleep readily. Neither Bess's soothing hand nor the soft bed superinduced slumber. He was modest, and "Mr. Clegg" haunted him. He could not see the connection between his impulsive rush forward to check the yeoman's plunging steed, and his employer's recognition of the service rendered.

"I only did my duty," he debated with himself, as he lay there, with a mere streak of light from the glimmering rushlight showing between the closely-drawn curtains—"I only did my duty. Any-one else would have done the same in my place. If I had once thought of consequences and grasped the reins deliberately, there would have been some bravery in *that*. But I never thought of the sword, not I. I only thought of poor old Mr. Chadwick and Molly; and I'm sure Mr. Mabbott's ready hand did as good service as mine. Only, I happened to get hurt. Yes, that's it!

And they are sorry for me. I wonder if that ruffianly fellow did know whom he was striking at? I hardly think he did, he was so very tipsy. If I fancied he did, I—but he could not. He was just blind drunk. What a pity, for such a handsome fellow, not older than I am, and a gentleman's son, too! Forgive him! I don't think I've much to forgive. I'd bear the pain twice over for all the kind things that have been said and done since! Tea in the parlour with Parson Brookes and all! And this handsome bed-room [handsome only in untutored eyes]. And all the thanks I have had for so little. And, oh! the bliss of holding Augusta's delicate hand in mine, and hearing the music those white fingers made. It's worth the pain three times over. And Mr. Clegg, too! *Mr.* Clegg! How like a gentleman it does sound! Will anybody call me Mr. Clegg besides Miss Chadwick? How fond she must be of her father, from the way she thanked me!"

(Ah, Jabez! what oculist can cure blindness such as thine?)

If less consecutive, still in some such current ran the young man's thoughts, until chaos came, and his closed eyes saw innumerable *Mr.* Cleggs written on walls, and floor, and curtains, and a delicious symphony seemed to chorus the words, and "lap him in Elysium."

After that, once each day, Mrs. Ashton paid him a brief visit of inspection and inquiry, generally timed so as to meet the surgeon. Mr. Ashton, with less of ceremony, dropped in occasionally, to bring him a newspaper, book, or pamphlet to beguile the hours, and was not above loitering for a pleasant chat on matters indoors and out, the state of political feeling, and of business, in a manner so friendly Jabez was at a loss to account for it. Once or twice Augusta tapped at the door, to ask if Jabez was better, and to "hope he would soon be well," and the simple words ran through his brain with a thousand chimerical meanings.

Joshua Brookes paid him a couple of visits, brought him papers of sweetmeats and messages from Mrs. Clowes, and a Latin

Testament and a worn Æneid from his own stores, as a little light reading. Mrs. Chadwick, too, made her appearance at his bedside, with kindly and grateful words from her husband; and amongst them he was in a fair way of becoming elevated into a hero to his own hurt.

Simon Clegg (who pulled off his thick Sunday shoes in the kitchen, and went up-stairs in his stocking feet, lest he should make a clatter and spoil the carpets) counteracted the mischief, and somewhat clipped the pinions of soaring imagination.

Jabez, his arm bandaged and sustained by a sling, lay with his head against the straight, high back of his padded chair, between the window and the fireplace, which glowed, not with live coals, but a beau-pot of sunflowers and hollyhocks from Simon's garden. At his feet lay little Sam, fast asleep, with his fat arms round the neck of Nelson, the black retriever, which had somehow contrived to sneak past Kezia with his tail between his legs, and to follow Bess up-stairs, where he had established himself in perfect content.

Simon greeted his foster-son with bated breath, awed no doubt by the lamp-bearing statues in the hall and on the staircase, and hardly raised his voice above a whisper while he stayed. He had much to tell which the reader already knows, but he took his leave with quite a long oration, impressed no doubt by the comfort in that chamber, as well as by the grandeur in rooms of which he had caught a glimpse through open doors. Jabez, himself, being still feeble, had spoken but little.

"Moi lad," said he, "this is a grand place, but dunnot yo' let it mak' yo' preawd; an' aw hope as yo'r thenkful yo'han fallen among sich koind folk."

"Indeed I am."

"Yo' did nowt but whatn wur yo'r duty, moi lad, as aw trust thah allays wilt; and thah's getten a mester an' missis i' ten theawsand, to mak' so mich on a cut in a 'prentice's arm—ay, tho it *wur* got i' savin' one o' theer own kin! Luk yo', Jabez: o' th' mesters aw ever saw afore thowt as 'prentices, body an' soul, wur theer own; an' yo've lit on yo'r feet, aw con tell yo'. An' yo' conno' do too mich for sich folk. Aw see they're makkin' a man on yo', an' dunnot yo' spoil o' by thinkin' yo' han earnt it, an' han a reet to it. We're unprofitable sarvants, th' best on us. An' dunnot yo' harbour anny malice agen th' chap as chopped at yo'. Them Yowmanry Calvary wur as drunk as fiddlers, an' as blind as bats. Thah tuk' thi chance wi' the ruck, an' came off better than some folk. So thenk God it's no waur, an' bear no malice; an' thenk God as sent yo' theer i' the nick o' time."

In little more than a fortnight Jabez was downstairs again, although his arm, not being thoroughly healed, yet needed support, and he was not hurried into the warehouse. Neither was he again invited to join the family, Mrs. Ashton having objected to Mr. Ashton's proposition.

"It would lift the young man out of his sphere, William, and do him more harm than good. Only very strong heads can stand sudden elevation; and it is well to make no more haste than good speed."

But Mr. Ashton's "Just so" was less definite than ordinary, and he took a second pinch of snuff unawares, with a prolonged emphasis, which supplied the place of words. To the observant, Mr. Ashton's snuff-box contained as much eloquence as did Lord Burleigh's celebrated wig. He had taken a liking to the lad from the first, paid very little deference to Mrs. Grundy, and gave Jabez credit for a stronger head than did his more cautious and philosophic lady.

Yet, Jabez, to his surprise, found that his little room down stairs had undergone a transformation. It was no longer a bare office, fitted only with a desk and stool. Desk and stool were there still, but a carpet, hanging shelves, a few useful books, and other furniture had been introduced, the result being a compact parlour. Mrs. Ashton had her own way of showing good-will.

His previous application to work in that room, when his fellow-apprentices in over hours were cracking jokes on the kitchen settle, lounging about the yard, tormenting or being tormented by Kezia, had served somewhat to isolate and lift him above them, albeit he took his meals in the kitchen with the rest. This separation was now confirmed by orders Kezia received to "serve Clegg's dinner in his own room," orders which Kezia resented with asperity, and at least three days' ill-humour, and which James declined to execute. He was "not goin' to disgrace his cloth by waitin' on 'prentice lads!" Ready-handed Cicily came to the rescue, and took the office on herself, amid the banter of the kitchen, which the quick-witted maid returned with right good will and right good temper.

Permission to receive his friends in his own room occasionally had been graciously accorded by Mrs. Ashton herself, with the characteristic observation—

"They are worthy people, Jabez Clegg, and you owe them a son's duty; besides, you need some relaxation—'The over-strained bow is apt to snap,' and 'All work and no play makes Jack a dull boy.'"

Altogether he was more than satisfied. He was not demonstrative, but his heart swelled as he felt within himself that all these little things were stepping stones upwards; and he mentally resolved to mount them fairly. He recognised that he was rising, and ere the week was out he found that others recognised it also.

His blood-stained garments had been removed, whither he knew not, and he had to fall back on his grey frieze Sunday suit. Be sure he began to calculate the chances of getting a fresh one.

As he was able to go out, he was employed on out-door business until his arm should regain its full vitality, and one of his errands was with a note to Mr. Chadwick's tailor, in King Street. At first he thought there was some mistake when the fraction of a man proceeded without more ado to take his measure.

Saturday night proved there had been no mistake. On his bed, accompanied by a very kind note from Mr. Chadwick (written with his left hand), lay not only a well-cut, well-made suit of clothes, but a hat, white linen shirts, neck-cloths, and hose.

Did ever a young girl turn up her back hair, or young man assume his first coat indifferently? To Jabez—the foundling—the Blue-coat apprentice, this was not merely a first coat, not merely a badge of approaching manhood,—the whole outfit, provided as it was by his master's brother-in-law, seemed a recognition of the station he was henceforth to fill. No clerk in the counting-house was so well equipped as he, when he stood before his oval swing-glass (for the first time far too small), and endeavoured to survey himself therein, that fine September Sunday morning.

I will not presume to say that he looked the conventional gentleman in that suit of glossy brown broadcloth, and beaver hat; I will not say that he did not feel stiff in them. Only use gives ease; but this I will say, that a more manly figure never gave shape to garments, or a more noble head to a hat, albeit there was more of strength than beauty in the face it shaded.

His forehead was broad and well developed; the reflective as well as the perceptive faculties were there. There was just a slight defensive rise on the else straight nose; the eyebrows were full save where a scar broke the line of one. Firm but pleasant were mouth and dimpled chin, and the lower jaw was somewhat massive; but his full grey eyes, dark almost to blackness, and standing far apart, were clear and deep as wells where truth lay hid, though deep emotion had power to kindle them with the luminosity of stars.

I am afraid he was not the only one on whom Parson Gatliffe's eloquence was thrown away that Sabbath morning. If he looked up at the Blue-coat boys in the Chetham Gallery with their quaint blue robes and neat bands, to throw memory back and imagination forward, others were doing likewise, from old Simon in his free seat to his envious fellow-'prentices in the pew, whose mocking grimaces drew upon them the sharp censure of the beadle.

Party spirit was then at a white heat. Had Peterloo been written on his forehead it could not have marked him out for curious eyes more surely than his sling.

Greetings, not altogether congratulatory, followed him through the churchyard. But old Simon caught his left hand in a tremulous grasp, his eyes moist with proud emotion. Tom Hulme beamed upon him, and Mrs. Clowes, energetic as ever, overtook them a few yards from the chapter-house, just as Joshua Brookes emerged from the door.

"Well, my lad, I'm glad to see you at church again!" she exclaimed, shaking him warmly by the left hand. "I hardly knew you in your fine clothes. They've made quite a gentleman of you. We shall have to call you Mr. Clegg now, I reckon."

"Now, Mother Clowes, don't you give Jabez *humbug* of that sort; it's sweet, but not wholesome. 'Fine feathers make fine birds.' He's as proud as a peacock already. *Mr.* Clegg, indeed! and him a 'prentice lad not out of his time! Let him stick to the name we gave him at his baptism—it's worth all your fine Misters." And Joshua turned off, muttering, "Mr. Clegg, indeed!" as he went away.

Neither the old woman in her antiquated gown and kerchief-covered mutch, nor the old parson in his cassock and square cap, modulated their loud voices. Jabez blushed painfully. Both had touched sensitive chords.

But others had heard the "Mr. Clegg," and *he* heard it again, from Kezia and the apprentices, in every tone of mockery and derision. Thence it travelled into the warehouse. He bore it with set teeth through many a painful week, until the title stuck to him, and the taunt was forgotten in the force of habit.

CHAPTER THE TWENTY-THIRD.

IN THE THEATRE ROYAL.

IT has been said that Madame Broadbent had various subtle ways of advertising her "Academy" (as the directory has it), by which she generally contrived to "kill two birds with one stone." One of these would scarcely have been practicable in any but a theatrical town like Manchester, where not even the fierceness of party politics could close the theatre doors. She was particularly fond of a good play, and as particularly careful of her own pocket. So she watched for such occasions as a special benefit or "Bespeak' night, to engage one of the dress-boxes, and take tickets for a select party of her pupils. The young ladies—apart from all natural love of amusement and display—were taught to regard their admission to Mrs. Broadbent's train as a high honour—a mark of exceeding distinction; and few were the parents so stern or so niggardly as to refuse the four shillings for a box-ticket when Madame invited and Miss pleaded.

The then Theatre Royal, in Fountain Street, which was opened in 1807, under Macready's management, and brought to the ground by fire in 1844, was, in 1820, a building so capacious—so solidly built—it might not fear comparison with Drury Lane. Stage, scene-rooms, dressing-rooms, were all on an extensive scale. There were three tiers of boxes, a large pit, and an immense gallery breaking the line of the third tier. With the exception of the large side boxes, which were partially on the stage, all these boxes were open to the view, having only a divisional barrier the height of the parapet, light iron pillars supporting the weight above. There were no chairs—only narrow, baize-covered benches, innocent of backs. And the theatre was lighted by sperm-oil lamps, those round the auditorium being suspended by cords over pulleys, so as to be lowered for lighting, trimming, &c. But the glory of that theatre, of which it was shorn at a later date, was its box-lobby—a lofty, open promenade, wide as a street, and long in proportion, for its one grand entrance was in Fountain Street,

HENRY HUNT.
From an Engraving.

the other in Back Mosley Street. Only for the step or two at either end, carriages might have driven through, or, depositing their living loads within at the saloon doors, have turned easily and driven back.

This lobby was naturally a lounge, as well as a waiting-place for servants and others with wraps and pattens, neither carriages nor hackney-coaches being numerous, and the streets being—well, not quite so clean or well-paved as at present.

The ten days' trial of Henry Hunt and his compatriots at York had, as is well known, resulted in sentence of imprisonment for different terms, to the discomfiture of one party, the exultation of the other. Close upon the promulgation of this sentence came Easter week, at the beginning of April, 1820, when Jabez had little more than a month to serve of his apprenticeship. Edmund Kean was then playing at the Theatre Royal, supported by Sophia M'Gibbon—daughter of Woodfall, the memorable printer of "Junius"—a favourite on the Manchester "boards."

Either to mark their satisfaction at the result of the trial, or their admiration of the great tragedian, the officers of the Manchester Yeomanry Cavalry bespoke "Othello" for the Wednesday evening, and Mrs. Broadbent made the most of the glorious opportunity. She engaged a box close to the centre of the dress-circle, on terms well understood, and as small people take less room than large ones, and her front row was very juvenile, she contrived to make it a profitable investment, even though she took a teacher with her (at a lower rate). The young ladies assembled at the school, and made quite a procession to the theatre, where Mrs. Broadbent's own maid took charge of hats and cloaks, and waited drearily in the saloon. Then, duly marshalled by Madame Broadbent and Miss Nuttall, they filed into the box decorously and took their seats, the youngest in the van—the whole programme having been rehearsed and re-rehearsed for a day or two beforehand.

A bouquet of white rosebuds they might have been called, white muslin was so general; but one young lady blushed in pink gauze, and Augusta Ashton's lovely head and shoulders were set off by delicate blue crape. There were round necklaces of coral or pearl, long loose gloves of cambric or kid, and every damsel in her teens had her fan. But of fans, commend me to Madame Broadbent's. It was no light trifle of ivory or sandal-wood, but of strong green paper, spotted with gold, with ribs and frame of ebony, and it measured nearly half-a-yard when closed. Her well-saved, long-waisted, stiff brocaded robe and petticoat might have been her wedding-dress kept for state occasions; but that fan, slung by a ribbon from her wrist, was part of her individuality—the symbol of her authority inseparable from her walking self. A relic of her younger days, she employed it—citing Queen Charlotte as her examplar—to arrest attention, to admonish, to chastise; and woe to the luckless little lady on whom it came in admonition!

The box was filled to the very door, where Miss Nuttall kept guard. Madame Broadbent displayed her own important person on the third row above the curly heads of the smaller fry, and to Augusta Ashton—being a profitable pupil of whom she had reason to be proud—was allotted a seat next to herself.

The house was full and fashionable, both stage boxes being occupied by members of the Manchester Yeomanry, resplendent in silver and blue. Laurence Aspinall, John Walmsley, and Ben Travis were of the party. In the pit were the critics, pressing as closely as possible to the stage. Nods and smiles from friends in different quarters of the theatre greeted the component parts of Madame Broadbent's bevy of innocents, and smiles responded.

Then rose the green curtain upon Edmund Kean's Othello and Mrs. M'Gibbon's Desdemona. The audience was enthralled. Act by act the players kept attention fixed, and all went well until the last scene. But, as Othello pressed the murderous pillow down, one of Madame Broadbent's white-frocked misses in the front row, with whose relatives Desdemona lodged when she was not Desdemona, started up, and cried out piteously—

"He's killing Mrs. M'Gibbon! He's killing Mrs. M'Gibbon!"

The clear voice rang through the house to the consternation of the actors, the amusement of some, and the annoyance of the audience. Some of the officers laughed outright in the very face of the tragic Moor; but Madame Broadbent was furious, all the more that she was bound to suppress her passion then and there.

For the credit of her "Academy" she, however, felt bound to resent so flagrant a breach of decorum. Tapping the tearful culprit on the shoulder with her ready fan, in a stern whisper, scarcely less audible than the child's impulsive tribute to the great tragedian, she asked, "How can you bemean yourself so far, miss, to the disgrace of the school?" and beckoning the child forth, she was passed to Miss Nuttall at the very back of the box, sobbing more for Mrs. M'Gibbon than for Mrs. Broadbent.

This caused a change of places, which brought Miss Ashton more prominently into view. Laurence Aspinall, an ardent admirer of beauty, put his hand on the shoulder of the officer before him, and said—"Good heavens, Walmsley! Do you see that lovely creature in Mother Broadbent's box?"

"Which?" was the obtuse answer.

"Which!" (contemptuously echoed.) "The divine beauty in celestial blue. Who is she?" And his admiring gaze brought a conscious blush to the young lady's forehead, although the querist was beyond her hearing.

"In blue?" And Walmsley lazily scanned the group. "Oh! that's Charlotte's cousin, Augusta Ashton! Yes, she is rather pretty;" and the married man turned away to the stage.

"Rather pretty! She's an angel! You must introduce me!"

"Well, well!" answered the other testily, anxious to end a colloquy which distracted his attention from the tragedy, "I'll see. But she's only a schoolgirl—not yet sixteen!"

"Egad! but she looks seventeen, and she'll mend of that disqualification every day;" and still he kept his eyes on Augusta in a manner extremely disconcerting, though her romantic little heart fluttered, for in him she recognised the "Adonis" who had reared his horse so threateningly in front of her Uncle Chadwick's house.

The green curtain came down amid universal plaudits. Ladies rose to rest themselves and chat, as was the custom. Gentlemen quitted their seats to join friends elsewhere, to lounge in saloon or box-lobby, or to take a hasty glass at the "Garrick's Head" adjoining.

Amongst the latter were Walmsley and Aspinall; but they did not return when the prompter's bell rang the curtain up. There was a *pas de deux* of Tyrolean peasants by the chief dancers of the company. Then followed an interlude, and then a comic song, all before the last piece; but the comrades did not return; and Augusta found herself wondering whether the handsome officer, with the rich copper-coloured hair, would come back at all.

They did make their appearance during the progress of the drama (Monk Lewis's "Castle Spectre," in which Mrs. M'Gibbon gave ocular demonstration that she was not killed), both seemingly exhilarated, but they left again before the drama concluded.

Well drilled as were Madame Broadbent's pupils, they could not quit their box in the same order they entered it—big people so seldom recognise the right of little ones to precedence. They straggled into the saloon, separated by the crowd. There Madame Broadbent, assisted by Miss Nuttall, collected her brood, and passing on to the box--lobby, they looked around for their respective attendants.

There was one—a fine young man, in height some five feet ten—who sprang forward with shawl and calesh for Miss Ashton, at the same time bowing deferentially to the pompous dame with the big fan. He proceeded to adjust the shawl round the dimpled shoulders so very precious to him, and said—

"I hope you have had a pleasant evening, Miss Augusta."

Then bowing again to Mrs. Broadbent, he offered his hand respectfully to the young lady to conduct her home.

On the instant they were intercepted by Aspinall and Walmsley, neither so sober as he might have been.

"Augusta, here's my friend, Aspinall; deuced good fellow—quite struck with you," was Captain Walmsley's unceremonious introduction—at a time, too, when introductions were somewhat formal.

"Quite, Miss Ashton," he assented. "'Pon my soul, I am! Your charming face has quite captivated me, and those eyes pierce my heart like bullets. Permit me to escort you home."

There was an amusing consciousness of his own attractions in this free expression of his admiration. A woman of the world, with her weapons ready, might have dismissed him either with hauteur, badinage, or cool indifference; but to Augusta Ashton, almost a child in years, it was bewildering and disconcerting.

Her eyes fell—her colour rose. She stood silent, abashed, and confused. Native modesty took alarm.

Jabez came to her relief.

"Miss Ashton is under my protection, sir; she requires no other escort."

The words were cool as those of a man who, having his temper well under control, did not choose to quarrel, though his pulses were beating like drums. With cool effrontery his old antagonist looked him full in the face.

"So it's you again, yellow-skirt! A nice fellow to protect a pretty girl: a fellow without skill to defend himself, or spirit to resent an insult;" and the speaker's red lips curled with derision.

The eyes of Jabez kindled and his teeth set. There was no lack of spirit, but not the spirit of which common brawls are made. He was anxious to get the trembling Augusta away from the gathering crowd.

Madame Broadbent, shorn of half her pretty train, came up aghast.

"Young lady! Miss Ashton! What is——"

A wave of the silver-braided sleeve set her aside, chafed and indignant at the freedom and impertinence.

"BRAVO CLEGG!"

"Keep out of the way, Mother Broadbent. Look after the rest of your lambkins. Miss Ashton's cousin and I propose to see your pupil home."

"All right, Augusta," said Walmsley, thickly; "we'll see you home."

But she clung in dismay to the arm of Jabez, and not Hercules himself could have torn her from him. Ignoring the coarse taunt of Lieutenant Aspinall, he endeavoured to lead her past them, simply saying to Captain Walmsley—

"Mr. Ashton committed his daughter to my care. I am answerable for her safety."

Aspinall, mistaking his calmness for pusillanimity, again intercepted their passage, and would have taken Augusta's hand. But a will strong as his own—an arm strengthened by lifting and carrying heavy burdens—was opposed to him. Jabez struck no blow; he thrust out an arm with muscles like leather, swept the offensive lieutenant aside, and down he went on the stone pavement of the lobby.

"Bravo, Clegg!" exclaimed a voice from the rear, and the burly form of Ben Travis parted the curious crowd, as leviathan parts the waves, before the infuriated Aspinall could rise or Walmsley interpose. "That's right; take the young lady away, and leave these gallant bucks to me. I'll guard the honour of our corps."

The terrified young lady and the inebriated young bully were alike in sure hands. But consequential Madame Broadbent, ignored, forgotten, had received a blow to her importance she was not likely to forget or overlook.

CHAPTER THE TWENTY-FOURTH.

MADAME BROADBENT'S FAN.

THEY had made their exit from the Fountain Street end of the box-lobby to avoid the rush from the gallery door in Back Mosley Street, which somewhat lengthened the short distance Jabez had to convey his precious charge, who appeared more apprehensive of offending Madame Broadbent by scant and unceremonious leave-taking than troubled by the impertinence of the young officers.

Truth to tell, the whole adventure had a savour of Miss Bohanna's circulating library about it, and she felt herself elevated into a heroine by the occurrence. But her appearance before Madame Broadbent in the morning would be very real and unromantic, that lady resenting nothing so much as disrespect.

"You see, Jabez, I did not even make a curtsey to her as we came away. I am afraid she will be displeased."

"If you think so, Miss Ashton," he replied, respectfully, "I will hasten back as soon as I have seen you safely home, and bear your apologies to Madame Broadbent. She may not have left the theatre. Besides, I feel that I also owe an apology for leaving a lady of her age unprotected in the midst of such a scene. It was very remiss on my part," he added, "but, indeed, at the time I thought only of placing you beyond reach of further insult;" and Augusta could hear him mutter between his teeth, "The impertinent puppy!"

The distance even from Fountain Street was very inconsiderable, and they had reached the broad steps of the door in Mosley Street, and his hand was on the lion-headed knocker when this ejaculation escaped him.

Service from Jabez was so much a matter of course that Augusta regarded his care for herself, and his proffer to run back at her bidding, only in the light of apprentice-duty; but that muttered exclamation spoke of smothered passion, and before James was roused from his doze in front of the far-away kitchen fire by that peal on the knocker, and sleepily opened the door, she had added a caution as an addendum to her message to Madame Broadbent.

"I hope, Jabez, you are not going back to—to interfere or quarrel with Mr. Walmsley and the other officer. If they are not quite sober, you must remember *they are gentlemen*."

"I will forget nothing I should remember, Miss Ashton," said he, as James unclosed the door for her entrance, and he darted off, the emphasis she had laid on her closing words having stung him keenly with a sense of his social inferiority in her sight. "She evidently thinks the apprentice College-boy has no right to raise his hand against gentility in uniform, however drunk or disorderly it may be," he thought, as he ran along, spurred by a manly desire to show that it was not cowardice which had caused him to leave his prostrate enemy in the hands of a deputy.

He was not three minutes in reaching the box-entrance in Back Mosley Street; but for all that, the short walk home, and the brief delay caused by sleepy-headed James, had given ample time to empty and close the theatre, from which more than half the audience had dispersed before they left. Even the oil lamps over the doors were extinguished; and though a few stragglers loitered about—the natural hangers-on to histrionic skirts—and there were brawlers in the neighbourhood, he saw none of those he went to seek.

The fact was, Captain Travis had hauled Lieutenant Aspinall from the ground with little ceremony, and with a sharp reproof for "the disgrace he was bringing on their corps by insulting a young lady in a public place, as if sufficient odium did not attach to the Yeomanry already," forced him into a waiting hackney-coach, giving the driver orders to bear him home to his father's house on Ardwick Green, heedless of the young officer's remonstrance to the contrary. But Jehu, who knew his fare drove him instead to the "George and Dragon" on the opposite

WHITE HART, WHALEY BRIDGE.

side of the Green, and Mr. Aspinall saw nothing of his hopeful son that night.

Nor would Charlotte Walmsley have seen much more of her husband, had not kind-hearted Ben gone far out of his own way to land John safely at home. Perhaps it would be hardly fair to calculate too nicely how far he was influenced to that by the relation of the Walmsleys to Ellen Chadwick, since the secret springs of action often lie too far down even for self-knowledge.

As for Madame Broadbent, no sooner had Miss Nuttall disposed of the last of the budding misses than she hid her indignation in the deep shadow of her large calesh, and with an access of importance, left the theatre, slightly in advance of her humble dependants, and made her fearless way through Fountain Street and High Street, with a step which augured unpleasantness for all beneath her roof if her supper were not done to a turn and served to a nicety.

Augusta was somewhat loth to leave her pillow in the morning, after the night's unusual dissipation, and was still more reluctant to encounter her lessons and Mrs. Broadbent; and she for the first time remarked to Cicily that she thought she was "quite too old to go to school." As if the world was not one huge school, wherein the dunces get punished most severely, and even the best and brightest do not escape the rod. But Augusta Ashton, buoyant, blooming, cherished, admired, adored, could not see that her real schooling would begin when Madame Broadbent's reign ceased.

No doubt Mr. Ashton would have been coaxed into granting an extension of his darling daughter's Easter holiday, and suffered her to remain at home that Thursday morning, but he was at Whaley-Bridge; and mamma met her request with :—

"No, my dear, you have had quite holiday enough. It would be setting a bad example to infringe Madame Broadbent's rules. Go, my dear, and go cheerfully. I will send Cicily for you at noon. The streets will be rather rough this week."

She went, though not cheerfully, and Cicily was duly despatched to bring her home; but neither Cicily nor Miss Ashton had returned when dinner was put upon the table at half-past twelve o'clock. Then Mrs. Ashton recalled her. own words respecting the rough streets, and the insult offered as unwelcome tribute to Augusta's beauty over-night; and, though by no means a nervous woman, the mother grew restless and apprehensive—a lovely daughter who is an only child is so very anxious a charge. As she sat down to her solitary meal, another thought crossed her mind.

"James, ask Mr. Clegg to oblige me by stepping this way."

Mr. Clegg was with her in an instant: the summons was unusual.

"Jabez, I'll thank you to ascertain why Miss Ashton has not returned from school at the usual time. Cicily has been gone almost an hour. Should Madame be keeping her in for any breach of etiquette last night, pray offer an apology for me and my daughter also, but at the same time politely insist on Miss Ashton's immediate return to dinner."

"I believe I owe Madame Broadbent an apology myself," answered Jabez, smiling. "I shall be glad of an opportunity to discharge the debt."

* * * * *

The schoolroom door was midway down the dark, narrow, arched entry. Groups of girls, with slates and bags in their hands, loitering on the pathway at the entrance and in the passage, made way for him, with curious looks and whispers among themselves (Jabez was not unknown to some of the senior pupils). The schoolroom door stood ajar; the whole place was in a commotion unprecedented in that precise establishment.

Madame Broadbent, holding by the copy-slip axiom, "Familiarity breeds contempt," preserved her dignity and that of her high office by avoiding personal contact with her pupils, save at stated hours. Her assistant-governesses were at their posts from nine until twelve, from two until four; but Madame herself only sailed into the long room from the house door across the entry at eleven o'clock to receive reports, inspect work, dispense rewards, or administer reproof and chastisement. "Spare the rod and spoil the child" had not been abolished from the educational code fifty-five years back.

The double shock her importance had received at the theatre sent her home to quarrel with her supper; and, as a meal despatched in an ill-humour does not easily digest, Othello and the Castle Spectre haunted her pillow, and broke her rest with nightmares.

She rose late, and stepped into her schoolroom later than usual, to visit her accumulation of disagreeables on minor delinquents, as well as on the primary offenders.

Let us be just. Madame Broadbent had gracious smiles and approving words to dispense to the ultra-good, and their very rarity made them valuable. But if she rewarded any that day, it was only that severity might stand out in contrast. Little hearts beat, little fingers plied industrious needles, little eyes bent over work, when Madame's step was heard in the entry; but when her august presence fairly filled the room, every little damsel rose simultaneously, and saluted her entrance with a low, formal, deferential curtsey.

Two rooms had evidently been thrown into one to give required space, the back portion being curiously lit by a narrow small-paned window extending along the side, high above the rows of racks and pegs. It was the writing end of the room. Madame Broadbent occupied a seat in the front portion, almost opposite to the door; and as she marched towards it with more than ordinary loftiness, and beat her fan on her table with one peremptory tap, instead of a short rapid quiver, to enforce her command, "Attention, ladies!" the very youngest of those ladies could interpret the signs portentously. Lucky was the young lady whose work passed muster that morning; so many were condemned to stocks, backboard, columns of spelling, recitations from the "Speaker" and Thomson's "Seasons," lengths of open hem, back-stitching, or seaming!

At length Madame Broadbent, having dismissed ordinary business, rapped her fan upon the table, and, in a sharp, peremptory tone, called "Miss Ashton!"—and Miss Ashton, who had been expecting the summons all the morning, came forward at her bidding, but not with the ordinary alacrity of pupilage. She had left her childhood (I had almost said her girlhood) behind her in the box-lobby of the Theatre Royal.

"Miss Brookes!" cried the same sharp voice; and, with a painful start, the little girl who had committed such a terrible breach of decorum before a whole theatre as to utter her impromptu commentary on the tragedian's art, rose, trembled, burst into tears, but was too agitated to obey with sufficient promptitude. Her seat was on a low front form. Madame took a step forward, stretched out her arm, and dragged the child by the ear to the side of Augusta, then gave her a smart cuff as an admonition to more prompt obedience another time.

Then with another rap of her fan on the table, which set all hearts palpitating, she began an inflated harangue to the mite of a child and the budding woman, in which she reproached them both with bringing disgrace on the "Academy," hitherto so irreproachable. The one had drawn the attention of a whole theatre to her ill-breeding and want of proper training; the other by "boldness of look and manner had licensed the free speech of loose men;" and, as if that were not enough, had "been the cause of an unpardonable insult to herself." She, Madame Broadbent, so highly honoured and respected by the chief people in the town, to be called "Mother Broadbent!"—it was an outrage not to be endured!

Her temper interrupted her oration; she shook Augusta violently, and condemned her to remain in school until she had learned one of Mrs. Chapone's letters by heart. Then she darted on the smaller Miss as the primary cause of all, shook her till the little teeth chattered, and dragged her by the lobe of the ear towards a dark closet, set apart for heinous offenders.

Something akin to rebellion had been growing in Augusta's breast all the morning. She was a girl of quick impulses and sympathies, and was not only struck by the disproportion of punishment meted out, but by the terror on the little one's face. She threw herself in their path, and to the utter astonishment alike of pupils and teachers laid hold of the child to release her, exclaiming as she did so, "You shall not lock her in the dark! you will kill her with fright, you cruel Madame Broadbent!"

If Madame Broadbent had been wrathful before she was furious now. Never in her long experience had she been so braved. Without thought, without premeditation, she raised her heavy fan and struck sharply at Augusta. The blow fell on her beautiful bare neck, the collar-bone snapped, as it will do with a very slight matter, and Augusta dropped!

Cicily, waiting outside at the time, heard Madame's raised voice and Augusta's impetuous remonstrance; then a thud, a fall, and a suppressed scream from the girls; and without pausing to knock, she pushed open the door. Cicily had been too long the recipient of Augusta's school-girl confidence to stand in much awe of Mrs. Broadbent at best of times. Now she darted forward to raise her young mistress, whom she almost worshipped, and certainly did not consult either Madame's feelings or dignity in the epithets she launched at her.

No one had been more electrified at the effect of that stroke with the fan than Mrs. Broadbent's self. She seemed petrified, and Cicily's indignant outburst fell on deaf ears; but as Miss Nuttall ran for water, and Cicily cried out for a doctor, she roused to self-consciousness, and closed the school-room door as if to keep the outer world in ignorance of what was going on inside.

A wide latitude was then allowed for school discipline; but even Madame Broadbent was sensible that the blow which had felled Mr. Ashton's only daughter was a blow to imperil her seminary.

Augusta did not revive. Miss Nuttall suggested that the school should be dismissed, and a doctor fetched; and, before either could be effected, Jabez was on the spot. He took in the scene at a glance; Augusta, white as her frock, her hair all in disorder, lay extended on a form, her head supported by the kneeling Cicily, whilst excited girls and teachers flocked helplessly around.

"Good heavens! what is the matter? What has happened to Miss Ashton?" was his hurried and agitated inquiry.

One said one thing, one another. Wrathful Cicily came nearest to the mark. "That old wretch has struck ar darlin' wi' her great fan. A'm afeared her neckbone's brokken!"

"Impossible! She could not be so heartless!" he cried, as the group made way for him to pass, and he knelt down opposite to the sobbing Cicily, on the other side of the form, and sprinkled the pallid face so dear to him with water some one had brought in.

There was no sign of revival. "My God! this is terrible! Oh, madam, how could you do it? Mrs. Ashton will be distracted!" and he started to his feet, inexpressible anguish in every feature. "But this is no time for revilings. Where is the nearest doctor?"

"There is Mr. Campbell in Hanover Street—and——"

Brushing unceremoniously past his informant, he was with the Scotch surgeon before Miss Nuttall had recovered from her surprise, or Madame from her stupor.

Mr. Campbell was quickly on his way to attend this new patient, and Jabez speeding towards the top of Market Street. There he hired a hackney coach from the stand, close as he was to home, and drove straight to Dr. Hull's. He bore the doctor from his unfinished dinner with impetuosity, brooking no delay. They found Augusta Ashton faint, pale, but restored to consciousness, in Madame's own dingy parlour, where the author of the mischief was doing her best to put a favourable colour on the disaster.

CHAPTER THE TWENTY-FIFTH.

RETROSPECTIVE.

SEDAN CHAIR.

THE collar-bone was broken; there was no mistake about that; but Jabez, mindful of Mrs. Ashton's protracted anxiety, lingered no longer where he would fain have remained than to see the surgeon prepare—under Dr. Hull's supervision—to reduce the fracture; a delicate process, since to the collar-bone no splints can be applied.

Augusta's affection for her mother overcame her pain.

"You will be careful how you tell mamma, Jabez, I know; do not frighten her more than you can help; she will be so terribly distressed," faintly murmured she, as he again departed.

With all his haste and care, so much time had been spent, Mrs. Ashton's fears had already conjured up all manner of evils, all, of course, wide of the mark. That something was wrong she felt assured, and he found her dressing to follow her dilatory messengers. The stoppage of the coach and his evident agitation were confirmatory; but the absolute facts roused as much indignation as grief.

Yet Mrs. Ashton never forgot herself; and though the waiting coach bore her to Bradshaw Street to add her maternal reproaches to the wrathful utterances of Cicily, the rough rebukes of Dr. Hull, and the prickings of Madame Broadbent's own conscience, the natural dignity of her manner more overawed and impressed the resentful schoolmistress than all which had gone before. She was as profuse in apologies as in extenuating pleas, but she was not prepared to combat Mrs. Ashton's proverbial argumentation.

"Facts arc stubborn things, madam, and she who cannot govern herself is not fit to govern others."

Neither coach-making nor road-making had reached the acme of perfection, and Augusta's removal home, without the displacement of the bone, had to be considered.

A sedan chair—one of the last in the town—was still kept for invalid use behind the Infirmary. Jabez was aware of this, and before Dr. Hull could make the suggestion, he had proposed to go for it, and was back with the black, brass-nailed sedan long before the doctors thought their patient fit to be removed.

As the unfamiliar vehicle waited at the "Academy" door, it attracted the notice not only of neighbours and returning schoolgirls, but of passers-by, until Madame Broadbent was in a fever. The reputation of her school was at stake, and she felt that every extra moment that hand-carriage and wheel-carriage remained standing there, the bruit of the lamentable occurrence was spreading farther afield.

There had been no cessation of afternoon school duties, albeit the teachers alone presided, and discipline was somewhat relaxed. But when patient, doctors, friends, and vehicles had gone their way, and the school was soon after dismissed, the harassed, agitated, and prescient disciplinarian surrendered herself to alternate fits of hysteria, passion, lamentation, and overweening assumption.

That first outburst over, the self-important dame stood on her "right to maintain discipline," even when confronted by Mr. Ashton, no longer the easy-going, pleasant parent of a paying pupil, but the angry father of an injured only child, who had posted from Whaley Bridge on the first intelligence of the mischance, leaving his business incomplete.

Not alone to the inmates of the house in Mosley Street was Augusta Ashton precious. Notwithstanding her sometime waywardness (the result of her father's over-indulgence), she had endeared herself, by her affectionate heart and winsome ways, to a wide circle of friends; even Joshua Brookes was less grim with Augusta; so no wonder Jabez was secretly devoted to her heart and soul. Great and general was the sympathy expressed on the occasion.

Mrs. Chadwick and Ellen were with Mrs. Ashton before the afternoon was out, and at Augusta's eager desire her cousin remained behind, not only for companionship, but as chief nurse' an office for which Ellen had that peculiar fitness observable in some women, coupled with the deftness and experience gained in long attendance on her father.

And now, leaving Augusta in the hands of love and skill, with all that affection and wealth can lavish upon her in furtherance of recovery, let us step backwards to the previous September, when Peterloo was fresh, and Jabez yet wore his left arm in a sling.

Whaley Bridge has been mentioned more than once, for in that village, near the high road from Manchester to Buxton, Mr. Ashton possessed a water-mill on the picturesque banks of the river Goyt, which there divided the counties of Cheshire and Derbyshire. It had been established in the previous century, together with another in the contiguous vale of Taxal, by a speculative ancestor of Mrs. Ashton, whose old hall was in the locality. The two places had been chiefly colonised by his workpeople, many of whom had been pauper apprentices from Manchester and Warrington.

Besides the mill, Mr. Ashton owned the "White Hart" Inn, close to the bridge, where the Buxton coaches stopped; and Carr Cottage, a long, low, rough-cast building, nestling under the shadow of a fine old farmhouse which crowned the elevated ridge of Yeardsley-cum-Whaley, lang-syne the Gothic stone Hall of the warlike Yeardsleys.

From this farmhouse Carr Cottage was separated by a retired walk at the back, which—itself a wilderness of nettles, gave access to the cellarage and a clear well—led the adventurer away

CARR COTTAGE—PRESENT DAY.

up the hill between the cottage grounds and the farmer's tall high-banked hedges, which almost overtopped the cottage roof. And on the left of the cottage (as viewed from the high road) spread the granaries, stabling, and farmyard, enclosed by remains of the ancient wall, and entered by a step or two through an ancient Gothic doorway, over which ivy and honeysuckle clambered in luxurious rivalry.

The cottage, which on each floor contained four capacious rooms in its length, was on the ground divided in the middle by a respectable lobby—the house-place and kitchen lying on the left, the parlours to the right as you entered. There were two staircases, one at each end of the building, the one running upwards in the kitchen itself, the other from a small enclosed space at the back of a parlour, containing also a china closet door, and lit by a low window close to the foot of the staircase, whence it was possible to step out into the garden, unseen by anyone in the house. Otherwise, both chambers and parlours had doors of communication from end to end of the building, the two middle chambers being only accessible through the others.

The lower windows in the front—at least, those of the large parlours—were brought close to the ground, and overlooked a charming landscape; descending, at first suddenly, from the widespread flower garden (with its one great sycamore to the right of the cottage for shade), then with a gradual slope to a beanfield below, to a meadow crossed by a narrow rill; then, after a wider stretch of grass, the alder and hazel fringe of a trout stream, skirting the high road, on the far side of which tall poplars waved, and in autumn shed their leaves in the wider waters of the Goyt fresh from the bridge, where the road bends. Rivulets, road, and river ran parallel. And from the road a broad wooden gate gave access (over a bridge across the trout stream) to a wide, steep avenue between trim hedges, rising to the level of the cottage, in itself as delightful a retreat as any wearied denizen of town could desire. To Mr. Ashton it was necessary as an adjunct to his factory; an occasional home for his family in the summer, a lodge for himself when a visit of inspection was desirable.

Hearing that the general discontent was spreading amongst his own workpeople at Whaley Bridge, Mr. Ashton, without waiting for the stage coach, put himself into a long-skirted drab overcoat, with high collar and small double cape, ordered reluctant James to "find another for Clegg," and having stowed away a carpet bag and a case of pistols, lest they should be molested on the road, he mounted his high gig, with Jabez by his side, and set off to "take the bull by the horns," as Mrs. Ashton had advised.

Away they drove through the mild September air, up London Road (where houses had been growing in the years since we scanned it last) and past Ardwick Green Pond, where a dashing young buck, booted and spurred, lounged at the door of the quaint "George and Dragon," and followed them curiously with his eyes; yet not so swiftly but Jabez had time to recognise with accelerated pulse his former assailant, Laurence.

Longsight, Burnage, Fallowfield left behind; Stockport Bridge gained, they went walking by their horse's head up the steep hill, between frowning houses, to the "Pack Horse" in the Market Place, where the beast was baited, and the travellers dined at the same table, Jabez not for one moment forgetting the social distance between his master and himself.

Again seated, they quickly left the smoke-begrimed, higgledy-piggledy mass of brick and mortar called 'Stockport' behind, and were away on country roads, where yellow leaves were blown into their faces, where brown-faced, white-headed cottage children were stripping blackberries from the wayside brambles, or ripe nuts from the luxuriant hazels which have since changed the very name of the Bullock Smithy, through which they drove at a gallop, to Hazel Grove.

It was a glorious treat for Jabez, was that drive, and Mr. Ashton, conversing with him as they went, was surprised to discover his love of Nature, and his knowledge of her secrets. This induced reminiscences of the early years of Jabez when Simon took him pick-a-back into the fields on Sundays; and Mr. Ashton led him on to dilate on his childhood among his first friends, until he had a closer insight into the young man's heart than in all the years he had served them.

But the object of their journey had not been forgotten; and at Disley, hearing Mr. Ashton remark that they were but three miles from Whaley Bridge, Jabez ventured to suggest—

"Do you not think, sir, as I am unknown in Whaley Bridge, I might make enquiries, and ascertain the feeling of the people better if I went on foot, having no apparent connection with you?"

"That is a wise thought of yours, young man. Just so. I will put you down at the next milestone. Here is a guinea for your expenses at the 'White Hart.' But country people are inquisitive; what do you propose to be?"

"Well, sir, I took the liberty to bring a sketch-book with me—I don't get many such opportunities—I could represent myself as an artist; or I could cram my pockets with plants and roots as I went along, and say I was a botanist in search of specimens."

"Stick to the artist, Jabez; our country botanists would soon floor you on their own ground—they know more of plants than pencils, I'll warrant." And Mr. Ashton, handing the reins to Jabez, took a pinch of snuff on the strength of it

Mr. Ashton, putting up the collar of his topcoat, drove direct to Carr, much to the surprise of his unprepared overlooker and wife, who had charge of the cottage. He said nothing of any companion; and Jabez some twenty minutes later walked into the bar of the "White Hart," dusty and weary, as if with long walking; called for bread-and-cheese and ale; intimated his intention to remain the night, if he could have a bed; talked of the scenery, and led the host to tell of the best points for sketching.

Professing fatigue, he kept his seat in the bar-parlour the remainder of the day. The sling, not yet wholly discarded, drew attention, as he expected it would. The incomers, eyeing him askance, talked politics before him, and finding him less glib than themselves, whispered that he was a refugee from Peterloo, and, to show their sympathy with the party to which he was supposed to belong, freely discussed the political aspect of the district before him.

He was young, free with his money, and they were not reticent. He found that the overlooker had made himself, and his master through himself, obnoxious to his weavers, and that only prompt measures would prevent an outbreak.

The next morning Mr. Ashton put his head into the inn, greeted "Mr. Clegg" as some one he was surprised to meet in so remote a spot, and invited him to Carr Cottage.

Jabez accepted the invitation for the afternoon, saying he could not spare the morning. Under pretence of sketching, he took his way by the Goyt to the neighbourhood of the mill with pencils and sketch-book; women and children flocked inquisitively round him in their dinner-hour, and talked to him; then he rested in a weaver's cot, and when he found his way to Carr in the afternoon, and sat with Mr. Ashton for privacy under the dropping keys of the sycamore, he had brought with him the key to the prevailing discontent.

Mr. Ashton listened, took an enormous quantity of snuff, dropped an occasional "Just so," and, knowing the sore, set about healing it. He drove back to Manchester, leaving Jabez as his temporary deputy—high honour for so young a man—and the overlooker was required to render up his accounts.

A fortnight later, as Jabez was midway up the avenue to Carr in the afternoon, he turned, hearing the blithe bugle of the coming Buxton coach, and watched its dashing progress along the road. To his astonishment it stopped at the gate. He himself reached the spot at a run.

His eyes had not played him false. Simon Clegg, in his best clothes, was there on the box seat; Tom Hulme and Bess and little Sim sat close behind him. Mr. Ashton was himself an inside passenger.

In the bustle and confusion of alighting, and dragging boxes from the boot and from the top, curiosity was kept on the stretch. It was not until the entire party were under the roof of the cottage that Jabez was enlightened. Tom Hulme was the new overlooker, Bess the new caretaker of Carr Cottage, which was henceforth their rural rent-free home; and to Simon, long disqualified by rheumatism for the wet and slush of the tannery, was given the charge of the garden, with a boy under him. And of all the group old Simon and little Sim were most delighted.

Some eight months before, Sim (then about two years old) had slipped on the frosty stones in the old Long Millgate Yard, and, rolling down its rugged declivity, was supposed to have injured his spine, and he had been too delicate ever since to run about freely. To the child, therefore, whose shoulders seemed unnaturally high, the change from the stifling court was something too exuberant for expression. To Simon Clegg, who, in losing his crony Matt, had felt the old haunts oppressive, the bountiful expanse of nature before him, and the comfortable fragrant home, were matters for deep thankfulness.

"Moi lad," said he to Jabez, when the latter was about to depart with Mr. Ashton, after they were fairly inducted, "ar Bess said thah would be a Godsend to us, an' thah has bin. This Paradise o' posies has o' grown eawt o' thy cradle. God bless thee!"

"I think, my dear, the experiment will succeed. There is a matronly air of respectability about Mrs. Hulme that will help to uphold her husband's position amongst the workpeople, and I can trust his soldierly discipline for keeping the rebellious in order."

Thus said Mr. Ashton to his good lady, sitting by the fireside after supper, the night of his return home. Then, after a little pondering and trifling with his snuff-box, he added, as if reflectively—

"It is all very well, my dear, to serve the young man's

friends and ourselves at the same time, but I should like to do something for Jabez himself. It is entirely to his clear head and his tact that we owe the preservation of peace at Whaley Bridge. I should like to give *him* a rise."

"My dear William, make no more haste than good speed, and never do things in a hurry," replied his calm proverbial philosopher. "We must not excite the envy of his fellow-clerks, or we shall surround him with enemies from the first. In removing his humble friends you have cleared one barrier to his advancement."

Mr. Ashton did not say "Just so!" for a wonder; he turned his gold box round and round in his fingers, and at length gave utterance to a thought which took Mrs. Ashton by surprise.

"If we remove all the young man's old associations, don't you think we ought to provide him with new ones?"

"I think, William, we ought to 'leave well alone;' smooth paths are slippery paths. The young man will be out of his time in six months; you can then advance him if you think proper—in the warehouse—but I do not feel disposed to open our drawing-room to him, if that is what you are driving at;" and she drew herself up as if her dignity had received a blow.

"We-ll, no—not exactly!" and Mr. Ashton, unable to express what he did mean exactly, shuffled and fidgeted till he upset his snuff on the Brussels carpet.

CHAPTER THE TWENTY-SIXTH.

ON THE PORTICO STEPS.

BETWEEN that expedition to Whaley Bridge, with its terminal connubial conversation, and the breakage of Augusta Ashton's collar-bone, rather more than six months intervened—six months during which Mr. Clegg, as his good master had anticipated, felt the solitary state of his trim sitting-room somewhat oppressive, the permission to receive his old friends becoming a nullity on their removal. He occupied a position midway between parlour and kitchen—above his old associates of the porringers, the fireside settle, and the sanded stone floor, and beneath the family seated round the tea-urn on cushioned chairs and Brussels carpet. Towards the former he cast few backward looks of regret—he had put his past behind him—but, oh! who shall tell his unuttered longings for the "Open Sesame!" to that paradise of which he had had one rapturous glimpse, and one only—that paradise where his master's daughter, so high above him, moved like a seraph, and filled the air with harmony!

I am afraid that at this time he brooded over his orphanhood and that unknown father who had disappeared so mysteriously, and strained his soaring thoughts in their flight towards possibilities more than was good for him. He was too much alone for one of his years, and there were times in those long, candle-lit winter evenings when books and pencils dropped from his wearied hands, and for lack of a companion he held dreamy converse with the fire.

Of course his library was restricted, and there were no institutions in Manchester at that time where young men of his class could meet for mutual improvement, or that mental polish caused by the attrition of mind upon mind. Occasionally, at long intervals, and at first to the utter confusion of James, Captain Travis had inquired for "Mr. Clegg," and been shown into the little sitting-room with a disregard to "caste" very creditable to both of them; and now and then Mr. Chadwick and Mr. Ashton would drop in together for half-an-hour's chat, the gratitude of the former being deeper than the surface.

But rarely did a feminine face save Cicily's brighten up his solitude, and she, devoted to her young mistress, had always something to say about Augusta, if only what she wore or how she looked, which sent him off into dreamland immediately.

Sunday was a very chequered day; when he missed his old friends most. True, he followed the family to church, perhaps carried Augusta's prayer-book, exchanged a word of kindly greeting with old Mrs. Clowes and Parson Brookes, who was not as hale as he had been; but there was no old Simon to grip his hand, no Bess to give him a motherly smile, and unless the weather was fine enough for a ramble in the fields with Nelson for companion, the rest of the day was very dull indeed.

The fan which broke Augusta's collar-bone broke down a barrier for Jabez. No personal sacrifice attended the service he rendered. He but went and came as an active messenger. But he went and came with intelligence and promptitude, and exercised for mother and daughter both the care and forethought of a much older man.

In the father's absence the father was not missed. What came under Mrs. Ashton's own eye Mrs. Ashton could appreciate, and the commendation of Dr. Hull was not without its weight. He had said—

"Capital fellow to send for a doctor, that messenger of yours, Mrs. Ashton! A determined, persistent fellow! Would see me and haul me off with only half a dinner, though I protested and he had already got a surgeon there before me!"

His thought about the sedan chair, which he had accompanied to Mosley Street to insure care on the part of the chair-men, and had ordered into the very lobby of the house, the cautious manner in which he had lifted Augusta thence and borne her to the ready couch, coupled with his protection of her daughter in the theatre the night before, weighed down the scale already trembling in the balance, and Mrs. Ashton's "Jabez, I am deeply indebted to you," was not mere words. He was her messenger to the Chadwicks, her amanuensis to Mr. Ashton, and when Ellen and her mother arrived somewhere about tea-time for the second occasion he was invited to join their party; and one, if not two, pair of cheeks burned as the invitation was given.

Then, the night Mr. Ashton returned home, to find Augusta an invalid, he was gratified to see Jabez again at the tea-table, and after that at odd times, until the restraint upon him gradually wore away, and he would read to Augusta and Ellen, as the latter sat at work, and do his best to make the time pass pleasantly.

Next Mr. Ashton took it into his head to teach him backgammon and cribbage, to help to make his own evenings at home more lively.

And Mrs. Chadwick, who for some occult reason had resisted her husband's desire to show courtesy to his preserver, could scarcely be less gracious than her grander sister, who owed him so much less; so now the green-parlour door in Oldham Street was opened to him, and as Jabez refreshed his memory with Hogarth's prints, he felt that he had made another step up the ladder.

Those were halcyon days; while Augusta, too tall to be robust, recovered so slowly, and was so much gratified by his attempts to entertain her. Halcyon days for more than one.

Yet, ere Jabez was out of his apprenticeship, or Augusta had left her pillowed sofa, a pebble was thrown into the stream which broke the surface of the tranquil waters, and disturbed them for ever.

Mr. Ashton was one of the original shareholders in the Portico, a classic stone building erected in 1806 as a library and reading-room, on the other side of Mosley Street, which, with its pillared *facade* and flight of steps, like an Ionic temple, looked down on the plain red-brick front of the Assembly Rooms, though its opposite neighbour stood quite as high in repute, and was equally exclusive in its constitution.

Mr. Aspinall, the Cannon Street cotton-merchant (who dined with the Scramble Club, instituted by business men whose homes were in the suburbs), was likewise a shareholder in the Portico; and from constant meeting at the long tables within the book-shelved, galleried walls of its lofty reading-room, he and Mr. Ashton had a tolerably lengthy acquaintance, although it had never ripened into intimacy—the men were so dissimilar.

Charlotte Walmsley was naturally troubled by the result of Madame Broadbent's notions of discipline, and not unnaturally (considering the condition in which Ben Travis had taken him home) blamed her husband as the primary cause. As naturally he shifted the onus to the shoulders of Laurence Aspinall, and, taking him to task, plainly told him he ought to apologise. Laurence snatched at the proposal.

"My dear Jack, nothing would please me better! I'll make a thousand apologies, if you'll only introduce me."

John Walmsley had had quite enough of introductions; besides, he stood in some awe of Mrs. Ashton, and did not know how she might take it, especially as his friend Aspinall had acquired the character of a "wild spark." He emphatically declined. But if Laurence Aspinall once set his mind on a thing he would attain it, if within the range of possibility, whether by fair means or foul, whatever might be the consequences.

For a few days he was on his best behaviour at home; and having won his father over by expressions of deep contrition, and promises of reformation, and the assurance that he would never again do anything "unbecoming a gentleman," he prevailed on him to introduce him to Mr. Ashton, with a view to making his own apologies in person.

"Well, Laurence, you can go with me to the Portico to-morrow morning, and if Mr. Ashton is there we will see what can be done;" the tone in which this was said clearly implying, "If *we*

BY THE PORTICO STEPS.

seek an introduction to the Ashton's for the purpose of making the *amende honorable* as befits gentlemen, there can be no doubt of its acceptance.

But when they met Mr. Ashton on the steps of the Portico the following morning, the self-complacence of the lofty gentleman received a slight but uncontemplated check. Mr. Ashton nodded to Mr. Aspinall with a beaming face, and would have passed his acquaintance with a mere "Good morning," but the other stopped, and after shaking hands, and remarking that trade was slack, presented, with due formality, the handsome, elegant, six feet of dandyism who bore him company.

"Mr. Ashton, let me make you acquainted with my son, sir—Mr. Ashton, my son Laurence; Laurence, Mr. Ashton."

The young gentleman raised his stylish beaver from his rich coppery curls, and bowed with courtly grace in acknowledgment of Mr. Ashton's formal bow, whilst his father continued, almost in the tone of one who confers an honour—

"The fact is, my son, sir, desires an opportunity of expressing to Miss Ashton his deep regret for the indiscretion of which he was guilty in the lobby of the Theatre Royal, some ten days back."

The smile faded from the face of Mr. Ashton, who, with a reserve very foreign to him, put his hand into his pocket for his snuff-box instead of extending it to the young man, and, tapping it with a little impatience, caught at his words.

"Indiscretion, sir? What you are pleased to call 'indiscretion' has placed my daughter in the doctor's hands with a broken collar-bone."

Before Mr. Aspinall could reply, Laurence, better skilled to temporise, interposed.

"So, to my infinite regret, my friend Mr. Walmsley has already informed me, sir. And I assure you, I take shame to myself that any word or action of mine should have led to consequences so lamentable. No one, sir, can deplore the injury Miss Ashton has sustained, more than myself—the unhappy cause. It is this, Mr. Ashton, which impels me to seek an opportunity to express the sensibilty of my grave offence, and my extreme regret, to Mrs. Ashtcn and Miss Ashton in person. I cannot rest until I have implored their pardon!"

The tones in which this apolegetic speech was delivered were at once so suave, remorseful, and sympathetic that Mr. Ashton, whose sternness was seldom of long duration, was considerably mollified. He looked at the handsome, dashing blade before him, whose blue eyes seem full of gentleness and pity, and felt as though the boy he had seen torturing old Brookes, and the yeomanry officer who had slashed at Mr. Chadwick and Jabez Clegg, could never be one and the same. He reverted to the latter circumstance—

"I think, young sir, you owe an apology to someone else under my roof—the young man who received the sabre-cut you designed for my brother-in-law, Mr. Chadwick."

Aspinall's handsome face flushed. His father's quick reply gave him time to think.

"You surely, Mr. Ashton, would not expect *my* son to apologise to an apprentice-lad, a mere College-boy."

"Just so! I would expect him to apologise to *anyoue* he had injured, were it a beggar!"

Here the son interposed: "My good sir, do not remind me of the horrors of that dreadful day! I shudder when I recall it. We acted under orders, and I swear I was utterly unconscious and irresponsible for my actions throughout the whole affray."

And Laurence seemed desirous to wash his hands of the responsibility.

"The fact is," said Mr. Aspinall, coming to his son's rescue, "Laurence had taken more wine than his young head would stand on both occasions. It takes years to season a cask, you know, Mr. Ashton, and we must not be too hard on young fellows, if they slip sometimes. We have all had some wild oats to sow."

This was a platitude of the period, but Mr. Ashton's "Just so!" was not a cordial assent; and Laurence, fearing the conversation was taking an unfortunate turn, led it back to its original request.

But Mr. Ashton tapped his box, and, offering it to his interlocutors, took a pinch himself, and then a second, before he came to a decision. It was evidently a debatable question.

"I will mention your request to Mrs. Ashton, young gentleman, and if I find her agreeable to receive you, I can take you across with me to-morrow morning, provided you meet me here. Good day."

Mr. Aspinall's "Good day" was somewhat stiff. He had held his head very high all his life, metaphorically as well as physically, and was not disposed to be snubbed by one whose status he considered scarcely on a par with his own. He was disposed to look on his son's peccadilloes as some of those "wild oats" which young gentlemen of spirit were expected to sow, and considered his fine figure and beautiful features, his education, accomplishments, and prospects, passports to any society; and that Mr. Ashton should for one moment hesitate to open his heart and his doors to *his* son, was an indignity not to be borne.

"The fact is, Laurence, that, if you make an apology to those people after this, you have less spirit than I take you to have!" was his conclusion.

"Never you mind, father, I know what I'm about. I want to get my foot in there," answered subtle Laurence. And he managed it.

Mr. Ashton went home to dinner full of his conversation on the Portico steps, and set his romantic daughter's heart in a flutter by mooting the point at issue in her presence.

"Oh, papa! do bring him; I want to see him again, he is so handsome!"

"'Handsome is that handsome does,' Augusta," was Mrs. Ashton's commentary on that young lady's impulsive exclamation.

"Charlotte says he is very wild," remarked Ellen, "and I feel as if I should shudder at the sight of him, after his conduct at Peterloo."

"You don't shudder when Captain Travis calls, and you don't shut the door in John Walmsley's face, and they may have done things just as bad, if you did but know it, Ellen," retorted Augusta, standing on the defensive for the absent "Adonis."

"Just so my dear, so they might," admitted Mr. Ashton, whilst Ellen held her peace, silenced by something in her cousin's retort.

"Yes, William, but look on the poor bandaged neck and shoulders of our child, and think of that ruffian's cruelty to Jabez and others when a schoolboy. I don't think either John Walmsley or Mr. Travis could have done anything so bad."

"Well, but, mamma," argued spoiled Augusta, "Jabez forgave him; and I think Madame Broadbent is more to blame than Mr. Aspinall—he only offered to bring me home."

Mrs. Ashton shook her head as she rose from table.

"Besides, mamma, he says he only wants to apologise, and you know you need not invite him again unless you like. It would be so rude to refuse.

"Just so, just so," assented Mr. Ashton, willing to humour his pet in her invalid state, and perhaps it might do the young fellow good to see the consequences of his folly.

As usual, where Augusta enlisted her father on her side, Mrs. Ashton's dissent grew feebler.

The next day Mr. Ashton made at least *one* false step in his life, and brought over his own threshold a blight.

Faultless were the curves of the stylish hat, faultless the fit of pantaloons, and coat, and Hessian boots, and York-tan gloves; graceful the figure they adorned; graceful the apology tendered so adroitly—more to the mother than to the daughter—but if ever a graceless good-for-nothing cast a shadow on a good man's hearth, it was the wolf in sheep's clothing whose hungry jaws were watering for the pet lamb of the fold, and who made so courtly an exit full in the sight of Jabez, as he crossed the end of the hall to his solitary dinner in his own room.

CHAPTER THE TWENTY-SEVENTH.

MANHOOD.

YOUNG as he was, Laurence Aspinall was wont to say he "wouldn't give a fig for any man who could not be anything in any society;" and the Laurence Aspinall of the cock-pit, the ring, and the bar-parlour, was a very different being from the Laurence Aspinall of the Assembly or drawing-room. He could be a blackguard amongst blackguards, a gentleman amongst ladies.

Nature had done much for him, art had done more. Nature had given him at twenty-one a symmetrical figure, and art an easy carriage. Nature had given him the clear pink-and-white complexion which so often accompanies ruddy hair, and art had trained his early growth of whisker to counteract effeminacy of skin. Nature had given him a lofty forehead, art had clustered his bronze curls so as to hide how much that brow receded. Nature had given an aquiline nose, eyes of purest azure, flexile lips with curves like Cupid's bow; and art had taught that eyes set so close, whose hue was so apt to change as temper swayed him, and lips so cruelly thin, might be tutored to obey volition, and contradict themselves, if so their owner willed. To crown all, Nature had gifted him with a flexible voice, and art had set it to music.

The Liverpool schoolmaster had obeyed Mr. Aspinall's instructions to the letter; all that education and accomplishments could do to polish and refine the physical man into the gentleman, as the word was then understood, had been done for him; but under the stucco was the rough brickwork Bob the groom had heaped together, and which no trained or loving hand had removed.

Be sure Laurence Aspinall did not carry this analysis into society, written on his forehead. Instead, he had cultivated the art of fascination; and in the brief space occupied by that apologetic introductory visit in Mosley Street, he not only contrived to dazzle the romance-beclouded eyes of Augusta, but, what was almost as much to his purpose, to win over Mr. Ashton, and to weaken the prejudice of Miss Augusta's less pliant mamma. Ellen Chadwick was the only one on whom he made no impression, the only one who retained a previous opinion—confirmed. Possibly, as Charlotte Walmsley's sister, she knew something of his life below the surface, and had imbibed that sister's notion that he "led John Walmsley away." Possibly, too, as Charles Chadwick's daughter, she contrasted the silken speech of the drawing-room dandy with the hectoring, sword-in-hand, yeomanry cavalry lieutenant who, in striking at her father, had wounded Jabez, his deliverer, instead.

At all events, she met the enthusiastic admiration of Augusta after his departure, the gratified encomiums of her uncle, and the more subdued approbation of her aunt, with the unvarying expression, "He would have murdered my dear father but for Jabez Clegg, and Mr. Clegg is worth a hundred of him."

Mr. Laurence knew better than to presume on that introduction all at once. From their gardens and greenhouses at Ardwick and Fallowfield, he sent small baskets of early flowers and fruit to Mrs. Ashton, for her daughter, with courteous inquiries; but he allowed several days to elapse before he presented himself in person, and then his call was of the briefest.

He knew he had prejudice to overcome, and worked his way gradually. Meanwhile Augusta progressed favourably; and if Aspinall grew in favour with the family, so did Jabez.

May, sweet-scented month of promise, brought to Jabez Clegg in 1820 his natural and legal heritage—manhood and manhood's freedom. He was no longer an apprentice bound to a master by the will of others. He had a right to think and act for himself, subject only to the laws of God and of the realm. True, that free agency brought with it a train of responsibilities, but the new *man* was not the one to overlook or ignore the fact. He had thought long and keenly of the coming change, and all it might involve, months before it came.

His fixed wages as an indoor apprentice, according to

indenture, were no great matter; but, supplemented by coin he extracted from his paint-box after business hours, he had found a margin for saving, besides contributing to the humble wants of his early fosterers. The latter duty he had never neglected, but Simon was as sternly just as the lad had been gratefully generous, and, even when poverty bit the hardest, would never accept the whole of his earnings.

"Si thi, Jabez, if thah dunnot keep summat fur thisel' to put by fur a nest-egg, thah'll ne'er see the good o' thi own earnin's, an' thah'll lose heart in toime," the old tanner had been wont to say, when sturdily limiting the extent to which his foster-son should open his small purse.

So Jabez, leading a steady, industrious life, spending little on personal gratification, save what he invested in books, had quite a little store laid by—the result of very small savings—against the time when he might have to shift for himself. Two things had troubled him—the possibility of having to find a situation elsewhere (Mr. Ashton having said no word of retaining him, though, on the contrary, he had said nothing of his removal), and the necessity for quitting the house which had been to him a home so long that even the grumbling cook and the affectionate dog had welded themselves into his daily life, how much more the kind master and mistress, and that beatific vision, their beautiful, bewitching daughter, who had held him in vassalage from the very day of his apprenticeship, and tyrannised over him as only a wayward, spoiled beauty—child or woman—could.

The bright morning of the fifth of May set this at rest. He was called into the inner counting-house, and passed the high stools of inquisitive-eyed, quill-driving clerks, with a palpitating heart, conscious how much depended on the issue of that interview.

As he opened the curtained glass door, to his surprise he found himself confronted by, not only Mr. Ashton, but Mr. Chadwick, and Simon Clegg, who had been brought from Whaley Bridge for the occasion.

Business men, as a rule, are not demonstrative over business, and, after the first salutations and surprised greetings, the congratulations of the day were soon said, and the stereotyped "And now to business" put sentiment to flight. And yet not entirely so, as will be seen.

There was nothing luxurious in that counting-house of the past. Besides the high desk and stool, it contained an oilcloth-topped hexagon table, with a deep rim of partitioned drawers, three wooden chairs, a sort of fireguard fender, and a poker; but there was neither carpet nor oilcloth on the floor, and the walls had but a dim recollection of paint.

Mr. Ashton, snuff-box in hand, occupied one of these chairs; Mr. Chadwick, resting hands and chin on a stout walking-stick, another; the third, a little apart, had been assigned to old Simon, now on the shady side of seventy). Jabez remained standing.

Mr. Ashton, as was his manner, tapping his fingers on his snuff-box lid whilst he spoke, opened fire, "No doubt, Jabez, you have been expecting me to say something respecting your prospects and position when your indentures are given up?"

"Well, sir," answered Jabez with a frank smile, "I believe I have."

"Just so! I knew you would. It was but likely. And I should have spoken to you some time since, but for brother Chadwick here. Both Mrs. Ashton and myself have watched your conduct and progress, during the whole term of your apprentice ship, with entire satisfaction."

Here a pinch of snuff emphasised the sentence, and both Simon and Jabez felt their cheeks begin to glow.

"You have been unusually steady and persevering—have not been merely obedient, but obliging, and your rectitude does full credit to the 'honourable' name Parson Brookes gave to you."

This was quite a long speech for Mr. Ashton; he paused to take breath; and old Simon, proud of the young man as if he had been his own son, feeling the encomium as some sort of halo round his own grey head, exclaimed—

"Aw'm downreet preawd to yer [hear] yo' say it, sir. It'll mak' ar Bess's heart leap wi' joy."

But Jabez, blushing, half ashamed of hearing his own praises rung out as from a belfry, could only stammer forth—

"I've endeavoured to do my duty, that is all, sir."

"A—ll!" interjected Mr. Chadwick, in his imperfect speech, "Nelson sa—said du—u—ty was all Engla—and expected of ev—ev'ry man, but it w—won the b—battle of Tr—Trafalgar!"

"Duty wins the battle of life, brother," put in Mrs. Ashton, who had quietly entered the counting-house by the door behind Jabez.

"Just so, just so!" assented Mr. Ashton, as he rose and handed his chair to the lady whose stately presence seemed to fill the room; "and Jabez has only to continue doing his duty to win his battle of life, I take it. But to our business.—You have hitherto served us well, Jabez, in the warehouse and out of it; you have been doubly useful to me as a designer and as a detector of the roguery and mismanagement of others. Then, to my daughter, who is far dearer than either warehouse or trade, you have rendered more than one service."

"Oh, sir, do not name it, I beg. It has been my highest pleasure to serve Miss Ashton—or yourself," Jabez exclaimed, the two last words rising to his lips simultaneously with the thought that his sudden outburst might fail of appreciation by Miss Ashton's wealthy relatives.

"Just so! but I must name it, Jabez, as a reason for my proposal to retain you in my employ, and for assigning to you a situation and salary higher than is usually accorded to an apprentice just out of his time. But as you have shown stability and judgment beyond your years, and I know you to be honourable in *all* respects, I feel I am justified in making the offer."

Mr. Ashton then stated, with a little seasoning of snuff, the salary he proposed to give the young man, and the duties he required as an equivalent, if Jabez accepted his proposition.

The eyes of Jabez sparkled and his cheeks glowed. As for Simon, he seemed dumb with delight and astonishment at the good fortune of the foundling.

"IF!" cried Jabez, "there can be no 'if,' sir; you overpower me with an offer so far above my deserts. I accept it most gratefu——"

"Stay, Mr. Clegg," interrupted Mrs. Ashton, as Mr. Chadwick raised his head from its rest on his hands and stick, and made an ineffectual effort to speak. "'Think twice before you speak once,' my bro——"

"Oh, madam! there is no need," Jabez began, but she silenced him with a mere gesture of her raised hand; and Mrs. Ashton, acting as interpreter for her slow-tongued brother-in-law, resumed—

"You have done *us* some services, Mr. Clegg, but 'a man will give all he possesses for his life,' and Mr. Chadwick feels that his debt to you is greater than ours."

Jabez looked from one to another, bewildered.

Mr. Ashton took up the thread—"Just so! and that brings me to the point we have been driving at. You see, Jabez, Mr. Chadwick is not so capable of managing his business as he used to be; things go wrong he scarcely knows how, and he is desirous to bring some one into his warehouse on whom he can rely. He therefore offers to take you at a higher salary than I think at all suitable for so young a man, and if you prove your competence to take the management within a reasonable time, to give it over into your hands, and ultimately—it may be in a very few years—to give you a small partnership interest in the concern."

It is difficult to say whether Jabez or Simon was the most completely stunned.

"You must not look on this altogether as a testimony to your business qualifications, Jabez, I think," continued Mr. Ashton, "but as the outflow of a grateful heart, and the proposition of a man who has no son capable of keeping his trade together. Is not that so?" turning to Mr. Chadwick.

"Cer—certainly!"

Jabez looked from one to another, then to Simon, but no help was forthcoming from that quarter.

Mrs. Ashton came to his relief: "I think, Mr. Clegg, you had better 'look before you leap.' Whatever decision you make will equally satisfy us. But I see you need time to consider. Suppose you consult your foster-father, and give Mr Ashton your decision at the outcome-supper to-night."

The hesitation of Jabez was only momentary. We are told that all the marvels and glories of Paradise were revealed to Mahomet before a single drop of water had time to flow from a pitcher overturned in his upward flight; and even whilst Mrs. Ashton spoke, Jabez had time to think.

"Thank you, madam," said he, "but I need no deliberation. I know not for whose kindness to be most grateful; but I do know that I should be most ungrateful if I were to quit the master and mistress to whom both myself and my dear friends owe so very much for the first tempting offer made to me. Mr. Chadwick overrates my service; Mr. Mabbott rendered quite as efficient aid; besides, I have no acquaintance with the manufacture of piece-goods, and have no right to take advantage of Mr. Chadwick's extreme generosity, knowing my own disqualifications. And, pardon my saying so, if Mr. Chadwick has no mercantile son, he may some day have a son-in-law better fitted in every way for the office and promise held out to me. I trust, Mr. Chadwick, you will not consider me ungracious in declining your liberal offer, but, indeed, I have been trained to the smallware manufacture, and here lies my duty, for here I feel I may be able to render something of a *quid pro quo*."

Before anyone had time for reply, the Infirmary clock struck twelve, and, as if simultaneously, there was a rush from the warehouse into the yard, an outcry and a din, as if Babel had broken loose, the sacred precincts of the counting-house was invaded, and Jabez was carried off *vi et armis*.

CHAPTER THE TWENTY-EIGHTH.

ONCE IN A LIFE.

CROWNING JABEZ WITH PUNCH-BOWL.

CUSTOMS change with the manners of the times, and as the apprentice is no longer the absolute bond-slave of his master, release from the seven years bondage is now seldom accompanied by the active and noisy demonstration which of old marked that epoch of a tradesman's or artisan's career.

But if the sudden uproar, which chased quiet from the precincts of Mr. Ashton's warehouse and manufactory when the Infirmary clock told noon, broke prematurely upon the conference in the counting-house, it was not unexpected. Every apprentice had been similarly greeted at the same period of his life. Until the clock proclaimed twelve, business routine had been undisturbed, but those twelve beats of the timekeeper's hammer had been the signal for every apprentice and workman on the premises to rush pell-mell into the yard, each bearing with him some implement or symbol of his trade, anything which would clash or clang being preferred. Remnants of fringe, bed-lace, and carpet-binding waved and fluttered like streamers from the hands of the women; umbrella sticks were flourished; strings of waste ferrules, brass wheels, brace buckles, button and tassel moulds, cops, and spindles were jingled and jangled together; tin cans were beaten with picking-rods, punches, hammers, leather stamps, and other tools by apprentices and men; whilst Jabez himself, hoisted on the shoulders of the two smallware-weavers who had seized and borne him from his master's presence, claiming him as one of their own body, a recognised lawful member of their craft, was paraded round and round that inner court-yard with the crowd in extemporised procession, amid shouts, hurrahs, songs, and that peculiar instrumental accompaniment which was—noise—not music.

The household servants had crowded to the scullery door; clerks stood aloof under the gateway, where Simon Clegg kept them in company in an ecstasy of satisfaction; Mr. and Mrs. Ashton and Mr. Chadwick surveyed the proceedings from the counting-house window, whilst even Ellen and Augusta were curious enough to look on from those back hall steps where they had once before received the hero of that scene, wounded—from a very different one.

More than six years had elapsed since the last indoor apprentice had been borne in triumph round that yard (Kit Townley's indentures had been prematurely cancelled), and Jabez may be pardoned if he contrasted the two occasions, and construed the wilder excitement and enthusiasm of this in his own favour, when his employers and their daughter noticed it also.

"It is easy to tell what a favourite Jabez must be in the warehouse, by the uproar. The last outcome, I remember, was quite tame beside this."

"Well, Augusta," answered Ellen, "I believe he deserves it. I know my father thinks there is not such another young man as Mr. Clegg in all Manchester."

"Yes, he's very kind, and obliging, and clever, and persevering, and all that, and I like him very well; but then you know, Ellen, he is not a gentleman, and he is not handsome by any means," responded Augusta, in quite a patronising tone.

Ellen looked grave.

"He is all that is good and noble, if he was not born a gentleman; and *I* think him handsome. He has a frank, open, expressive countenance, and a good figure, and good manners, and what more would you have?"

Augusta turned her head sharply, and looked up archly in her cousin's face.

"It's well Captain Travis does not hear you, Ellen, or he might be jealous of the prentice-knight," she said, banteringly.

Ellen coloured painfully.

"When shall I make you understand that Mr. Travis is nothing to me?" asked she.

"When my cousin makes me understand that she is nothing to Mr. Travis," was the quick reply, as Jabez was being borne past for the last time, and the young ladies once more waved their handkerchiefs in salutation.

It may be very gratifying and very triumphant to be borne aloft on other men's shoulders, but it is neither dignified, nor graceful, nor comfortable; and Jabez, being carried off bare-headed, had neither hat nor cap to wave in return. He made the best use of his right hand, his left being required to steady himself, yet I am afraid he was more desirous to make a good impression on the romantic young lady muffled in a shawl—to hide the swathing bandages—than on his less-attractive and elder champion by her side.

It was half-past twelve; the dinner-bell rang, Jabez was lowered to *terra firma*, and there was a general rush to the packing-room, which had been cleared out to receive tressels and planks for the tables, and an abundant supply of cold meat, cheese, bread, and ale, provided by the master.

And then and there, before a mouthful was cut, Mr. Ashton, standing at the head of the table, having Mr. Chadwick by his side, and Simon Clegg close at hand, presented Jabez with his indentures, with many expressions of his good will and his good opinion, and an intimation to those assembled that Mr. Clegg would in all probability continue in his employ, an announcement which was received with loud acclaim; and the hungry operatives set to at the collation with right good will.

This was the master's feast; that of the apprentice, for which it was customary to save up long in advance, was at night, and held at the neighbouring "Concert-Hall Tavern" in York Street, opposite to the then "Gentleman's Concert-Hall."

Prior to that, however, Mrs. Ashton had somewhat to say to the young man, and she chose his own sitting-room to say it in. Of course, his apprenticeship over, it behoved him to shift his quarters; and he had looked forward to his abdication with regret undreamed of by Mrs. Ashton, or she would certainly have hesitated ere she made the proposal she did.

As it was, she kindly and thoughtfully considered that Jabez had no good parental home to return to; that she had no other use for the rooms he occupied, so she proposed to him that he should continue to occupy them whilst he thought fit, since he had elected to remain in their service.

He had already looked at lodgings in Charlotte Street, close at hand; but this unexpected proposal came like a reprieve to an exile, and he was as prompt in his acceptance as he had been in that previous decision which had so thoroughly swamped all Mr. Chadwick's plans for his advancement. His eager "Oh, madam, you cannot mean it! You overwhelm me with kindness. Remain under this roof! It is a privilege I had not anticipated, and I shall be proud to embrace it!" sent Mrs. Ashton away well pleased.

It was doubly satisfactory to find the comforts of their home appreciated after seven years' experience, and to be able to refute Mr. Ashton's theory that "all young men like to shake a loose leg, and Jabez would be too glad to escape from grumbling Kezia's jurisdiction to accept the offer."

Mr. Ashton, however, did not abandon the opinion he had formed. "I'll wager my gold snuff-box against a button-mould," asserted he, "that Clegg only said 'Yes' because gratitude would not let him say 'Nay!' It's not likely a young man would care to be always under the eyes of a master or mistress, however steady he may be."

Ah, but neither Mr. nor Mrs. Ashton knew there was a magnet under their roof, stronger than all the ordinary inducements which might otherwise have drawn him away—and perhaps it was as well for him they did not.

Simon, who was present at the time, seemed literally overpowered with gratitude for all the good which was falling into the lap of the child of his adoption. He, however, took his own views of the matter, views not calculated to puff Jabez up in his own esteem, and when Mrs. Ashton was gone he broke out—

"Eh, Jabez, lad! but thah's lit on thi feet! Thah's bin a good lad, aw reckon, an' thah's sarved thi master gradely; but thah sees many a lad does that as never gets a lift such as thah's getten. An' aw canno' but thenk it o' comes o' that prayer o' thy Israelite namesake, as aw towt thee when thou were no bigger than sixpenn'orth o' copper. Yo' hanna furgetten it, aw hope?"

No, Jabez had not forgotten it! It would be strange if he had. Nay, only that morning, in the flush of success he had carried from the counting-house, with the buoyant presumption of youth, a conviction that it was not so much a prayer as a prophecy nearing fulfilment.

Simon brought his soaring pinions down from their Icarian flight.

"Well, lad, it may be 'the Lord has enlarged thi coast,' but if so be He han, thah sees theer's moore room fur thee to slip as well as to stond, and theer's moore rayson whoi thah shouldn be thenkful and humble! for the big book says, 'Let him that stondeth tak' heed lest he fall,' an' aw shouldna loike t' see thi young yead torned wi proide."

His lecture was somewhat of a cold shower-bath to Jabez in his hour of triumph, but no doubt it was salutary in its ultimate effects. At all events, it kept the vaulting ambition of the new man a little in check.

People—especially work-people—then observed early hours. At seven o'clock the outcome supper was on the tables at the "Concert Hall Tavern;" and the elder apprentices, and all such of the workmen as were absolutely engaged on the premises, were there to partake when Jabez found old Simon a seat, himself taking the head of the table, with the two senior apprentices on his right hand and left.

The cost of such suppers usually fell on the apprentice, but sometimes, as in this case, the master added his quota. If plain, the provision was substantial and ample. Rounds of beef and legs of mutton, piles of floury potatoes, and red cones of carrot on pale beds of mashed turnip, smoked on the board, and the two-pronged forks and horn-hafted knives were flanked with earthenware jugs and horns of ale.

It was the first essay of Jabez in the art of carving, and no doubt he made rather an unskilled president. But in the then condition of the lower classes a large joint of meat was a rare sight to a working-man, and so he cut away with no fear of critics. Amidst the rattle of cutlery and crockery, and the rapid play of jaws, beef and mutton disappeared, and were succeeded by a tremendous plum-pudding—the contribution of old Mrs. Clowes—and half a cheese, which came to the table in the then common japanned receptacle locally known as a cheese-biggin.

Appetite and the viands fled together, the noise of tongues succeeded to the noise of knives and forks, and Lancashire humour vented itself in jest and repartee, sometimes coarse, but seldom mischievous. Old Simon enjoyed it immensely. It seemed like a renewal of his own youth.

It was not, however, until the supper-table was cleared that the chief ceremonial of the evening took place. Then an arm-chair was mounted upon the table, in which Jabez was enthroned, the two eldest apprentices standing also on the table on either hand as supporters. An immense bowl of steaming punch was brought in, which was held over the head of Jabez by the one apprentice (when he was said to be crowned), whilst the other, wielding the punch-ladle as a symbol of authority, with many a theatrical grimace, began to ladle the odorous compound into the glasses of the guests; and the head overlooker of the manufactory, from the opposite end of the table, prepared to propose the health of the late apprentice, as a new member of their craft.

At this juncture in walked their master, Mr. Ashton, closely followed by Mr. Chadwick, leaning on the arm of the Rev.

Joshua Brookes, who with many a "pish" and "pshaw!" and "pooh!" had professed to come reluctantly "to see a sensible lad make a fool of himself." Their entrance, and the volley of cheers which greeted it, made a momentary pause in the proceedings. Then Mr. Ashton, being duly supplied with a ladleful of punch, took his overlooker's place, and, the glass serving as a substitute for his snuff-box, he proposed and drank "Mr. Clegg's health and prosperity," and welcomed him among the confraternity of small-ware weavers.

This was succeeded by a prolonged cheer, and then, as one by one each man's glass was filled, ere he touched it with his lips he sang separately (with whatsoever voice he might happen to have, musical or otherwise) the following toast to proclaim the released apprentice a freeman of the trade, the chorus being taken up afresh after every repetition of the quatrain:—

Here's a health to he that's now set free.
  That once was a 'prentice bound,
And for his sake this merriment we make,
  So let his health go round;
Go round, go round, go round, brave boys,
  Until it comes to me;
For the longer we sit here and drink,
  The merrier we shall be.
    Chorus—Go round, go round, &c.

Mr. Ashton had ordered up another bowl of punch, and that being distributed with like ceremony over the new small-ware monarch's head, Jabez, from his temporary throne, with all the warmth of freshly-stimulated gratitude, delivered a very genuine oration on the excellence of the master then present, and proposed, as a toast, "Mr. and Mrs. Ashton, our worthy and esteemed master and mistress."

Nowadays I'm afraid the master would have been dubbed a "governor," and the mistress ignored altogether; but, though it is only fifty-five years since, servants were not ashamed to own they had masters and mistresses, and, consequently, were not above being amenable to rule.

During this digression, at a hint from someone (I believe old Simon), Jabez, whose eloquence must surely have come from the punch-bowl, dilated on the spiritual relation between the reverend chaplain and the party assembled, there being scarcely an individual present who had not been either baptised or married by the Rev. Joshua Brookes; and he wished "health and long life to him" with much sincerity.

A general shout rose in response, but Joshua made no other reply than to turn on his heel (the better to hide his face), and growl out, "Long life, indeed! Ugh! pack of tomfoolery!" as he hurried from the room, before either Mr. Ashton or his paralysed brother-in-law could follow. Yet, in spite of his gruff disclaimer, he added another bowl of punch to the "tomfoolery"—at least, one was brought in soon after, and no one there was called upon to pay for it.

Relieved from the restraining presence of the gentlemen, tongues wagged freely, long pipes were introduced, song, jest, and toast succeeded each other, and, as the fun grew and the smoke thickened, they mingled confusedly, until at length clear-headed Simon drew his arm through that of the novice, and, watching his opportunity, led him unnoticed into the open air, with his head spinning like a teetotum.

Jabez awakened the next morning with a terrible headache, and a dim recollection of having encountered stately Mrs. Ashton in the hall overnight, when the very statues had seemed to shake their heads at him, and her mild, "Fie, Jabez!" followed him upstairs, apparently carpeted with moss or indiarubber for the nonce. It was his first dissipation, *and his last.* He never forgot it. And if anything was wanting to destroy the germs of self-sufficiency and elation, it was found in the consciousness of his own frailty, and the sense of shame and self-reproach it engendered.

Experienced heads knew that the surrounding fumes of liquor and tobacco had been more potential than the small quantity of punch he had imbibed. But he did not know it, and by the hail-fellow-well-metishness of those workmen who were most inclined at all times to keep Saint-Monday, and who came to their work, or stayed from their work, unfit for their work, was a sensitive chord of his nature struck, far more than by the quiet caution of Simon, the light badinage of Mr. Ashton, or the jeers of captious Kezia.

In making light of it, Jabez felt they made light of him, and he was long after afraid lest those whose opinion he held in esteem should make light of him also—Augusta Ashton chief of these.

CHAPTER THE TWENTY-NINTH.

ON ARDWICK GREEN POND.

IT was in vain Madame Broadbent waited on Mrs. and Mr. Ashton and solicited Miss Ashton's return to her establishment on her ultimate recovery. The pupil was not more shudderingly reluctant to be replaced under her despotic rule than the parents were peremptory in their refusal.

When her plea for the "maintenance of discipline" failed, and she tried cajolery as ineffectually, she gave way to the expression of her natural fears that it would "be the ruin of the Academy" if Mr. Ashton did not reverse his decision. He loved his daughter too well to yield, and Mrs. Broadbent went back to Bradshaw Street to find, as years rolled on, that she had been a true prophetess.

The injury done to Miss Ashton's collar-bone had been bruited about, and slowly but surely it helped to sap the foundation of the once-flourishing seminary. It continued to exist for some years, but its prestige was gone, its glory departed. Yet she maintained her personal importance to the last, and exhibited her flock in the "lower boxes" of the Theatre Royal on Mrs. M'Gibbon's benefit nights with undiminished dignity through successive seasons.

The rapidly-ripening young lady had her will; she had done with the schoolroom for ever, and her lessons on the harp from Mr. Horobin, and on the piano from George Ware, the leader of the Gentlemen's Concerts, came under quite another category. Nor did she think it beneath her aspirations to retain her place in Mrs. Bland's fashionable dancing-room, where she practised cotillons, quadrilles, and the newly-imported waltz, with partners on a par with herself. But these were *accomplishments*, and we all know, or ought to know by this time, that accomplishments require much more prolonged and arduous application than the merely useful and essential branches of knowledge, theorists for the higher education of women notwithstanding.

Miss Augusta was desirous to be captivating and shine in society, and so proud was Mr. Ashton of his beautiful daughter that he fell in readily with the expansive views of the incipient belle, and new steps or new melodies were paraded for his gratification week by week. But Mrs. Ashton, telling her daughter that "knowledge was light of carriage," sent her to Mr. Mabbott's to take lessons in cookery and confectionery, and into the kitchen to put them in practice under the eye of Kezia; and, exercise being good for health, according to the same sensible mother, she was required to assist in bed-making, furniture polishing, dusting, and general household matters, for which the young lady had little liking, and was not to be spurred into liking by any citation of her cousin Ellen's qualifications in these respects. She preferred to dress with all the art at her command to make her beauty more bewildering, and to take her place at harp or piano, or embroidery frame, ready to receive visitors either with or without her mother, and to be as fascinating as possible, especially when Laurence Aspinall was the caller; or she would sit in déshabillé in the retirement of her own chamber and read Moore and Byron because they were tabooed, and the handsome lieutenant quoted them so enchantingly, whilst Cicily, who had something to answer for in this respect, bustled about and overworked herself to spare her darling Miss Augusta, who, with all her faults, must have been a loving and lovable creature to win such devotion from a dependent.

It happened that the young lady received visitors alone more frequently than was desirable, Mrs. Ashton being usually tied to the warehouse in consequence of the interest Mr. Ashton took in the establishment of the Manchester Chamber of Commerce and in the project for the widening of Market Street and other of the cramped thoroughfares of the growing town, which necessarily took him much from home and his private business, to say nothing of the excitement consequent on the trial of Queen Caroline during its long progress.

But the year 1820, which had opened only to close the long volume of George the Third's life, and to open that of George the Fourth's reign at a chapter of regal wife persecution which has few parallels, had itself grown old and died, and 1821 had thrust itself prominently forward.

It came with a white robe and a frost-bitten countenance, which grew sharper and more pinched as weeks and months went by. It looked down on the currents of rivers and canals, on the secluded still waters of Strangeways Park, the oblong pond in front of the Infirmary, and the leech-shaped lakelet within the area of Ardwick Green, until their ripples curdled under the chilling glance of the New Year.

Sterner grew its aspect as the shivering weeks counted themselves into months, and the shrinking waters spread first a thin film, then a thick and a thicker barrier of ice between them and the freezing atmosphere. Every gutter had its slide, along which clattering clogs sped noiselessly; every pool its vociferous throng of boys, and every pond its mingled concourse of skaters and sliders. Of these, the Infirmary and Ardwick Green waters were most patronised; the former having the more numerous, the latter having the more select body of skaters, and consequently the more fashionable surrounding of spectators.

The amusements of the town were then on so limited and exclusive a scale that long frost was quite a boon to the younger portion of the community; and during the sixteen weeks of its continuance, the Green became a promenade gay with the warm hues of feminine attire, as ladies flocked to witness and extol the feats of husbands, brothers, cousins, or particular friends. There was no fear of vulgar overcrowding (except on Sundays); working-hours were long, and there were no Saturday half-holidays, so that only those whose time was at their own disposal could share the sport or overlook it.

Amongst these, much to the annoyance of Mr. Aspinall, his son Laurence chose to enrol himself, with less regard to the fluctuation of the cotton market, or the comparative value of

American or East Indian staples than the Cannon Street merchant thought necessary to fit him for his future partner or successor. The younger man had chosen to construe liberally the word "gentleman," which had been the be-all and end-all of his training, and to regard elegant idleness as its synonym. What availed his fine figure and proficiency in arts and athletics, if he had no opportunity for the display of his person or his skill? And to throw away the rare chance the winter had provided was clearly to scorn the gift of the gods.

Accordingly he spent more time on Ardwick Green Pond than in the counting-house, varied occasionally with a visit to the Assembly Billiard-room in Back Mosley Street, or a morning promenade in the Infirmary Gardens, from the open gates of which he generally contrived to emerge as Miss Ashton descended the steps from Mr. Mabbott's, and just in time to hand her courteously and daintily across the roadway, and bear her company to her own door, discoursing of recent assemblies or concerts, from the former of which she had hitherto been debarred, and of the last occasion on which he had the "exquisite pleasure of seeing her at Ardwick Green"—occasions which were seldom reported at home, any more than the chance meetings on her way from Mr. Mabbott's; and the reticence, be sure, boded no good.

Dr. Hull had long ago advised "out-door exercise" for the rapidly-growing girl, and there was no embargo on her walks abroad, Mrs. Ashton suspecting no danger, and no surreptitious meetings. Her visits to the Green during the long skating season were quite as unrestrained, except that an escort became a necessity. Occasionally her mother accompanied her, sometimes Mrs. Walmsley and John (then there was generally a nurse and baby in the rear), sometimes Ellen and Mrs. Chadwick; and Augusta had always returned so exhilarated by her country walk, and so delighted with all she had seen, that once or twice, when imperative business withheld Mrs. Ashton from bearing her daughter company, as promised, rather than disappoint, the lady had made Mr. Clegg her deputy, an honour on which he perhaps set far too high a value.

Mrs. Ashton would have drawn herself up with double dignity, and repudiated as an insult the suggestion of any other of their salesmen or clerks as an escort for her beautiful daughter; but Jabez lived in the house, had lived there so long, had even from her childhood been the girl's frequent guardian, and proved himself so worthy of the trust, that she committed her to his care now much as of old, and perhaps all the more readily because she saw, or fancied she saw, a disinclination on Miss Augusta's part to be so accompanied.

In March the cold was as intense as in January, and Miss Ashton as eager to watch the skaters. One afternoon towards the close of the month, when the breaking-up of the frost was anticipated, quite a family party had gone to the Green, wrapped n fur-trimmed pelisses of velvet or woollen, with fur-rimmed hats and Brobdignagian muffs.

It was not yet closing time when Mr. Ashton, always disposed to be friendly with Jabez, accosted him.

"The ladies are gone to the Green, Clegg. Suppose you lend me an arm along the slippery roads, and we go to meet them, eh?"

The sparkling eyes of Jabez confirmed his ready tongue's "With pleasure, sir," as, sensible of the honour done him, he left the sale-room, whistled his black friend Nelson from the yard, and they set off at a brisk pace, to keep the blood in circulation, the dog leaping, bounding, and barking before them, in token of good fellowship. As they passed the Infirmary pond, Jabez remarked that the ice began to look watery, to which Mr. Ashton replied,

"Yes; I think Jack Frost's long visit is near its end, and there must be some truth in the old saw that 'a thaw is colder than a frost.'"

At that moment Mr. Aspinall's carriage rolled past them, bearing the merchant homewards in distinguished state (private carriages were by no means common), whereat Mr. Ashton observed with a shrug,

"How pride punishes itself! Fancy a tall fellow like Mr. Aspinall cramped up in a stifling box upon wheels on a day like this, when he has the free use of his limbs!"

Contrary to expectation, they did not come in sight of the ladies until they gained the Green, which they found a scene of wild hubbub and commotion; skaters and spectators gathering towards the centre of the Green, whence came a confused noise of voices, shouting, crying, and screaming.

The quick eye of Jabez was at once arrested by the figure of Augusta on the opposite bank, the centre of an appalled group, wringing her hands in the very impotence of terror, and as he penetrated the excited crowd, he saw the hatless head of a man, whose body was submerged, resting with its chin upon a ledge of the ice, which had apparently broken under him. At the first glance he failed to distinguish the head from the distance, and rushed forward, apprehensive lest it should be that of either Mr. Walmsley or his friend Travis, whom he knew to be of the party.

Recognition came, accompanied by a shock that staggered him. If the ice had attractions for Aspinall and Walmsley, Ellen Chadwick had certainly as great attractions for Ben Travis; but it is certain that neither cousins, nor mother, nor aunt were sensible that they had been drawn thither simply as a sort of decorous train to Miss Augusta Ashton, whose inspiriting had in turn been the fascinating lieutenant, the most graceful and accomplished skater on the pond. Perhaps she hardly knew it herself, not being given to searching her own heart for its motives. But a hint from him had set her longing for "another sight of the skating before the chance was gone," and her imperative will no less than her persuasive voice had swayed the rest.

Laurence had made the most of the occasion, glad of an opportunity to cultivate the acquaintance of the whole family, and display his graceful figure, and his skill to the best advantage. Now and then he joined the Chadwicks and the Ashtons on

ON ARDWICK GREEN POND.

the bank, anon darted off, wheeling hither and thither, so swift in his evolutions, the eye could scarcely follow him.

Amongst the skaters the man and his feats stood out. He was the observed of all observers, and not vainer was he of his accomplishments than was Augusta at being singled out for attention in the face of so many damsels of his acquaintance, all, as she foolishly supposed, equally desirous to bask in the sun of his smile.

A small match will kindle a large flame if combustibles be there. Fired by her too apparent satisfaction, and Mrs. Ashton's presence, his excessive vanity induced him to perform what, with the imperfect skates of the period, was a distinguished feat. He was ordinarily proud of his calligraphy. Now, he wound and twisted, lifted his skates or dashed them down, until he had scored upon the ice an alphabet in bold capitals; but whether he had miscalculated his space, or the strength of the ice—broken into for the use of cattle at the upper end—or the crowd of inquisitive or envious followers had been too great for its resistance, as he made the last curl of the letter Z, the ice gave way, and he was plunged in up to the neck, amid the shrieks of women and the shouts of men. His chin had caught upon the ice with a stunning blow; but it rested there, and, aided by the buoyancy of the water beneath, upheld him until, with returning sense, he struggled to bring his shoulders above the surface, and upheave himself. He trod the water, and it sustained him, but the *ice* would not. He was forced to content himself with the use of his hands beneath as paddles, to relieve the pressure on his chin, and wait for help, which seemed an eternity in coming.

He had been in the water some time when Jabez and Mr. Ashton appeared on the scene, amongst women shrieking with affright, and men rushing about without presence of mind, or paralysed to powerlessness. Mr. Travis alone appeared to have a thought, and he had sent for ropes and hatchets to cut a way to him through the ice itself. But there was a question, would his strength hold out?

"Will no one save him? Will no one save him?" cried Augusta, piteously.

"Fifty pounds to him who will save my son!" was the cry of the frantic father, who had witnessed the accident from his own carriage window. "A hundred!—two hundred pounds!—five hundred pounds to anyone who will save him!"

"It's noan a bit o' use, measter," said a working man, with a shake of his head. "Men wunna chuck their lives aweay fur brass; an' yon ice is loike a pane o' glass wi' a stone through it."

Unfortunately, impulsive Ben Travis had darted forward to his rescue at the outset, and his ponderous weight had cracked the already broken ice in all directions. He had himself retreated with difficulty; and now no offers of reward would tempt men to put their own lives in peril, though Kit Townley was there, urging others to the attempt, and Bob, the ex-groom, had rushed for ropes they had neither pluck nor skill to use, since a noosed cord, flung like a lasso, would have strangled him.

"Oh! save him; save him, Jabez!" implored Augusta, as he and her father came up.

Jabez looked at her strangely. His head seemed to spin. His face went livid as that on the ice. Had his secret devotion no other end than this? True, she had called him "Jabez," but so she had called him in his servitude. She had appealed to him as one she trusted in implicitly; but the appeal sounded as made for one she loved, and that was not himself, but he who, as boy and man, had wounded him in soul and body. The very tone of her cry was as a knell to his hopes and himself. It was his foe and his rival who was perishing! Was he called upon to risk his life to warm a serpent to sting him again? The conflict in his breast was sharp and terrible. "If thine enemy hunger, give him food," seemed to float in his ears.

There was a small gloved hand on his arm, a pale, sweet face looking up into his. The moments were flying fast.

"Oh! Jabez, Jabez, do try!"

"I will," said he, hoarsely.

Had he not often declared in his secret heart that he would give his life to serve her?—and should he be ungenerous enough to shrink now?

"It is folly to attempt. I forbid it!" exclaimed Mrs. Ashton, laying her hand on his arm. And Ellen Chadwick, pale as Augusta, tried to stop him with—"You must not! you must not! You will perish!"

Even strangers from the crowd warned him back. But he was gone ere Mrs. Chadwick softly recalled her daughter to herself. "Hush, Ellen! This is not seemly. Mr. Clegg will attempt nothing impossible."

He hurried to the side nearest Laurence; called to him, "Keep up; help is coming!"—asked for ladders; gave a word or two of instruction to Mr. Ashton and Travis; sent Nelson on the ice to try its strength; secured a rope round his own waist; then, lying flat on the cold ice, cautiously felt his way to the farther side of Aspinall, whose eyes were closed, and whose strength was ebbing fast. He hardly heard the words of cheer addressed to him."

Two long ladders had been lashed side by side to give breadth of surface. These, by the help of cords and Nelson, whose sagacity was akin to reason, he drew across the cracked and gaping ice; and crept slowly from rung to rung, watched from the land breathlessly, until he reached his almost insensible rival. With rapidly benumbing fingers he secured strong ropes beneath each shoulder, sending Nelson back to the bank with the main line, in case his own strength was insufficient to lift the dead weight of Laurence, or that the ice should yield beneath the double weight.

Someone sent a brandy-flask back by the dog.

"Can you swallow?" he asked. There was no answer, but a gurgle.

He moistened the blue lips, while the head bent slightly back, introduced a small quantity of the potent spirit between his set teeth; and, having warmed himself by the same means, essayed to lift the freezing skater, who was almost powerless to aid. But the latter with an extreme effort raised an arm above the ice, and grasped recumbent Jabez. And now Nelson proved his worth. He set his teeth in Aspinall's high coat-collar, and tugged until their united strength drew him upwards and across the ladder sledge, almost as stiff and helpless as a corpse.

To lessen the weight, Jabez crept from the ladders; they were drawn to the side with their living freight before he himself was out of danger; for the heavy pressure and the swift motion set the ice cracking under him, and with extreme difficulty he dragged himself to the bank to sink down on the hardened snow, overcome by the strain of mind and muscle, whilst the approving crowd set up a shout, and Augusta Ashton thanked him tremulously.

"I'm afraid, Clegg, you've spent your strength for a dead man," said Travis, grasping his hand warmly, "and Aspinall was scarcely worth it, alive or dead."

But Jabez made no reply. He rose slowly and painfully, shook off the congratulatory crowd of strangers and friends on the plea of needing to "warm and dry himself," refused point blank to accept the grateful hospitality of Mr. Aspinall, and, taking the proffered arm of Travis, turned towards the "George and Dragon," as little like one who had done a noble action as could be imagined.

Mr. Ashton followed, tapping his gold snuff-box in wonder and perplexity. He saw that something was wrong, but knew not that Augusta's hasty thanks had closed the young man's heart against all but its own pain.

CHAPTER THE THIRTIETH.

BLIND!

SO white, so cold, so still was the rigid figure borne from the pond to Mr. Aspinall's house, Travis might well count him "a dead man," as the rumour ran concerning him, and feeble old Kitty sent up a lamentation as over the dead.

Mrs. Ashton, who knew that to be a home without a thinking woman at its head, volunteered her services, and entered the house with the bearers, leaving the trembling Augusta with their friends. She gently put the old woman aside, and felt pulse and heart.

"There is life," said she, "and while there is life there is hope. Keep tears until there is time to shed them; now we must act." Then, turning to the scared and scurrying servants, she gave her orders much as though she had been in her own warehouse, and with a stately authority there was no disputing.

The butler was bidden to "bring brandy, quick!" The footman was required to "wheel this sofa to the fire and pile up the coals!" A maid was asked for "hot blankets without delay!" and moaning Kitty was set to work to "help to strip her young master and chafe his limbs." And so promptly were her clear, cool orders obeyed, that when the doctor arrived in hot haste with Mr. Aspinall, half his work was done. The pulse had quickened and the limbs began to glow, though the eyelids remained closed.

Most grateful then was Mr. Aspinall for the efficient matronly service rendered to his motherless boy by the stately lady, who was drawn nearer to him in his helplessness by her own kindly act than by all the conciliatory visits and peace-offerings with which Laurence had himself sought to propitiate her. And for *once* Mr. Aspinall accepted a kindness as a favour, not as a tribute to his personal importance, and he placed his carriage at the disposal of Mr. Ashton and herself for their return home without a sign of his usual self-inflation.

His importance received a considerable shock, however, when

he called at the house in Mosley Street the following day to report progress, and relieve himself of his obligation to his son's preserver by paying over the five hundred pounds he had in his extremity offered as a reward.

"I do not think Mr. Clegg will accept a reward," said Mr. and Mrs. Ashton in a breath.

"Not accept it!" and the portly figure seemed to swell! "five hundred pounds is a large sum for a young man in his position; only a fool or a madman would refuse it."

"Just so, just so," replied Mr. Ashton, offering his open snuff-box to his visitor, whilst Mrs. Ashton stirred the fire as a sort of dubious disclaimer; "but I think, for all that, you will find we are right; Mr. Clegg is not a common man, and is not actuated by common motives.—My dear?" He nodded, and Mrs. Ashton pulled the bell-rope.

Mulberry-suited James answered on the instant.

"Mr. Clegg is wanted."

Mr. Clegg, labouring under the disadvantage of a cold caught the previous afternoon, to which any huskiness of voice might be attributed, obeyed the summons. He was presented duly to Mr. Aspinall, and much to that gentleman's surprise, was invited to take a seat.

"Absolutely invited to take a seat;" as he afterwards recounted in indignation to a friend; "these Whigs have no respect for a gentleman's feelings."

Nor had Jabez. He was pale enough when he entered, but his face flushed, his lips compressed, and the scar on his brow showed vividly, as Mr. Aspinall drew forth a roll of crisp bank-notes from his pocket-book, and loftily offered to him the reward he had "earned by his bravery."

He flushed, put back the notes with a movement of his hand, and said, coldly: "You owe me nothing, sir. The meanest creature on God's earth should have freely such service as I rendered to your son. I cannot set a price on life."

But I offered the reward, and the fact is, I must discharge

the debt. Reconsider, young man, it is a large sum; many a man starts the world with less."

"A large sum to pay for your son's life, or for mine, sir?" interrogated Jabez, drawing himself up stiffly; adding, without waiting for reply, "I do not sell such service, sir. You owe me nothing. Let your son thank Miss Ashton for his life; he is her debtor, not mine."

The words seemed to rasp over a nutmeg-grater, they came so hoarsely, as did his request for leave to withdraw; and he closed the door on the five hundred pounds, and on the smiles of husband and wife, before the rebuffed cotton merchant could master his indignation to reply.

The notes in his palm were light enough, but lying there they represented liberality contemned; a debt unpaid; an undischarged obligation to an inferior; and not thrice their value in gold could have pressed so heavily on Mr. Aspinall as that last consideration. The frigid manner of Jabez he construed into Radical impudence; he resented the salesman's repudiation of reward as a personal affront, and did not scruple to express his views openly, then and there, winding up with a question which startled his interlocutors.

"What did the singular young man mean by his reference to Miss Ashton?"

Had they followed the "singular young man" across the hall to the sanctuary of his own sitting-room, seen him dash himselt down into a chair, and bury his head in his hands on the table with unutterable anguish on his face, and heard burst from his lips—more as a groan than embodied thought—"Oh, Augusta, adored Augusta, what a presumptuous madman I have been!" —they would but have had half the answer. But had they mounted the polished oaken stairs to the dainty chamber where Augusta Ashton lay in bed with a "cruel headache," brought on by the fright, and eyes red with weeping at the catastrophe which had befallen her adorable admirer, the gallant lieutenant, and heard her half-audible lamentations, the answer might have been complete.

Mrs. Ashton had heard Augusta's frantic appeal to Jabez at the pond, had seen him stagger and turn livid as if shot, noted the inward struggle ere he said, "I will;" but she had ascribed it to old and unforgiven injuries, and thinking it hard that he should be called upon to hazard his life for his known enemy with chances so heavy against him, had herself forbidden the attempt. This was all the solution she had to offer Mr. Aspinall. In the excitement of the accident and the rescue, she had overlooked Augusta's excessive emotion, but now her mother's heart took alarm. Could it be that the younger eyes of Jabez had seen a preference for the handsome scapegrace which she had not?

The matter was talked over by husband and wife long after Mr. Aspinall had left; and the anxious mother questioned the maiden in the privacy of her own room, to come thence with the sad conviction that Augusta had prematurely been led captive by a handsome face and a dashing air, irrespective of worth or worthlessness. Yet she consoled herself and Mr. Ashton with the reflection, "It is, after all, only a girlish fancy, and will die out."

"Just so, and as the young rake is laid by the leg for one while, there is all the more chance," assented Mr. Ashton.

"If his immersion does not convert him into a hero," added the matron, with a clearer knowledge of her daughter. Yet neither asked themselves how the intuitive perception of Jabez came to be more acute than their own, nor what power impelled him to risk his life for an enemy at the mere bidding of Augusta. Indeed, they set the hazardous exploit down to the score of magnanimity and bravery only.

Equally unobservant were they of Ellen Chadwick's remonstrance, or her feverish watch of every perilous turn Jabez and Nelson had taken on the ice, or of the caresses she lavished on the dog when all was over. Only Mrs. Chadwick had seen that, as she had seen fainter signs years before; but she held her peace, and, having a leaven of her sister's pride, "hôped she was mistaken."

There were three young hearts consumed by the same passion—

that which lies at the root of the happiness or misery of the world, —one nursing the romance, two fighting against its hopelessness in silence and concealment; but "the race is not always to the swift, nor the battle to the strong."

Jabez Clegg could not tell when he had not loved Augusta Ashton, from the time when she was young enough to play about the ware-rooms, or to be lifted across the muddy roadways in his strong apprentice arms, when it was his pleasant duty to protect her to and from school. But he could trace back the time when Hogarth's prints gave to that love a definite shape, and he began to look upon his master's daughter as a prize to be attained. All things had tended to confirm his belief in its possibility, and love and ambition had gone hand in hand, and fed each other. The child had come to him for companionship and entertainment, the girl under his protection had confided to him her school-day troubles, and come to him for help in difficulties, with lessons on slate or book. She had looked up to him, trusted him, clung to him; and though she was as a star in his firmament, he had had a sort of vague impression that the star which shone upon him from afar would draw nearer, and, as he rose to it, come down to meet him.

His first sharp awakening was her reminder that the pair of intoxicated officers who had insulted her in the theatre were "gentlemen," and so not to be chastised by *him*. His second—and then jealousy added a sting—was meeting Aspinall face to face in the hall, when the latter smilingly bowed himself out on his first visit. And now he brooded in despair over the final dissipation of his dream beneath the icicle-hung boughs on Ardwick Green; for the first time conscious that she belonged to another sphere.

Never by look or word had he done himself, or her, or her parents, the dishonour of giving expression to his ambitious love; and now another had looked on his divinity, and won he for himself. It came upon him like a flash when that white-faced agony, that piteous cry, called him to imperil his own life,

—worthless in the scale against another, and *that* other. It came upon him with a flash that scathed like lightning. He had forgiven the boy Aspinall long ago; and the man—well, Augusta's happiness demanded the sacrifice, and he had made it. Out of his very love for Augusta he had saved the rival's life she had prayed for. And he had been offered *money* for the act which wrecked his own life. Thank God he had rejected it with scorn!

A kind hand laid on his shoulder interrupted a reverie which had induced torpor.

"Mr. Clegg, you are ill—your cold requires attention. You had better seek repose: you are quite feverish."

Repose! The man's soul was on fire, as well as his body. Yet from his chamber a fortnight later emerged a grave business man, without an apparent thought beyond the warehouse.

And what of Laurence Aspinall, whom we left with closed eyes, wrapped in blankets, on a sofa? He had hung suspended in the water for an hour by the clock in the tower of St. Thomas' ivy-clad church; and, notwithstanding he had kept his limbs and the water in motion so long as he had power, the chill had extended upwards, and though life had been called back, sight and reason were in abeyance.

Shorn of his rich curls, for weeks he raved and struggled in the grasp of brain fever; and old Kitty, forgetting everything but her promise to his dead mother, watched and tended him night and day, albeit nurses from the Fever-Ward relieved each other in their well-paid care of him.

The frost was gone; vegetation, bound so long, had leapt upwards from its chains. Lilacs and may buds greeted him with perfume through the open windows, and even the daffodil and narcissus sent up their incense from the brim of the garden pond when he began to show signs of amendment.

"Better," "Much better," were the answers to inquirers (among whom may be cited Kit Townley, and Bob, their sometime groom); but the lilac and the hawthorn ripened and faded, and the daffodils gave place to the wallflower and carnation, and the rosebuds opened their ripe lips to June, yet the rich cotton merchant's son saw nothing of the glow.

Over the blue eyes of Laurence the lids were closed, and not an oculist in the town had skill to open them. Dr. Hull, the consulting physician of the Eye Institution, and his surgical colleagues, Messrs. Wilson and Travers, had laid their heads together over a case peculiar in all its bearings, but the lids remained obstinately shut.

At length, when Hope had folded her drooping wings in despair, and Mr. Aspinall was borne down with grief for his sightless son, someone suggested that, as water had done the mischief, water in action might cure it.

"Can he swim?" asked rough Dr. Hull curtly of Kitty.

"Swim? ay, he can do owt he shouldna do," replied the old woman, having no faith in the value of her charge's peculiar accomplishments.

"Is he a good swimmer?"

"Aw reckon so! He used to swim fur wagers i' Ardy (Ardwick) Green Pond when he wur quoite a little chap."

"That will do."

Mr. Aspinall was conferred with, and the next day's mail coach took the blind patient, his father, Kitty, and one of the surgeons to Liverpool. After a night's rest at the York Hotel, they were driven down to St. George's Pier, a very humble presentment of what it is in this our day. Like Manchester, Liverpool has vastly swelled in size and importance within the last fifty years, and her docks have grown with the shipping needing shelter. The Mersey was not the crowded highway it is now—there were fewer ships and *no* steamers to cross each other's track, and set the waters in commotion, defying wind and tide.

Mr. Aspinall had engaged a boat to be in readiness. The sightless athlete was rowed a short distance from curious spectators on the pier, and then, his face being turned towards Birkenhead, he plunged into the swelling river, which he breasted like a Triton, so welcome and native seemed the element to him. And as the salt wave buoyed him up, or dashed over his cropped head, he appeared to gain fresh strength with every stroke.

Anxiously his three attendants followed in his wake, lest cramp should seize him, or his impaired strength give out before the river—there rather more than a mile in breadth—could be crossed. Yet not a yard of the distance bated he.

By instruction he had bent his course slightly down stream, so as to meet the opposing tide, then rolling in with a freshet. He struck out boldly, the very dash of the salt waves invigorating him as they broke over his bare poll, or laved his naked limbs. Still well in advance of the boat, he seemed at last to cross the current as a conqueror. He touched the shore at Rock Ferry, and—miracle of miracles!—his eyes were opened. Laurence Aspinall, who for weeks had cursed his darkened existence, could once more see!

CHAPTER THE THIRTY-FIRST.

CORONATION DAY.

MISFORTUNE binds closer than prosperity. The calamity which tied Laurence Aspinall down in a strait-waistcoat to a bed of fever, with shaven head and sightless eyes, touched the Ashtons in a tender point. Themselves the parents of an only child, the very crown and glory of their lives, their sympathies went forth to Mr. Aspinall in spite of his haughty assumption. Indeed, distress brought him down to the common level of humanity, and having neither sister, aunt, nor cousin to undertake the care of his sick son for love, and not for fee, he learned the comparative powerlessness of wealth, and hailed with all the gratitude in his nature the occasional visits of Mrs. Ashton, in whose stately bearing, no doubt, he recognised a sort of kinship.

It was, however, not Mrs. Ashton the business woman, not Mrs. Ashton the lofty lady, but Mrs. Ashton the mother who laid her cool hand on the young man's fevered forehead, questioned the nurses, made suggestions for the benefit of the invalid, and by means of a "Ladies' Free Registry" in Chapel Walk, found a staid woman of experience to act as housekeeper and bring the disorganised household into order without treading on the toes of attached but incapable Kitty.

The head of Antinous shorn of its glorious locks, swathed in lotion-cloths, tossing in delirium, would scarcely appear so attractive as to fill the most timid mother with fears for a romantic daughter's heart, and so, whilst sympathy was awake, vigilance slumbered. Yet never need vigilance have been more awake. She saw him as he was—Augusta, as he had been. Through other channels than the maternal she heard of his condition from day to day, and how in his delirium he had mixed up her name with the slang of the cock-pit, the race-course, and the prize-ring; but with strange infatuation she ignored all that should have warned, and clung to all that was pleasant to her own self-love. Never had she been so assiduous in her visits to her aunt Chadwick and her cousin Walmsley, and her smiling "I've brought my work and come to sit with you this afternoon," should have been translated, "I hope John or Mr. Travis will drop in. They are sure to have something to say about Mr. Laurence; it is so dreadful not to know how he is going on."

And pretty generally her calculations were correct. The two gentlemen were interested in Aspinall as a member of their yeomanry corps, apart from private friendship, and were constant in their inquiries, even finding their way to his bedside; and Mr. Benjamin Travis, who could not very well every day manage to meet Mr. Chadwick accidentally on his way from the warehouse and lend his stout arm as a support, appeared only too glad to be the bearer of bulletins from Ardwick as an excuse for calling in Oldham Street and hovering about the chair or the window where Ellen Chadwick sat at her sewing or knitting and grew silent on his entrance, blushing when she heard his footstep or his voice in the hall, from motives sadly misinterpreted.

There was no mistaking the true purport of his frequent visits and assiduous attention to the crippled old gentleman, so Augusta, having settled in her own mind that Ellen was either too reserved or too shy to give her big, good-natured, but timid lover proper encouragement, took upon herself to play into his hands and make opportunities for his wooing.

"What a delightful afternoon for a walk!" Whether he or she made the observation, the other was sure to assent, and then wilful Miss Augusta, unaccustomed to be gainsaid, and seconded by her aunt, also a secret ally of Ben Travis, would drag her cousin forth in defiance of any excuse or protestation, to the undisguised satisfaction of their magnificent cavalier.

It was remarkable that on these occasions, whether they took their way up Ancoats, or Dale Street, or Piccadilly, or Garret Road, they would eventually be led so near to Ardwick Green that it would have been unkind had not Mr. Travis "just stepped across to see how Mr. Laurence progressed."

And so, too, whenever she went abroad with Cicily at her

heels, or when Cicily was sent on errands, nothing would content her imperative young mistress but that she should hasten (whether in her way or out of it), with "*Mrs.* Ashton's compliments," to ascertain the condition of the invalid scapegrace.

Many a scolding did breathless Cicily get in consequence from angry Kezia, the queen of the kitchen, which Augusta paid her messenger for with coins, or ribbons, or kerchiefs, or smooth words, as might be most convenient at the time. And Mrs. Ashton was accredited by the Aspinalls with a degree of attention never contemplated by herself.

But there was one person in the house Augusta avoided from that afternoon at the end of March, when her fascinating hero would have lost his life but for a much humbler hero, of less pretension and fewer attractions. She might have been blind as father and mother to his attachment until that afternoon; but that one wild, impassioned, agonized look of Jabez into her eyes had opened them for ever: she felt she had tasked him beyond human endurance, and was ashamed to look him in the face.

The presumption of the ex-apprentice paled before his devotion and self-abnegation, but, self-conscious, after that first outburst of thanks on the Green, she had shrunk from meeting him in hall or on staircase, and had always a reason ready why he should not be invited to their own tea-table when father or mother proposed it.

Public events march on irrespective of private joys or sorrows, and no individual goes out into the world after three months' seclusion to find things just as he left them. The first use Laurence Aspinall made of his eyes was to look at himself in a mirror; the second, on his return to Manchester, to select a substitute for the clustering curls of which he had been despoiled. Closely shut in the carriage which Mr. Ashton had lightly designated a box, he was driven down Market Street, to discover that the Spirit of Improvement, "fell bane of all that's picturesque," had touched the ancient, many-gabled, black-and-white houses with which his earliest recollections were associated, and they were crumbling into dusty ruins before the potent incantation "Space."

It was the beginning of a very necessary widening of the main thoroughfares of the growing commercial metropolis; but the blanks in the narrow street took Laurence by surprise.

There was a newspaper the more for his restored sight to scan, albeit the *Manchester Guardian*, which Jeremiah Garnett and John Edward Taylor first gave to the world on the fifth of May, was scarcely likely to take his view of party politics, or of his share in the "Peterloo massacre," which was still a disturbing element in the town. Just now the paper, which he found at the perruquier's, was given over to the discussion of the approaching coronation of George IV., which likewise formed the theme of conversation, not only at the wig-maker's, but whithersoever he turned when once more presentable.

Somehow, though he found his way to the warehouse, and the Cockpit, and the Assembly Billiard Club, and to Tib Street, where Bob the groom had a pretty daughter very much at the young man's disposal, he did not present himself at his Mosley Street friend's as soon as might have been expected, considering all things; and Augusta, in the most becoming of morning robes, watching with eager expectation for his coming, began to pant and chill with the sickness of hope deferred. He was by no means the only admirer of the lovely heiress, and was sufficiently desirous to complete his conquest before other competitors were fairly in the field; but he was in perplexity how to deal with Jabez Clegg, who stood in his way after another sort. He was grateful—after a fashion—for the preservation of his life; but *ungrateful*, inasmuch as Jabez was the preserver.

"Hang it!" said he, in conference with himself, as he tied on a neck-cloth at the glass, "if the fellow had but taken the five hundred pounds, there'd have been an end of it; and one could have wiped one's hands of him. What right had the beggarly charity-boy to refuse a reward, as if he were a gentleman, I should like to know? I wonder what Kit Townley and Walmsley were about—the cowardly ninnies—to let an upstart like that pull me out of the hole. I'd almost as lief have been drowned."

And away went a spoiled cravat across the room in his temper, and he rummaged for a fresh one, to the detriment of linen, as he went on—

"There's one thing positive, I must either bring down my pride or give up the girl, and be d——d to it! That old Ashton, with his 'Just so!' like a cuckoo, would certainly shut the door in my face if I neglected to make a set speech and thank his precious *protegé*, who knocks you down with one hand and picks you up with the other. Well, I don't feel inclined to surrender the finest girl in Lancashire, and with such a fortune as she'll have, so I'm in for it. I must make a virtue of necessity. Egad! I'll write to this Mr. Clegg. No, I won't. It would be a feather in his cap to have a thanksgiving letter of mine to exhibit."

Having at length determined his course, Mr. Laurence betook himself to Mosley Street, made his bow duly and gracefully to Mrs. Ashton and the young lady, keeping the hand of the latter as long within his own as etiquette would permit, and sending the warm blood mantling to her cheek, with a supplicating glance of devotion as potent as words. Then, with some little prolixity, he professed his desire to "thank his noble preserver" for the life he had saved; and at his request Mr. Clegg (whom he might just as well have thanked in the warehouse without ceremony) was sent for. Coming into the parlour all unwittingly as he did, to find Laurence Aspinall, handsome as ever, and more interesting from illness, standing under the lacquered-serpent chandelier in close proximity to Augusta, sparkling with animation, and blushing like the rose he had just offered her with a pretty simile, his emotions so overmastered him that the polished gentleman had him at a disadvantage, and shone in comparison.

Both Augusta and her mother noted the contrast between the elegant manner, suave tones, and rounded periods of Laurence Aspinall's thanks and the curt disclaimer of Jabez, though their deductions were different. Augusta was in raptures with the rose-giver.

"Ah! my dear, all is not gold that glitters. There is more sterling metal in your father's salesman, mark my words, than in the tinselled lieutenant," was the summing-up of the elder, as she replaced cake and wine in sideboard and cellaret. She was clearly no friend to Aspinall now that he had recovered sense and sight.

The town, which had been strong and outspoken in its condemnation of the new king during the trial of Queen Caroline, was now all alive with preparations to celebrate his coronation with befitting magnificence, one branch of trade vieing with another which should make the greatest display in the coming procession to the Green, the like of which never had been, and never would be again. And this competition, productive of marvellous results—due, in a great measure, to trade rivalry and an ambitious desire to outshine—was set down by historians, rightly or wrongly, as a proof of the excessive loyalty of the Mancestrians.

In all classes, from the highest to the lowest, something was being done, and nothing was talked of, thought of, dreamed of, but the coronation and the procession. In courts and alleys there were making, and mending, and washing; and no little pinching was undergone by hard-working fathers and mothers to provide the girls with white cambric frocks, tippets, and net caps, or the lads with fresh jackets and breeches and shoes, so as not to disgrace the Sunday schools under whose banners they were to walk.

The finest horses of the Old Quay Company and Pickford's were put into new harness and the finest condition, and every lurry (a long, flat, sideless waggon) was called into requisition. Smiths, saddlers, sign and scene painters, were at work day and night for weeks; and such was the request for banners that ladies undertook the work when skilled labour was not to be found.

The important ceremony was fixed for the 19th of July. On the 17th a deputation of small-ware weavers waited on Mr. Ashton in despair. They could get neither flag nor banner; the painter had thrown over the order at the last moment.

"An' Tummy Worthington's getten a foine un, measter. It'll be a sheame an' a disgrace to us o' if we let Worthington's cut us eawt."

[The said Worthington was a rival small-ware manufacturer.]

Mr. Ashton had recourse to his snuff-box, and then to his wife.

"My dear, what is to be done? There will be no flag. The painters cannot execute the jobs in hand. Worthington's have a fine one I hear."

"No flag! That will never do. We must have a flag. Let me consider."

Ellen Chadwick was busy helping Augusta to make favours for the men. She looked up.

"Do you not think Mr. Clegg could paint you one?" she suggested.

Mr. Ashton brightened, but his "Just so!" was nipped in the bud by the recollection that there was no time.

"Where there's a will there's a way," said Mrs. Ashton, and sought out Jabez.

"It is quite out of my line, but I can try. It would be a pity to disappoint the men," answered he.

"And nothing beats trying but doing," added Mrs. Ashton.

Silk and colours were procured. There was no leisure for complex design or elaboration. At that time the dark blue covers of the Dutch tapes in gross bore the symbolic device of the flax plant within a rude scroll. This Jabez transferred in colours to his silk on a colossal scale, both sides bearing the same emblem of their trade, more effective on its completion than any elaborate work. He had bargained to be left without interruption. The men fidgeted about the warehouse in a state of nervous trepidation (it was an important matter to them), but at dawn on the 19th it was finished, and borne off by the weavers in triumph and exultation.

Market Street Lane being in ruins at one end, and a narrow

gully at the other, Mosley Street became the natural course for the procession (two miles and a half in length) from Peter's Field to the Green, where a royal salute was to be fired; and like every other house on the line of route, Mr. Ashton's was filled with guests, and from garret to basement every window had its streamer, and was crowded with gaily-dressed spectators, mostly feminine, the gentlemen of the town taking part in the procession, officially or otherwise. The Chadwicks and Mrs. Walmsley were there of course, and Mrs. Clough amongst others; and on another floor Jabez—who being above the warehousemen, and not a master, did not walk—had as a companion good Bess Hulme, who with her husband had come over from Whaley Bridge, where there was, of course, a holiday. To Tom had been assigned the honour of chief standard bearer.

In all such processions the military element, with its brilliant uniforms and stirring music, prevails. But here (where every item of the cavalcade had its own brass band) were also all the dignitaries of the church, with every silver badge of office resplendently burnished for the occasion; the borough-reeve, and other magistrates, and constabulary, in new uniforms; the lamp-lighters with new smocks, carrying their ladders and cans; the firemen and fire-engines, bright as paint and polish could make them; the gentlemen of the town, all with favours; the Sunday-school children, marshalled under their respective banners or tablets, walking six abreast; the Ladies' Jubilee School; the Green-Coat School; and the Blue-Coat School, on which Jabez looked down with curiously-mingled feelings.

But the marked feature of the magnificent procession was the display made by the trades, with their banners, a lurry accompanying each, bearing well-dressed workmen and machines in full operation.

At the head of these came two figures, representing Adam and Eve, in a perfect bower of greenery, as representatives of the primitive condition before dress was invented. They were followed by a lurry, on which tailors (whose art is the first on record) sat cross-legged, and stitched and pressed, as if on a shopboard, whilst a select band of journeymen walked after, bearing minature garments on wands, or ferruginous geese and sleeveboards.

The blacksmiths wrought on their anvil, and carried also on long poles, horse-shoes, &c. The brass and copper smiths, likewise at work, had a bright array of kettles, candlesticks, and a mounted man in armour, as had also the tin-plate workers. The glass-blowers made a goodly array, and gave away tokens as they went. The men wore hats and caps brittle and brilliant, with wavy plumes of spun glass, whilst birds, ships, goblets, and decanters on their poles glistened in the beams of the hot sun. A printing-press distributed appropriate verses, worked off in the course of the procession. And St. Crispin's followers waxed their threads and plied their awls on boots and shoes as they and their benches were borne along, followed by their leather-aproned fraternity, holding aloft their productions, from the most gigantic of Wellingtons to the tiniest infant's slipper.

All branches of the cotton trade were represented. There was cotton in bags; twist in bales; carding, roving, spinning, weaving, all going on under the eyes of the onlookers, with the workpeople following in their best and brightest.

Shouts and hurrahs attended the whole line of march, not wholly unaccompanied by hisses; but as the small-ware weavers passed Mr. Ashton's the cheers were deafening. A loom was at work weaving lengths of binding for garters, on which was inwoven "God save King George IV.," with the date, and these were lifted on long wands to the ladies at the windows on their way, or scattered to others in the street; and as Tom Hulme caught the eye of Jabez, he pointed proudly to their banner, which had no rival in all the elaborately painted flags waving in the wind, and the impromptu artist was well satisfied. But the brightest day has its cloud. As the Manchester Yeomanry went prancing past, Travis and Walmsley alike saluted the ladies at the drawing-room window, but to the pain of Jabez and the indignation of Mrs. Ashton, Lieutenant Aspinall had the audacity to kiss his hand to Augusta.

CHAPTER THE THIRTY-SECOND.

EVENING: INDOORS AND OUT!

AUGUSTA AT HER HARP.

THE two-miles-and-a-half-long procession was not the only popular demonstration which made the Coronation of George IV. memorable in the annals of Manchester. There were no telegraph wires to flash intelligence to the supporters of Queen Caroline that she had been repulsed from the Abbey gates, and driven thence to die broken-hearted and uncrowned. So, in the absence of a cause for indignation, loyalty, or its substitute, contrived to add a pendant of disorder and excess only to be recorded as the dung-heap out of which grew flowers of promise.

As in most of the private houses along the line of route, a cold collation had been prepared for the refreshment of the friends who crowded Mr. Ashton's open windows. But no calculation had been made of the space the unwonted pageant would cover, or the time it would occupy in passing; and Mrs. Ashton, having discovered that sight-seeing in the dust and glare of July was parching and fatiguing, issued orders for tea to be handed round when the last banner had disappeared, and before her less intimate friends should rise to depart.

In giving these orders, she unwittingly stirred the kitchen fire into a white heat. Lavish hospitality was a characteristic of the time, and when a family of good position professed to keep "open house," it was generally equal to the most extravagant demands. As a rule, Mrs. Ashton had little leaning towards impromptu parties, and Kezia considerably less, preferring those grand and formal receptions which involved elaborate preparation, and placed imaginary feathers in the caps of mistress and maids.

Kezia herself considered the honour of the house involved in everything under her control being "in apple-pie order;" and the surprise which put her on her mettle, put her also in a fume.

Recalled from the window—whence her head had been poked far as the farthest—to provide tea and its concomitants for an indefinite number of strangers, she accompanied her erratic movements about her domain with explosive outbursts of spleen at "bein' takken unawares when nowt's ready to hand."

"Here's missus bin an' ordered tay fur the whole boilin' of folk up-stairs; an' theer's Cicily and t'other wenches a' agog ower th' crownation, an' not worth 'toss of a pancake!"

She jerked out her anger in the ears of Bess Hulme, who, seated on the settle, had just lulled to sleep Mrs. Walmsley's crying baby, which (neglected by its gaping nurse) had commemorated the day by a fall from a high bed.

Bess made a temporary couch for the baby in a snug corner, and quietly came to Kezia's assistance; then Ellen Chadwick, intuitively perceptive of kitchen troubles, busied herself in bringing reserves of china, glass, plate, linen, and sweetmeats from closets and store-room; Cicily and Dolly came down in due time; and the credit of the establishment lost nothing in Kezia's hands, even though there was an additional influx of visitors, and a supper also to provide.

That was Mr. Ashton's affair. He had tired of his processional march in the broiling sun by the time they had skirted Ardwick, and defiled into Chancery Lane. The two friends by his side, Mr. John McConnell and Mr. John Green (both cotton-spinners with whom he dealt), being of the same mind, they had fallen out of the line in Ancoats Lane, and turned down Canal Street to the house of the latter, to refresh themselves with something less dry than snuff or road-dust.

Mr. Green was the uncle of Henry Liverseege the artist, fragile of form and spiritual of face, but the latter was then only a

HENRY LIVERSEEGE.
From an Engraving.

genius in his nineteenth year—with fame and an early grave dimly foreshadowed. They found him on the doorstep, with his fusssy and fidgety, though kind-hearted aunt, just back from Mr. Gore's in Piccadilly, whence they had seen the show. The gentlemen's requirement, a "draught of ale," was soon supplied, accompanied by a spasmodic comment on the "gand display," and the exhibition of a pair of the loyally inscribed fillets she had secured as the smallware-weavers passed.

"By-the-bye, that was a wonderfully effective banner of yours, Mr. Ashton," interposed the thin voice of Liverseege. "Who painted it?"

A young fellow in my employ, who occasionally designs for us," answered Mr. Ashton, handing his snuff-box to the group in rotation—"quite a self-taught artist!"

"Indeed! It was not much like an amateur's brush. I should like to know him. You see I do something in that way myself." The young painter, conscious of his own latent power, was sensitively alive to undeveloped art in another.

"Would you? Just so! Then you shall. Come along, all of you, and finish the day with us. Mrs. Ashton will find us a dish of tea, and I am sure, Mrs. Green, she will be proud to see you also." Turning to the gentlemen, who had by this time emptied their talboy glasses, he added, "And I think I have a few bottles of rare old port waiting among the cobwebs for us to drink the King's health."

It was a period of much pressing and many excuses, but the excitement of the day had so far destroyed ceremony that even Mrs. Green, who was somewhat punctillious, after a little nervous trepidation anent the fitness of her last new cap for company, consented, and accepted the arm Mr. Ashton gallantly offered to pilot her across the crowded street, along which the tail of the procession had only just trailed.

Graciously, though with her natural stateliness, Mrs. Ashton received the new comers; Mrs. Green, finding the company generally in morning visiting dress, was at ease about her cap;

the tea was exhilarating, the viands toothsome, the wines excellent; there was one common topic for discussion; the ice of ceremony had thawed hours before; and genial Mr. Ashton, having locked the doors to prevent the escape of a guest before the supper he had bespoken was demolished, was thoroughly in his element.

Mrs. Ashton was not quite so much at ease, though she was too well-bred to manifest her disquiet, which had two sources. In the first place, the presumptious salutation of Augusta by Lieutenant Aspinall had jarred a sensitive nerve. In the second, Mr. Ashton, generously impulsive, had introduced Mr. Clegg to their friends, and *as* a friend of whom he was himself proud. She thoroughly appreciated Jabez, and equally contemplated his advancement; but she was for "making no more haste than good speed," and considered it more prudent to raise him by insensible degrees. And as she watched her husband, radiant with goodwill, cross the room with Jabez (discomposed at the very doorway by the wondering eyes of Augusta), and present him to Mr. Green and Mr. Liverseege, thus ran her thoughts:—

"Dear me! William is very inconsiderate! He will turn the young man's head, and insult our visitors at the same time. I hope Mrs. Clough will not recognise him. How indignant she would be if she thought we expected her to associate with one who once wore her son's cast-off clothes! Certainly he is well-conducted, and worthy in all respects, but—people don't forget such things! If Mr. Green and Mr. McConnell only knew William was introducing our Blue-coat apprentice, what would they say?—I am glad, however, to see young Mr. Liverseege so affable with Jabez."

To her surprise, at this juncture Mr. McConnell drew his chair close to Jabez and Mr. Liverseege, and, attributing the evident embarassment of the former to the newness of his position, endeavoured to dissipate it by taking part in the conversation, to which quiet Mr. Green occasionally added a word. The lady, who was so afraid of touching the dignity of her friends, had not heard her less exclusive lord whisper to the two cotton-spinners, "I'm afraid I've committed a grave misdemeanour in Mrs. Ashton's sight by bringing young Clegg among our party; but kings are nct crowned every day, and I thought it a good opportunity to bring a worthy lad out. You and I"—and he tapped his snuff-box—"know what Manchester men are made of, and that young fellow has good stuff in him! He was made to rise, sirs."

Mr. Ashton's friends nodded in acquiescence, and willing to humour their kindly host, and perhaps desirous to test the calibre of an aspirant so introduced, wittingly or unwittingly did their part in helping him to "rise" by the very distinction of their prolonged attention. It was an act quite in the way of John McConnell, who had already given a lift to his rising young countryman, Fairbairn, the engineer.

Presently Mr. Chadwick, beckoning attentive Ellen to his side, and using her shoulder as a support, involuntarily seconded his brother-in-law by joining the group, and, putting out his hand to Jabez (who rose at his approach, and offered his own seat to the paralytic gentleman), said:—

"Wha-at inter-rests yo-you so m-much, M-Mr. Clegg, th-that you f-forget old f-friends?"

"No, sir, I had not forgotten you, nor Miss Chadwick either" (Ellen coloured), "but Mr. Ashton having honoured me with an introduction to Mr. Liverseege and these gentlemen" (bowing to them), "I was not at liberty to break away, had I felt so disposed."

"We were discussing the influence of art on our local manufactures," added Henry Liverseege, and thereupon the subject was resumed, Ellen, necessarily in close attendance on her father, standing there with sparkling black eyes, an animated and attentive listener, well pleased that Mr. Clegg's merits (as seen by her) had at length found recognition.

Meanwhile Augusta, the centre of a group of young people, indulged in sentimental chit-chat, and, trifling with her fan and human hearts, completed the enslavement of her last admirer, a fair-haired Mr. Marsland; while Jabez, from his distant seat, looked and longed in vain.

Cards were, as a matter of course, proposed for the amusement of this extemporised party, and in filling up tables for whist or loo, Mrs. Ashton's fears for the sensibility of her friends were forgotten. They were utterly put to the rout by a loud rat-tat-tat at the street door, followed by the entrance of Mr. Clough and the Reverend Joshua Brookes, the latter less vigorous than of yore, but in a state of unusual excitement. His loud voice was heard before he was seen. "Hogs, sir, hogs! They are no better than hogs, sir!" he was saying even as he came into the drawing-room. He appeared too much ruffled to respond composedly to the kindly greetings of his many friends; even Augusta, who put forth her little white hand with her most winning smile, attracted no more attention than a hurried "How d'ye do, lass? How d'ye do?"

"What is the matter, Mr. Brookes? You seem——"

He interrupted Mr. Ashton's inquiry with—

"Matter, sir? Waste and riot, intemperance and indecency, are the matter. These old eyes have seen that which is enough to bring a curse upon the coronation and a blight upon the town."

Conversation was arrested, flirtation forgot its part, cards were laid down, save by three or four inveterate players, and young and old were alike on the *qui vive*, crowding round the speaker.

"Permit me," said Mr. Clough, commencing an explanation. "I suppose you are all aware that the new market in Shude Hill is the chief station of the nine appointed for the distribution of meat, bread, and ale to the populace?"

"Populace, indeed!—the very scum and dregs of the town—say rather the lowest, roughest rabble!" broke in old Joshua.

"Well, Parson, for the credit of our working population, let us hope so," chimed in Mr. Clough, resuming—"Whilst Mr. Brookes and I were at tea in his sanctum, Tabitha ran in breathless to tell us that the platform erected for recipients in front of the storehouse had given way, that several persons were injured, and one had been killed on the spot."

"Ah!" said the Parson, drawing a long breath between his teeth, while Jabez, unobserved by either, drew nearer to listen, and the ladies put up their hands in horror.

"It was not our most direct route, but either curiosity or compassion took us round by Shude Hill Market on our road hither, and never shall I forget the scene we witnessed. Loaves and junks of meat were being pitched high and far amongst the crowd from the warehouse doors and windows, as if flung to hounds."

"Hounds, sir!" burst in impatient Joshua, "don't slander the better animal. Only the commonest curs would have yelped, and scrambled, and struggled, and fought for their rations, as did the human beasts we saw clutching and gripping from weaker women and children that which had fallen within their reach, or trampling in the mud underfoot the food they were too greedy or too drunk to devour. Ay, mud, for the very kennels ran with ale thrown in pitchers-full amongst the people, to be caught in hats, and bonnets, and hollowed hands, as if it were rain in an African desert. Ale! the atmosphere reeked of ale! Men, women, and children of all ages carried it away, or drank it from all sorts of vessels; reeled, hiccoughed, and staggered under their burden, or sank down by the wayside; whilst others, shouting like maniacs, drained the half-empty mugs. I tell you, sirs, Captain Cook never fell in with greater savages. Even death and disaster in their midst had not awed them! Ugh! I say again they are hogs, absolute hogs!"

As Joshua paused to take breath, and sank into a chair, Jabez modestly put the question to the excitable chaplain—

"Do you not think the distributors are most to blame for this wanton waste and excess, to say nothing of the loss of life? Surely the arrangements of the committee must have been defective."

The Parson's harsh tones softened as he put out his hand to grasp the speaker's.

"Ay, Jabez, lad, is that thee? I'm glad to see thee *here*"—and he laid emphasis on the word—"Ay, the distributors are answerable for——"

But the personal recognition had created a diversion. The question Jabez had mooted was talked over by separate knots of individuals in different quarters of the large room, whilst Mr. Clough, to Mrs. Ashton's amazement—yes, and gratification also—shook the salesman warmly by the hand, and congratulated him on his apparent success. Moreover, he bore him away to Mrs. Clough, at the loo-table, and called her attention to the change time had effected in the old tanner's foster-child, in the most cordial manner.

Thanks to Mr. Ashton, Mr. Clegg had truly got his first foot into Manchester society that coronation-day, and his old hopes might have revived, had not a disturbing element crept into the room during the denunciatory oration of his clerical friend.

John Walmsley, not finding his wife at home when released from yeomanry duty, had come in quest of her, bringing two of his comrades; and when Mr. Clegg retired from the loo-table with a bow, his eye fell first on the conspicuous figure of Captain Travis, in the silver-and-blue glory of uniform, bending deferentially to address Miss Chadwick; and in another moment on the elegant Adonis he had dragged from icy death, toying with Miss Augusta's carved ivory fan, and whispering low to her, whilst she hid her Indian-muslin robe and too eloquent face behind the screen of her convenient harp, and drew her flexible fingers lightly across the chords.

The lustre of that evening's introduction was dimmed for Jabez. Augusta scarcely looked at him as she brushed past to supper, leaning on the arm of Lieutenant Aspinall, her white dress in strong contrast to his dark uniform; and no doubt his pain was pictured on his face, for Ellen Chadwick sighed, as she too passed him with her martial cavalier, and half turned to look pitifully as she went.

There was no lack of ladies, so Mrs. Ashton paired Mr. Clegg off with a chatty damsel of thirty or thereabouts, and he did his best to listen and make himself agreeable, but not even the novelty of his situation could keep his thoughts or his eyes from wandering where they should not.

Along the whole course of the procession the Manchester Yeomanry had been greeted with more hisses and groans than cheers. This had chafed their noble spirits, and on disbanding they had sought consolation in the wine-cup, which temperate Jabez was not slow to observe, although their degree ot exhilaration was not then considered a disqualification for the drawing-room or for the society of ladies.

Mr. Ashton's strong home-brewed supper-ale was not a sedative, yet still Augusta smiled on Laurence, in spite of her mother's frowns, driving Mr. Marsland to desperation, and Jabez to despair.

Indeed, he was glad when the repast was over, for then Joshua Brookes rose to depart, sober as when he sat down, and the Chadwicks also. He had thus an opportunity of escaping from his torment, by offering his escort to tottering Mr. Chadwick and the Parson in succession, if the latter did not object to the slight detour. Jabez foresaw that Mr. Travis was ready to do Miss Chadwick suit and service; but in offering his arm to assist the slow feet of the disabled father, he little dreamed how gladly the daughter would have made an exchange; nor, had he been wiser, would he have thrust himself in big Ben's way, any more than would Mrs. Chadwick, who openly favoured the "personable and unimpeachable" captain.

CHAPTER THE THIRTY-THIRD.

CLOGS.

HOUSE OF GRAMMAR-SCHOOL MASTER.

LEAVING the Chadwicks at their own door, where Captain Travis would fain have lingered had he been encouraged, Jabez and he fell back as guards to their reverend friend, whose excitability might otherwise have involved him in some unpleasantness, so disorderly a riff-raff occupied the streets.

Turning down Church Street, they pursued their dimly-lighted way along Cannon Street (so named from dismounted cannon said to be captured from "rebels" which served as corner posts), through Hanging Ditch to Hyde's Cross, thence past the deserted Apple Market and Dr. Smith's ancient labyrinth of a house, to the Parson's less antiquated domicile in the corner by the Grammar School and those College gates which had been the portals of peace and promise to Jabez, and not only to him, but to hundreds besides.

The excitement of old Joshua had been toned down amongst the wax-lights and pleasant faces around the Ashton's well-spread supper table, and at first he was disposed to be conversable, after his own peculiar manner. They had purposely avoided Shudehill Market by an ample circuit; but stragglers of both sexes from the scene of riot lay maundering or asleep in their path, or crossed it at every turn, in all stages of inebriation and disorder, until the natural irritability of the chaplain (increased by failing health) broke forth in loud-voiced indignation, ending in a wail that he was "getting old and powerless," or he would "rise like another John Knox and denounce the wickedness rampant in the land."

"A good man lives there, Jabez," said he, pointing to the black-and-white home of the head-master, where lighted windows told of hospitality awake, "a good man, but for whom I should not be alive to tell you; but there are those in the pulpit, my lads, whom the Church ought to spew out, lest they poison the flocks it is their duty to feed. Can the stream be pure if the fountain be polluted? And how shall we rebuke the gross excesses of the untaught rabble whilst chambering, gluttony, and drunkenness defile the high places of the land? Ugh! There wants another flood to wash Europe sweet and clean. The sin on the earth was not greater in the days of Noah!"

They were crossing the space before the two closed gates when he paused for lack of breath, and Travis, with no thought but to change the subject, observed to Jabez, over the head of the panting Pastor——

"How quiet this little nook of ground is now! Yet to me, and no doubt to you, Mr. Clegg, it is haunted by ghosts of old times!"

That set Joshua off again.

"Ugh! to hear a lad of five-and-twenty talk of old times! What's the world coming to? Ghosts, indeed! It had like to have been haunted by ghosts of something more than old times, as Jabez and I know to our cost. I've never been right since the young ruffians had me in their clutches! And mark you, my lads, and think of it when you have young ones of your own to rear: there's no worse sign for a country or a family than when the young jibe and jeer, mock and scorn their elders. When grey hairs fail to command respect, virtue, principle, and religion are at their lowest ebb."

He stood within his own gate as he said this, and as Tabitha opened the door for her master, he checked all reply with——

"There! you've had a sermon for nothing. Ugh! you'll forget it when the old man's back turns. Good night, lads! See you steer clear of brawls, and give drunken fools a wide berth."

Leaving the young men so abruptly dimissed to retrace their steps towards Hyde's Cross, it may be as well if we throw a light on some of Parson Brookes's dark allusions. Time had not smoothed the old man's eccentricities, nor modified the antagonism between the Grammar School boys and the ex-master. They were always at war, and there never was wanting a *casus belli.* The previous September he had been more than usually irritated by a lampoon which began——

"O Jotty, you dog,
Your house we well know
Is headquarters of prog——"

the purport of which was to fix on him the stigma of inviting a friend to dine, and regaling him with a black-pudding only.

Lashed to fury, he burst into the Grammar School when the first and second-form boys were assembled in the afternoon to rehearse the speeches which, according to custom, they were to deliver in public at the annual commemoration in October. He braved them in his hottest style, winding up with, "You are a set of blockheads! I would not come to hear your speeches if you would pay me for it!"

There was a general cry, "Turn him out! Turn him out!" But Jotty would not be turned out. He stuck himself in the doorway with his legs against the door-post, and his back against the door itself, to the extreme risk of broken limbs, whilst his young and vigorous opponents brought their strength to bear upon the door to force him out.

With such odds he was sure to be overcome; but, driven into the yard, he fought with his antagonists like a mastiff at bay, and they, like the cowards they must have been, to have assailed in a body an old man (under any provocation), by sheer force of numbers, bore him backwards to the wall, and, but for the opportune arrival of Dr. Smith, would have repeated the outrage perpetrated on Jabez Clegg eight years before.

He might well say Dr. Smith had saved his life. Such a fall, whether in high or low water, to so old a man, would have been certain destruction. They broke his heart, I think, if they did not break his limbs, for he never was the same man afterwards. Even old Mrs. Clowes used to rally him on his frequent "fits of the dumps."

Whether Jabez and Ben Travis had, or had not, lost sight of the Parson's homily, they were linked arm in arm, the rich yeomanry officer and the unpretending smallware-salesman, just as, nearly nine years previously, the big, raw-boned youth, with a heart large enough to match his frame, had linked his arm in that of the poor Blue-coat boy, as a friend and protector, when as yet his admittance into society was undreamed of.

Where the four roads met at Hyde's Cross, a staggering Charlie (as the watchmen were called, much as, at this day, they are Bobbies) passed them, with his horn lantern and staff, and his rattle in his belt, proclaiming—

"Past ten o'clock!" (hiccup). "And a foin moonleet neet!"

The two stood for a moment; then, animated by a desire to ascertain if Joshua Brookes had spoken sooth, or, in his spleen exaggerated, they turned up Shudehill, all alive with people who were ordinarily at that hour in bed, and made their way to the market.

Exaggerate! Joshua Brookes had seen but in part, and painted but in part. Every avenue to the market was a scene of debauchery. Hogarth's print of "Gin Lane" was feeble beside it. The distribution of food was over, but that of drink continued. The oil lamps of the street, the dying illumination lamps, and the misty moonlight showed a picture of unimaginable grossness; whilst their ears were assailed with foulness which would have shocked a hardened man of the world—how much more these inexperienced young friends!

Children, men, and women, their clothes torn or disarrayed, lay singly, or in groups, on the paths, or in the gutters, asleep or awake, drunk, sick, helpless, exposed; there was fighting and cursing over the ale yet procurable; there were loaves in the gutters, and meat trampled in the mire; food which, properly distributed, would have gladdened many a poor, hard-working family, too self-respecting to join that clamorous mob.

The two young men turned away sick and disgusted.

"Henry Hunt, in advocating the disuse of excisable liquors," said Jabez, thoughtfully, "may only have designed to cripple the Government; but surely no one could witness scenes like these, whether Whig or Tory, without feeling that some restriction on drink is absolutely necessary for the safety of the State and the comfort of the people."

"You are right, Mr. Clegg," responded Travis, heartily. "Men of all politics ought to meet on this ground. I shall see how far my little influence goes to check intemperance henceforth. Something must be done, and that promptly."

"Whatever I can do to second you, you may depend on, though beyond our own warehouse my opportunities are small," said Jabez; "still, if I can influence one within our walls, that one may act on two outside, and so we may prevail in the end."

"Yes," added Travis, "and if this night be not eloquent in its protest against drink, all humanity must be equally debased and brutalised."

Some caution had been necessary to cross the Market, so as to avoid insult, the captain's bulk and uniform rendering him conspicuous, and his corps being in anything but good odour. They had kept well within the shade of the pillared piazza which extended along the side to their right, and, stunned by the uproar of brawling and fighting crowds, picked their way between degraded humanity in heaps on the pavement, crushed hats and bonnets, torn caps and shawls, boots and shoes which had done duty as drinking vessels, sodden meat and bread, and had much ado to avoid splashing through puddles of ale and other abominations. They had emerged into Oak Street, glad to have got tolerably clear of the clamour and brutality, when a cry from the direction of Tib Street, "Watch! Help! Watch!" fell on their ears in tones which had a strangely familiar ring to Jabez.

Hastening on at a run, they came upon a decently-dressed man struggling against three or four drunken ruffians with heavy clogs on their feet. They had got the man down, and were vociferating with oaths not to be repeated here.

"Gie him a lick wi' thi clog!" "Punce him well!" "Shut up his tater-trap fur him!" "Purr him i' th' bread-basket!" "Fettle his mug wi' thi clog!"

Before Jabez and his companion could prevent it, a heavy thud, followed by a groan, told of a brutal kick; the two only dashed among them in time to arrest the other clogs, already on the backward swing for force; and saved the prostrate man by turning the fury of the savages on themselves. The cowardly brutes, however, stood little chance against sobriety and skill, backed by the muscular frame of Jabez and the herculean one of Travis, even though they carried weapons of offence on their feet, and plied them vigorously; and before a droning watchman hove in sight to spring his rattle for assistance, they were over-mastered or put to the rout.

Most thankful was Jabez for the impulse which had directed their steps that way when, on raising the fallen man, the light of an adjacent oil-lamp projecting from the wall fell on his blood-stained face, and revealed Tom Hulme, who had been drawn into that unusually disorderly neighbourhood by like curiosity with their own, and had been set upon without provocation. He walked with pain, and they supported his steps to the Infirmary, not finding Mr. Huertley, on whom they called, at home. But so fertile had that evening been of serious injuries, he was some time before he could obtain attention. Thirteen far more urgent cases had preceded his. At length his head and cut lip were plaistered up, a reviving draught administered, and after some examination of bruises, and poking and pressing of his body, three of his ribs were pronounced "broken." His defenders were disposed to smile at the surgeon when, besides an embrocation for bruises, he prescribed " a succession of oatmeal poultices applied internally"—in other words, a cushion of as much oatmeal porridge as the patient could consume, to press the crushed ribs gently into position.

It was, however, not much of a laughing matter to Tom Hulme, or to loving Bess, who looked aghast at this deplorable termination of a day's jollity. Nor was there a trace of mirth on the face of Jabez when, at parting with Ben Travis on the Mosley Street door-step, he gripped, more in pain that pleasure, the big hand extended so cordially.

It was after midnight, but from the open windows of the still-lighted drawing-room the thin quick ears of Jabez had caught the sound of Augusta's melodious voice blending with that of Laurence Aspinall in a popular duet, although the notes of the latter were neither so clear nor so steady as they might have been. The pallor on her foster-son's face Bess attributed to tender-hearted sympathy for her injured husband; but Jabez hurried away from her oppressive thanks to the solitude of his own chamber, where he could bury his face in his quivering hands, and unseen wrestle with emotions of which she had no conception.

Never had he known a day so chequered. The same sun which had looked down at noontide on the triumph of his amateur brush, had beamed on Augusta Ashton's conscious cheeks, as she accepted his rival's familiar act of gallantry without so much as a frown. The evening had made a man of him—lifted him into a new sphere—brought him, so to speak, nearer to his divinity, within the radius of her smiles, the music of her voice. She had put her small white hand within his, and blessed him with a word or two of shy recognition; but Laurence Aspinall had again come like a cloud between him and his sunbeam; her sweetest smiles, her softest tones, were for the intruder; her arm had rested willingly on his, her voice had blent with his in sentimental song, and darkness once more shut out hope from Jabez.

"Common sense might have taught me that my love was folly, presumption, madness!" he argued with himself; that the heiress of a wealthy man would not stoop to her father's Blue-coat apprentice. But oh!" he groaned, "I had hoped to raise myself step by step nearer to her level—to make myself worthy of her as a man, if I had not riches to lay at her feet. She is young, and what might I not accomplish with industry ere she came of age? but now——"

He tore his neckcloth off, and cast it from him, stripped off coat and vest, and flung them aside, as though they held his passionate folly, and he had done with it, then sank into a chair, the very impersonation of listless hopelessness. He had gone through all this struggle once before, and thought he had overcome his weakness; but at the touch of the enchanter's wand love had blazed up afresh, and was not to be smothered.

His reverie was broken into by the tread of many feet on the staircase below, and the murmur of voices calling one to another; the hall-door shut with a clang, and then a light foot came tripping up the stair alone, and from heart and lips dropped unconsciously the soft refrain of that too well-known duet. She, too, was carrying to her chamber memories of the night, and bearing the burden lightly.

He listened until a door closed upon step and song. Then, as if its echoes pierced his soul, he set his teeth and clenched his outstretched hands in mute agony. There was more than hopeless love in this—there was jealousy also. Then he murmured half audibly, "If he were only worthy of her I could bear it better; but to see her cast her heart at the feet of one who will trample on it, is beyond mortal endurance."

He started to his feet. A bright thought irradiated his face.

"Coward that I am! I am quitting the battle without striking a blow. I am myself unworthy of Augusta if I surrender her to a heartless profligate without an effort to save her. 'Faint heart never won fair lady.' Women have stooped lower, and lowly men have looked higher ere now. I am making way, but I must make money too, if I would look above me. Father and mother look on me with favour, and why not the daughter? She may learn the worthlessness of the fine gentleman in time. Courage, Jabez! Work with a will; do your duty. Miss no opportunity, and the gold and the goddess may both be yours in the end, and honestly won."

He sprang into bed fresher and lighter than he had been all day, the prayer of that other Jabez rising from his heart with the fervour of old times.

CHAPTER THE THIRTY-FOURTH.

BIRDS OF A FEATHER.

PALACE INN.

THE "Palace Inn" on the north side of Market Street Lane was the last relic of that cramped thoroughfare to disappear at the bidding of Improvement. Possibly, because its many eyes and bald dark-red-brick face looked out on a space so much beyond the twenty-one yards assigned by Act of Parliament to the regenerated street that the Improvement Committee had no powers to meddle with it, for surely its historic associations were not sufficient to protect it. Prince Charles Edward had been hospitably lodged and entertained beneath its roof by its owner, Mr. Dickenson, long ere it became an inn; he had harangued his devoted followers from the stone plateau of its double flight of steps, with his hand perchance on its smooth rail of unornamented iron; but in isolated dignity rather than palatial pretensions lay its chief safeguard. Be that as it may, fourteen or fifteen years elapsed between the first act of demolition for widening (at the shop of a Mr. Maund), and that last feat of narrowing, which blocked up and darkened history (as represented by the Palace) with common stone warehouses for every-day merchandise. Alas! Clio and all her sister muses *must* succumb when Mammon is on the march!

But Mammon had only got his first foot in the street on that Thursday morning in July, which blushed at the doings of the Coronation night, and the "Palace Inn" yet held its head high as beseemed its historic state. The open space in front was enlivened by the newly-painted London stage-coach, the "Lord Nelson," the fresh scarlet coats of coachmen and guards, the assembling of passengers and luggage, the shouting and swearing of half-awake ostlers and porters, the grumbling of the first-comers (shivering in the raw air) at the unpunctuality of the stage, the excuses of the booking-clerk, the self-gratulations of the last arrival that he was "in time," the dragging of trunks and portmanteaus on to the top, the thrusting of bags and boxes into the boot, the harnessing of snorting steeds the horsing of the vehicle, the scrambling of the "outsiders" to the top by the ladder and wheel, the self-satisfied settlement of the "insides" in the places they had "booked for," the crushing and thrusting of friends with last messages and parting words, the crack of the whip, the sound of the bugle, the prancing of horses, the rattle of wheels, and the dashing off up Market Street Lane of the gallant four-in-hand, amid the hurrahs of excited spectators.

Every morning witnessed a somewhat similar scene of bustle and excitement at five o'clock, when the London coach started, but every morning did not see Jabez mounted on the box-seat with the coachman. Nor did every morning see the coach an hour behind time, or the driver's face quite so red, or the spectators so heavy-eyed, or so much handing up of horns and glasses to the passengers, to be returned empty, or leave Mr. Ashton standing there when the "Lord Nelson" had bowled away.

That Coronation Day had much to answer for.

When Tom Hulme should have risen at four o'clock to return home, his bruised limbs were so stiff and sore that the soldier, who had borne the fatigue of many a campaign, who had bivouacked on the battle-field, after a forced march, and being ready with the sun for the day's duties, had to confess himself "fettled" by Lancashire clogs, and unable to stir. There was no alternative but to acquaint Mr. Ashton. The mill could not be left without a manager.

After the night's unwonted dissipation, Mr. Ashton slept heavily, and was with difficulty aroused. When once he comprehended the state of affairs, he was on the alert.

"It's a bad business!" said he to his wife, as he dressed in haste.

"'There is nothing so bad, but it might be worse,'" was her consolatory reply. "Never bewail a loss till you have done your best to repair it. Can you not send Mr. Clegg to Whaley Bridge for a few days?"

"My dear, your counsel is invaluable, but I fear there is not time to catch the coach; it is twenty minutes past four now."

"It is sure to be late this morning, and Jabez will catch it if it is to be caught," was her quick rejoinder.

Bess had already awakened Jabez, and he, fully dressed, met Mr. Ashton at his bedroom door with "Can I be of any service, sir?" A prompt commentary on Mrs. Ashton's declaration.

A few necessaries hastily crammed into a carpet bag; a bowl of milk and a crust of bread as hastily swallowed; and Jabez, accompanied by Mr. Ashton, was on his way to the Palace coach-office confident they were in time, not having heard the guard's bugle, or met the coach. There was, however, barely time to claim for Mr. Clegg the place already booked for "Mr. Hulme" (Mrs. Hulme's seat was forfeited), and for him to take his seat, before they were off in a canter, and Mr. Ashton's business mind was relieved.

As the manufacturer, satisfied that the mill-hands at Whaley Bridge would not be left altogether to their own devices, stood within a short distance of the high steps looking after the vanishing coach, a party of roysterers came swaggering out of the inn, hallooing with all their tipsy might. One in advance of the rest, observing an elderly gentleman below, pointed him out to his companions as fair game, and leaning over the rail to steady himself, cried out—

"Halloo, old fogey; are you a Tory or a Radical? D—— me, take your hat off before gentlemen!" and, suiting the action to the word, extended a riding-whip he carried, and jerked Mr. Ashton's hat off into the dust; whereupon his worthy comrades set up a loud guffaw in admiration of the feat.

Naturally Mr. Ashton, his brief reverie disturbed, stooped to

BIRDS OF A FEATHER.

pick up the fallen beaver, and making due allowance for the unwonted occasion, turned to remonstrate good-humouredly with an excited stranger who had evidently drunk the king's health too frequently.

It was not with more surprise than annoyance that he recognised four of the hilarious party in the doorway and on the steps of the inn, which had apparently been open the night through. Not one of the four was in a condition to recognise him, although two of them, John Walmsley and Laurence Aspinall, had supped overnight at his own table, although the third, Kit Townley, had good reason for remembrance, and Ned Barret was anything but a stranger.

Loud laughter hailed the fall of the hat. A second attempt to "uncover the obstinate old fogey" was made, but dexterously avoided by Mr. Ashton, in his absolute astonishment, stepping backward beyond range.

"Young gentlemen, do you know whom you are insulting?"

There was another laughing chorus. Aspinall almost toppled over the rail as he leaned forward, impotently striking out with his whip.

"I protest the old rad's demnibly li-ke the lovely Augusta's snuffy old dad," drawled out he, in a sort of tipsy wisdom.

"Just so!" appended Walmsley, mimicking the old gentleman's peculiarity.

Mr. Ashton, though a reasonably temperate man himself, was not so greatly shocked at these young carousers as we might be. Long usage blunts sensibilities. It was a glorious distinction to be a three-bottle man; the inability to drink a solitary bottle of wine at a sitting was a sort of disqualification for good fellowship; and it was considered a fine thing for a boy of seven to "toss off a glass like a man;" so the genial old gentleman was inclined to allow some latitude for the special occasion. But they had touched him on a tender point. The light mention of his darling daughter's name roused his blood.

"John Walmsley," he cried angrily, looking up, "what brings

you, a married man, with these young rakes at this hour of the morning?"

"Pray wha-at brought y-you here, old fogey?" hiccoughed Aspinall, answering for the other.

One of the ostlers—Bob, the ex-groom—squeezed between the rollicking fellows to whisper in the ear of Laurence. He was impatiently thrust back with an elbow.

"Tchut! don't believe it. Old snuff-an'-tuppeny's fast 'shleep in bed shuresh a gun. I know b-better. I say, you——"

But "old snuff-an'-tuppeny" had turned on his heel, too wise to enter into contention with a set of inebriated boobies, though not proof against the disrespectful epithets of Laurence, or the derisive laughter of his boon companions. His irritation half emptied his snuff-box before he got home, so often he tapped smartly on its golden lid, and so often his finger and thumb travelled between it and his nose with a touch of ruminant displeasure.

Neither he nor Mrs. Ashton was disposed to overlook the fact that Kit Townley and Ned Barret—scapegraces by repute—were of the party, nor that Augusta's name had been familiarly used in their midst.

"'Birds of a feather flock together,'" said the lady; "and if Mr. Aspinall's son associates with that reckless and dishonest Kit Townley, he is a very unfit friend for John Walmsley, and still worse for our dear Augusta."

"Just so; for a dashing blade with a handsome face, who sports a uniform, talks poetry, and sings sentimental songs, is just the fellow to take a silly girl's fancy, before she is old enough to think. I know I regret I ever brought him *here*," said Mr. Ashton seriously, as Augusta came in the room to breakfast, entering at the door behind her mother's back.

"Well, William," observed Mrs. Ashton loftily, her hand on the china coffee-pot, "you can imagine *my* annoyance when John and Mr. Laurence walked in arm-in-arm last night, after the liberty he had taken in the morning—kissing his hand to our daughter from the public procession in the face of all our friends, as if Augusta had been a flaunting barmaid. I was most indignant!"

Augusta said "Good morning," and took her seat with a heightened colour. Such a construction of the gallant officer's salute had not occurred to her, and native delicacy took alarm.

Mrs. Ashton continued to pour out her thoughts along with the coffee. It was fit Augusta should know her sentiments on this head.

"It would have been a breach of hospitality to resent it before our friends, and not good policy either. But I shall put a stop to his visits henceforth."

"Oh! mamma," exclaimed Augusta dropping her hands at this climax, "you cannot mean that?"

"Yes, my dear, I do. If Mr. Aspinall has depraved associates, he must be depraved himself; and I am sure my daughter"—she drew herself up proudly—"would not choose her friends from those of Christopher Townley."

Augusta's colour suffered no decrease. She paused as she was taking her dry toast from the silver rack, and half-hesitatingly remonstrated.

"Of course I should not wish to associate with Mr. Townley's friends. But papa may be mistaken. I do not think Mr. Aspinall would mix with them. People meet and mingle at coach-offices who are strangers."

"Just so, my dear; but——" interposed her father.

"Why, mamma," the persistent young lady went on, "no more perfect gentleman enters our doors than Mr. Laurence Aspinall. His manners are most refined. Then he talks enchantingly, and sings divinely. And"—this she thought conclusive—"is he not intimate with Charlotte and John?"

"Just so," quickly answered Mr. Ashton, glancing across the table at his attentive wife, "and all the worse for Charlotte and John. I shall have a word with them on the subject. I called in Marsden Square on my way home, and found Charlotte with red eyes. John had not been home all night." And Mr. Ashton battered the top of an egg whilst delivering what he regarded as a crushing argument.

Breakfast and the discussion were unusually prolonged, the only impression left on the young lady's romantic, impressible, and inexperienced mind being that her parents were unaccountably harsh to her and unjust to Mr. Laurence, in her eyes the beau-ideal of a man. Such a figure and such a face could only enshrine divinity. And if he was a little wild, so were all heroes at his age.

Let not the inexperienced young girl be over-much condemned for this. The opinion generally prevailed in her day; she had heard the sentiment expressed in farces on the stage, in society at home and elsewhere; even her own father's hospitality trended in the same direction.

Mrs. Ashton was a woman of her word. The door in Mosley Street was closed against Mr. Laurence Aspinall, and James was incorruptible.

But the teaching of Miss Bohanna's library being that Love was far-seeing and parents were blind, it followed that Miss Augusta (who would have resented any supposition of wilful disobedience or intentional disrespect towards the good father and mother she loved so dearly) met the fascinating gentleman (always by chance) either at her cousin's in Marsden Square or in her walks abroad, and scented billet-doux came and went between the leaves of four-volumed romances which Cicily carried to and from the library. One of these fell into Mrs. Ashton's hands, when, finding her advice contemned, she took measures to check this premature and clandestine love-making, as she thought, effectually.

CHAPTER THE THIRTY-FIFTH.

AT CARR COTTAGE.

"WHITE HART" SIGN ON EASEL.

TOM HULME was most anxious to get back to Whaley Bridge and the mill, and motherly Bess was equally uneasy to return to her poor little Sim, afraid lest he should tax his grandfather's strength over-much, or meet with some fresh accident. Yet more than a week elapsed before her husband was fit to travel, and in the interim Mr. Ashton had himself gone thither to ascertain how the new substitute filled the post.

He was still at Carr Cottage when the "Lord Nelson" stopped at the end of the avenue, and Jabez, with fragile Sim mounted on his shoulder, trotted down to the gate to welcome Bess and her invalid home. They had travelled inside, but John Loudon MacAdam had not yet been appointed "Surveyor of Roads," and Tom Hulme had suffered severely from the jolting of the coach.

Bess clasped her child tenderly, and held him up for his father's kiss; but she put him down to waddle on before them (he could not run), whilst she and Jabez helped the injured corporal to ascend the steep incline. Old Simon, who seemed to have got a new lease of life from the invigorating country air and occupation, had already breakfasted, and was in the bean-field gathering the first ripe pods for a dinner of beans and bacon.

"Eh, Tum, lad," said he, as he entered the house-place, and saw his son-in-law's pale face against the blue-and-white check cover of the arm-chair, "whoi, thi feace is as whoite as a clout!

Tha'll noan be fit to wark fur one whoile. Thah's nobbut fit fur t' sit under th' sycymore tree, an' look at th' fleawers, an' watch me put th' garden i' fettle."

"Just so," said Mr. Ashton, bringing his pleasant face in at the door; "I think Mr. Clegg will have to do duty for you a while longer. And don't distress yourself about it, Mr. Hulme, for I fancy a little fresh air will do *him* no harm this hot weather; he has been overworking lately, and does not look too brisk."

"You are very kind, sir," responded Jabez, "but I trust a few days' rest will set Mr. Hulme on his feet again." He said nothing of himself.

But Tom Hulme had received unsuspected internal injuries, and many weeks went by before he was stout as before—weeks pregnant with fate for Jabez; and not Jabez alone.

Factory hours were long, but the summer days were longer, and he was glad after work was over to ramble away through the valley of the Goyt, following the winding of the stream, or over the larch-clad hills above Taxal, whence he would return with the rising moon, bringing pockets full of the crisp-brown fir-cones for Sim to play with. In the pine-woods, alone with nature, he could give vent to his emotions, or indulge in meditation at his will.

Mr. Ashton, however, found him other occupation for his spare hours. The landlord of the "White Hart," bearing in mind that Mr. Clegg had come under his roof first as a travelling artist, had expatiated to Mr. Ashton with much pathos on the deplorable condition of the inn sign, not without sundry broad hints that Mr. Clegg's temporary residence on the spot was a glorious opportunity not to be neglected. Mr. Ashton had smiled, said "Just so," taking a pinch from the immense snuff-box lying on the bar-parlour chimney-piece, then falling back upon his own, had gone away, and forgot the dingy sign altogether, until another hint from his tenant refreshed his memory.

As he stood at the inn door waiting for the Manchester coach, an upward sly glance of the jolly host's caused him to say to the young man by his side, "Do you think you could manage to paint a new sign for the 'White Hart,' to oblige Chapman and me?"

Jabez hesitated, not from unwillingness.

"I'm afraid, sir, to attempt. It's not in my line, and——"

"Oh! you can do it well enough. Remember the banner."

"I've no materials here, sir, else——"

"If that is all, you shall have them in a day or two."

In a few days an easel, a new sign-board, and colours were sent by the Manchester and Buxton carrier, and Jabez set to work, to the especial wonder and admiration of little Sim, who delighted to stand by his side, and grew rebellious when "bedtime" was announced. Jabez was, however, but an untaught artist, and his painting hours were few; the *couchant* hart was rubbed in and wiped out over and over again before he was satisfied even with the outline; but then it grew in fair proportion under his brush, until he felt there was something in him beyond the region of tapes and braces.

The graceful animal, resplendent in golden collar and chain, looked mildly out from the easel in the parlour nearest to the passage (used, when the family was there, as an eating-room), and little Sim gravely reported to his elders it only wanted "gass, an' tee, an' ky," when the inmates of Carr Cottage were startled by the arrival of unexpected visitors.

It was the second week in August; the air was heavy with the perfume of clove carnations, honeysuckle, mignonette, lavender, musk, and mint. Golden sunflower and crimson hollyhock were in their glory; bees and wasps hovered over balsams and china asters, or hid themselves in the blue Canterbury bells or the amber nectary of the stately white lily. Fruits were ripe for the gatherer, grain was falling under the sickle. Bess, in a fair white muslin cap, a large check apron over her dark chocolate-and-white-print gown (her blue bedgown days were over), was moving quietly about the house-place, preparing their early breakfast, no longer restricted to oatmeal porridge.

Tom, looking worn, but clean and neat as loving hands could

make him, leaned back in his soft arm-chair, and watched her with well-satisfied eyes. Little Sim was already in the garden with his grandfather, helping to gather raspberries and currants for preserving.

The tall oak-cased clock struck seven, and then, true to time, the guard's bugle announced the coming of the coach from Manchester. Instinctively Bess went to the door, as was her wont, when the coach came in. She uttered an exclamation of surprise.

"Eh, Tum! aw declare t' coach is stoppin' at ar gate. Happen theer's a parcel or summat for ar Jabez."

And off she set past the kitchen window and the farm-yard Gothic doorway, and down the avenue, with the light foot of a younger woman. Before she reached the avenue gate, the stuffy vehicle had yielded up three ladies and two bandboxes, and the guard having unlocked the capacious boot (a kind of closet at the back), dragged thence, with much superfluous puffing and straining, two hair trunks of moderate dimensions. Yes, there stood Mrs. Ashton, grandly calm; bright-haired Augusta, tall, slim, and, it must be added, unamiably silent; and Ellen Chadwick, whose black eyes had an absolute glow of expectancy in their depths. Bess put up her hand in amazement.

"Eh, Mrs. Ashton, madam! Yo' han takken us unawares! An' theer is na a bit o' flesh meat i' th' heause, an' th' butcher's cart wunna be reawnd agen till Setterday! But awn downreet glad to see yo' an' th' young ladies (she dropped a respectful curtsey) an' a' lookin' so weel. Aw wur afeard yo' wur no' comin' this summer."

"Never mind the butcher's meat, Mrs. Hulme; having come to Carr, we must do as Carr does. I do not doubt we shall fare very well," said the stately lady, reassuringly. "I trust we shall find your good husband free from pain, and Mr. Clegg and your family in health."

Bess thanked Mrs. Ashton for her kind inquiries, but somehow she boggled over the "Mr. Clegg." She was proud enough of his advancement, but to her he was still "Jabez," and he did not seek to be otherwise.

There was a difficulty about the luggage, no men being about. By this time old Simon was nearly down the hill, little Sim following at his heels, his face, hands, and pinafore stained with fruit.

"I run for Joe," cried crippled Sim, as Bess tried the weight of a trunk, and Ellen interposed. Run, indeed! It was the very travestie of a run!

"Well, yo' see as heaw o' Moore's folk are eawt i' th' fields cuttin' whoats [oats]. Feyther an' me con carry one on 'em atween us. They're noän so heavy," said Tom, who had followed in the wake of Bess.

Mrs. Ashton would not hear of it. Just then little Sim came back with Joe—his most particular friend, to whom he was chief patron—a drivelling idiot, a man in frame, a child in heart and brain. He was a pitiable object, the scoff of the rabble, but he had sense enough to know his protectors. At the instance of the four-year-old child he shouldered the box with a vacant chuckle, and Sim, loaded with an oval pasteboard bandbox half as big as himself, waddled after him as fast as his deformity would permit.

Before the travellers could reach the top of the avenue Jabez Clegg was with them, the other trunk upon his shoulder. He had heard at the "White Hart" of their arrival, and had almost sacrificed the dignity of his position in *his* desire to run.

There were more greetings, accompanied by a cordial shaking of hands, and Bess and Simon looked on with pleasure, not unmixed with pain, that the foundling they had adopted and reared had mounted far above their heads, albeit in rising he had drawn them up too.

He breakfasted not with them in the house-place, but with the new-comers in the parlour, and Bess herself waited upon them, Meg, her little maid, being off in the harvest field gleaning for a bed-ridden mother.

She heard him conversing freely, if deferentially, with the lofty Mrs. Ashton on topics, and in a language her provincial tongue could never compass. She saw him turn to answer the arch sallies of Miss Ashton, and the quieter observations of Miss Chadwick, and noted that the dark eyes of the latter kindled when he spoke, and her cheeks had a warmer glow, as if they caught their hue from the flushed face of Jabez.

Breakfast over—little Sim had sat on the doorstep to share his with Crazy Joe, whilst Ellen and Augusta retired to unpack—Mrs. Ashton graciously accepted the escort of Mr. Clegg to the mill, and they trod the avenue and the high-road side by side, discussing business matters, her dignity losing no whit by the companionship. Mrs. Ashton was one of those who could lift up without stooping.

Clouds never lingered on Augusta's face; she had been transported thither, as she said, "with no more ceremony than a bale of twist," but she put off her displeasure with her travelling bonnet, and danced into the kitchen airily as a sylph, to help Bess out of the quandary caused by their advent.

"I am afraid our arrival has been very inauspicious," Augusta said, "but I can assure you I was not consulted, and am not to blame." (She had certainly not been consulted—blame was another matter.) "And now what can I do for you, Mrs. Hulme?"

Augusta tucked up the sleeves of her peach-coloured gingham dress, borrowed a linen apron from Bess, who confessed to being "rayther a heavy hond at paste," and soon the matron was at ease respecting pies, and tarts, and custards. Simon Clegg brought in a dish of trout fresh from the stream, the larder supplied savoury ham and eggs, the garden furnished peas, so Mrs. Ashton was not far wrong.

It was but a spurt on Augusta's part; her tender impressionable heart had melted at Mrs. Hulme's first look of dismay, but, the impulse over, there was no more tucking up of sleeves or handling of paste pins. Fortunately for their digestion, Ellen

Chadwick had no less skill, since, quiet as she was, she seemed to lack an outlet for superabundant energy, and, obtrusively restless, helped Bess she hardly knew how, or how much.

Augusta wandered about cottage and garden, or sat for hours under the shade of the great sycamore tree, singing low-voiced plaintive ditties; feeling herself the most ill-used and wretched being in existence, separated from her adorable lover; and the more she brooded, the more discontented and melancholy she became. It was all very real and very much to be deplored. No knife cuts so keenly at the heart-strings as the sharp edge of a first love turned in upon itself; and Augusta was as much in love as ever was maiden of seventeen.

Mrs. Ashton went daily to the mill, but a casual remark of Mrs. Hulme's on "Miss Ashton's mopin' an' malancholy" aroused the attention of the energetic mother, and she did her best to counteract morbid fancies with long sharp walks in the early morning (extending, on one oecasion, as far as Shawcross Hall, where she astonished her relatives by an informal visit), and a repetition of the dose in the evening, when Mr. Clegg made one of the party, thus unconsciously adding fuel to the fires which, unknown to her, consumed alike her niece and her warehouseman.

At the end of ten days, Mrs. Ashton returned to Manchester, leaving the girls behind. She had extorted a promise from Augusta that she would not write to Mr. Laurence Aspinall, and relied on that promise being faithfully kept. Moreover, after some debate with herself, as they walked from the mill together on the last afternoon of her stay, she committed her daughter and niece to Jabez Clegg's care.

"You are a very young man for so important a charge," she said, "but you are steady as old Time, and of your integrity and fidelity we have had many proofs. Miss Ashton's health demands a prolonged stay on this breezy hill-side, but I fear she feels it dull after Manchester. If you will endeavour to amuse her when you see her drooping, I shall consider myself your debtor, sir; and should anything *unusual* attract your notice, I depend on your calling our attention to it."

"I feel honoured by the trust you repose in me, madam," replied he, a grave consciousness of his own danger stirring at his heart; "you may depend on my watchfulness over Miss Ashton and her cousin."

But of any danger to Miss Ashton beyond that arising from a sensitively delicate frame, which might need the sudden summons of Dr. Hull to allay the fears of parents anxious for their only child, he had no suspicion or perception. He had no more clue to Mrs. Ashton's hidden meaning than she to his secret emotions. It had been wiser to have been more explicit. Without that charge he might have made it a point of honour, if not of duty, to hold aloof from the young ladies, lest he should be obtrusive; as it was, the more he pondered, the more he became satisfied that it was only a delicate way of giving sanction to a companionship he might otherwise have regarded as presumptuous.

Accordingly, he constituted himself their cavalier after business hours, fulfilling to the letter his instructions to endeavour to amuse Augusta whenever he found her drooping, well rewarded if he could win back a smile or a peal of the rippling laughter he had heard so oft in her school-girl days. His attentions to Miss Chadwick were tinctured with the profoundest respect, but there was no effort to entertain or be agreeable; on the contrary, it was Miss Chadwick who kept the light shafts of her cousin's wit within bounds when they were likely to wound—as they did sometimes.

The "White Hart," to Sim's disquiet, would have suffered long from dearth of herbage, had not thunderous clouds emptied their reservoirs amongst the hills, until brooks became rivers, and roads almost impassable. Then Jabez resumed his brush, Sim clapped his thin little hands with delight, whilst the sedate young lady of twenty-four, and the bewitching damsel of sweet seventeen, varied the monotony of piano, book, or embroidery-frame, with an occasional criticism of his work.

It was a time fraught with intoxicating delight, but of terrible temptation to Jabez. The frequent fits of languor which bowed Augusta down like a drooping lily, made her only more dangerously dear to him, and it needed all his strength to remember that she was his master's daughter, and confided to his care. If he now thought of Laurence Aspinall and his fascination, it was only as a butterfly beau, for whom no sensible maiden could entertain a permanent liking. Not even when, turning back one forenoon for something in the closet which he had forgotten, he found her in tears on the low ledge of the open window at the foot of the staircase.

"Good heavens! Miss Ashton, what is the matter? Are you ill? Is anything troubling you?"

"Nothing," sobbed she, the clear drops falling faster.

"Nothing! oh, Miss Ashton, this cannot be for nothing," and he sat down on the window-ledge beside her, not daring so much as to touch her hand, his own were in such a quiver.

"Miss Ashton—Augusta—you told me your troubles when you were a school-girl, am I less worthy your confidence now? Can I do anything to serve you? I would lay my life down to save you from pain;" and the earnest tenderness of his voice spoke volumes.

She had subdued her emotion. Gathering herself up with a reflex of her mother's stateliness, she said haughtily, "It is nothing, sir, I am better," and swept past him up the staircase, leaving him to set his teeth and turn away with clenched hands, alike exasperated at his own loss of self-command and grieved for her grief.

On the narrow landing which ran parallel with the staircase like a balcony, Augusta found her cousin Ellen, with one hand on her side, leaning against the chamber door-post, as if for support, with closed eyes and pale lips. She had been "overcome by the heat"—so she said.

CHAPTER THE THIRTY-SIXTH.

THE LOVERS' WALK.

JABEZ held a responsible post, and had no more leisure than other business men for emotional indulgence. He hurried out of the cottage, and down the avenue, shutting up his bitter feelings within the door of his heart as he went. But the process closed his eyes and ears to external sounds, and the old postman, with his long tin horn, which had been echoing through the straggling village a full quarter of an hour, passed him in the avenue and said, "Good day," without so much as arresting his attention.

At the mill he found letters waiting—one, which had been post-paid as a double letter, conspicuous amongst the wafered business communications, not only because of its thick, gilt-edged paper, and crimson disk of crested wax, but from its curious folding, as if to baffle prying eyes.

It was signed "Ben Travis," and was so long, it went into a pantaloon pocket, to be read when his multifarious duties allowed him more leisure.

When the hands were dismissed at noon, and the one clerk had left the counting-house, he took out the voluminous epistle, which was dated September 10th, and certainly found therein matter of interest. Amongst a few preliminary items of news, he learned that the excesses of the Coronation night had created so much disgust in the minds of thinking men that many of those who had denounced Henry Hunt's advocacy of abstinence and at the public expense had formerly disseminated printed laudations of good brown ale, the "old English beverage," as "a cheering and strengthening drink," no longer branded the water-drinkers as "enemies to the corporeal constitution of Englishmen," but had given their countenance to social gatherings whence intoxicating liquors were excluded. Travis himself was doing what he could to promote these temperate meetings, and looked for the earnest co-operation of Mr. Clegg on his return to Manchester. (And reformers saw in advance how universal would become the temperance movement of which this was the unpretending precursor.

The letter went on to say—

"*Miss Chadwick and her fair cousin were spirited away mysteriously. At first I blamed myself as the unhappy cause. I have since discovered my mistake, through a quarrel between Mr. Walmsley and Mr. Laurence Aspinall, when both were slaves to Bacchus—"In vino veritas!" I suppose you know that Mr. Aspinall the elder is a martyr to the gout, and has been driven by his enemy to the Buxton baths. The cause, I have heard, was a gentlemanly debauch in a fit of passion or wounded pride. His son joins him to-day. I scarcely think he will call on your young ladies after what has occurred.*"

"What has occurred?" repeated Jabez, "what can he mean by that? I wish correspondents would be more explicit!"

He pondered over this sentence, but could make nothing of it, and after reading a little way, came to the real object of the letter, prefaced as it was with much circumlocution.

"*It may seem strange that a great, big, burly fellow like myself should be such a booby as to seek the intervention of a third person in an affair of the heart. Yet, if I have any insight into your nature, I think I may confide in you, and depend on your good offices. After so many months' dangling, and craven hesitation, I summoned up courage to make my pretensions known to Miss Chadwick. I know I did it clumsily and ungracefully; the very strength of my passion fettered my tongue. I shall never forget the pitiful look of the sweet girl as she burst into tears, assured me of her esteem, but declined my suit. Her tears unnerved me, and I had not power to plead my own cause. Do not despise me, Clegg; neither Samson nor Hercules was any stronger. I cannot resign myself to that verdict. I would throw myself again at Ellen's feet, and beseech her pity, but that I dread its repetition. Can I count on your good offices to move her in my behalf? I know the value Miss Chadwick sets on your opinion, and how highly she esteems you, or I should not think of asking this. The trust I repose in you is the best proof I can give of friendship. Do not hesitate to tell me the worst. I hope I am brave enough to bear my fate—when I know it. Mrs. Chadwick does not believe her daughter's decision final."*

This was a disquieting letter. Mr. Travis had been his firm, true friend, in spite of difference in position and fortune. He had overlooked that difference from the first, but would Miss Chadwick, his employer's niece, overlook it, if he stepped beyond privileged bounds? From the depths of his own conscious heart he felt grieved for his friend, but how to approach so delicate a subject to serve him was perplexing. He never thought of shirking the trust.

It was late when he got home to dinner. Ellen and Bess were both on the look-out for him. He quickened his pace, fearing some evil to his beloved Augusta, whom he had last seen in tears.

"What an anomaly is woman!" he thought, as he found her fingers rattling over the keys of her piano in accompaniment to the merriest ditty he had heard from her lips since she was a child.

There was a strange sparkle in her eyes, a vivacity in her manner so opposed to her sadness that he asked himself if he had been dreaming before, or was dreaming then. She blushed over her willow-pattern plate as she took her seat, but, after that first token of susceptibility, chatted with a volubility unusual to her, and curiously in contradistinction to the silence and reserve of Ellen Chadwick. In the morning he had debated whether that secret trouble came within the category of "unusual" things Mrs. Ashton required to be informed of, and, behold! it was gone!

She rallied both Jabez and Ellen on their gravity, and at length, as if on a sudden inspiration, asked, playing with her green-handled, two-pronged fork—

"Shall you be very busy at the mill this afternoon, Mr. Clegg?"

It was an unusual question. He answered—

"Rather. Some bales of twist have come in from Messrs. Evans, of Darley-Abbey Mills. I must see them unpacked, and compare the twist with samples. But—your motive for asking?"

"Oh, if you are busy——Well, perhaps after tea will be better; it will be cooler. I wish you would just take Ellen a good long walk; I found her fainting with the heat this morning."

Ellen coloured vividly.

"Augusta!" she remonstrated.

"And yourself, Miss Ashton?" questioned he.

"Oh, I have a heap of clear-starching to do. My frills and laces are in a woeful plight. I shall be clap, clap, clap, all the afternoon, and this sultry weather prohibits ironing until there is a cool evening breeze to fan me through the window. Without it I should be as likely to faint as Ellen."

Miss Chadwick made light of her faintness, and objected, if not too strenuously, to be so disposed of; but Augusta, in her old wilful way, insisted, and Jabez, with his friend's letter on his mind, was not likely to throw opposition in the way. So, notwithstanding his recent rebuff, he was once more "Miss Ashton's humble servant to command."

After an early tea, which was but a fiction to all three, Augusta was left behind, busy with her box-iron and her lady-like laundry of lace and muslin in the house-place, whilst Ellen Chadwick and Jabez went rambling with the winding waters of the translucent Goyt, under umbrageous trees on pleasant mountain slopes, where foxgloves nodded and horsetail grasses bent before them, and only an occasional reaper or gleaner crossed their path.

Had these two been incipient lovers, no more embarrassing silence could have fallen upon them. If Jabez, her junior by two years, had had a tussle to keep his love within bounds, there had at least been a glimmer of hope in the distance, and the struggle was upwards. Ellen had been trained from her childhood to keep her naturally strong feelings under control, but there was a war in her breast between maidenly shame and unsought, hopeless love, and the two hacked at each other and at her heart in the rayless dark, and the struggle was downwards.

Here she was, for the first time, alone with the man she loved with all the strength of a strong heart, with the newly-gained knowledge that he "would die to save her cousin pain;" and he, conscious of a sacred and delicate mission, all unaware of her secret love for himself, was perplexed how best to approach the subject and take advantage of the opportunity so afforded him. At length——

"I had a letter from my friend Captain Travis to-day," he began.

With little perceptible emotion, she replied——

"Indeed! I hope he was in good health. You are honoured in your friendship, sir. Mr. Travis is a noble gentleman, and I esteem him highly."

This paved the way for him to expatiate on Ben Travis's many good qualities. He told the story of the big, raw-boned youth's first patronage of himself, and found an attentive listener as he traced the growth of their friendship upwards, and related favourable anecdotes which have no place in this history. But no sooner did he begin to plead his friend's cause with all the warmth of young friendship, than her manner entirely changed. Her colour came and went; she panted as if for breath, and, gasping out, "Oh—h! Mr. Clegg, for mercy's sake, don't—don't!" was seized with a sudden faintness for the second time that day.

A lichen-covered old tree trunk, shattered and uptorn in the late thunderstorms, was at hand; he seated her upon it, bringing water to revive her from a runnel near; but any attempt to renew the subject only seemed to give her exquisite pain, and he desisted on her telling him, in a suffocating voice——

"Honour forbids that I should listen to Mr. Travis; I—I—love another."

Something in her tone or manner told him that her love was as hopeless as his own for Augusta, and nothing could be more respectful and gentle than his bearing towards her on their homeward way, thus adding fuel to the fire which consumed her.

The evening shadows were fast closing in when they reached the cottage, and she, with a simple inclination of the head, left Jabez on the threshold, and, passing through the parlours, carried her overmastering emotions upwards to her room, to be grappled with in the silence of the night.

"Wheere's Miss Ashton?" asked Bess. "Hoo said it wur too hot to bide i' th' heawse, and hoo put her irons deawn, an' after tittivatin' hersel' oop a bit, went eawt a-seekin' yo'."

In some surprise, not unmixed with alarm, for the hour was late—as times and country went—and the harvest brought rough strangers into the neighbourhood, Jabez set off at full speed down the avenue, and ere he had reached the first brook, saw her lithe figure advancing buoyantly, and, if his eyes and the gathering mist did not deceive him, a second figure parted from her at the gate.

She was the first to speak. "Whichever way did you people ramble off?"

"Oh! down by the Goyt, Taxal way, Miss Ashton," answered Jabez.

"Ah! and I went up the Buxton Road; we were certain to miss."

"I thought I saw you part from some one at the gate? Could I be mistaken?" half-questioned her interlocutor.

"Oh, Crazy Joe! that was all!" and he took her reply in all sincerity, not believing Augusta Ashton capable of untruth.

A day or two went by, during which Jabez wrote to tell Ben Travis he "must arm himself with fortitude"—that "the world was full of disappointments"—that "Miss Chadwick loved elsewhere"—but there was "something more for men to do than die of disappointments or blighted love."

And yet another day or two, during which Augusta's moods were as variable as the gusty shadows of the sycamore, changing from wild exuberance which rallied Ellen on her depression, and condescended to play or dance for Sim, to a moping, moody melancholy, enlivened by frequent showers. She was given to snatch up her hat and "run out into the garden for a breath of fresh air," but she generally came in panting, as if the "run" had been literal; and sometimes she would be found in the house when supposed out of it, and *vice versa.*

The "White Hart" had not yet walked away, although Jabez considered it complete. It waited Mr. Ashton's coming and his verdict, and stood on the easel in the dining-room.

The morning post had brought a message to Simon Clegg concerning fruit and vegetables for the Manchester home, and having sought him in the kitchen-garden to deliver it, Jabez entered the house at dinner-time by the lower staircase window (frequently used for entrance and exit). His passage through the best parlour was arrested by voices in the room beyond, one of which he knew too well. It was that of Laurence Aspinall. His painting was evidently under free criticism, and had been for some time. There was some jesting at the sign-painter.

"You see, Miss Ashton, what a few touches can effect!"

The speaker had apparently made free with Clegg's colours and brushes, and there was a murmured sound of assent from Miss Ashton.

"Well, Barret, *Nec scire fas est omnia; Ne sutor ultra crepidam.* What say you?"

"Yes; let the cobbler stick to his last. If this Clegg would be an artist, let him stick to his brush; if a tradesman, let him stick to his trade. If a man means to succeed, he must never flirt with either art or trade. It's just as bad as wooing two women at once."

Jabez heard no more. The blow which had been aimed at his art-pretensions drove him back by the way he came, and he paced the long terrace parallel with the "Lovers' Walk" for fully half-an-hour. When he turned the corner of the cottage, and went in at the front door, the critics were gone, but Aspinall's "few touches" remained. They had indeed given life to the "White Hart." Henceforth the "cobbler" resolved to "stick to his last."

Ellen Chadwick had been away, with little Sim by the hand, to take some substantial comforts to Meg's bedridden mother. She appeared annoyed when she heard of their masculine visitors from Buxton. Her evident displeasure set Jabez wondering what Travis meant by "after what has occurred," and he wrote that afternoon for enlightenment, sending his letter as a packet by coach, there being no second post.

It has been said that the cellarage of the cottage was only accessible by flights of steps in the portion of the weed-grown "Lovers' Walk" which lay at the windowless back of the long low building, where nettles grew so thick and rank that even the square unused trap over one set of steps was half hidden by them. The path was rarely used, the farmer having made a nearer cut from the farmyard to his ancient dwelling.

Tom Hulme was slowly recovering, under the care of a Buxton doctor who came thrice a week. He could walk about the garden with a stick, but there was no sending him to the dark cellar for anything. The doctor had ordered him port wine, and Bess, who kept the key, had asked Mr. Clegg to fetch a couple of bottles from the cellar.

Tea was over, but he fancied there was sufficient light to guide him without a lantern. He had got the wine, and was approaching the cellar door at the foot of the sunken steps when he heard the sound of voices coming along the walk from the direction of the moor.

Every pulse in his body seemed to grow still as he recognised the tones of Augusta Ashton and Laurence Aspinall, and heard with deepening anguish the unmistakable sound of kisses interchanged. They had apparently paused close to the stair-head for that embrace; and then he heard—and thanked God that he was there to hear, though that hearing blighted every hope he had—his rival, with every argument which passionate love or skilful sophistry could employ, persuade her to elope with him the following night.

Backwards and forwards they walked in the gathering dusk, but never beyond the length of the premises; and now and then they stopped, and drove him mad with their caresses. The place was so retired and lonely, precaution was neglected; and Jabez, chained to the spot as it were, gathered that proposals for her hand, made by Laurence himself, had been peremptorily rejected by Mr. Ashton, who was set down as a despot and a tyrant for refusing to surrender a silly girl of seventeen to a rake of two-and-twenty. He heard her tell that Jabez Clegg had found her sobbing at the separation, even whilst her darling's letter was at the gate. And he heard it said that the elder Aspinall not only countenanced this secret courtship, but had furnished funds for the proposed elopement. This generosity was set against the cruelty of her own parents; her affection, her pride, the romance in her nature were appealed to, but still Augusta's better angel held her safe, until, coward that he was, Laurence terrified her with a threat to "blow his brains out" if she refused him.

She wept her assent upon his breast, and then Jabez, already half-stunned, heard the details of evidently previously concocted arrangements for their elopement and marriage at Gretna Green, professedly with his father's sanction.

CHAPTER THE THIRTY-SEVENTH.

A RIDE ON A RAINY NIGHT.

A MIDNIGHT ALARM.

JABEZ, bottles in hand, his mind a chaos, had walked in at the wash-kitchen door precisely as Augusta, stealthily creeping through a gap in the privet hedge, made her way to the convenient staircase window, shivering more from fright than from the chill drizzling rain which had begun to fall. Putting her head in at the parlour-door, where Ellen was sewing, with a brief "I'm off to bed," she hurried upstairs in the dusk to lave her flushed face, smooth her disordered hair, crush it under a nightcap, and place her head on a pillow, to still her heart's flutterings under the screening counterpane, and hide her emotions from her cousin under the semblance of sleep, though sleep was an absolute impossibility,

In 1821 the village of Gretna Green, on the Scottish border, was the general resort of runaway lovers, who, being in their minority, could not be married legally in England without parental consent, whereas in Caledonia a mere promise to marry made in the presence of witnesses was held binding. At Gretna a man not in holy orders, but metaphorically called "the blacksmith," because he riveted the chains of matrimony, lived in the first house beyond the bridge which spanned the river Sark, and, with a ceremonial as unseemly as it was brief, married all comers, often with pursuers at his very doors; and the marriages so contracted were not to be set aside. For more than half a century Gretna Green weddings had figured largely in the literature of the stage and of the circulating library; and there is no doubt that the halo of romance thrown around an elopement to Gretna blinded to the impropriety of the prenuptial flight many a foolish or headstrong girl whom the actual ceremony shocked and startled.

Augusta Ashton, with all her sentimental romance, all her petulant wilfulness, all her resentment at being exiled from home and her Adonis, yet loved her parents well, although her reverence and filial obedience had been gradually undermined by the plausible sophistry and impassioned eloquence of her ardent lover. But if she loved them much, she unfortunately, loved Laurence more. He was, to do him justice, terribly in earnest; and in the inexperience of her seventeen years she could not be expected to sift and analyse that passionate earnestness for its many components. With her *all* was *love*, and *love* was *all.*

His proposition had, nevertheless, come upon her with a shock. She was not prepared to ignore the prudent teaching of her mother, or to brave the indignation of her indulgent father, or to forfeit her own self-respect, and nothing could have moved her to consent but that appalling threat of suicide. and he knew her tender heart well when he made it?

But neither that threat nor her promise could reconcile her to the rash step, and she lay in bed shuddering with her own fears, and, strangely enough, her first thought was—"What would Jabez say if he knew it?" Not her father, not her mother, but the Jabez whom she had rebuffed only a week before, yet of whose opinion she somehow slood more in awe than of all else besides.

What did Jabez think, seeing that he did know? Think? He scarcely could think. Feeling seemed to overpower thought, reason, perception. When after a stagnant time he emerged from the stairhead, it was more as a culprit than Jabez Clegg. He put down the bottles and escaped again into the open air, cowed alike by the knowledge which had overpowered him, and by a sense of dishonour at having played the unworthy part of a listener, albeit the listening had been involuntary, seeing that the shock of his discovery had stunned him like a blow from a sledge-hammer, crushing his own long-cherished hopes to death. His next thought was of intense thankfulness that by any means the schemes of Aspinall had been bared to him, and in time to attempt the rescue of his idolised Augusta from the clutches of a villain.

Unacquainted with the events which had preceded Augusta's removal to Carr—unaware that the Mosley Street doors had been closed against Laurence, or that a formal proposal for the young lady's hand had been made by the elder Aspinall on behalf of his son, and peremptorily declined by the Ashtons; ignorant that imperious Mr. Aspinall, in his gouty wrath, had sworn "upon his honour" that his son *should* "marry the girl in spite of the paltry beggars'-inkle-weaver," and having no faith in the man himself, Jabez regarded the use of the father's name only as a proof of his greater perfidy, and gave him no credit even for an honourable intention or an honest emotion. The time was past for Clegg to find excuses for the wrong-doing of his adversary

Now, with every nerve unstrung, he was required to act, and that promptly. To-morrow would be too late. What if he should take Miss Chadwick into his confidence? But no, he could not lower Augusta in the eyes even of her own cousin; and neither she nor anyone there had authority to detain Miss Ashton against her will even if her foot were on the step of the post-chaise. It was imperative that he should reach Manchester immediately, yet how to do so without exciting alarm perplexed him. There was a horse in the stable at the mill, but as he had a bed in Simon's room, and could neither leave it nor return to it in the night without passing through the Hulmes' sleeping apartment, there was a difficulty in quitting the house unknown.

"I must be at the mill before daybreak to-morrow, having something of importance to attend to, so I will sleep on the squab in the house-place, Mrs. Hulme. If I am not in for breakfast, do not wait for me," said he; and no one questioned him, although Mrs. Hulme and her husband were of joint opinion that "Jabez looked terribly put eawt," and wondered what business he could have on hand of so much consequence.

No one thought of locking country cottage doors. By nine o'clock all the inmates were in bed and asleep. Before ten Jabez, sad at heart, had quietly left the cottage for the mill, had saddled Peveril, and, though no great horseman, was speeding past the "White Hart" along the highway to Manchester, fast as the steady-going roadster would travel. The wind had risen, and the rain came down persistently; but, heedless of discomfort or danger, with the one thought paramount in his mind—the preservation of his master's daughter—he set his teeth and rode on with feverish impatience, which at length communicated itself to Peveril, and quickened the beat of the sensible animal's hoof; impatience which would have sent him flying over the toll-gates, had either he or his steed been equal to the exploit, and which could barely brook the delay of drowsy tollkeepers.

Nevertheless as he turned from Piccadilly into Mosley Street, the muffled-up old watchman, catching the echoes of the Infirmary clock, bawled out, to mark his own vigilance, "Just one o'clock, an' a dark, rainy neet!" and the Ashton household had closed its eyelids and its account with the day at least a couple of hours.

It is never pleasant to be the bearer of ill-tidings, so no wonder Jabez hesitated with the lion-headed knocker in his hand ere he sent its reverberations growling through the silent house. His hesitation must have influenced the knocker, for the lion had to roar again, and louder, before he heard the window above unclose, and saw Mr. Ashton's night-capped head thrust out, to ask, in alarm, "Who's there? What's the matter?"

Jabez stepped back to the kerbstone to let the dull rays of an oil lamp fall upon his face.

"It is I, Jabez Clegg, sir; I have a matter of importance to communicate."

"Good heavens, Clegg, you! Surely the mill's not been

burned down?"

"No, sir, all's right at the factory. There's no harm done anywhere at *present.* If you will please to come down, I hope there may be time to prevent that which is threatened."

"Just so; I'll be down directly."

There were no lucifer matches with which to procure instantaneous light, but during this brief colloquy Mrs. Ashton had been groping on the tall chimney-piece for their precusors, the Prometheans, and having found them, by dipping a small chemically prepared match into a tiny bottle of fluid, she obtained a light as soon as the window was closed and the draught shut out.

Too uneasy to waste much time in dressing, before many minutes had flown Mr. and Mrs. Ashton, whose fears had equally pointed to their daughter—the one in a roquelaire, and the other in her warehouse overall—were both listening with agitated and anxious faces to Mr. Clegg's communication, made with a discomposure great as their own.

"Elope!" both parents exclaimed, simultaneously.

"Elope!" reiterated the mother. "Our daughter consent to elope, and with a reprobate like him? It is not possible!"

"So I should have said, madam, yesterday," rejoined Jabez, sadly, as he sank on a chair, overpowered more by the strain on his feelings than by the fatigue of his long, wet, midnight ride, "and I would have given the *world* to have been able to doubt the evidence of my own ears."

Mrs. Ashton, with clasped hands up, sat opposite to Jabez; Mr. Ashton, lacking the consolation and inspiration of his snuff-box, walked about the room with one hand to his head in a state of distressing perturbation. He stopped in his walk to ask, "What's to be done?" as Jabez made this declaration, unconscious of its force.

The light of the chamber candle fell upon the haggard face and drenched garments of the young man. The elder one looked full at him, paused, then drawing near and laying his right hand heavily on the other's wet shoulder, asked in a troubled voice, with an inquisitorial, but not unkind manner——

"My lad, did no other motive than duty to your employers bring you eighteen miles through the rain this dark night to save Miss Ashton from an imprudent marriage?"

Jabez had not stopped to analyse his own motives. Thus questioned, it was not without embarrassment that he answered, "Mrs. Ashton desired me, sir, to watch over Miss Ashton, and acquaint you with any matter affecting her welfare. But apart from that, sir, I could not see Miss Ashton in the toils of a libertine without an attempt to rescue her. I should have been a dastard to sit passive, and even now I feel we are losing time."

"Just so, just so," assented Mr. Ashton. "That reminds me, Peveril is in the street, and you are soaked to the skin. My dear"—turning to his wife—"will you arouse the servants, and see that neither horse nor rider suffers in our service more than we can help?"

Having thus got rid of his wife, of whom he stood somewhat in awe, he resumed his searching catechism of Jabez.

"And so, Clegg, you have no motive beyond a chivalrous desire to save your master's daughter, no *interest* to serve beyond your duty to us?"

The ordeal was terrible. Jabez rose, his features working convulsively.

"Mr. Ashton, you are torturing me. Humble as I am, I love Miss Ashton with my whole life and soul. But knowing the distance between us, I have striven to keep the secret in my own breast. And I protest I had no double motive in my journey hither."

The genial smallware manufacturer, to whom that night had brought two revelations, looked Jabez steadfastly in the face as he made his avowal; then, taking him kindly by the hand, said—his eyes swimming——

"Just so, just so, my lad! I believe you. And, Jabez

Clegg, let me tell you that I would rather give my daughter to an upright, persevering man like you, without a penny, than to a spendthrift like Laurence Aspinall, though he rolled in riches. But it is no use saying that *now*."

Indeed there was no use, and time was flying. A glance of grateful attachment, and a mute pressure of his liberal master's hand, were the sole acknowledgment of Jabez. But a new bond was established between the twain.

Mrs. Ashton had come back to discuss with her husband and Jabez the best mode of procedure. She was not less shrewd than her lord, and had not failed to perceive that the young man's heart was in the service he now rendered them. The blow dealt by Augusta to her pride dashed down the impalpable barrier between them and she took counsel with him as a tried and true friend.

Mr. Clegg pointed out the necessity for his return to the mill before it should open, and he be missed; and taking a proffered glass of brandy and water to avert cold, he hurried, whilst hot coffee was preparing, to change his soaked garments preparatory to the ride back; his elders also taking the opportunity to dress and prepare for departure with the morning coach.

Not a moment was wasted, but though Peveril had been well groomed and fed, he was not so fresh to the road as he had been; still the journey was homeward, the rain had abated; day began to dawn as he left Stockport behind, and without much use of the whip, Jabez had his horse back in the stable before the factory bell began to ring. And then the *beast* was allowed to rest. The jaded *man* had to rouse himself to another day's work, another day's trial and excitement, without a moment for repose.

To everybody's astonishment, Mr. and Mrs. Ashton stepped out of the "Lord Nelson" coach that morning at the bottom of the avenue, with a carpet-bag for luggage. The difference of their reception by daughter and niece was palpable, and they could not fail to observe how much the former was disconcerted by their arrival.

"Oh, aunt and uncle, this is a pleasant surprise!" exclaimed Ellen, running down the avenue to meet them.

"*You* do not appear very well pleased to see us, Augusta," remarked Mrs. Ashton, as she met her lazily sauntering through the garden towards them, as captivating in her printed morning dress as a sleepless night, an anxions headache, and her unmistakable confusion would permit the recognised beauty to be.

"Oh, yes, I am pleased enough, but I should have been better pleased if you had written instead of coming upon one so suddenly. It is quite startling!" and the petulance of her tone gave effect to the pettish frown on her brow.

"My dear, ill thoughts make ill looks," said Mrs. Ashton, gravely, with a searching glance. "What is the matter with you this morning? Nothing serious, I hope."

The very inquiry apparently annoyed her.

"Oh, I've got a headache, that's all. I heard a man's foot on the gravel-walk long after everyone was in bed, and I got a fright."

"I think it was only Crazy Joe—he hangs about at all hours," put in Ellen, who had not heard the crunch of Mr. Clegg's heel on the gravel, as he stood for a moment under their window, to breathe a prayer for the safety and well-being of the supposed sleeper, before he turned away swiftly on his errand.

Almost Mr. Ashton's first inquiry was for Mr. Clegg.

"He's at the mill, sir. He was off afore any on us was up; an' he said happen he mightna git whome fur breakfast, he wur so busy," was the reply of Bess.

But Mr. Ashton, setting off towards the factory, encountered Jabez on the way, and they returned together to breakfast, as if they had met for the first time that morning. On Mrs. Ashton's suggestion, Augusta was neither questioned nor accused.

"We should only tempt her to deny, and perhaps provoke ill-will towards our informant, with no good end," she said. "Better wait and ascertain beyond question what her intentions are."

Jabez would fain have spared her the pain and shame of exposure, but the matter was out of his hands.

The day passed unmarked save by Augusta's restless look-out for Crazy Joe, and the way she hung about her mother, as if half afraid of the rash step she contemplated.

Mr. Ashton meanwhile, to cover his distress and agitation, busied himself about the transfer of the "White Hart" (which he pronounced "admirable") to its place over the inn-door, and managed to elicit from Chapman, the gossiping landlord, without direct inquiry, that a fine young spark in hunting gear had put up his horse there several times within the past week, and was ike to make the fortune of Crazy Joe, he gave the poor softy so many half-crowns; but Joe was "deep, and never let on what he got them for."

CHAPTER THE THIRTY-EIGHTH.

DEFEATED.

ATTEMPTED FLIGHT.

JABEZ CLEGG and the young ladies occupied adjoining chambers (the two inner rooms of the suite), but the door of communication was locked, and they were attained by different staircases. Thus, as he was compelled to pass through the 'Hulmes' sleeping apartment, so Ellen and Augusta were constrained to go backwards and forwards through that of Mr. and Mrs. Ashton—an arrangement to which long use had probably reconciled them.

It was this fact which had so much disconcerted Augusta, since she foresaw a difficulty in escaping unheard; and not meeting with Joe (that most unpromising of Cupids), she was as equally unable to convey a message to her expectant lover. She repented her rash promise, and would fain have availed herself of a pretext for delay, but the night came, and, haunted by imaginary pictures of Laurence with a pistol to his head, she dared not disappoint him. She had promised to meet him at that entrance of the Lovers' Walk which opened below Yeardsley Hall Farm into Moor Lane, whilst, the lane being a steep declivity, he was to keep the post-chaise in waiting at the foot.

Her headache served as an excuse for retiring to bed earlier than her cousin, and scarcely could her father and mother restrain themselves as she kissed them lingeringly before she went. Indeed, Mr. Ashton would much have preferred to "have it out with the girl at once, and have done with it," there not being much "waiting" blood in his veins.

He had kept out of her sight most of the day, fidgeting over one thing and another, whilst his waistcoat and shirt-frill bore testimony to the constant raid on his snuff-box.

"I don't like to see my poor lass trapped like a bird in a cage," he said in confidence to Jabez, whose opinion he already knew agreed with his own, as did the desire to "thrash the infernal scoundrel within an inch of his life."

The last straw had broken the camel's back, and Jabez was no longer inclined to be passive.

Laurence had bid Augusta take no care for her wardrobe; his purse was ample, and he would dress her like a queen if she would only consent to fly with him. So, after collecting a few immediate necessaries and trinkets, and placing the reticule which contained them out of sight, she crept into bed, to lie and listen for the household to follow her example. How lazily the hours lagged! She heard old Simon shuffling about, and the creaking of his camp-bedstead as he settled his old rheumatic bones for the night, but the firm foot of Jabez she did not hear, though the house clock struck nine, and Ellen came up with the last stroke.

In answer to a question, Ellen said that Mr. Clegg was asleep on the squab, and that she understood he had slept there the previous night, to be able to go to the mill very early without disturbing anyone else.

"I saw him as he lay there, where he had fallen asleep shortly after tea, and I have been speaking to my uncle about him; he looks so dreadfully worn and jaded, I am sure he is either killing himself with overwork or has some great trouble on his mind," and a deep sigh followed this expression of opinion.

Augusta was silent. Something within her secret heart whispered that the trouble of Jabez Clegg would be intensified sevenfold by her act of that night, and, haughty as she was betimes, she pitied him. And whatever were her compunctions, fears, or emotions, Jabez certainly shared with her parents in her thoughts.

Ellen slept. The clock struck ten. Father and mother entered their room, and through the door which Augusta had artfully requested Ellen to "leave open on account of the heat" came the sound of their voices in low but earnest converse—"You leave her to me, William," spoken with decision, being the only words she could distinguish, though she heard her father walk about for some time. Indeed, she thought he would never go to bed.

Eleven! She slipped stealthily from the side of her sleeping cousin, and by the light of the moon, clear enough to-night, dressed as noiselessly and rapidly as her trepidation would permit. From habit she knelt to pray, but as she came to the passage, "Lead us not into temptation, but deliver us from evil," a new meaning seemed to flash through the words, and she half wavered in her purpose.

"Poor Jabez!" she murmured to herself, as she caught up her shoes and reticule, and listened in the open doorway for the deep breathing which came from behind the dimity curtains of the four-post bed. Re-assured, she stepped lightly across the room in her stocking-feet, turned the drop-handle of that chamber door as silently as the squeaking latch would permit, and fled swiftly down the stairs, sitting down at the bottom to put on her shoes.

She had raised the sash, and was in the very act of stepping over the low window-sill, when a foot was heard on the stair, and, turning her head, she saw her mother fully dressed, close by her side, and felt her slight wrist grasped as in a vice.

"Is this your filial love and obedience, misguided girl? Is this the result of Madame Broadbent's training? Have you no more sense of honour and decency than to elope at midnight with any man, least of all with the worthless reprobate who has caught your silly fancy? Could you not think that chastity is the brightest jewel in a woman's crown, and the soonest dimmed, that you were ready to leave your character at the mercy of every gossip who had a tongue to wag?"

She had drawn Augusta, too much stunned to speak, into the parlour close at hand, and had shut the doors—a needless precaution, seeing how remote were all sleepers. A few words of gentle motherly inquiry might have softened impulsive, tender-hearted Augusta to tears, and turned the whole current of her life; but Mrs. Ashton's stateliness had become sternness, and, fresh from the evil teaching of Laurence Aspinall, her daughter's proud spirit rose in rebellion, and answered her.

"We are going to be married. And I was not going with Laurence alone. Cicily was to travel with us. Laurence himself proposed it."

"Infatuated girl!" exclaimed Mrs. Ashton, "Cicily was in Mosley Street last night."

"And so were you, mother," was the smart retort, "but the coach which dropped you here carried her to Buxton. Outside passengers were muffled up, but she waved her handkerchief as she passed, as a sign to me."

"Sign to you, indeed! I marvel you are not ashamed of yourself and your hero, who is not content with corrupting my daughter, but must corrupt our servants also! A fine hero indeed, whose qualifications are all external! I cannot see what there is to admire in him."

"Not see what there is to admire in that exquisite figure and beautiful face? Why, I shall be the envy of half the girls in Manchester when I marry him!" Augusta exclaimed, with anything but the air of a culprit just detected.

"But you are not likely to marry him, you forward chit. You go back to Manchester to-morrow, and I will take good care you don't marry either clandestinely or openly a man so sure to make your heart ache, if he were thrice as handsome!"

"But I WILL marry him, mamma—*I'll please my eye, if I plague my heart!*"

"*Then as you make your bed, so must you lie, miss,*" answered Mrs. Ashton, gravely and deliberately. "But take my word for it, neither your papa nor myself will give our consent. And now go to your room, Augusta, and thank God you have been saved from disgrace this night, and thank us that we have kept you from open exposure. Not even your cousin has a notion of this last folly. Our daughter's honour is dearer to us than to herself," and the mother's tone softened as she spoke.

"Your daughter's honour has never been in any danger," said Augusta, haughtily, as she swept from the room, to encounter at the foot of the stairs, flooded by moonlight through the open window, her father—and Jabez.

Up to that moment she had stood on the defensive, her wayward spirit upholding and arming her for retort. The sight of the father who had indulged her every whim, and of Jabez, whose esteem she valued more than she herself knew, gave a sudden shock to her overwrought nerves, and she fell forward into the arms of Jabez in a deep swoon.

Tenderly, respectfully, sadly, he bore her into the parlour, and placing her on the sofa, relinquished her to her mother, divesting himself of his shoes in order to procure water to restore her without creating alarm.

When she recovered he was gone; she was alone with the parents whose counsels she had despised, whose love she had wounded; herself detected and humiliated.

A greater humiliation had fallen to the lot of elate, enamoured, and self-satisfied Laurence Aspinall, when, leaving his friend Barret with the post-chaise, their saddle-horses, and Cicily at the bottom of Moor Lane, he mounted the hill and whistled softly at the entrance of the Lovers' Walk, to call forth—not a blushing maiden, half afraid of her own temerity, but—two justly incensed and indignant men. His low-voiced "Augusta—" died upon his lips; he recoiled, stammered—

THE MIDNIGHT STRUGGLE.

"You! I—I did not expect——D—nation! What brought you here? I thought——"

"Just so, you atrocious scoundrel, you thought God had left our pet lamb to the fangs of the wolf, and that neither father nor friend was near to protect the innocent!" exclaimed Mr. Ashton, raising the stout bamboo with which he was provided.

"If that infernal Cicily has betrayed us, I'll——"

The threat was not completed, for Jabez interrupted him with—

"No, sir, it was not Cicily. You betrayed yourself. You laid bare your whole scheme in this walk within my hearing, Mr. Laurence Aspinall, and the sophistry which misled a simple, confiding girl could not delude one who knew you as I do."

"D—nation!" hissed Laurence between his teeth. "You infernal charity-school whelp! Am I to meet you at every turn? I suppose you want Miss Ashton for yourself, but I'll baulk you yet!" and, but that Jabez had a quick eye and hand, his riding-whip would have seamed the latter's manly face.

Jabez dexterously caught the light whip, and wrenched it from him, a simultaneous sharp blow of Mr. Ashton's bamboo on Aspinall's shoulders tending to loosen his grasp. And then the two young men, with all the fever of jealousy added to old animosity, closed and grappled with each other as might a lion and a tiger in the arena. And Mr. Ashton, his love of fair play yielding to his exasperation, made good use of his bamboo whenever he could deal a blow without harming Jabez.

The two combatants were not unequally matched; there was little difference in size and weight, but the scientific skill of Laurence had more than a counterpoise in the nerve and muscle of Jabez, strengthened by exercise and a temperate life, whilst vicious courses had somewhat impaired his own athletic frame.

The struggle on the steep hill-side was too deadly for noise. At length Laurence—himself booted and spurred—in striving to take an unfair advantage and rip the unprotected calves of Jabez with the rowels of his spurs, lost his foothold, and was borne to the earth, falling heavily. He lay on the ground stunned and motionless. At once Jabez, with a swift revulsion of feeling, knelt down by the side of his prostrate foe, and raised his head, Mr. Ashton bending over them inquiringly, just as Barret, whom curiosity and impatience had drawn from his post below, came on the scene. A stifled groan, and a muttered curse, having assured Clegg that his rival was not mortally injured, he called to Barret—

"Here, sir, take charge of your worthy principal; and be careful, when next you plan an elopement, that you have not a man to deal with instead of a credulous girl."

Mr. Ashton's "Just so!" coming sharply in as chorus, the young man put his arm in that of the elder and drew him away, leaving Barret and the postilion to restore Laurence Aspinall, and assist him into the post-chaise by the side of Cicily, whose trepidation would have been very much increased could she have seen how the blood was trickling down from a wound in his head, staining still more the torn, miry coat, and the disordered shirt-frill over which he was usually so fastidious.

Barret, leading his companion's horse, rode on in advance of the vehicle, to prepare the pompous gentleman, laid up with the gout in Buxton Crescent, for the reception of his gentlemanly son in a highly gentlemanlike condition—hatless, wigless, dirty, dilapidated, bruised, bloody—and unsuccessful. The hat had rolled downhill, to be crushed under the wheels of the chaise; the wig and broken whip were found the next morning by Crazy Joe, who exercised his witless head respecting them and the trampled ground to small purpose; then brought them to his friend Sim as playthings. Had they fallen into the hands of a reasoning mortal, much more perplexity, and a very serious mystery, might have been the result.

Buxton being only five miles from Whaley Bridge, Barret again made his appearance in the neighbourhood of the "White Hart," whilst the new sign still attracted rustic admirers; and, finding no rumours current respecting the occurrence of the preceding night, he rode off again, having first committed to Crazy Joe a scarcely decipherable missive from the discomfited lover to the not less disconsolate damsel.

The evening coach bore the Ashtons and Ellen back to Manchester; Augusta, still in a rebellious mood, the cause of which, being hidden from her cousin, occasioned the latter no little perplexity. There was something, too, in the manner of her uncle and aunt to Jabez, and of Jabez to all, which, being undefinable and impalpable, struck her as peculiar. He seemed suddenly to have risen to another footing. How was it they had taken *him* into their confidence?

Not until the last moment—when attention was distracted by the bustle at the inn-door, the disposal of the luggage, and the taking of seats—could Crazy Joe (with cunning worthy a better cause) contrive to slip the billet-doux into Miss Ashton's reticule unseen by all but herself.

Not until she reached her own room in Mosley Street, could she scan its characteristic contents, which ran as follows:—

"*Crescent, Buxton,*

"*September* ——, *1821.*

"*Adored Augusta,*

"*Excuse this scrawl; I can scarcely hold my pen in consequence of a ruffianly attack made upon me by your father's favourite factotum, Jabez Clegg, in Moor Lane last night. Can you disclose to me the strange fatality which kept you from my expectant arms, and revealed our plans to that upstart foundling? Had not Mr. Ashton also struck at me with a stick, I could readily have disposed of his assistant; but my foot tripped over a stone, and falling, I lay at their mercy. Yet, sweet Augusta, if my blood flowed it was for thy sake, and for thy sake I endure.*

"*Be constant, be firm; let no tyranny coerce you, and I will make a way for our union, if I steal you from their very midst.*

I have a dislocated ankle, a bruised and swollen hand, a plaistered crown, and I write painfully. I shall feel every hour a year until I hold you in my arms again. But if my angelic Augusta be only true to her promise, she will soon, in spite of spies and informers, be the adored wife of her

"*Most devoted*

"*Laurence.*"

CHAPTER THE THIRTY-NINTH.

LIKE FATHER, LIKE SON.

IT is no uncommon thing for a woman to gild a block, wreathe it with flowers, and then fall down and worship the idol she has adorned. Augusta's hero needed no outward embellishment, so she fitted the fair exterior with the perfections and virtues of the high-spirited, noble, generous Mortimers and Mowbrays, whose acquaintance she had made in print, and had set him on a very elevated pedestal, in spite of all warnings. With that misleading letter of his before her, no wonder if the "blood shed for her sweet sake" converted the hero into the martyr, and placed Jabez and her father in the category of cruel persecutors. It did more. It erected a barrier against reconciliation. In vain her placable father held out a flag of truce; she kept aloof resentfully, though in the solitude of her own chamber she gave way, and wept at her isolation from all who loved her.

Mrs. Ashton, whose sense of propriety had been outraged, whose maternal pride had received a terrible shock, was less readily disposed to condone her daughter's offence; and, being a better business woman than a psychologist, her tactics showed none of her ordinary shrewdness.

The failure of Augusta's banishment to Carr should have taught her that romance is nursed in solitude, and that conciliation is better than coercion. Had she spared a few hours from the warehouse to arrange a dance, or a gipsy-party to Dunham Park; chaperoned her lovely daughter to assembly, theatre, or concert-room; invited her companionship in a stroll through St. Ann's Square and King Street, calling at Mrs. Edge's fashionably-frequented library by the way; joined the after-morning-church promenaders in the Infirmary Gardens, or given a little time to morning calls, she would have brought Augusta into contact with young people of her own age, and with the attractive of the opposite sex, and so have supplied an antidote for the poison Laurence and ultra-sentimental literature had instilled.

Instead, never was the golden fruit of the Hesperides more vigilantly guarded. She was kept much within doors. There was no Cicily to sympathise or convey clandestine billet-doux. The modern notion that a daily airing is indispensable had not been promulgated, or had not become the creed of the manufacturing community. Mrs. Ashton had "no leisure for gadding," and Augusta cared little to drive in the gig with only James for her charioteer, or even to walk with Ellen, so long as the mulberry-coloured livery was in attendance. (It might have been otherwise, had not the said James held it as much "beneath his dignity" to accept a bribe as he had formerly done to wait upon Mr. Clegg.) From her old bedroom, which overlooked Mosley Street, she was relegated to one in the rear, which commanded no wider prospect than their own courtyard, nor anything more interesting than Nelson and his kennel—by-the-bye, Nelson had been in favour since the sad accident on the ice. Then, visits to Marsden Square were prohibited, lest she should there meet John Walmsley's undesirable friend; and, altogether, her escapade had converted home into a cage, in spite of its gilding.

As might have been expected, the high-spirited wayward girl, so long her father's pet, so long indulged in her caprices, chafed and rebelled against every fresh token of restraint, and contrasted the dull monotony of her life with the freedom and gaiety promised so frequently by Laurence as the certain concomitants of wifehood with him.

With all her haughty spirit, she had a clinging, affectionate nature, tinged though it was with poetry and romance, and now that her father looked so unusually grave, and her mother so frigid, and she felt herself an alien from both their hearts, instead of bewailing her premeditated flight as a crime, the tendrils of her love only clung closer to him who professed so much, and the more she was isolated from them, the more she brooded on the ill-used and maligned Laurence, his manly beauty and accomplishments, his lavish generosity, his fascinations of voice and manner. and the fervour of his passion for her.

Meanwhile, Tom Hulme had resumed his duties at Whaley Bridge Mill, and Jabez returned home to his. Much to Augusta's surprise, he was .not only invited to dine with them on the day of his return, but to take his place henceforth at their board as one of the family.

With Laurence's misrepresentations fixed in her mind as truths, she construed the daily association thus thrust upon her as a deliberate affront, and resented it with a silent scorn which cut Jabez to the soul. He knew nothing of Aspinall's letter, or that he was accused of a "ruffianly attack;" he only felt that he would have died to serve her, and had done what he had to save her from life-long misery, without a single thought of keeping her for himself.

A few more days, and back to Manchester came Mr. Aspinall, senior, having left a little of his portliness with his gout in the Buxton Baths. Back with him came his son, and his son's congenial companion, Mr. Edmund Barret; the former still smarting under his defeat at Carr, and all the more resolutely determined to carry off Augusta, jealousy adding a new element to his love, a new aliment to his hate.

Sitting idly by the parlour window on the third of October, with her head leaning against the frame, meditating on her own unhappiness and her parents' harshness, Augusta suddenly started to her feet with a suppressed cry of delight, a vivid glow upon her cheeks, a brilliant sparkle in her eye. Laurence Aspinall, mounted on Black Ralph, his favourite hunter, was riding up the street, the dislocated ankle apparently not affecting his enjoyment of equestrian exercise. As he raised his new beaver in graceful salutation, even the flutter into which she was thrown could not prevent her missing his glorious curls. He had not deemed it necessary to replace his wig, and the poll shorn during fever had not yet grown a fresh crop ripe for harvest. The unfavourable impression passed with the moment, as he brought his obedient steed on the flagged pavement close under the window, and, without a moment's hesitation, she raised the sash, and leaned forward to speak with him, glad of the opportunity.

"Oh, Laurence!"

"My own Augusta, this is indeed fortunate!"

Their hands clasped upon the window-sill—the elevation of the house raising her to his level—her tearful eyes looked up in his for traces of suffering after the "ruffianly attack," and found there, mingled with the fierce light of violent love, a bitter sense of defeat, a resolve to obtain her by fair means or foul.

Each had the separate experience of that memorable September night to relate, coloured as passion or prejudice prevailed; but neither could fully enlighten the other as to the share Mr. Clegg had had in preventing the elopement.

He could tell her that Jabez had avowed overhearing their conversation in the Lovers' Walk, though where he could have been to overhear, or what strange fatality could bring Mr. and Mrs. Ashton to Carr in time to become the recipients of his eavesdropping and defeat their plans, was a puzzle to both.

Be sure Laurence put the worst colour on the encounter in the lane, and urged all he had himself endured to strengthen his claims upon her—claims she was quite willing to admit, had she the power to concede to them.

Having shown with very evident annoyance, how impossible it was for her to meet or give him a private interview, he exclaimed with indignation—

"What! not allowed to visit a relation, or to go abroad without a gaoler! My dearest Augusta, this is a cruel state of captivity. But my bird must not be allowed to fray her beautiful plumage in beating against the bars of her cage. I must devise a better plan for her escape. Any means are justifiable to obtain release from tyranny like this. What says my love? Is she still willing to trust her Laurence?"

"To the death!" she whispered, emphatically.

"You are alone here every morning?"

Her lips could barely frame a "Yes," when a voice and step in the hall warned her to close the window with a hurried gesture to him; and before Mrs. Ashton, who had lingered to give an order to James, could enter the room, Black Ralph was cantering towards the Portico, and Augusta occupied with the third volume of "Alinda, or the Child of Mystery."

Very little escaped Mrs. Ashton's eye. The clatter of hoofs on the flags, audible through the thick front door, had left no sensible impression on her brain, but the heightened colour of Augusta attracted her attention at once. She brought her work-basket from the panel-cupboard, took thence a strip of cambric muslin, and handed it to her daughter.

"My dear," said she, quietly, "'all play makes no hay.' Your eyes are younger than mine, and I think it will do you more good to hem your father's shirt-frills than to pore over sentimental books from morning until night. So much romance reading is not good for you. I see that you are quite flushed and excited over the one you are perusing now."

There was a sharp rat-tat on the lion's head, and in burst Mr. Ashton, much more flushed and excited than his daughter. He had met Mr. Laurence on Black Ralph just as he was quitting the Portico, after an angry discussion with Mr. Aspinall the elder.

"You are quite right, my dear, in saying, 'Like father, like son,'" cried he, "for I'll swallow my snuff-box if that pompous old cotton-merchant did not justify his scapegrace son in his attempt to carry off our Augusta! He said that 'the end justified the means,' that we 'ought to be proud of such an alliance'"—Mrs. Ashton's lip curled—"that 'he was glad Miss Ashton had more discernment than her parent,' that 'his boy had set his heart upon her, and should not be thwarted in his choice by any beggar's-inkle-weaver in England.' And no sooner had I left him in the reading-room, to digest *my* opinion on the subject, and put my foot on the steps of the Portico, than up rode young Hopeful, and took off his hat to me, bowing down to his black horse's mane."

Having delivered himself of this explosive intelligence, Mr.

Ashton walked about, and sought a sedative in his snuff-box; and Augusta, who, folding the hem of the frill, had not lost one word, said, drily,

"I think Mr. Aspinall's justification of his son's design may at least be taken as a vindication of Mr. Laurence's *honourable* intentions, of which so many doubts have been expressed. And the bow equally absolves Laurence from a charge of malice."

With a proud toss of her shapely head, she walked towards the dining-room, rejecting the proffered arm of Jabez, who had entered the parlour whilst Mr. Ashton was speaking, and thus closed a discussion which could not be continued in the presence of servants.

* * * * * *

Jabez, on his return from Carr, had found his rough old clerical friend confined to his room seriously ill. Tabitha was worn out with his humours and eccentricities, and was glad when the young man offered to relieve her twice or thrice a week; and old Joshua welcomed him as a relief from the monotonous garrulity of an unlettered old woman. Jabez could bring him news of another stamp. Through Ben Travis (who had discovered that activity was the best antidote to melancholy), he kept him informed of the progress of the incipient temperance movement, in which the Parson took uncommon interest; through Mr. Ashton, he kept him *au courant* of town politics, and for general intelligence he brought newspapers with him to be read, interrupted by many and unique commentaries. In order that Tabitha might obtain repose, Mr. Clegg usually remained until a late hour, Mrs. Ashton herself entrusting him with a latch-key on these occasions.

One night, towards the middle of October, when Joshua had been more than ordinarily crusty, and Jabez did not quit the classic corner until the "wee short hour ayont the twal," he was struck as he turned the corner from Market Street into Mosley Street to find Mr. Aspinall's carriage in waiting with four horses and postilions.

He stood still for a moment to re-assure himself, but carriages were not so common that he should mistake that particular one; and his heart drummed an alarm within his breast.

Hurrying on with sad misgivings, he passed two tall figures muffled in cloaks, whom he had no difficulty in recognising, from build and walk, to be the Aspinalls, father and son; and increasing his speed he gained the door, inserted his key in the latch, and was on the stairs before the cloaked individuals had finished their speculations respecting his being a robber escaped from a constable.

Formerly, Augusta had to pass his room door to reach her own, on the opposite side of the long corridor. Her new chamber was next to his own, and nearer to the staircase. A thin stream of light shot through the key-hole, and a bright narrow line cast upon the opposite wall showed the door ajar. He stood still in his surprise.

As if a tipsy, musically-disposed man were going past, the refrain of a rollicking song was trolled out in the street; and then Augusta, equipped as for a journey, came forth from her chamber to descend the stairs. She had calculated on the signal an hour earlier, and expected Jabez an hour later. As she stole on tiptoe down the stairs Jabez confronted her and barred her progress. Her silver candlestick dropped from her hand, with the one word "Again!" and rolling down with a clang, awakened Mr. and Mrs. Ashton, the only sleepers on that floor, and set Nelson barking furiously. They were in the dark, but he had caught her hand.

"Miss Ashton, this is infatuation—madness."

"No matter, sir, let me pass; you have no right to detain me!"

"But I have, miss," said her father coming behind, guided by their voices, his scant apparel as invisible in the gloom as himself. "Is this another attempt to disgrace us by eloping? Oh, my child, my child, you are breaking your poor old father's heart!"

"And mine!" floated like the echo of despair's last sigh from the lips of Jabez.

But the utter hopelessness of the old man's tone touched a sensitive chord of Augusta's soul, and turning, she fell upon his neck crying tearfully, "Oh, forgive me, father, forgive me. I did not think you would take it so much to heart."

The appeal of affection to affection had accomplished what reason and authority had failed to effect.

CHAPTER THE FORTIETH.

WITH ALL HIS FAULTS.

A DYING GIFT.

AUGUSTA'S penitence exhaled like dew from a flower. In the light of her mother's lofty displeasure her tears dried, and self-will once more exerted its pre-eminence. She locked herself in her own room, and resolutely refused to come forth.

"So long as that odious meddler, Jabez Clegg, remains under our roof, I will stay here; and if you will not consent to my marriage with Laurence Aspinall, I will starve myself to death!" was her angry declaration, as she closed the door and turned the key.

"Leave her alone," said Mrs. Ashton, "she will want her food before her food wants her; and a little wholesome solitude is good for reflection. She will change her mind before the day closes."

This was at mid-day; but night came, and another noon, yet there was no sign of Miss Ashton's appearance; and Mrs. Ashton had made no overtures to her refractory daughter. The tender-hearted father was in a pitiable state of perturbation. In and out the warehouse he was twenty times in the day—as Kezia observed, "For a' th' world like a hen on a hot griddle;" and his snuff-box was hardly ever out of his hand. Business seemed altogether beyond his grasp; he answered questions at random, or was unconscious when addressed.

To this state of trouble Jabez unintentionally contributed his quota. Over the tea-table, unenlivened by Augusta's sparkling presence, though she was the one sole topic of conversation—he said, and not without an effort—

"It has occurred to me, and I have thought the matter well

over, that since my unfortunate position in relation to late events has made my very presence obnoxious to Miss Ashton it might be better for all concerned if I were to shift my quarters without delay. There are lodgings vacant close at hand; and I have no right to linger here and disturb the peace of any one member of your kind family."

"Jabez Clegg," remonstrated Mr. Ashton, with wide-open eyes.

"Have you any *other* reason to be dissatisfied with present arrangements?" asked Mrs. Ashton stiffly.

"Oh! Mrs. Ashton, how can I have? This house has been my home for years, and such a home as rarely falls to the lot of the fatherless. To you, my benefactors, I owe everything—almost myself; and I should ill repay your uniform kindness by remaining to create discord."

"If your only desire to remove is to gratify Miss Ashton's whims, you will oblige me, Mr. Clegg, by remaining," replied Mrs. Ashton, with grave decision; whilst Mr. Ashton, looking the very picture of consternation, laid his hand upon the young man's sleeve, and said slowly—

"My lad, you have been one of the household for many years; do not be the first to make a breach in the family. If the child of our blood and our affections goes forth to strangers wilfully, and repudiates us, do not let the son of our adoption leave us to lament her loss in solitude."

This was strong language, but Mrs. Ashton did not gainsay it, and Mr. Clegg could not longer press the point, though his own pain was intensified by the fear of adding to the distress of Augusta, who, he was confident, regarded him as an interloper and a mischief-maker.

Little had been seen of Ellen since the return from Carr Cottage. A message despatched by Mrs. Ashton to her sister, in her dilemma, was answered by another to pray them to "excuse Miss Chadwick, who was not well enough to go out."

This somewhat disconcerted Mrs. Ashton, who, more alarmed

than she would admit, and disturbed by the restless uneasiness of her husband, had looked for Ellen to act as a mediator without any compromise of her own dignity.

At the close of the second day, as Augusta pertinaciously refused to open the door, at the instance of Jabez the lock was forced; and even then a barrier of chairs and boxes had to be thrust back by sheer strength. She was exhausted from want of food, but her will was indomitable, and neither her father's entreaties, nor her mother's commands could induce her to partake of the viands spread before her.

Jabez was in agony. Delicacy and her obvious dislike had kept him from intruding upon her privacy, but as hour after hour was added to the night, and Augusta persistently dashed aside the food placed to her lips, he joined his prayers to those of her father, and neither availing, rushed out of the house, and in less than a quarter of an hour returned with Dr. Hull. *He* was not a man to stand any nonsense.

"Here, sir,"—to Jabez—"you are young and strong. Hold the silly child's arms whilst her teeth are forced apart. If she will not take food, she shall take physic, and see which she likes the best."

But the struggle to nourish her frame through set teeth was prolonged and painful, and the parents were likely to yield before the child.

Servants may be faithful, but they have eyes and ears, and not always discreet tongues. Family matters discussed freely in the kitchen before apprentices found their way into the warehouse and beyond it, and Mrs. Ashton's nerves tingled when she became acquainted with the rumours afloat.

From Tim, the Ashton stable-boy, Aspinall's emissary (Bob the groom, once more in his old service) had no difficulty in obtaining all the information his young master required.

Laurence waylaid Mr. Ashton, inquired anxiously after the obstinate girl's health, and, having paved the way by as much contrition as he thought necessary, called at the house the following morning, in company with his father, to renew proposals for Miss Ashton's hand.

Worn out by Augusta's obstinacy, which she and Laurence agreed to call "constancy," father and mother were in a different frame of mind to receive this proposition than when they had given their former peremptory rejection. They were not one whit more convinced by Mr. Laurence's assurance that he meant to "reform," or Mr. Aspinall's quotation of the adage, "A reformed rake makes the best husband;" but, rather than see their child starve herself to death before their very eyes, they yielded, and Laurence Aspinall, profuse alike in thanks and professions, was permitted by aching hearts and reluctant lips to introduce Augusta to his father then and there as his bride-elect.

It was a moment of triumph for Laurence when Augusta refused to come down stairs without an assurance under his own hand. He pencilled on a card, "My Augusta, I wait for you,—Laurence." And presently, supported by a maid-servant, she entered the room, her dress of purple poplin serving to show how wan and transparent her fair skin had grown, how unnatural was the brilliance of her eyes,

She would have fallen, as much from weakness as emotion, on her entrance into the parlour, but that Laurence darted forward and caught her in an embrace which brought back somewhat of her lost colour; and if anything could have softened the pain of that hour to her parents, it was the apparent ardour and sincerity of the lover, the hope that a genuine passion might tend to wean him from his old habits and associates.

Mr. Aspinall's reception of Augusta was characteristic.

"My charming Miss Ashton, I see my son has brought back the roses to your cheeks. May they never fade again, but bloom perennially without a thorn! I rejoice to kiss your hand paternally on this auspicious occasion, and to assure you that I shall be proud to welcome such beauty, and such constancy, as the wife of my noble son."

Consent once obtained, the Aspinalls were as eager to press forward the marriage as the Ashtons were to retard it, neither her father nor mother affecting a satisfaction they did not feel.

"My dear," said the latter to Augusta one day, when her eyes were sparkling over a costly present just received from Laurence, "your father was in hopes you would have fixed your heart on some good steady man like Jabez Clegg, who would have been a comfort and a credit to all of us, and have kept the business in the family after we were in our graves."

"Pshaw, mamma? how preposterous! I am surprised at my father's infatuation for that young man. I esteem him quite sufficiently for a friend, but"—and she locked an emerald earring in her delicate ear—"I could not exist with a husband whose heart was in his business. My husband's heart must hold me, and me only; and I must have something to look at as well as to love."

"Ah! Augusta, it must be a very small heart indeed which cannot find room both for a wife and a business to maintain her fittingly. The sheen of a dress which must last a life is of less consequence than its durable texture."

"Well, mamma, so long as the material pleases my eyes, I will take the wear upon trust. And do not be surprised that *your* daughter prefers a fine man and a gentleman to one whose fortune is in the clouds, and whose origin is so obscure he has not *even a name* to call his own."

She was standing to admire herself and her new jewellery in the Venetian glass between the windows as she said this, and her mother's figure filling in the frame, Jabez Clegg came and went unseen, a pang in his heart and an intensified resolve to make both fortune and name for himself even though his master's daughter vanished from his vision.

Nothing would induce Mr. Ashton to part with his child until she was at least eighteen; and in that particular he was proof against the importunities of Laurence and the cajoleries of Augusta. So for ten months (during which the lawyers had ample time to quarrel over the settlement of Augusta's £18,000, so that too much or too little should not be tied down on the lady) the dashing young blade was on his trial, so to speak, and contrived to beguile both father and mother of their prejudices; whilst to Augusta a new world of gaiety was opened out.

As her daughter's chaperon, Mrs. Ashton renewed her acquaintance with the yellow satin cushions of the Assembly Rooms, the Gentlemen's Concerts discoursed sweet music in their ears, Miss Ashton could take her seat in the boxes of the Theatre Royal without fear of Madame Broadbent's fan, and Kezia was in her glory, so many balls and parties had to be catered for; and Mr. Laurence Aspinall was in the ascendant.

All this was inexpressibly painful to Jabez, but as he had written to Ben Travis that "there was something more for men to do than die of disappointment or blighted love," so he set his face like a rock against the breakers, and gave himself entirely to business. He said to himself it would be cowardice to flee from that which must be borne and mastered, so never another word was heard of his seeking a home elsewhere. If he was brave, he was not foolhardy enough to court pain in the sight of his rival's triumph, and though in his determination to "stick to his last," he had eschewed all art which came not within the scope of pattern designing, to that he turned with redoubled assiduity after business hours, having found a profitable market apart from Mr. Ashton's firm, as his account with the Savings Bank in Cross Street had borne witness from the date of its establishment in January, 1818.

But for a brief space, and that whilst the wound was raw and new, his ministrations to the dying chaplain of the Old Church not only carried him out of sight and hearing, but in a measure drew his thoughts away from his own sorrow.

Once only did Joshua scarify the sore. In an interval of pain he said with his customary abruptness—

"And so that pretty lass of thy master's is going to throw herself away on the wild rascal who pitched thee over the wall?"

Jabez could not trust himself to answer save by a movement of his head.

"Ugh! she'd better ha' takken a fancy to thee!"

Half-an-hour or more elapsed. Waking from a doze, he said—

"Dost thou remember my telling thee to look at 'Hogarth's Apprentice' in Chadwick's parlour?"

"Indeed, I do! Those pictures have influenced my life," answered Mr. Clegg with a sigh, pouring out a dose of medicine as he spoke.

"More physic, eh? Ugh! doctors kill more than they cure with their stuff! Ay, lad, thah'st mounted up, thou'lt be a master thyself some day, if thou dost not forget that *Jabez* must be an *honourable* man!"

"I never did forget it sir, even though the apprentice boy was mad enough to aspire to his master's daughter! But losing her, I have learned a new lesson. The prayer of the olden Jabez, which has been mine night and morn from boyhood, was a prayer for *self*, and *self* only, and I had no right to look for an answer to all the hopes I based upon it. If I have not been 'kept from evil,' and it *has* 'grieved me,' I prayed for myself *alone*, and in grief I have my answer. Prayer should take a wider range."

"Right, lad, right! now let me sleep."

When he waked again he remarked—

"It's time for thee to be off, Jabez; but time is running faster with me than thee, lad. Here, reach yon "Terence" from the bureau. It is the Edinburgh edition. Keep it for the sake of the rough old Parson who gave thee thy name. And take care of it. Good night. How thick the fog is!" He had lost the sight of one eye, and the other was rapidly going.

That was the ninth of November. When Jabez came again on the eleventh, the fog had cleared away from Joshua Brookes's sight for ever; and fountains of tears ran freely from many eyes for the hot, hasty, single-minded, and learned Parson whose name was a household word in the town, and who had ever been a kind friend to Jabez. In his life he had been at war with huckster-women, street-urchins, school-boys, and his ecclesiastical brethren. In his death the wide parish, and more than the parish, united to reverence his memory, those who had laughed loudest at his eccentricities being foremost to bewail him,

Even the November clouds hung thick and heavy as a pall over the Old Church and churchyard, crowded with mourners, when his silent remains were carried to their bed in the cross aisles his feet had trodden so many active years, and if others besides Jabez shed tears over the open and honoured grave, there was many an old creature mourning in solitude, besides the queer old woman, in kerchief and mutch, who sat amongst her sweets in a closed shop, and lamented that so young a man as Parson Brookes should be carried off before her.

"Well-a-day! and only sixty-seven! He'll want no more humbugs, and no more cakes for his pigeons. Poor Jotty!"

There was no mention of Jabez in his wiil, but when the young man took the old worn "Terence" sadly and reverently down from the shelf where he had first placed it, on turning over its leaves he found a banknote for £300 pinned to the fly-leaf, on which was inscribed his own name and that of the eccentric donor.

CHAPTER THE FORTY-FIRST.

MARRIAGE!

HAD Jabez been vindictive, the opportunity, or at least the promise of revenge on his successful rival was not wanting. Various efforts had been made to call the Manchester Yeomanry to account for their doings at Peterloo, and many had been the overtures and suggestions to Jabez Clegg by members of the Radical party to join in the prosecution of the offenders. But he resolutely refused to identify the trooper who struck him, saying——

"I forgave the man at the time, believing him to be drunk, and incapable of discrimination. If I have since had reason to think otherwise, I cannot be so mean as to allow private feelings to influence a public act."

It would be false to say there never was a tug at his heart-strings when the tempters were again at his elbow, before they made their final attempt in 1822. But he said to himself——

"If it would have been revengeful at the time when the bodily injury was fresh, it would be doubly revengeful, mean, and dishonourable now that he has supplanted me in love. And in striking at him I should wound Augusta, and that must never be."

The temptation to expose his adversary was set aside, and thus it was that Laurence Aspinall's name was not added to those of the four defenders on the record of the trial at Lancaster in April; and as that trial, after the examination of nearly a hundred witnesses of all ranks, terminated unsuccessfully for the prosecution, the forbearance of our friend Jabez spared him at least the mortification of defeat.

The year rolled on. At the instance of Mr. Ashton, Jabez withdrew the bulk of his deposits from the Savings Bank, and adding to Joshua Brookes's gift the £200 he had accumulated by working late and early, and saving small sums even during his apprenticeship, placed all in his master's hands to be invested in the business and so return him a higher rate of interest. And this was the first absolute start of Jabez as a capitalist.

The joyous excitement attending Augusta's own preparations for her approaching nuptials was somewhat damped by the unaccountable condition of Ellen Chadwick, whose health, instead of improving during her visit to Carr Cottage, had appeared to decline still more perceptibly. A constant pain at her chest, frequent headaches, uncertain spirits, and increasing langour gave Mr. and Mrs. Chadwick real cause for uneasiness; but Ellen would not hear of a doctor, and maintained that it was "nothing to trouble about," she would "be better soon."

She did not get "better soon," and when the first August sun shone on Augusta's birthday and bridal, it taxed her powers to the utmost to sustain efficiently her part as bridesmaid.

Had Captain Travis accepted his lieutenant's invitation to be groomsman, she would have found it still more difficult; but a comparative stranger, a Mr. Joseph Bennett, of Gorton, filled the post, the bride's father having objected very decidedly to bold Ned Barret.

Yet Ben Travis and Jabez Clegg were both among the guests, albeit it cost each a struggle. The two had mutually strengthened each other as such friends should, arriving at the Spartan decision to "suffer and be silent, facing their fate like men." And indeed, old Mr. Ashton had wrung the hand of Jabez at least a week before, and said—

"I'm sorry for you, Clegg; I am, upon my soul; and I'm sorry for our poor lass, too, for she's made a mistake. But keep a brave heart, and don't let that slashing yeomanry fellow crow over you. As Mrs. Ashton would say, 'What can't be cured must be endured,' and we must all of us show the best face at the wedding that we can."

If that meant elaborate display in dress and decorations, and provision for the bridal breakfast and dinner, then the face exhibited was a shining one. Mrs. Hodgson, the fashionable mantua-maker and milliner, of Oldham Street (where two or three of the private houses had already been converted into shops), had kept her apprentices at work almost night and day for weeks, executing bridal orders from the Ashtons and their friends. A very snowstorm might have passed through the workroom, such heaps of white French crape and satin, lace and organdi, lute-string and gauze, littered and covered available space, putting matronly brocade, velvet, and llama quite into the shade.

The warehouse saw little of Mrs. Ashton for a week or ten days previously. Cicily, who had gone over to the Aspinalls, had begged to be allowed to help Kezia for that occasion, and she roasted her own face in spinning gold and silver webs and baskets from sugar for the table, making "floating islands," syllabubs, trifles, jellies, and blanc-mange to supplement the solid dishes Kezia dressed with so much skill. And Mr. Mabbott sent in a sugary "Temple of Hymen" and a bride's cake prepared six weeks in advance.

The bride, alternately radiant and tearful like an April day, veiled with lace and crowned with white rosebuds and orange-blossoms, wore a low-bodiced dress of white satin, festooned round the narrow skirt with costly lace, whilst on neck and arms, and in her tiny ears, were negligé, bracelets, and earrings of pearl, the gift of the gallant bridegroom's gallant father.

The bridegroom was scarcely less resplendent in his high-collared blue coat and gold buttons, his white waistcoat buttoned to match, his glossy white trousers, and low shoes tied with a bunch of silk ferret. An oblong brooch set with a rim of pearls held down his broad fine shirt-frills; from his fob hung a huge bunch of gold seals pendant from a flat gold watch chain; and in his hand (not crushing his elaborate curls, now clustering richly as ever) he carried a hat of white beaver of the newest shape.

To Mr. and Mrs. Ashton it was a matter of open regret that Joshua Brookes, who had christened Augusta, should not have lived to marry her also; but Mr. Aspinall, whose reminiscences of the old chaplain were of another order, was much better satisfied to see his own personal friend, Parson Gatliffe, the *bon vivant,* behind the altar rails.

If the bride was tall and graceful, with sunshine in her eyes and in her classic curls, tall and stately was the bride's mother, whose long train of purple silk velvet swept the aisles, though trains had ceased to be general. There was no faltering over the responses. There was a glow of modest pride on the cheek of Augusta; a look of mingled ardour and exultation on the face of Laurence; his "*I will*" was pronounced with a force which was almost fierce, yet, as she faintly promised to "obey," he pressed her hand with smiling significance.

The ceremony over, the bride did not faint, but turning to her tearful-eyed father, threw her arms around his neck and clung to him, whispering how grateful she was that he had given her the man of her choice, and that he should see what a good wife she would make; and the impromptu embrace sent a shower of snuff over white satin and lace.

Yet some one fainted, whom Ben Travis caught in his strong arms and carried to the church door for air; a dark-haired, black-eyed bridesmaid, whose face was white and skin transparent as her own robe.

Custom had not set its imperative seal on the wedding tour as a necessity, but after a magnificent solid dinner, to which the party did full justice, and an elaborate dessert, during which the cake was cut, and Mr. Aspinall proposed the health of the bride in an inflated toast, demanding that it should be drunk in bumpers, "and no heel-taps," the wedded pair drove off in Mr. Aspinall's carriage to the family mansion at Fallowfield, there to spend the honeymoon.

"Good-bye, Jabez," said Augusta, putting her small soft hand into his as they left the house; "you will comfort my father and mother, will you not? I trust them to you."

And he replied with the fervency of truth, "I accept the trust willingly. Good-bye, Mrs. Aspinall" (how the word choked

COURTYARD, BARLOW HALL.

him!) "May God bless you, and the marriage you have contracted. Good-bye!"

He did not kiss her hand, had not taken the common liberty of guests to kiss the bride's lips in church; he did but press her hand as any old friend who had grown up with her under the same roof might have done; but before the carriage had well dashed from the door, or the bridegroom had fairly settled himself on his seat, Laurence turned to the fair young wife, whose prophetic tears were now falling fast, with the sharp rebuke—

"What was that foundling fellow mumbling over your hand? You will please to remember that that hand is mine now, Mrs. Aspinall. You have promised to *love* and *obey* me—ME your LORD and MASTER. And MASTER I mean to be. I have borne the fooling of your friends and your own pretty caprices long enough. It is my turn now; and if any man so much as dares to look at you I'll pound him to a jelly! And now dry your eyes and give me a kiss!"

And that was the inauguration of Augusta Apinall's married life.

It has been said that the bridesmaid fainted. Every lady carried a smelling bottle, and means to revive her were not far to seek. She soon recovered, and with a sensitive blush withdrew from the arms which had been so proud to sustain her, casting her eyes round as if in search of some other whose service might have been more acceptable. But she suffered no relapse. She was ready to wait upon the bride, to sign "Ellen Chadwick" in the church register, and to assist a Mr. Joseph Bennett in cutting up the cake for distribution, with cards and gloves, to friends not present. It was an arduous task, and she succumbed before it was half completed.

"Miss Chadwick, you are not well; let me relieve you," said Jabez, coming to her assistance after the "happy pair" had driven off, and whilst peals of laughter, shouts, and hurrahs came from the dining-room, where gentlemen were honouring the bridal by drinking themselves senseless and speechless.

Ellen remained with her aunt a few days longer, during which Jabez, exceedingly pained to see the ravages hidden disease had made in so estimable a young lady, was pitifully attentive.

He could not, however, fail to see that his attentions distressed her; and, on the whole he was not sorry when Augusta's parents and he were left to themselves, to talk of their own dear one and speculate on her future.

Weeks went by. Mrs. Aspinall visited her old home, but never without her husband; and seldom was she allowed to remain more than an hour. Her spirits seemed exuberant, but somehow her unusual vivacity jarred on her mother's nerves, and she suspected that her spirits were forced.

Meanwhile Ellen Chadwick faded. Dr. Hardie, called in at last, watched his patient with curious and attentive eye, perplexed and dubious. He had been friend as well as physician since Mr. Chadwick's attack of paralysis, and was a close observer. Now he came and went in a gossiping sort of way, to put his patient at ease, and off her guard. He was there one day when Jabez was announced, and saw a sudden spasmodic action of the face, a dilation of the pupils, a scarcely perceptible pant and parting of the lips, and then he watched her closer. He introduced Mr. Clegg's name, as if casually, whilst his fingers were on her pulse. The result of his observations were told to Mr. Chadwick the same day.

"Your daughter has no specific disease, Mr. Chadwick, she is simply *love-sick*."

"L-love-s-sick?"

"Yes; and her secret passion is consuming her. Medicine cannot save the patient's life if her affection be not returned, and that right speedily."

Mr. Chadwick was aghast.

"I feared as much," said Mrs. Chadwick, with a sigh.

"Then you will have an inkling who is the desired object?" said the doctor.

"I think so."

"Does your maternal instinct point to Mr. Clegg?" he asked, with a curious look.

"It does; but he himself has no suspicion, and I am sure regards Ellen only as a friend—a friend elevated a little above him."

"Is the young man courting?

"I believe not."

"Then," said the doctor, sententiously, "the sooner he is, the better for Miss Chadwick. Her life is not worth a month's purchase unless Mr. Clegg become the buyer. But let not Miss Ellen hear a whisper of my opinion. Good day."

And, snatching up his hat, the doctor departed, leaving them to their reflections.

Here was a delicate subject to be dealt with, and that without either loss of time or the sacrifice of their beloved child's sensitiveness and reserve.

Unknown to Ellen, a family conclave assembled under the Mosley Street roof, to discuss the momentous question, and deliberate what was best to be done. Long and grave were their deliberations. At length, taking Mr. Chadwick's imperfect speech into consideration, Mr. Ashton consented to lay the case before Jabez, and leave his brother-in-law to supplement it, if necessary; though opinions were divided as to the result.

It was after business hours, and Mr. Ashton found Jabez in his own room, doing his best to dissipate thought by hard work, mind and hand being busy with a chintz pattern for calico-printing.

There was a nervous plunge into the gold snuff-box, and a consequent flourish of a gay bandana, and some time spent in examining the incomplete design on the desk before Mr. Ashton could fairly enter on his embassy. After a little prelude, in which, whilst enlarging on the serious nature of his niece's illness, he elicited from Jabez that he held the young lady in the very highest esteem, and was deeply grieved to hear of her perilous state, he put down his snuff-box on the table before him, and drawing up his chair so as to bring their heads closer together, looked steadfastly into the other's clear eyes as he put the question—

"And what should you think of *love* as the cause of her malady?"

"LOVE!" echoed Jabez, his mind running off to the agonised confession made to him on the Taxal hillside.

"Yes, *love*, and for the very man whose merits *my* foolish child failed to see."

Jabez looked at him vaguely.

"Surely, not Mr. Marsland!"

"Pah! no!" exclaimed Mr. Ashton, as if disgusted at his obtuseness. "Yourself, man—Jabez Clegg."

Jabez fixed his eyes on his informant in blank amazement, a monosyllabic long-drawn "*Me!*" being his sole response.

"Just so!" assented Mr. Ashton, and he took a pinch of snuff on the strength of it.

"Oh, sir, there must be some mistake! How has this been ascertained? Has Miss Chadwick made——"

"No, Clegg, the poor lass has never said one word, except with her eyes and pulse. Dr. Hardie has made the discovery now, and it turns out Mrs. Chadwick suspected it long ago."

"Oh, dear! dear! this is very terrible!"

He was estimating the pain in Ellen's heart by that in his own.

"Very terrible indeed, Clegg, for Hardie says the lass's life is not worth so much as a yard of filleting if her love meet no return."

The head of Jabez sank in his open hands upon the table. What would his friend Travis think of all this? Presently he raised his face, over which a strange change had passed.

"Mr. Ashton, what would you have me do?"

"Whatever Jabez Clegg thinks he ought to do," he answered steadily, adding in another tone, "I would have been glad to have given thee my own child; my brother-in-law implores thee to take *his* child, to save her life."

After a prolonged silence Jabez spoke.

"Mr. Ashton, I hold that love alone can sanctify marriage; my love has blossomed and died fruitless. Yet so highly do I esteem Miss Chadwick, and so proud am I of the great honour she has done me in her preference, that I place myself in your hands. If I can spare so amiable a young lady the pain I suffer from rejected love, I should be a brute and a savage to refuse her the remnant of a valueless life. We may at least soften its asperities for each other."

The Chadwicks went home with minds relieved, but Jabez had stipulated that nothing should be said to Ellen of their overtures to him, no hint given which could alarm her shrinking modesty.

The following day he called to inquire about her health, made his genuine anxiety apparent, and noted, as he had never done before, how her lip trembled and her eyelid drooped. Gradually, as his attentions became more marked, her health and spirits rose, and when at last he proposed to her calmly, quietly, as though he sought a haven when the frothy waves of a first passion had subsided, she accepted him as God's best gift, all unaware that his offer was not spontaneous, or that her cousin Augusta was yet deeply shrined in his secret heart.

He had been at first greatly concerned about Ben Travis, but the generous fellow, to whom he felt in honour bound to explain his conduct, only wrung his hand, and said—

"I could not resign her to a worthier."

CHAPTER THE FORTY-SECOND.

BLOWS.

AUGUSTA DRESSING.

RICHARD CHADWICK, who had served as a midshipman under Admiral Collingwood, and shared in the victory of Trafalgar, was a midshipman still, and his vessel had long been away on a foreign station. Few, brief, and far between had been his opportunities to visit home and friends. Ships had been paid off, but he had been exchanged, several years had elapsed since he had set foot in Manchester, and the hearts of his kin yearned towards their sailor.

His very whereabouts was unknown to them, and when written communication was necessary, letters had to be forwarded through the Admiralty.

Ellen's engagement and prospective marriage called forth a voluminous epistle, crossed and recrossed like a trellis, from Mrs. Chadwick to her son, whose presence she craved, if leave of absence could possibly be obtained. The letter was a singular compound of gratulation and apology, through which a thin undercurrent of dissatisfaction meandered like a stream. His sister's strange malady and infatuation for a man of apparently low origin, whose name and parentage were alike unknown, were set forth to be deplored. Still, since the sole remedy for Ellen's ailment rested with this obscure Mr. Clegg, whose career upwards, from his floating cradle to his honourable position in the Ashton house and warehouse, was circumstantially detailed, his personal worth was a matter for congratulation; and the deep obligation of the whole family to him for the service rendered on Peterloo Day seemed dragged in as a sort of extenuating circumstance. Clearly the Mr. Travis, whose name and pretensions cropped up here and there throughout the letter would have been a more acceptable son-in-law in the sight of Mrs. Chadwick and his other sister, Charlotte Walmsley, and just as clearly it was made apparent that his paralysed father (hale and strong in all other respects) was as much infatuated with the young man as was Ellen, having "positively offered to take him into partnership on his entrance into the family." And even there Mrs. Chadwick felt "constrained to admit that the clear head, business tact, and energy of Mr. Clegg would be a great acquisition."

This item of news closed the missive, which must have gone a circuitous round of red tape it was so long upon its travels. Months came and went; Father Christmas shook his snowy locks over the town; but neither the midshipman nor a written substitute put in an appearance.

Meanwhile Jabez, who had crushed down in the garden of his heart those roots of his love for Augusta which mocked his strength to eradicate, did his best to plant and foster above them a grateful affection for the one who had chosen him, and hoped in time that the newer growth might utterly extinguish the old. His attentions to Ellen were more assiduous than, under the circumstances, might have been expected, but he argued with himself—

"I must endeavour to atone to her for a proposal in which love had no part. She must never have occasion to suspect the truth. I should be a brute did I remain insensible to the unconquerable love she has so long cherished in secret for me. Augusta's face, alas! was more divinely fair, her manner more enchanting; but Ellen, though she is older than myself, will doubtless make the better wife for a business man who has to carve his way to fortune, and *she loves me!*"

Ellen, too, had her seasons of doubt and perplexity. She

had been so sensitively alive to the silent homage of Jabez Clegg to her younger and fairer cousin that at first her mind had refused to realise the fact that he desired to marry her, even though his proposal had been preceded by direct and palpable attention. She had been at first inclined to attribute his many acts of kindness and courtesy to friendship and compassion for her failing health. And when he had spoken of being won by her many estimable qualities to seek her for a wife, she had listened incredulously; then, overpowered by contending emotions, sank back amongst her cushions in a state of insensibility. Even her tremulous acceptance had been uttered as in a blissful dream, which might vanish all too soon. From time to time she perplexed herself with questions of the motive for so sudden a change in one so steadfast as Jabez, and at last wavered between the two suppositions that Augusta's wilfulness had wearied him, or that she owed her lover to pique. Of the real state of the case she had no inkling.

She was not alone in her latter supposition.

"A happy new year to you, Mrs. Clowes!" said our friend Jabez to his friend the old confectioner, as at one stride he took the two steps to her confined shop on the bright frosty second of January, 1823, and extended his hand to her across the counter, where she still kept up a show of activity in spite of age and wrinkles.

"Same to you, Mr. Clegg."

She had been one of the first to recognise his right to the prefix, and, with all her old-fashioned familiarity, never dropped it.

"Eh, but now I look at thee, thah doesn't look ower bright an' happy;" and she peered into his face inquiringly.

He smiled.

"Looks are not always to be relied on. I ought to be happy, for I am about to be married, and my errand hither is to——"

She interrupted him with—

"So I've heard. But what o' that? Is she th' reet un? For I wouldna give a mince-pie for thi' happiness if she isna."

The blood mounted painfully to his forehead.

"Miss Chadwick is all that is estimable and amiable, Mrs. Clowes," he answered steadily, "and if I am not happy with her it will be my own fault."

The old dame was not satisfied. The white linen lappets of her antiquated mutch flapped like a spaniel's ears as she shook her head.

"Eh, well!" sighed she, opening and shutting a drawer in the counter abstractedly, "you should know best, but both me and Parson Brookes (dead and gone as he is) thought you'd set your mind on th' lass that rantipollin lad Aspinall snapped up. I hope thah's not goin' to wed th' cousin out o' spite," and she looked up in his face, over which a cloud had swept. "It would be the worst day's work you ever did, either for her or you."

He had mastered his emotion, and answered cheerfully—

"Make your mind easy, Mrs. Clowes. I am not marrying from any unworthy motive, and I think our prospect of happiness is about the average. I came to ask you, as the oldest friend I have in the town, to be present on the occasion."

Mrs. Clowes was overpowered.

"What! Mr. Clegg! Me, in my old black stuff gown and mutch, among your grand folk? Nay, nay; I'm too old to don weddin' garments. But I tell you what"—and her face puckered with pride and pleasure—"you shall have the finest wedding-cake that ever was baked i' Manchester, and the old woman will mebbe look on the weddin' from some quiet nook, out o' the way. It's a thousand pities Jotty is not alive to marry you."

"There will be no grand folk, Mrs. Clowes; I am but a poor man struggling upwards, and Miss Chadwick has not had good health of late; so we shall be married very quietly on Wednesday week. Only very near relatives or old friends are invited."

Customers interrupted the colloquy. When the shop was clear she asked where he was going to live after marriage, and was told with his bride's parents.

"Eh! but that's a bad look out. Now, I've built some houses in a new street off Oxford Road as they call Rosamond Street, an' I'll tell you what, you shall have one to live in at a peppercorn rent, and I'll lend you the money to furnish it. Young folk are best by themselves."

Clear and bright were the eyes that met hers in reply.

"Thank you, Mrs. Clowes, thank you heartily for your kind offer; but I think you lose sight of Mr. Chadwick's infirmity. He has acted very liberally towards me—in fact, has offered to take me into partnership—and I should ill repay him by removing from his hearth the good daughter on whom he relies. It is rather my duty to add to the comfort of his declining years."

"Oh!" said she, sharply, "if that's how you raise your crust I'd best keep my fingers out of your pie."

Jabez was going. The shop was full.

"Stay, Mr. Clegg," said she, beckoning him into her parlour, and closing the door. "It's hard cheese for a man to owe everything to his father-in-law. I've got £500 hanging on hand. It's not much, but the least bit of capital would make you feel independent, and it's heartily at your service; and if you don't like to take it without interest you can pay me one per cent., and repay me when you've made a fortune; and if that doesn't come till I lay under a stone bed-quilt, you can hand it over to my first godchild."

That same evening Augusta Aspinall stood before a large oval swing-glass in her luxurious dressing-room, the blazing fire shed its warm glow on polished furniture, amber silk hangings, bright fireirons, costly mirrors, and expensive toilet ware (of execrable shape). She was robing for a ball at the Assembly Rooms, and Cicily, who, although cook, insisted on retaining her post as lady's-maid on such occasions, had just fastened the last hook of a delicate lilac figured silk as soft as it was lustrous, with swansdown fringing skirt, sleeves, and bodice, as if to show

how fair was the symmetrical neck of the wearer to stand such test.

In came Laurence fresh from the Spread Eagle in Hanging Ditch, where he, a newly-elected member of the Scramble Club, had spent the afternoon with one or two others, forgetful that the origin of the club was the fourpenny pie and glass of ale, or at most the slice from a joint despatched in a hurry or "scramble" by business men to whom time was money.

Neither time nor money seemed of much value to Mr. Laurence, who was equally lavish with both, taking as much from his father's business and adding as little as could well be imagined. His step on the threshold caused Augusta to turn round, beaming and beautiful, and dart towards him, exclaiming—

"I'm so glad you've come!" simultaneously with his "Clear out, Cis!" and a warm embrace which somewhat disarranged the dainty dress. His wife was yet a new toy, and his passion had not had time to evaporate. She was a something to admire and exhibit for admiration as a possession of his own; and though her love had received one or two rude shocks, he was still a glorified being in her eyes, and she clung to him as a true wife should cling. She was still but a girl in her teens, proud of the admiration she excited. Disengaging herself, she cried—

"Oh, Laurence, see how you have crushed my swansdown! and now, dear, do make haste and dress, we shall be so late," and putting the fluffy trimming in order, she unlocked a small jewel case on the table, and took thence the pearls she had worn on her wedding-day.

"What will you say for these, Augusta?" cried he, dangling before her eyes a gossamer scarf and an exquisite ivory fan, whilst his other arm thrown over her white shoulders again threatened the elastic down.

"Oh, Laurence, you are a darling! Where did those beautiful things come from?" and she gave him more than one kiss in payment.

India, my love; they are 'far-fetched and dear-bought,' and

so must be good for you, my lady. I met your uncle Chadwick with an old sea-captain, from whom I bought them. By the way, matrimony seems catching. We are invited to a wedding," and he began leisurely to undress as he spoke.

"A wedding! Whose?"

He laughed.

"Ah, woman all over! I thought I had news for you. Guess!"

In small things as well as great it was his delight to tantalise, so he kept her guessing whilst he proceeded with his toilet, and she began to clasp her pearls on arms and neck, and in her pretty ears.

"Well," said he at length, "who but your cousin Ellen!"

"Ellen?" She had gone so little near her own family that this was indeed news for her.

"Yes; I thought she meant to die an old maid, but it seems she's not too proud to wear your cast-off slippers."

"My cast-off slippers? What do you mean?" and she paused whilst clasping her bracelet with a look of bewildered interrogation.

"Now, Augusta, pray don't look so innocent! Your father's favourite fetch-and-carry, that sneaking, canting fox, Jabez Clegg, finding that Miss Ashton was a sour grape, has straightway gone wooing to Miss Ashton's cousin as fruit ripe enough and near enough to drop into his vulpine jaws, and, by G——, the girl has had no more spirit than to drop when he shook the boughs, rather than hang on untasted!"

The speaker's lip and nose had curled with contempt as he began, then his nostril dilated, and he struck his wet hand on the washstand with a force which threatened the earthenware and set it jingling.

Augusta was not yet schooled to silence; her generous spirit rose to repel these allegations.

"Oh, Laurence, how can you? Ellen has had plenty of admirers; she has no need to wear anyone's cast-off shoes. And as for Mr. Clegg! He is no cast-off slip"——she checked herself; a thousand trivial and forgotten things flashed across her mind at once; there was no doubt that Jabez had aspired to her own hand—he must have offered himself to Ellen in pique, to look as if he didn't care; she could not add the "of mine," which should have rounded her sentence; she substituted, with barely a moment's pause, "He is neither a sneak nor a cant, and if Ellen marries him she will have a good husband;" adding with marvellously little tact or knowledge of her own husband, "I am sure, Laurence, dear, you have no right to speak ill of the man who saved your life in the very pond that is frozen over now before our doors! And you cannot really think him mercenary, when he refused the £500 your father offered as a reward for his bravery."

Not lightning was more quick and scathing than the fury which flashed from her husband's eyes and almost paralysed his tongue as the last words fell from her lips. With the damp towel in his hand he struck across her beautiful bare shoulders with a force which traced red lines upon their snow; then marked her round arm with a band as red by tearing away the suspended fan and scarf, which he threw behind the fire without one thought of either "far-fetched" or "dear-bought."

"Soh, madam!" he hissed, rather than spoke, whilst Augusta shrank from him in affright, "soh! you dare defend the wretch who played the spy on us at Carr—attacked me, an unarmed man, with a stick, like a coward, and left me bleeding there for dead, hoping to win the heiress for himself!"

From her father and Cicily both she had gathered the truth of that night's exploits. His misrepresentations no longer misled; but for very fear she held her peace. He went on—

"Madam, that night's savage attack cancelled every debt of gratitude I owed the calculating knave who turned his back on my father's £500, thinking to multiply it by thousands from *your* father!"

"It is not true!" she dared to say, her sense of justice and her spirit of resistance rising in defence of one she knew to be foully aspersed. Not because he was Jabez Clegg, but because he was an absentee maligned.

A shriek rang through the big house, and servants came scurrying up, with Mr. Aspinall in their midst; and Cicily, the first to dash between them, caught on her well-covered back the blow from the madman's brace, which would else have fallen afresh on the naked shoulders of his wife, already scored by it with livid welts.

Carry away the fainting lady—soothe the infuriated savage—apply raw beef to shoulders as red, if not as raw—let the brute steep himself in brandy unto stupefaction. The morning will come, when the fumes of passion and brandy will alike have passed away, and the man will repent him of his cruelty. But the sting of groundless jealousy will remain, and the broad livid stripes across the white shoulders. Time and care will efface those marks, but neither kisses, nor caresses, nor presents, nor time itself can obliterate the hieroglyphics stamped with that buckskin brace on the young wife's heart. He has fixed the name of Jabez Clegg there, and in conjunction "brute" and "liar," as equivalent to his own.

It might have been expected after this that the Aspinalls would have been conspicuous by their absence from the cousin's wedding, or that Augusta might have laid her wrongs before her mother. But, no; your jealous man never spares himself a pang if he hopes to inflict one; and the wilful woman who finds she has made a mistake in marriage is the last to confess it.

Cold weather and recent indisposition served as an apology for the violet velvet spencer which, worn above the pale lilac silk, covered bust and neck; and it was far from unbecoming to the young matron or the occasion.

Old Mrs. Clowes—who had kept her word anent the cake, which was a triumph of confectionery skill—from some long-closed coffer brought forth a stiff brocade of ancient make and texture, placed a bonnet on her unaccustomed head, and from a far seat in the choir watched Jabez Clegg enter with his college

GEORGE PILKINGTON.
From a Photograph.

friend and groomsman, stalwart George Pilkington, though she did not see them linger to read the inscription over the grave of Joshua Brookes, or look up with grateful remembrance to the Chetham Gallery, where they had worshipped together. But she remembered them as boys in long blue gowns and yellow underskirts, and could not help contrasting the college dress of the past with the high-collared bright blue coats, the gilt buttons, lemon-coloured vests, light trousers, and white kid gloves, in which they found their way to her to shake hands, whilst waiting for the trembling white-robed bride and her friends.

And there Mrs. Clowes sat and listened to the irrevocable words which bound Jabez to "love and cherish" the woman who loved him with her whole soul; whilst in spite of himself his very brain was reeling with memories of that other wedding-day, when Laurence Aspinall and Augusta Ashton, now standing calm and beautiful in the background, had breathed the selfsame vows before that altar; and somehow the old dame had a secret misgiving when all was over that it was "*not* the reet one after all."

"All over!" had been the cry from the heart of Jabez then. "All over!" was the echo now, as the last "Amen" sounded, and he registered a silent oath, not down in the rubric, to keep the troth he had plighted, although no electric thrill answered the shy touch of Ellen's hand, or the dumb devotion of her glance, and although Augusta's greeting of her new "cousin" jarred a still sensitive nerve.

All over! so men delude themselves. "All over!" they say, when disappointment closes the door of the past, and veils their eyes to the vista of the future. "All over!" when the curtain falls on the prologue of life's drama. Yet it rises again, and they find that the play has but just begun.

CHAPTER THE FORTY-THIRD.

PARTNERSHIP.

BY dint of persuasion old Mrs. Clowes was induced to place her well-saved brocade at the table graced by the wedding-cake she had manufactured; though, as she afterwards said confidentially to Jabez, "I must have had as much brass in my face as I had i' my pocket to sit down cheek-by-jowl wi' grand folks with foine manners, who might come into my shop th' next day to be served with a pound o' gingerbread; but I'd not ha' missed Mester Ashton's toast for summat. And I don't know as annybody turned up a nose bout it wur that spark Aspinall, who owes me for manny a quarter a pound of humbugs."

Round that hospitable and substantial wedding breakfast, which owed much of its success to the bride's own deft fingers, also gathered the Cloughs, who had watched the career of the bridegroom with interest from his cradle—Miss Clough as bridesmaid; Mr. John M'Connell and Henry Liverseege, who had cultivated his friendship from their first introduction; John Walmsley and Charlotte, who privately chafed at his reception into the family; and Augusta, whose brilliancy was somewhat dimmed by the overt watchfulness of too courteous and attentive Laurence; but there was no Ben Travis, and missing him, Jabez was disposed to gravity. But though there were uncongenial elements present, George Pilkington's cheery voice and lively sallies sufficed to set mirth afoot and keep her dancing; whilst Mrs. Ashton, stately and proverbial, seemed to share some pleasant secret with which Mr. Chadwick and her husband were on the *qui vive.*

It was the age for toasts and sentiments. Some smart and witty things had been uttered, but not until the cake was cut and commended, and a post-chaise at the door waited to convey the newly-married pair to Carr Cottage and the earliest friends of the bridegroom, did Mr. Ashton rise to his feet, snuff-box in hand, and, with a merry twinkle in his eye, propose—

"Success to the new partnership!"

"Stop, my friends!" said he, as glasses were elevated in honour of the toast; perhaps I had better explain what is meant by the new partnership."

"I should think that was pretty obvious," whispered Laurence to his friend Walmsley across the table, but he changed his opinion presently.

"There are partnerships for life," continued Mr. Ashton, "where the contract is attested in church, as we have had the pleasure of witnessing to-day, and, I am sure, with the best of wishes for its success; and there are partnerships in business, which are usually signed, sealed, and attested in a lawyer's office; and it is to such a one I now refer, in conjunction with the former."

He paused to consult his snuff-box, and smiled to see how suddenly inattentive heads were eagerly bent forward to listen.

"It may not be generally known that my dear *nephew* Jabez, at the close of his honourable apprenticeship, declined an eligible offer from brother Chadwick, in order to remain with us."

(Walmsley and Aspinall exchanged glances. Mrs. Clowes looked knowing.)

"It may not be generally known that he has a small amount of capital invested in our concern at present."

("Small enough, I should say," muttered Laurence.)

"Now, there being no likelihood that his son Richard will ever leave his ship for a warehouse, Mr. Chadwick proposed to take his son-in-law Jabez into equal partnership, considering his integrity, his business tact, and energy to be equivalent to capital."

"Hear! hear!" in which Mr. Chadwick's stumbling tongue was loudest, and "Success to the new partnership!"

(The snuff-box closed, the bandana was disposed of, the speaker's beaming face was all in a glow.)

"Stop! stop! gentlemen! not so fast. You will have to fill

your glasses afresh. We have not yet got to the new partnership."

("What the d——l is he driving at?" was Aspinall's polite query to Walmsley, who shook his head in token of ignorance.)

"Brother Chadwick had concluded that Mr. Clegg was wholly without capital, whereas he happens to have more than a thousand pounds at his disposal."

(Broadcloth made sudden acquaintance with chair backs. George Pilkington grasped his friend's hand; there was a puckering of Mrs. Clowes's wrinkles; there were lowering brows from Laurence and John.)

"And Mr. Clegg being perfectly satisfied with his present investment, and anxious to join the gingham manufacturer without quitting the smallware manufacturer, proposed"—pinch of snuff—"that the *two concerns should be amalgamated*, and he have a share. Gentlemen and ladies, the proposal was hailed as an inspiration; and, as soon as the change can be legally effected, the firm will be gazetted as 'Ashton, Chadwick, and Clegg!' And now let us drink—'Success to the new partnerships, matrimonial and commercial!"

Aspinall's voice alone remained silent amongst the enthusiastic cheers with which the toast was drunk. Ellen, with humid eyes, escaped to change her garments, and Augusta also rose; but as she passed the new Manchester man, around whom friends crowded with congratulations, she put out her hand with a smile, and said, "Cousin Jabez, I wish success to both your partnerships with all my heart."

Laurence was at her elbow, apparently to lead her with courteous ceremony from the room, and whilst offering one hand with a graceful inclination of his head, he contrived with the other to pinch the upper part of her arm, and to whisper in her ear, between his set teeth—

"D—n you, madam! You shall smart for this!"

An irrepressible ejaculation of pain burst from her. More than one turned round. There was real concern on the brow of Jabez as he asked—

"What is the matter, Mrs. Aspinall? Are you hurt?"

She made light of it.

"Oh, nothing, nothing. I struck my foot against a chair—that was all."

But Jabez saw the white, frightened face, and felt there was something more; and that scared look haunted him for many a day.

Laurence attended his wife to the staircase, smiling blandly whilst within sight or earshot. Ere he left her at the stairfoot he gripped her tiny hand till her jewelled rings cut the flesh; and the smile became satanic as he whispered—

"You are discreet, madam. I charge you to remain so—for your life!"

Once in Ellen's crowded bedchamber she became hysterical, to her cousin's great grief. But she overmastered her emotion by a violent effort, excused it on the plea of recent indisposition, and was consoled by her mother and other sagacious matrons with the remark that such affections might be expected. The newly-married pair were whirled away down Oldham Street and up Piccadilly; old Mrs. Clowes took her departure, and then Augusta, acting on Mrs. Clough's advice, lay on the drawing-room sofa to rest.

Not until night did the guests depart, Mr. Liverseege being the first to retire. There was a late dinner at six o'clock, and when the gentlemen rose from their post-prandial wine, and sought the drawing-room, all considerably elevated, Laurence Aspinall was too intoxicated to move. The Aspinall carriage had been waiting an hour. The coachman and Bob the groom grew anxious and impatient about the horses.

"Mr. Laurence drunk? Eh! that matters nowt!" exclaimed the latter. "Steve an' me 'll manage him." And taking the limp young Hercules between them, they somehow hauled him to the carriage, and ensconced him in one corner, with his head drooping on his breast.

Augusta shrank from joining him, afraid lest he should awake to malicious consciousness on the road.

"Oh! I dare not go home with him! Indeed, I dare not go home with him!"

"My dear," said her mother gravely, "I am afraid you *must*. A wife cannot absent herself from home because her lord and master indulges in too much wine, even though he may occasionally make a beast of himself. It is too late to think of this *now*. What cannot be cured must be endured. As you made your own bed, you will have to lie on it to the end. Those who leave the spring for the stream must expect muddy water. However, there is nothing so bad but it might be worse. Once is not always, and love overlooks lapses."

Augusta's persistence that she dared not be "shut up with him alone," caused Mrs. Ashton to say—

"Well, my daughter, the occasion has been so unusual that even your own father has taken more wine than his wont, or he might bear you company. That groom seems a steady man; suppose he rides inside to support his master; and, whatever you do, remember when wine is in wit is out; silence is a wife's safeguard, and you will have to make the best of a bad bargain."

A month back Augusta would have tossed her head, and laughed lightly at her mother's pet philosophy. That night she rode home from Jabez Clegg's wedding feast with a groom and a drunken man, pondering whether spirited resentment or tame submission was her best course. The morning dawned on a wife pinched black and blue, with hardly strength or spirit to sob.

Then followed a reaction, and a period of remorseful uxorious penitence, during which Laurence submitted with a tolerable grace to a lecture from Mr. Aspinall, senior, who saw that something was amiss; and chivalrous gallantry towards woman being part of this gentleman's creed, he did not spare his son.

Nor did Laurence spare himself. He knelt at his wife's feet, called her "an angel," and himself "a savage," implored her forgiveness, excused his jealousy on the ground of passionate love, lavished his means on extravagant gifts for her, and exhausted language in fair promises. But so proud was he of his wife's beauty, that he must needs exhibit at theatre and assembly the jewel he had won; whilst the admiration she excited set his jealous brain on fire, and she paid the penalty in the silence of night, or even in the close carriage driving home.

But his contrition and the old plea of "excessive love" for his jealous infirmity won her over, and not even Cicily more than suspected half his cruelty.

* * * * * *

Great preparations had been made at Whaley Bridge for the reception of Mr. and Mrs. Clegg; the factory windows were extra burnished; the landlord of the "White Hart" hoisted a flag; the mill-hands lined the road to greet them; the avenue gate was thrown open that the chaise might drive on to the cottage; somebody had put Crazy Joe into a new suit of clothes for the occasion, and he stood by the side of little Sim on the step of the Gothic arch (the greater child of the twain) to laugh and chuckle a welcome, as sincere in its way as the homely greetings of the orphan's fosterers.

It was a fine stalwart young man, of open but grave countenance, around whom Bess threw her motherly arms, while Tom Hulme helped the bride to alight, and marshalled the way for the pair, who followed arm-in-arm into the house-place, where Simon, stiff with age and rheumatism, kept possession of the padded chair set apart for the sick or aged.

In some way the knowledge that Mr. Clegg came as a master, and not as a servant, had preceded him.

"Eh, Jabez, lad," exclaimed Simon, tears of joy coursing down his cheeks, "that aw should ever live to see this day! Would annyone ha' thowt as th' little lass at' played wi' ar Jabez an' his toys, an' kissed him when he wur a babby, would come to wed him when he wur a mon—an' a gentlemon into th' bargain! An' neaw let thi wife goo an' tak' off her pelisse while thah talks to me; hoo'll be tired wi' th' lung journey, aw reckon. Theere's a fire i' th' best parlour, that's th' place fur gentlefolk, an' yo'r

MAN AND WIFE.

supper's laid theer."

Old Simon naturally concluded that young lovers wanted no society but each other. On five-year-old Sim such a consciousness had not yet dawned, and so he penetrated into the "best parlour," and, much to the relief of the bridegroom, broke into that first domestic *tete-a-tete* to exhibit some wonderful pictures he had drawn with red ruddle picked from the gravel-path.

They had been at Carr Cottage little more than ten days or a fortnight, the first week being wet; Jabez, without neglecting Ellen, busied himself with contemplated changes and improvements at the mill, and thus the great bane of the modern honeymoon was avoided. The occupation thus found for the mind and hand of Jabez at that particular epoch of his life was a blessing for which Ellen had need to be thankful in after years, if she had but known it.

As it was, she did fancy he might have given her a *little* more of his time, and not have needed her suggestion to re-visit Taxal and the spot where he had wooed her for another, and not for himself. Yet a very slight hint was sufficient, and, taking advantage of a clear, dry day, the two re-trod the old path by the Goyt, which awoke reminiscences that could but be flattering to that self-love of which every human being has a share.

Sitting down as man and wife on the lightning-scathed tree-trunk, which had never been removed, he remembered the confession wrung from her agony on that very spot. His arm stole round her waist in the pitiful compassion it evoked. A new emotion stirred within his breast. He folded his wife in his arms, and pressed upon her answering lips his first spontaneous kiss of dawning affection.

Half-way home they were met by Crazy Joe, who had been sent to seek them. A consecutive message was beyond his grasp. All they could make out was, "Back! Sharp! Quick!" And, hastening on in alarm, they at length discerned Mr. Ashton at the gate, on the look-out. His pleasant nod was reassuring.

"My dear," he cried to Ellen, as they advanced, "Dick has

got his promotion at last; Lieutenant Chadwick has been duly gazetted. Here is his letter to your mother, dated from Mal— Stop, my dear!"—Ellen had put out her hand for the thick, heavy missive—"A communication which called your old uncle Ashton out of his way to act as courier is not to be dealt with lightly. And before it is read I must know whether you would rather be Mrs. Clegg or Mrs. Travis?"

Closer she clung to the arm of Jabez.

"Oh, uncle! How can you ask?"

There was a sly gleam in the corner of his eye.

"Ah! just so. That's it. How *can* I ask?"

But his face sobered. He handed the letter to his new nephew.

"Jabez, I think you had better carry it to your own room for private perusal. I will communicate its contents to all whom it may concern besides."

Jabez had deep feelings, though he was not demonstrative, and long before he had mastered its contents he was thankful for the delicacy which had spared him an open display of irrepressible emotion.

The writer, who was stationed at Malta, after dwelling on his own promotion, and answering sundry maternal questions relative to himself, went on to say—

"And so our Nell's going to be married. Well, it's about time—she'll be twenty-six next April, or I've lost my reckoning.

"And so she was fretting herself to fiddle-strings for a fellow younger than herself, and without a shilling or a name, when she might have had a finer fellow, with name and shiners to boot. Bravo! Nell, for choosing a brave lad instead of a money-bag! She's the sister for a sailor, whatever Charlotte may think.

"But your story of the flood and the cradle, and your mention of Mr. Travis, coming both together, recall a story I had forgotten, which may perhaps furnish a name for Nell's hero of the Irk and Peterloo.

"We had a broad-set sailor on board the *Royal Sovereign*,

who was always getting into scrapes for chalking caricatures of the officers on the bunks and cabin-doors; but there wasn't a man fore or aft that hadn't at some time or other coaxed a picture or portrait out of him, to send to mother or sweetheart, and never a Jack Tar amongst them would split on good-natured Ben Travis."

Down dropped the shaking hand that held the letter. *Ben Travis!* What strange coincidence was this?

"His father had been a Liverpool shipbroker, and Ben took to me because I was a Lancashire lad like himself, though he was old enough to be my father. He had been pressed, and as I was the youngest middy, and he the master of the forecastle, many a time had he told me the sad story of his life. His father had died without a will, and Ned, his eldest brother, had laid his clutches on everything but a hundred pounds or so, which had been the mother's. Ben turned his back on Liverpool and his brother, and being smart with his pencil, took to that to get a living. He wandered about to pick up bits of scenery, and at Crumpsall fell in with a widow and her daughter, both named Ann Crompton, and went to lodge with them. After a while he married the lass, and thinking if he meant to earn a living for his wife and the child that was coming he'd best seek a large town, he removed to Manchester, and took an old cottage in Smedley Vale, where he hoped to turn his talent to account."

The paper rattled, and Jabez leaned against the window-frame, as much for support as light, as he read on with panting lips.

"He tried portrait-painting, but lacked a patron; he turned his head to pattern-designing, but no one would employ a raw beginner. His money was dwindling, and a birth was near at hand. He doted on his wife, and for her sake wrote to his brother, who was married when their father died. Ned wrote back enclosing a bank-note, and begging to see him at once. His wife had died, leaving a baby-boy, whom he had christened

Ben, after his runaway brother. Ned said her loss was killing him, and he wished to leave his boy in his brother's care before he died. Poor Ben Travis kissed his wife, and went by coach to Liverpool. Before he could reach his brother's office in Castle Street, near the docks, he was pounced upon by a pressgang, dragged on board a ship in the Mersey, and never saw brother, or wife, or home again. I have seen Ben's tears roll down his weather-beaten cheeks many a time as he told this. He was one of the first sent down to the cock-pit at the battle of Trafalgar, and when Admiral Nelson's glorious remains went home to be buried, Ben went likewise, to hospital, and I lost sight of him. When I was exchanged to the *Excellent*, Ben turned up again, hearty, but aged with grief. He had sought his dear ones, but a flood had swept through Smedley Vale in 1799, and left no trace of his home. A man at the dye-works remembered something about an old woman they called stiff-backed Nan being killed by the falling house in trying to save a baby; but Ben could learn no more, and his own impression was that wife, child, and mother-in-law had perished in the same catastrophe. He went to Liverpool. Death had swept off his brother; executors swept off the son Ben, his namesake. He went back to sea, and I saw the brave Ben Travis drowned in trying to save a bumboat woman, who fell overboard off Spithead.

"And now, mother, you used to be a good hand at patchwork—piece my story and your story together, and see if Ellen's poor cradle-friend is not near of kin to your rich friend, Mr. Benjamin Travis, with quite as good a right to be called Mr. Travis too.

"I should have a rough sketch of the old sailor, drawn with a quid of 'bacca on the fly-leaf of his Prayer-book. I'll look it up for Nell."

CHAPTER THE FORTY-FOURTH.

MAN AND BEAST.

THE January twilight had deepened into dusk, and from dusk to dark, before Jabez was sufficiently master of himself to descend into the light of the rooms below.

Whatever of surprise or satisfaction Richard Chadwick's letter had held for him, a wave of sorrow had passed over soul and countenance for the sad fate of the parents whom he had never known. As his footstep was heard overhead, Ellen flew to meet him at the foot of the staircase, and threw herself into his arms.

"My love! my own husband!" was all she said, but such an intensity of devotion and sympathy was in the act and tone that he felt he had indeed a true heart beating with his as he held her close, and his lips touched her forehead as a seal to a new bond.

It was but a single step to the parlour door, which opened on a room all aglow with light, and radiant faces. On Mr. Ashton's inspiriting, Simon's easy chair had been wheeled in from the house-place, there being no stately Mrs. Ashton at hand to demur at the innovation, or to whisper a syllable of class distinctions. And surely that was not—yes, it was—Ben Travis himself standing by the rheumatic old tanner, with both hands outstretched, to greet a new cousin in his long-time friend. And there was Bess, proudly glancing from his face to a piece of yellow paper. "It's as like as two peas," she cried for the twentieth time, handing to her tall foster-son a sketch which, though little more than a succession of brown smears, was a ludicrous resemblance to himself.

"Well, Jabez," said Mr. Ashton, sitting by the fire, with his handkerchief over his knee, after the first hubbub of congratulation had subsided, "it is as well our new partnership has not been gazetted. I suppose there will have to be a change of name, and Ellen there will be Mrs. Travis after all."

This was but a playful sally on his part, but Ben Travis

visibly winced, and quick-eyed Jabez saw it.

"No, sir," replied Jabez, calmly, with his hand on his wife's shoulder, "there will be no change. I bear the name of the kind friends who saved my infant life; fed, clothed, and kept me through evil report and good report, through pinching poverty, privation, and pain" (he glanced towards Bess); "as Jabez Clegg I was enrolled as a Blue-coat boy; as Jabez Clegg I was apprenticed to you, sir; as Jabez Clegg I married my wife; as Jabez Clegg I have been honoured with a place in your firm; and Jabez Clegg shall go with me to the grave. I had no name when that good man" (pointing to Simon) "lent me his; time has made it mine, and I mean to keep it as honourable as it came to me." He looked down: "Mrs. Clegg are *you* content?"

"Perfectly, Jabez."

A long-sustained pinch ot snuff spoke Mr. Ashton's approbation, whilst Simon could only reiterate, "Eh, lad, when aw tuk thee eawt o' the wayter, aw little thowt whatn a blessin' theaw'd be to us, or the credit theaw'd bring on ar neame! Aw nobbut wish Parson Brucks wur aloive neaw to yer thee."

"Our relationship will only bind our friendship closer, whatever name you bear," put in Ben Travis, warmly, in spite of himself pleased with the decision which would spare him the pain of addressing Ellen as Mrs. Travis.

"An' meals come reawnd whatever neame yo' ca' them by," supplemented Bess, who, like Martha, troubled with much serving, had been running in and out during the colloquy, whilst a combination of savoury odours, and a clatter of knives and plates, came from the adjoining room; "it's supper toime neaw, an' nobbody's had even theer tay yet."

"Just so, just so, Mrs. Hulme. But never mind the tea," said Mr. Ashton; "here comes your good husband in from the cellar, with a bottle or two of generous wine to drink to new relationships."

"I think I shall go abroad for a few months, Cousin Jabez,"

said Travis to him, as Mr. Ashton mounted first into the gig to return home next day. "I require to dissipate thought. If I were occupied as you are from morning until night there might be less necessity. But—I say, Chapman the landlord here tells me you painted his sign. I think the faculty must run in the blood, for I do a bit in that line myself sometimes. How is it I have not seen a brush in your hands latterly?"

"Well, I got a hint, through painting that very sign, that trade and art were incompatible, and seeing the force of the remark, as counselled—'the cobbler has stuck to his last.'"

"Look you, Cousin" (Travis seemed fond of the word), "the fabled shield had two sides—stick to your trade if you like, but don't let your trade absorb you. A business man who allows himself no leisure, and has no resource out of his business, is apt to degenerate into a money-grubber. I hope better things of you."

A nod, a shake of the hand, the gig rolled off with its occupants, and Jabez stood looking after them, hesitating whether to go back to the mill or to the cottage. The casual word of warning had come not one whit too soon. That which was sending Travis abroad had kept Jabez close to business. He had not sought so much to dissipate thought as to circumvent it by substitution. If he had given his leisure to the cultivation of art, it had of late been art only as connected with manufacture and money-making. Even his honeymoon he was casting into the mill as grist. He was ever ready to take a hint. He turned his steps towards Carr with something like a sigh.

"Well, perhaps, I might as well give my afternoons to Ellen whilst we are here. I did not come to work, and the poor thing does need some compensation for the lack of a lover's ardour. God forbid that she should ever suspect that I married her out of pity, or that I should become a money-grubber. I wonder if Travis thought I was likely to neglect her? It is a thousand pities she should set her mind on me instead of him. And why she should passes my comprehension. He has every advantage of face, figure, and fortune, to say nothing of his evident devotion. Ah! women are strange creatures, and men are not much better. I fear I am very ungrateful not to reciprocate her attachment more fully. Why, here she is running down the avenue to meet me, as if I had been gone a month. I really ought to love her better than I do. But love can neither be forced nor crushed. Heigho!"

* * * * *

Back to Manchester they went, rather sooner than expected; and then, though Jabez threw himself into business with a will, he bore in mind the parting words of Ben Travis.

The contemplated amalgamation was effected, not without extra draughts on Jabez and his leisure. But as partner of a large firm, even though a junior, it was obvious he could not work as designer for calico-printers, or for any other than their own house. Consequently, not being a man of pleasure, his evenings hung rather heavily on his hands, especially as neither Ellen nor he cared for the card-parties which formed the visiting staple. His very marriage had driven away his closest friend, and broken in upon plans and schemes which otherwise would have found sufficient occupation for his spare hours. Other friends, however, dropped in for an occasional chat, notably George Pilkington (to whom the wine trade had opened a road to fortune), with his reminiscences and jocularity, broke in on the monotony of married life, that monotony which is as much to be dreaded by young couples as is a first quarrel.

Ellen knew it not, but Augusta's image often and often rose up between husband and wife, and would not be driven back; whilst Ellen's very caresses were a source of pain to him, so much he felt himself a debtor to her love. There was a void in his breast which she could never wholly fill; he himself complained of a dearth of intellectual recreation, and when Henry Liverseege suggested a return to painting, he fell back upon his advice.

The fact is he needed to be alone, to have a place where

he could shut himself up with himself, whether to indulge in day-dreams or to discipline his soul, or to think out the ideas of art, trade, or social economy which floated through his brain, and were dispersed by actual business or fireside chat; such a sanctum as had been his so many years in Mosley Street; but, self-conscious, he had shrunk from making the proposal, afraid to wound his devoted wife by showing a desire to isolate himself. The young artist's open remark was enough for Ellen. At once a small room, or rather closet, partitioned off from a large one, at the top of the house, was set apart for his use. He shelved one wall for books, set up an office-desk, carried thither easel, papers, and painting materials; enclosed the fly-leaf of his father's Prayer-book within glass and a black frame, suspending it on the wall before him as a sacred relic, and there, after warehouse hours, he was wont to shut himself in, and almost forget that he was a married man. But this room acted as a safety-valve.

Luckily, in Ellen's eyes, Jabez could do no wrong; he was gentleness itself in all his comportment towards her, and the love which had sprung to life unsought, and lived so long without encouragement, asked but slight return to sustain it. It was treason for Mrs. Chadwick to hint that Jabez was "unsocial," or gave them "too little of his company." She was ever ready to resent it with the reply that—

"If he is not dull shut up there by himself, I am sure we three have no right to complain of dulness down here together;" yet if we analysed her heart very closely there were longings and yearnings for his society known only to herself.

It was judged advisable, for the further introduction and extension of Ashton, Chadwick, and Clegg's business, that one of the partners should travel occasionally as their commercial representative; and naturally this duty devolved upon the active junior, whose capacity for the undertaking revealed itself not only in heavy remittances and a full order-book, but in a paucity of bad debts. Of course he travelled with a horse and gig for the carriage of samples, and now and then he would take Ellen with him on a short journey, an indulgence which appeared to fill the cup of her delight. And altogether the marital yoke in a few months adjusted itself to their shoulders very naturally.

It was during their absence on one of the earliest of these journeys that an event occurred which set the indignant blood of Jabez on the boil, and showed there was a fire smouldering, not extinguished.

The Aspinall home at Fallowfield was an ancient, many-gabled grange, with mullioned windows, recessed window-seats, expansive two-leaved entrance arched above; noble hall, with trophies from the hunting-field; grand staircase, with massive carved oak balusters, flights of broad low steps, and wide square landings; long corridors, three or four rooms of magnificent proportions, and clusters of little ones grouped around unsuspected passages and stairs; open fire-places recently enclosed, and double doors to the chief chambers. Antiquity had set its seal upon the place, and filled the panelled rooms with quaint or obsolete furniture and adornments, as each successive generation had left its quota. High-backed chairs, sofas of grotesque device with dim worsted-work cushions and covers, heavy draperies of silk or velvet, and tables with legs of all possible patterns.

It had come to the former Mrs. Aspinall from her ancestors, and from her to her son on his marriage; consequently this was the home proper of Laurence and his wife, although they had a suite of rooms set apart for them at Ardwick, and Mr. Aspinall would fain have had his fascinating daughter-in-law abide there always, instead of making his house a mere convenience for visiting in town.

Stabling and other outhouses were attached, the gardens were well laid out, there was a good quantity of grass land, all enclosed within a high wall, and it lay away from the main road. Mr. Aspinall's carriage was a close one, for service as well as show. Mr. Laurence, on his accession to his mother's property and his wife's dowry, added to other extravagances not a like carriage, but a new Tilbury, and astonished the crowd by driving tandem.

Whitsuntide is the great annual festival of Manchester. It is the race week, the time when the Sunday-school children dress in their best to walk in procession and have excursional treats into the country. In 1823 Whit-Sunday fell on the 18th of May, when the hawthorn scented the air, and cherry-blossom snowed on the carriage which Mr. Aspinall sent for his daughter-in-law, that she might witness from his drawing-room windows the interesting spectacle on the Green, and preside over the hospitalities of his open house during the week. At that time, as now, Monday was the day set apart for the children of all the Established Church Schools to assemble at the Collegiate Church, sing anthems, and thence defile in long procession six abreast, attended by their respective clergy and teachers, until they reached the Green, where the girls, in their white caps and frocks, were ranged within the enclosure round the Pond, the boys forming a dark cordon around them, and the crowd a motley one beyond. And then from the multitudinous young throats poured forth anthems of praise in a volume of swelling harmony which hushed to silence the listening birds above them.

Augusta, not in robust health, lay on a couch by the window and looked on, her father-in-law watching her and anticipating her wants with the homage of old-world gallantry, for young Mrs. Aspinall was becoming an important person in his eyes.

Nor was Laurence much less attentive. He had been on his best behaviour for some time, and would scarcely let the wind of heaven blow too roughly upon her.

At that period Manchester races were held on Kersal Moor, an extensive tract of land generously set apart for the purpose by the owner, Miss Byrom.

"The glass of fashion and the mould of form," was the handsome man who patted Augusta's shoulders and stooped down to kiss her on Wednesday, the first race day; but it was with something more than a shade of anxiety she saw him draw on his buckskin gloves, take the long reins, and mount his high Tilbury, with Bob beside him, and dash round the lower end of the Green at a canter.

Evening came to verify her fears. Back from Kersal Moor came the tandem and the tandem's master, but the biped was *ebrius*. He was in that stage of self-satisfied elation which a contradictory word would change to fierceness, and the whim of the hour was to drive his wife to Fallowfield, and show her how dexterous a whip he was, and that not Ducrow could manage a tandem better than he.

It was in vain she or his father pleaded her delicate health, the height of the vehicle, the shaking she would sustain; he laughed at her fears, then fiercely insisted, and not daring to disobey, she was hoisted to her perilous seat.

In much alarm, Mr. Aspinall mounted Bob on a saddle-horse to follow. The roads were dotted with vehicles and people, the latter shouting and singing, or muttering tipsy oaths, as the fortune of the day inclined them. Laurence proved his dexterity in guiding his far-off leader through all intricacies, but so close did wheel often come to wheel that Augusta's heart seemed to leap into her throat, and her teeth chattered, although it was May.

After they turned off from the Stockport Road at Longsight, they "spun along at a rattling pace," as he said; but she had to hold by the rail to keep her seat, notwithstanding which, at the sharp angle by Birch Fold, the vehicle gave a lurch which almost pitched her off. At their own gate there was an abrupt stoppage for opening, their return being unexpected. Then the foremost horse refused to obey the rein and canter up the drive. Laurence plied his whip, which did not mend the matter, and but that Bob and the gardener were there to soothe the animals, and lead them to the house, worse might have followed.

As it was, Mrs. Laurence Aspinall was half-dead with fear and the shaking. She was lifted down and carried, almost insensible, into the house. Cicily and one of the maids got her to bed, whilst Aspinall himself, calling groom and gardener from the stables into the drawing-room, sat down to have a drinking bout with *them*.

Presently Cicily put a white face in at the door, and beckoned forth Bob, whom no drink seemed to affect, and sent him off as fast as four legs could carry him, to bring back a doctor, and acquaint Mr. Aspinall and the Ashtons that his young mistress was very ill.

In less time than might have been expected, Mr. Aspinall's carriage brought to the Grange that gentleman, Mrs. Ashton, and Mr. Windsor, a young Quaker practitioner from Piccadilly. A competent nurse from the Infirmary was on the box.

There was no doubt she was in a critical state, but the immediate danger was warded off; and though Augusta was not able to leave her room in the interim, the scent of June's roses came in at the open windows before her baby was born, when penitent Laurence went into raptures over wife and son.

For two or three days he hovered about the house, nervously anxious lest any sound should disturb the young mother. He saw that every domestic was shod with list, stopped the great hall clock, and had the rolled-up carpets laid down on the polished oaken stairs.

Four days sufficed. On the fifth he rode off to town on Black Ralph on a pretence of business; but very little did Cannon Street see of Mr. Laurence that day. With every acquaintance he met was a glass to be drunk, "to wet the child's head." At the Scramble Club, where he dined, he paid for two or three bottles of wine, also "to wet the child's head," according to the practice of the club. Riding home, he stopped at the "George and Dragon," Ardwick Green, and went through the same process.

There some one remarked that he was too drunk to stand, much less ride home, when he swore with an oath that he would show them how he could ride; he and Black Ralph were equal to anything. And then, amid roars of derisive laughter, he flung out another oath, and laid a wager which was regarded merely as the boasting of drunken braggadocio.

He had kissed his wife's pale lips on leaving in the morning, and she faintly implored him to be home early—she did not dare add, "and sober." Towards nightfall she began to listen for his return. Hour after hour went by, and at one in the morning she heard the great gates and the door thrown open for their impatient master by the watching servants, and the strong steed come tearing up the gravel—ay, and on up the broad, flat steps, clattering through the great oaken hall, and, urged with whip and spur, and a madman's voice, mount the freshly-carpeted stairs, cross the landing at a stride, and driving back the affrighted nurse, enter that sick chamber where, with her baby at her side, lay the fair young wife, gasping and shrinking with terror, and there stand with quivering flanks and panting nostrils, as the reckless rider on his back cried in exultation—

"By G—d, I've done it!"

He had done it. No matter what noise accompanied the removal of horse and rider, the wife, whom in his sober hours he professed to love so passionately, lay insensible to sight or sound, and wakened only to a morrow of delirium.

CHAPTER THE FORTY-FIFTH.

WOUNDS INFLICTED AND ENDURED.

THE spark lies cold in the flint until it is struck; and Ellen had not believed her quiet husband capable of so much passionate indignation as burst from him on the receipt (at Sheffield) of the details just given.

"Brute! ruffian!" burst from his lips, as the letter he had crushed in his grasp fell to the floor; and with a stamp he rose to his feet, pressed one hand across his knitted brows, and paced the dingy carpet from end to end in a state of restless perturbation, his wrath finding vent in epithets and invectives foreign to his tongue.

"Whatever is the matter, Jabez, love?" Ellen asked in amazement.

"Oh, Ellen, dear! that brute Aspinall——." He could get no further. Feeling choked his utterance.

She picked up the crumpled letter, and with almost equal exasperation and pain made herself mistress of its contents, in her womanly indignation and love for her cousin losing sight of her husband's excessive emotion.

Jabez left his journey unfinished, and drove back home with all speed. Ellen shared with Mrs. Ashton and her own mother the anxious watch in that large dim room, where the favourite of the family tossed her head from side to side, and muttered incoherent words.

In the sudden emergency, Bob the old groom's recommendation of his own daughter as a wet-nurse for the poor frail baby passed without cavil. Not until long afterwards was it known that Sarah Mostyn was the last woman to have entered that house, and on such a footing.

One month, two months wore out before Augusta rallied, and Mr. Windsor, whose medical creed was to "let nature take its course," pronounced her out of danger, and fit for the removal contemplated by her friends, and resisted by Laurence. Double doors, however, could not exclude outer sounds, and so long as she shrank and shuddered at every crunch on the gravel, every echo of his raised voice, recovery was retarded. So the elder Mr. Aspinall, exasperated with his son, and most solicitous for the welfare of his son's charming wife, added his dictum to that of the doctor, offered his own carriage for her conveyance, and threatened to disinherit Laurence if he interfered.

Once in her childhood's home she amended rapidly, but with increasing strength came maternal yearnings for her infant, still in charge of the wet-nurse at Fallowfield. A hackney-coach was sent to bring Sarah Mostyn with the child to its mother; but not a step would the nurse budge. She had no orders from her master, and the master paid her wages, and she "shouldna tak' orders from annybody else." Messages were sent, and notes were written to Laurence, which he tore to shreds; but he kept away from his wife, and kept back the child.

At length she pined so much for her "dear babe," that Mr. Ashton and Jabez together sought Laurence out in one of his haunts (a tavern near Cockpit Hill), to prevail on him to let Augusta have her boy with her.

"Mrs. Aspinall herself deserted her child," he replied, all the more haughtily, seeing that Jabez was Mr. Ashton's seconder. "When Mrs. Aspinall thinks fit to return home to her maternal and wifely duties, she will find the nursery door open, and her son in trustworthy care. A true wife's place is by her husband's hearth."

"Yes, sir, when the husband is a true man," replied Jabez, with decision.

"And who dares to say I am not a true man?" retorted Laurence boldly.

"I do!" promptly answered the other. "No true man would have imperilled his wife's life by a reckless drive in the dark night in a tandem Tilbury! Only a reckless madman or a ruffian would have forced a horse into a wife's sick-chamber, to drive her delirious with terror!"

"And pray, sir," haughtily responded the other, "how long has Mrs. Aspinall made *you* her confidant?"

"I have not the honour of Mrs. Aspinall's confidence," answered Jabez sturdily, looking him full in the face; "such facts are trumpet-tongued."

"Just so," put in Mr. Ashton, drawing his arm through that of his junior partner. "And the fact that Augusta shrinks at your name has spoken so loudly to us that if ever she sits on your hearth again it won't be with my consent. Come away, Clegg."

After this declaration, Aspinall changed his tactics. He wrote to his wife, requesting her return; then entreating it; and finally went in person to beseech her to "come back," vowing to "atone for the past with the devotion of a life."

The young mother yearned for her babe, the tender-hearted wife could not resist the appeal of the husband whom, with all his faults, she yet loved; and, regardless of the previsions of her mother, or the entreaties of her father, she allowed him to drive her home again to the Grange.

Her first thought was the nursery. There she found, in addition to her own boy, drawing its sustenance from the nurse's breast, a well-dressed child, some two years old, playing with a wooden milkmaid rattle on the rug. Something in the child's face and auburn curls made her ask, "Sarah, whose child is that?"

"Mine. Whose should it be?" was the pert answer; and the boldness of the woman's manner checked further inquiry. But Augusta's heart had received a shock which shook the pedestal on which her idol sat enthroned.

For a short space Laurence kept terms with his wife, and before her father or strangers he was her most devoted slave, but she underwent a species of slow torture in secret.

She soon found that Sarah Mostyn was mistress of the house as well as of the nursery, and that Sarah Mostyn's child was of as much importance as her own baby-boy.

Then Laurence filled the Grange with his riotous associates, and compelled his wife to do the honours of his table, though their oaths and conversation overpowered her with disgust. And if one, flushed with wine, or more bold than the rest, paid her a compliment, or looked too warm an admiration, he was sure to find his way to her side with his common undertone threat—"D——n you, madam, you shall smart for this!"—a threat always accompanied with sly pinches, which left their marks beneath her sleeves. Then, straightway, "my dear," or "my love," would be asked, in the blandest of tones, to sing a song, play a rondo, or perform some act of courtesy for the very guest who had excited his jealousy.

They had few lady visitors. The neighbourhood was remote from town, and sparsely inhabited. Mr. Laurence Aspinall's reputation was as a yellow flag to warn gentlewomen who had daughters or husbands to lose against close intimacy with their neighbours of the Grange. Pitying the isolation of one so formed to adorn society, Mr. Aspinall gave mixed parties at Ardwick Green in the name of Mrs. Laurence, when the splendour of her attire and the assiduous attention of her husband set rumour to contradict rumour. But save on an occasional family gathering, she saw few of her own sex at Fallowfield.

And her position in her own home was rendered intolerable by the continued presence of Sarah Mostyn, who, at first familiar, then impertinent, had become at last openly defiant.

It was not until all efforts to keep the nurse in her proper place had failed, that Augusta appealed to Laurence to discharge her, the woman having refused to take a dismissal from anyone but her master.

"Tchut!" said he, "I'll soon settle that business!" and forthwith stalked to the nursery, whence his voice was heard in loud command; but the result was not the woman's removal, only a temporary submission, to be followed by fresh rebellion, and the confirmation of Augusta's worst suspicions. How often did the aggrieved wife then recall her thoughtless declaration to her mother, that her "husband's heart must hold *her* and *her only*," not even business to share in its possession! And how thankful she would have been to have had no rival then but business! She was finding the bed she had made for herself a woefully hard one; but she did not succumb readily, she had high spirits and a buoyant nature, and would hardly admit to herself how much she suffered or how great a mistake she had made.

But Cicily, that most faithful of faithful followers, cognisant of her mistress's wrongs long before her mistress, paid Sarah Mostyn off in her own coin on various occasions, and took care that through one means or other the Ashtons should know what a life their darling led.

Amongst his other little peculiarities Mr. Laurence was an epicure, and one of his favourite tit-bits was that spongy lining of a goose's frame known as the *soul.* It chanced at a family dinner, rather more than a year after Augusta's return home, that a fine stubble goose formed part of the bill of fare, and Cicily, who had long owed him a grudge for his heartless treatment of her young mistress, determined to pay him off, and expose him before the whole company. A good caterer for a dainty palate, Cicily knew her power and privileges, but in this case she overshot the mark.

One of the accomplishments of that generation was dexterous carving, and Laurence prided himself on being able to dismember a large fowl without once shifting his fork. The goose was set before himself, and duly helped, but, lo! when his knife would fain have extracted his favourite morsel it scraped bare bones.

The flat bell-rope was pulled violently. Cicily was summoned, and Cicily, in clean linen cap and apron, stood in the doorway curtseying respectfully.

"What have you done with the soul of this goose?" he demanded, in a tone of suppressed passion.

Cicily came a step or two forward with an aspect of marvellous innocence. "Eh, sir, it's not a goose, it's a gonder, and *gonders have no souls.*"

Scarcely an individual present but took the covert innuendo, and glances were exchanged across the board; but the look he shot at the woman as, incapable of speech, he waved her to retire, was one never to be forgotten, so much demoniac wrath was concentrated therein.

From the time when Jabez was acknowledged on 'Change as a Manchester man, was admitted into Manchester "society," and had absolutely become a member of the same family as his son, Mr. Aspinall punctiliously invited him with his wife; and Laurence, with widely different feelings, followed suit.

It was not until after the noble exploit to which Augusta so nearly fell a sacrifice that Mr. Clegg could be induced so far to listen to Ellen's desire for conciliation, "now that they were all of one family," as to accept one of these invitations. After that event he was of Mrs. Ashton's mind that "as offenders never pardon," Augusta needed a friend to watch over her. So he left his books, and his brushes, and his schemes for the class amongst whom he had been reared, and (believing his growing affection for his wife, and the babe she had borne him, a sufficient guarantee to his own heart for his own good faith) when the Aspinalls next invited, he accepted.

As previously stated, Augusta had not dropped into tame submission all at once; her old wilfulness would have way at times, and the light shafts of her satire were frequently aimed with effect against her recalcitrant lord. More than once Jabez had averted disastrous consequences by checking her vivacity ere it went too far. But never had he been so thankful for his self-appointed guardianship as on the night when Cicily thought to pay back her darling's wrongs.

To his surprise and pleasure, Ben Travis, just returned from the Continent, was of the party. He had not yet called on the family in Oldham Street, and Jabez never asked him wherefore The cousins had much to talk over, and whilst Laurence Aspinall was pouring wine on his wrath, they discussed a project in which Jabez took an interested part, and which eventuated the following year in the Manchester Mechanics' Institution. But through all their discussion Jabez never once lost sight of Laurence, and from his excessively polite manner to her augured ill for Augusta when

BARLOW HALL.

the restraining presence of friends was removed. He communicated his fears to Travis, and when the good-byes were said, and the various conveyances rolled out between the great gates, a fee to Luke the gardener, who was also gatekeeper, kept them open. A whispered word was sufficient for those who had seen the look Laurence directed across the dinner-table from Cicily to his wife, and who knew the character and disposition of the man.

Mr. Travis's gig and the Ashton's hackney-coach were kept in waiting close at hand, Mrs. Ashton and Ellen, well wrapped up within, waiting anxiously for they knew not what.

Back towards the closed house went Mr. Ashton and the cousins, treading carefully over the gravel. There was a flagged footway round the building, and from the windows of dining and drawing rooms light was still streaming. The last owner had lowered the middle window of the drawing-room as a door of access to the lawn.

As if by accident the curtains had been dragged a little aside in each apartment, and now there were watchers at the apertures. The elder Mr. Aspinall had made an excuse and retired to bed early. Augusta, with a shawl wrapped round her, sat weeping on a sofa in the drawing-room, afraid to go to bed. High words had evidently passed whilst those outside had made their arrangements at the gate.

Presently, into the dining-room sauntered Laurence, with his arm round the shoulders of Sarah Mostyn, the shameless nurse. They sat down to the supper-table; he poured out wine into a goblet, and they drank from the same glass; he fed her with delicacies, and kissed and caressed her with an assured familiarity which told it was no new experience.

Long they lingered drinking and dallying, and the watchers might have thought no danger need be apprehended. Suddenly a word of the woman's, like a match to petroleum, set the whole man ablaze. He rushed from the room with a loud oath, the woman after him, apparently in alarm. The movement her friends made outside in gaining the other window caused Augusta to raise her beautiful head, and at that moment her husband stood before her, brandishing his cavalry sabre, and with his eyeballs glaring, fiercely vociferating, "I'll teach you, madam, to set my servants to insult *me!*" he made a fearful slash at her.

As she sprang aside with a terrified shriek, the old woodwork of the glass-door gave way, and before the tipsy madman could recover his guard to strike a fresh blow, his sabre was wrenched from him, and himself struggling in the grasp of three powerful men, his own gardener being one.

Poor Mr. Ashton's care was his stricken child, whose white shoulders, bathed in blood, were washed by a father's tears. Thankful then was Jabez to have been at hand, and on the alert, with so powerful an ally as Travis; thankful to have saved Augusta's life at any sacrifice of personal feeling; and only himself could tell what his presence under that roof cost him.

Even Laurence had no inkling of it; the marriage of Jabez had closed his jealous eyes. But now, finding in his old opponent an unseen watcher over his wife—her defender when he had least expected—his baffled rage was something terrible to look upon. He fought, struggled, vociferated, threatened, and foamed at the mouth; and Mr. Aspinall, coming thither in his dressing-gown, aroused by the uproar, could barely master his indignation and disgust as he ordered the men-servants, crowding in half-dressed, to "help to bind that murderous maniac down!"

It was well, too, that Mrs. Ashton and Ellen were close at hand, and a vehicle ready to despatch for a surgeon, for Augusta needed all their care.

Before three days were over there was a little coffin in the house, holding a still-born child, and there was a young mother, with a plaistered shoulder, lying, white as her pillow, in a state of coma.

Dr. Windsor having exercised his best skill, as was his wont, left nature to do the rest, and youth and nature between them, did their work effectually.

Fain would Mr. Ashton have removed his child once and for

all. He offered to set up a carriage for her, if she would but leave her husband, and seek a legal separation, insisting that she owed a duty to herself, as well as to her husband. Mr. Aspinall himself begged that she would take up her abode with him, at Ardwick, if only for her own security. He had ceased to find excuses for his son, and his son's charming wife stood high in his esteem.

But Laurence had been beforehand, and with plausible promises and penitential tears, and an adroit parade of her little Willie, also in tears "for mamma," won her over to pardon, and to give him another trial; and not all Mr. Ashton's eloquence, nor Mrs. Ashton's proverbial battery, could win her from her decision.

"My dear mother," said she, "remember you told me 'what could not be cured must be endured,' and that 'as I made my bed so must I lie.' 'It is a long lane,' mother, 'that has never a turn,' I have heard you say many a time; and who knows but Laurence may take a turn now, and reform? At all events, it is my duty to give him a fair trial, and keep my own wayward nature in check, so as not to provoke him; and I must not leave Willie alone with that woman. I think Mr. Clegg would say I am right."

I am afraid she overrated Mr. Clegg's magnanimity much as she overrated her wild husband's promised reformation, for her decision struck a pang into the heart of Jabez, little dreamed of by Ellen. Indeed, it cost him a sore struggle to subdue his concern for Augusta within the bounds of duty to his own wife, whose many virtues were gradually winning their way into his heart, and towards whom his attention never relaxed.

CHAPTER THE FORTY-SIXTH.

THE MOWER WITH HIS SCYTHE.

NEW BAILEY PRISON.

YEARS went by—Laurence had promised to remove Sarah Mostyn, but the woman laughed, refused to stir, and he let her remain—a thorn in his wife's side—training up the boy she had nursed, and whom he idolised, to scorn and jeer at his own mother; whilst her red-haired girl ran about the place wild as a young hare. He broke out from time to time, and his wife was the sufferer; he horse-whipped her, shot at her, and tortured her in every way that malignity could devise.

No wonder that so many tiny coffins of immature babes should be carried from the gates of the Fallowfield Grange. No wonder if Augusta began to compare her lot with Ellen's, and to repent her scorn of a true heart because of its plebeian origin.

Meanwhile, the firm of Ashton, Chadwick, and Clegg prospered beyond expectation, the business tact and integrity of the junior partner alike aiding the extension and stability of the firm. To make way for its expansion more warehouse room was required. The Ashtons, not without a sigh for old association, relinquished their house, and removed to another close at hand in George Street, little less commodious, however much Kezia might grumble at it. This was when Ben Travis, lacking employment for time, mind, and money, offered them to the growing establishment, and his influence as "Co." was accepted. This combination of capital and energy, as Jabez had foreseen, worked wonders for them commercially, enabling them to tide over the trade distress of 1826 with security and advantage. Long before then Jabez had offered to pay Mrs. Clowes her loan, with interest; but she told him she was going to render up her account where, not the coin she had, but that which she had given away, would be put to her credit; and so, as at first proposed, she made it over to her little godson, Joshua Clegg, before she was gathered to the great garner.

But the universal mower reaped a heavier harvest in 1828, when he swept his keen scythe over the bed of the river.

In 1822 Mr. Ashton (one of the first promoters of the Chamber of Commerce), notwithstanding his advancing years, took an active part in the formation of a New Quay Company, for the better navigation of the river Irwell. The company was established, quays were constructed, warehouses erected, boats built, traffic was extended, and the town generally benefited.

In the February of 1828, the axe, the adze, and the hammer made a busy noise in the boat-building yard of the company, and sail-makers were active with their needles; for a flat or barge, destined to convey cargoes of merchandise to and from Liverpool, was to be ready for the launch on the 26th, a day destined to send a thrill of horror tingling through the veins of Manchester, so sad was the catastrophe it closed upon.

The launch of the *Emma* was an event in the annals of the company, and of the town; consequently a large number of spectators assembled, a goodly proportion being admitted to the yard to take part in the ceremony, and to go with the flat on her trial trip under Captain Gaudy.

Mrs. Ashton, saying, "that when the cat's away the mice will play," had decided on remaining at home to watch the mice, but Mr. Ashton compensated himself by taking Ellen and her two elder boys, leaving baby with its grandma; Jabez, detained by business in the counting-house, promising to overtake them before they were on board. Mr. Aspinall, too, was there, and on his arm was his son's wife, and Laurence, with his boy Willie, close beside them. He was too jealous of the admiration she excited, to permit her to go into company, even with his father, unless he had also his own eye upon her, especially where there was a chance of meeting Jabez Clegg. He brought the boy for a treat.

It was quite a gala-day, and as the pleasant company mounted the deck, peered into the low cabin, and chatted gaily to one another, they little thought to how many that would be a launch into eternity.

The boat, a large flat, fully rigged, painted white above the water-line, and black below, with sails set and flags flying, rested in well-greased cradles, her head down; the shipwrights stood ready with their daggers; painters with their cans and brushes to dab her sides as she slid past them; a band upon the quay played lively tunes, and (fatal mischance) the people on deck flocked to one side to listen. The sponsor, a Miss Grimes, with her sister and our friends, advanced to the bows. The word was given; the ready daggers struck away the shores; the boat began to move; Miss Grimes caught firmly the bottle (suspended by a ribbon), and shattered it upon the vessel, proclaiming, with that baptism of wine, the boat was henceforth the *Emma.* Hurrahs and exclamations followed. The bows touched the water, which first splashed the faces, then lifted from their feet the christeners and the Ashton party. The flat had *dipped too deeply*, it heeled over on her *crowded* side, and *sank* with her living cargo clinging and fettering each other in the swirling waters, whilst shrieking spectators looked on helpless from bridge and bank, watching others braver and bolder, or better skilled, rush to the rescue to their own risk.

Who shall picture the horror and confusion of that moment, when some scores of holiday people—men, women, children—were precipitated at one fell swoop into the water, shrieking and clinging to one another with that tenacity of grip proverbial with the drowning?

The bridge, the Old Quay, the open space in front of the New Bailey Prison—railed off at an elevation far above the stream—the steep steps, and the towing-path beneath, were all lined with

NEW BAILEY BRIDGE.

spectators, though the fatal launch was made from a yard lower down the river on the Manchester side. (The New Bailey was in Salford.)

As the vessel struck the ground, shuddering from stem to stern, before turning over on her side, and the final catastrophe was imminent, Laurence (sober for once) snatched his darling boy up in his arms, whispered a hasty word of instruction and confidence, and, regardless of aught besides, sprang with him into the water in the contrary direction, far as possible beyond the eddy and suction, and keeping clear of the struggling wretches who were pulling each other down, swam with him to the towing-path. But not until he had placed Willie under safe charge, beyond danger from the scurrying throng, did he hasten back to attempt the rescue of wife or father; and then neither was to be seen.

Mr. Aspinall had been an able swimmer in his day, and made a bold effort for self-preservation; but cramp seizing his gouty limbs, he was one of the first to disappear and perish, though boats and swimmers had put out to the general rescue.

It was vain to search for individuals; though well was his son's prowess tested that day; more than one drowning wretch he clutched from behind by clothes or hair, and urged forward to the bank, where the Humane Society's men, with ropes and grapnels, were ably seconded by volunteer humanity, and strong hands were outstretched to haul the helpless up.

Ben Travis had waited for Jabez, detained in the warehouse by courtesy to Mr. Gregson, the buyer for Messrs. Leaf, of London, and the two, hurrying to make up for lost time, only reached the New Quay with Nelson at their heels as the hurrahs died out in appalling screams, and the waters of the Irwell closed over all the twain held dearest in life.

With the celerity of light, coats were doffed and shoes cast off, and the two leaped from the stone quay in hope and dread, but the good old dog was before them, its teeth in a child's coat, swimming to the shore. Almost as Jabez touched the water, a sinking woman clutched his legs. With a plunge he freed himself, then catching at her long hair, towed her behind him to the side, and swam back to seek and save his own wife and little ones, if that were possible.

A floating scarf, a mass of matchless brown curls, a hand and arm above the water, and Jabez knew that Augusta Aspinall was sinking there before him. A few strokes brought him to the spot; he dived; a youth was clinging to her skirts, and held her down. One or both must have drowned. With a blow which went to his heart, he freed her, and, catching her beneath the armpit, held her well from him as he made for shore. To the Humane Society's men he yielded her. So far gone, the men shook their heads over the lovely woman, as though she were beyond help. But they bore the dripping lady to the sail-room close at hand, whilst Jabez, taking the precaution to secure a rope to his waist, plunged boldly into the midst of the entangled mass in quest of his own.

It was a vain search; he brought one strange child, and then another to bank, and then a man; but he was again laid hold of when his strength was exhausted; and only for the precautionary rope, he would have given to the greedy river the life Simon Clegg had saved from it.

Travis had the good fortune to rescue Mr. Ashton, but he had been some time in the water, and the old man was far spent; but there was no trace of Ellen or her boys, even though he dived close by the sunken flat, and brought up lifeless bodies in their stead.

Jabez and he could only hope some other of the brave men, putting their own lives in peril, had saved them.

The governor of the gaol had opened his house doors, the recovered dead were carried into the gaol itself, the sail-maker's room was crowded, every tavern near was filled, but no trace was found of Ellen or their sons, and Jabez was like one distraught.

He was but one agitated atom in that seething, surging, frantic crowd, where women shrieked for their husbands, parents for their children, children for their parents; where passing strangers threw themselves into the water to save life, and lost their own; where ignorance lifted the hapless by the heels "to pour the water out" and extinguished the last spark of vitality; and where yelping dogs astray were caught and slaughtered, that medical skill might transfuse the warm blood of the lesser animal into the veins of the human, as a last resource to restore suspended animation. Even gallant old Nelson narrowly escaped falling a sacrifice to the surgeons.

Jabez entered the room where Augusta Ashton was lying, to all appearance, dead—ordinary means of resuscitation having failed, and a surgeon was about so to operate on her from a bleeding spaniel on the ground. Jabez shrank with a strange loathing; in an instant bared his arm to the doctor's lancet; and if he did not give his life to serve her, as he had once said, he gave his life's blood to save her; and as the warm fluid passed from his quick veins to hers, he saw the blue, quivering lids tremble, light pass into the brown eyes, breath part the blue lips once more, and from the depths of his anguished heart he thanked God as a faint "Jabez" indicated recognition as well as returning animation.

He had restored a wife to thankless Aspinall; but who should restore to him the darling boys who had crept about his knees and round his heart, and the good wife who had won a place there, in spite of fate, by her own patient, but intense, love?

The *Emma* was raised and floated, so little damaged that she was speedily ready for use, and continued so for many years. In her cabin were found the remains of Ellen and her sons, where the childish curiosity of the elder one had doubtless led all three; but they were raised from the water only to be committed to the earth, and covered up out of sight and hearing for evermore; and never did Jabez know fully all she had become to him until he stood with Travis by the side of an open grave, and heard the clods rattle on the coffin lid. She was all as one then to the man who had worshipped her, and the man she had worshipped; and though the babe she had left behind was nearer to the one, it would be hard to say to which little Nelly was the dearer in the aftertime.

MRS. ABEL HEYWOOD (MISS GRIMES).

From a Photograph.

Including the bodies found beneath the flat and those laid out in the gaol and elsewhere for inquest, thirty-three lives were sacrificed on the altar of the *Emma;* and of these must be reckoned the brave men who cast their lives away to rescue others.

Among the early saved were the Captain, Miss Grimes, and her sister, the two latter being hastily conveyed home in a private carriage (mayhap Mr. Aspinall's), with coats and cloaks wrapped around their saturated garments.

Good, kind, genial Mr. Ashton never recovered from the effects of his long immersion. He was a man far advanced in years, and the shock was too much for him. He hobbled about the warehouse, snuff-box in hand, a few months, and then dropped asleep in his easy chair after a game of cribbage with Jabez—never to wake again.

And then the excitement and agitation consequent on the loss of his dear Ellen and her romping boys having brought on Mr. Chadwick a fresh attack of paralysis, which left him still more helpless (though he survived many years to pet and spoil Ellen's baby-girl), Mrs. Ashton, lonely in her large house, proposed that her sister's family (Jabez included) should join her in George Street; but when she would have said "the more the merrier," the words died on her lips. Who were they but the survivors of two wrecked households?

After a little hesitation the offer was accepted, and the whole family gathered in their shorn proportions under one roof. But there was another proposition from another quarter, to which there was considerably more demur. Mrs. Hulme, in a warm, grey-duffle-cloak, for the preservation of her new mourning, travelled from Whaley Bridge, to ask as a favour that baby Nelly should be committed to her care.

"You see, Mrs. Chaddick, th' poor little babby'll thrive better yond than here i' th' smooak; an' aw'd fain do summat for Mester Clegg, he have done so much fur feyther an——"

Jabez interrupted her.

"Hush! Mrs. Hulme. I owe life, and all that life has given, to your father and yourself. What little I have done in return has been but dust in the balance. Yet as it is your desire, and I know baby would be best in your hands, if grandmother will consent to part with her, Nelly and her nurse shall go back with you for the coming summer months."

And so, though parting with Ellen's baby seemed parting with Ellen over again, the little blossom went away to other blossoms on the healthy hill-side.

Tom Hulme was no longer overlooker, but responsible manager at the Whaley Bridge Mill, with a good salary; and if Jabez gratefully traced his fortune back to his cradle, so too did the Hulmes trace their amended position to the same source. But Bess more immediately referred to the benefit Simon Clegg had derived from the Buxton Baths, whither Jabez had sent him year after year, for the relief of his rheumatism, and to his care of steadfast little Sim. He had first placed the crippled lad with a doctor celebrated for his treatment of bodily deformities, under whom the boy's bent body had strengthened and straightened considerably, and then removed him for education to the house of a married clergyman, where there were no rough boys to torment him. Jabez knew well what were the amenities of public schools.

CHAPTER THE FORTY-SEVENTH.

THE LAST ACT.

EMPTIES.

THE catastrophe which deprived Laurence Aspinall of a father, and had almost robbed him of a loving, patient wife, would have steadied any man less reckless and selfish than he. But that *he* should rescue strangers, and Jabez save his wife, and that through transfusion the blood of Jabez should course through Augusta's veins, formed a combination of mischances beyond parallel, and the honey was changed to gall. Nay, he was graceless enough to exclaim, in the first burst of his jealous rage, "I would rather she had died outright than have that fellow triumph in her restoration through his means. D—— him!"

And yet there were times when in his uxorious fondness he wholly persuaded himself, and half persuaded her, that his very extravagances arose from excess of love!

His fancied wrongs culminated when first the will of his father, and after a brief period that of Augusta's father, were read and proved.

The former set forth that, disgusted with the ungentleman-like excesses of his son, and convinced that his course of lavish extravagance would end in penury, he had determined to settle on his son's wife, Augusta Aspinall, for her sole use and benefit, the house and premises on Ardwick Green, with all therein contained, together with a sufficient sum in the funds to maintain a befitting state; in the event of her decease, the reversion to pass to any child or children she had or might hereafter bear to his son Laurence. To him he left the residue of his means, and the old business in Cannon Street, with a charge to apply himself to merchandise.

The latter will, though equally stringent, was a much more prolix affair. After a number of legacies, of which Jabez came in for one, Mr. Ashton bequeathed to his wife all other properties whatsoever he died possessed of, together with half his share in the firm of Ashton, Chadwick, Clegg, and Co.; the other half to his beloved daughter, limiting the annual sum she was to draw from the firm, and which was in nowise to pass into the hands of her depraved husband; and Jabez Clegg and Benjamin Travis were appointed executors for the due performance of its provisions.

Imagine the excitement and jealous fury of Laurence Aspinall on thus being set aside even by his own father and superseded by his wife; and as if that were not sufficient degradation, to have Jabez Clegg, whose charity-school face yet bore the impress of his foot, set as his wife's executor, to dole out what he called a "pittance" where he had anticipated a fortune!

It so happened that the early duties of his executorship called Jabez once or twice unexpectedly to Fallowfield, and that on each occasion the master of the mansion was from home.

It might be that the river had washed the roses from Augusta's cheeks so effectually that her complexion had never regained its tone; or it might be that her skin looked white in contrast with the blackness of her bombazine and crape; certain it was that Jabez was struck with the pallor of her countenance, and his inquiry, "Are you not well, Mrs. Aspinall?" was tinctured with alarm.

As a light flush tinged her cheek, then faded away again, and she received him with a timid indecision very unlike her former girlish freedom, a sense of her almost supernal loveliness brought something of the old ache into his heart, and out of respect for himself and her, he hurried over his business, and having obtained the signatures for which he came, mounted his horse and rode back to town, haunted by look, and voice, and manner.

Yet in the integrity of his own heart he had no conception

that her embarrassment was the result of fear—fear of the interpretation her jealous madman of a husband would put on so unwonted a visit.

He thought he saw a smile of malice in the corners of the mouth of the bold woman who met him in the hall, and nodded to him so freely as he passed her on his way out; but no prescient spirit whispered in his ear that his twenty minutes' visit on absolute business would furnish envy and jealousy with a pretext for foul-mouthed slander, for coarse vituperation, for the use of a whip, and for calumnious accusations which cut deeper than its lash.

Cicily, who intervened to save her mistress, might have conveyed some inkling of this to Mrs. Ashton, but Augusta absolutely forbade her sympathetic servant's interference.

"You would do no good, Cicily," she said; "the evil is beyond earthly remedy; you would only distress my dear mother to no purpose, and she has suffered too much on my account already. It cannot last for ever!"

On the next occasion Jabez was accompanied by his joint-executor, but even that fact did not save Augusta from her husband's wrath, and his vile aspersions went far to drive out the last lingering sentiment of affection or regard she had for him. But she clung to her child, and that bound her to her home and him whom in an evil hour she had chosen; though tears fell bitterly on Willie's curly head, when he, like his father, gave her back blows for kisses. And if at times her conscience smote her for her haughty repulse of Jabez by the stair-foot window at Carr Cottage, what wonder? Had not Laurence himself scored his rejected rival's name on her heart with his braces and whip-lash?

She shut the obtrusive memory out with a shudder, and, dropping on her knees, prayed earnestly for strength to bear and to forbear.

Yet much of the cruelty of Laurence at this time arose from another source than causeless jealousy. He had been living far beyond his private means, and was greatly involved. He had calculated on laying his hand on a good round sum, and was disappointed. In order, however, to raise the needful, he sold his father's old-established concern to their head clerk, far below its value. On the Fallowfield estate his friend Barret held a mortgage, and, had it been possible, he would similarly have disposed of Augusta's possessions. Here, however, he was doubly baffled, and he turned on her as the primary cause.

The old law which preserved the woman's absolute right over properties legally settled upon herself, by strange anomaly did not secure to her one guinea of the coin those properties produced.

Well did Jabez watch over Augusta's interest, but his heart ached as he saw her sad countenance, and the greedy triumphant eyes of ever-present Laurence when her dividends were paid in. For, before his very face, Laurence laid his hand upon the money, to squander it as he had squandered his own on Sarah Mostyn and other dissolute companions, leaving his wife without so much as would purchase a pocket-handkerchief.

Then, lest she should make her wrongs known, he kept her a close prisoner at Fallowfield, and, for all the pleasure she had of her Ardwick mansion, she might as well have been without it.

No wonder if each fresh act of personal violence snapped some bond between them, until the only one link to bind her to life and her husband was her boy Willie; whilst the only human trait of Laurence was his fondness for his son, whom he was rapidly ruining with false indulgence, as he himself had been ruined.

It was customary, when the hay-making season came round, for Laurence to gather such friends as his wife or he retained—the married with their children—for a frolic in the hayfields, and the bringing home the last waggon-load in triumph to crown or inaugurate a feast.

On these occasions he had the grace, or the diplomacy, to keep Sarah Mostyn in the background, though she flaunted boldly enough about the house in the presence of his wife, and her child mingled with the children.

The harvest-home of 1831 was attended with the customary festivities, Willie, a rough playmate, was half smothering Nelly Clegg in the hay, or chasing the Walmsleys amongst the haycocks, until the last load was ready, and then the boy insisted that he and his companions should be mounted atop. Shouts and cheers announced their coming to the party in the drawing-room; they came crowding to the windows, and, the glass-door being open, one or two sauntered out on to the flagged walk. Merrily they came along the gravelled drive, under the hot sun, dreaming of no danger, Willie clapping his hands and calling, "Look at us papa," when, right in front of the drawing-room window, the pin which held the body of the cart down, by some means became displaced, the cart tilted up, and hay and children were sent flying.

Beyond a few bruises, none of the children were injured but one; they had fallen amongst hay, or on the spongy lawn; but Willie, the one jewel in the Aspinall casket, pitched with his head on the flagged pavement, and was killed on the spot.

Draw we the curtain over consternation and bereavement, and pass on to results. If a change came over Laurence, it was not for the better. He drank incessantly, became alternately moody and defiant, and added a coping-stone to his offences by placing Sarah Mostyn at his table by the side of his wife, and boldly avowing that her child was his child also.

Then all the woman rose within Augusta, so long cowed and dispirited. She left the table, and, the insult being repeated, again retired in indignation.

Of the servants none had pitied her so much as Cicily, but for whom communication with her friends had been cut off. Often had the former waxed savage over indignities she could neither check nor prevent; but in many little ways the faithful domestic was enabled to ameliorate the condition of her mistress. Now that Mrs. Aspinall—more lovely in her sad womanhood than in her brilliant girlhood—was virtually supplanted, a prisoner under torture in her husband's house, with no tie of motherhood to bind her there, her old nurse, as the mouthpiece of Mrs. Ashton and her aunt Chadwick, had urged upon her once more the necessity for legal separation, and she no longer turned a deaf ear.

When Jabez came to hand over the next quarter's dividends Travis accompanied him, and then Augusta, in the presence of both her executors, demanded and claimed her right to a legal separation from her husband.

Laurence, taken by surprise, started to his feet, then, resuming his seat, said, with a scowl and a contemptuous sneer—

"You had better obtain a divorce, madam, whilst you are about it. Mr. Clegg will not object to the cost, if you can only be made Mrs. Clegg by Act of Parliament."

It was a cruel and uncalled-for sneer, and Travis, firing up, resented it for his friend, who appeared dumbfounded by the suggestion.

"If she *had* been Mrs. Clegg, sir, instead of Mrs. Aspinall, there would have been no necessity now for the interference of friends for her protection!"

"Of course not," sneered Aspinall. "Mr. Clegg is the white hen that never lays away; and now, having favoured you with one of Mrs. Ashton's pithy proverbs, perhaps, gentlemen, you will favour me by taking your departure; this house and this lady are alike my property."

The value he set upon the latter article of property was testified by an immediate application of a horsewhip, so savagely applied that even Bob, and Luke the gardener, drawn thither by Augusta's screams, wrenched the whip from him, and covered her escape, the latter declaring he would "no longer stay an' witness sich wark."

To this man, who was also gatekeeper, Cicily crept at nightfall, and offered him a goodly sum down, out of her own savings, promising a much larger one from Mrs. Aspinall, with the offer of a new situation at Ardwick, if he would only suffer her ill-used mistress to "get clear o' that brute's violence."

The man, to his credit be it told, refused the money, but opened the gate; and, when Laurence wakened from his sodden sleep at noon the next day, wife, cook, and gardener were missing.

The three had walked to Ardwick, and once there, though Augusta found sad havoc had been made in the place, all was her own, carriage included, and the domestics in charge welcomed her with gladness.

Without waiting for even the show of a breakfast, Augusta hurried like a frightened bird to her mother's nest in George Street, where alone she felt secure.

Jabez and Travis were summoned, and when Aspinall, recovering from his stupor, sought his human property at Ardwick, he found the trustee under his father's will—a Mr. Lillie—holding the place for Augusta in right of his trust. And in George Street he was refused admission, Mrs. Ashton justifying her daughter's flight with "self-preservation is the first law of nature. A good Jack makes a good Jill. It is the last straw breaks the camel's back. If you sow the wind, you must reap the whirlwind. He who beats his friend makes an enemy."

He threatened, and she answered—

"Threatened folk live long. You had best, Mr. Aspinall, keep your breath to cool your porridge. Augusta's friends will defend her from her only enemy. Pending separation *you* see her no more."

He never saw her more. The deed of separation was *sealed* but never signed.

With Augusta, all good angels seemed to have flown from Fallowfield. In his demoniac passion, he strove to blacken her character, to find himself met with laughter—his own life had been so chaste! Whilst, as if to refute him, when she took refuge with her mother, Jabez deemed it a point of honour to retreat. Accordingly he took up his temporary abode with Travis, in delicacy towards her, and as a check upon himself. No act, or thought, or word of his must give an evil tongue a chance to foul that spotless woman with its slime.

In the midst of all this, Aspinall's embarrassments increased. Creditors pressed; writs showered in upon him; Barret foreclosed, and men were put in possession of the Grange. He flew to his old remedy, and it drove him mad. Lancaster Gaol for debtors loomed upon him. From his chamber window he beheld a sheriff's officer approach with a warrant. His cavalry-pistols were in his dressing-room. A sharp report rang through the house. Laurence Aspinall, in the prime of life, delirious with drink, driven to desperation by his own profligate excess, set a blood-red seal on the deed of separation.

* * * * *

Ten years had passed from the partnership of Ashton, Chadwick, and Clegg—years in which money well employed had multiplied itself. Jabez was a rich man—a man of influence in the town; no longer the amateur artist, but the patron of art, as well Henry Liverseege and others could have told. As he had been one of the first promoters and directors of the Manchester Mechanics' Institution, so was he now the supporter of the Royal Institution for the Advancement of Art; and seeing farther than Mr. Ashton, who, as a member of the New Quay Navigation Company, had opposed the Act for a railway between Manchester and Liverpool, he threw his energy into the project, and helped to carry it out, his cousin Travis working with him.

His widowerhood had cast a gloom over him for a time, but he left himself small leisure for morbid reflection, and that was cheered by the prattle of his little Nelly. Then came the crash at Fallowfield, and when darkness set upon Aspinall and his deeds, light broke upon the path of Jabez Clegg—at first a mere ray, but he worked the more cheerfully in its light. It was not *hope* for himself; it was merely a joyful consciousness that there was hope and calm in the sky over the head of their fluttering and wounded dove, and that Augusta could now rest in peace with her mother in the house at Ardwick, with no dread of a brutal husband bursting on them unawares.

He came and went as friend and executor, but it was long before it flashed across his comprehension that the fearful ordeal through which Augusta had passed but brought his old master's daughter closer to him; or that the prayer old Simon had taught was being answered to the full. That which was "above rubies" had blessed his life, and kept his human heart warm whilst his "coast had enlarged;" he had been kept from the evil of a wilful and capricious wife; and at last when he had resigned all prospect of setting the purified pearl as a star on his own breast, it dropped into his hand, unsought, unsolicited.

He had schooled his heart, we know. He had married from a sense of duty and grateful compassion. He was a faithful husband to a true wife, and when he lost her he mourned her as a valued friend. But though all the early love of his being had been kept alive and in a ferment by the sufferings of Augusta, as an honourable man he suffered no word or look to betray more than a friend's sympathy. And still he kept as strong a guard over himself, though the tragic end of Laurence had set her free once more.

The last fatal act struck a sensitive chord in Augusta's nature. There was no exultation at release. For a time she lost sight of his profligacy and cruelty, and accused herself of having hastened the catastrophe by leaving him to his own unbridled will and the temptress by his side. She wept for the handsome lover who had captivated her young fancy; she mourned for the besotted soul gone to its account with all its imperfections rampant.

"Let her alone," said Mrs. Ashton to her sister; "the sharpest shower wears itself out soonest; she will come to her senses long before her crape is worn out."

Mrs. Ashton was a true prophetess. For a long time the Fallowfield tragedy cast a shadow over the house at Ardwick, and they led very retired lives. Then harp and piano were heard once more, visitors were admitted, and the mansion that Kezia and Cicily united in declaring "worse than a nunnery," grew bright and cheerful, though the widow's weeds were not cast aside. (Kitty had been laid under the mould whilst Augusta was yet a bride.)

Almost two years had elapsed. Suitors in plenty had been attracted by the wealthy young widow's many charms, her old admirer, Mr. Marsland, among the rest, yet Mrs. Aspinall showed no disposition to change her state; and the one man who had loved her longest and best was not of the number at her feet. He scorned to importune now in his widowerhood for the love withheld when they were both young. He counted age by events, not years.

It was for Augusta *now*, she who had been taught by her very husband's taunts and sneers to think upon the true man she had set aside, to think of him daily and hourly with rapidly strengthening attachment, and think of him as one who had dropped her from the book of his life for ever. Her whole thought was how could she become worthy the love of such a man; yet every day and hour the fear pressed heavily upon her that the quiet virtues of Ellen had driven her out of his heart altogether. Of all her guests he was the one most welcome, most desired, but he was the one she received with most reserve, the one whose stay was briefest, whose visits fewest. "Business" appeared to have more imperative claims on him than when he had his way to make; and Augusta, whose sables had long since been cast aside, seemed to wear them on her heart. The vivacity which had never wholly forsaken her in all her trials, forsook her now—she grew listless and melancholy.

Meanwhile Captain Richard Chadwick had come home on half-pay to brighten up the somewhat dull house in George Street, and comfort the old folk—to say nothing of astonishing Sim and Nelly with his long yarns and adventures. Sim always spent part of his vacations with Mr. Clegg, who well paid back to Bess all her early care for him. He indulged the boy's craving for books and pencils, first implanted by himself, and in which he saw the dawn of his future career. That which in his own case had been repressed and subordinated to trade and money-making, should not be so checked in that boy; and old Simon, to whom the lad appeared a marvel, never ceased to pride himself on his forecast in pronouncing Jabez a "Godsend."

It was during the second summer of her widowhood, when Augusta accompanied her mother (not a whit the less stately than of yore) to Carr Cottage for the first time since her attempted elopement, that the feeling of all she had cast from her, and all that she had brought upon herself, all that might have been, and now never would be, pressed heaviest upon her. She had gone thoughtfully over the old ground, had trod the nettle-grown Lovers' Walk, and sat down on the open window-ledge at the stairfoot as once before, and wept tears of penitent bitterness. How long she sat there she could not tell; she was weeping for a life lost and a love rejected. As once before, the voice of Jabez (whom she imagined eighteen miles away) broke upon her solitude, but now it thrilled through her.

There was a light touch upon her shoulder.

"Mrs. Aspinall?"

She shuddered.

"Oh! don't call me by that name—*here!*" broke from her, imploringly.

"What name shall I call you by?" half wonderingly; then, in in a lower semi-smothered tone of entreaty—"Augusta?"

Lower sank her head in her hands; but there was no answer save her sobs. It was thus he had addressed her there once before.

"Augusta!"—and this time the hand on her shoulder shook —"Augusta—dear Augusta, once on this very spot I found you weeping thus, and I begged to be allowed to share your grief. I told you I would give my life to serve you—what I said then I repeat now—I *would* give my life to serve you, and you *know* it!" He gently drew one hand from her agitated face. "Tell me your trouble,. as you would tell it to a brother!"

A brother—ah, that was it! She drew her hand back, but she

did not rise, and her sobs seemed to choke her.

Again he took her hand, and his other arm went round her soothingly, protectingly. "Oh, Augusta, this is inexpressibly painful to me. I love you, as never man loved woman. Can you not tell me what troubles you?" and the earnest tenderness of his voice made strange music in her ears.

He had seated himself on the narrow window-ledge beside her, and now he thought she was about to punish his presumption and quit him haughtily as before.

But no! She only slid from his arm to his very feet, and cried, with still covered face—

"Oh, Jabez—*dear* Jabez, forgive me all I made you suffer here; for oh! I have repented bitterly."

He was stunned, bewildered. His passionate declaration of love was made as a claim to her confidence, not to her affection; and now—"*dear* Jabez!" Did he hear aright? For an instant he was silent from very incapacity to speak. Her bent head touched his knees.

Slowly, reverently, as if she had been a saint, with every nerve of his strong frame trembling with emotion, he raised her from the ground; but no arm went round her now. He held both her hands in his, and looked steadfastly down upon her; but no answer made he to her plea for pardon. Constraint in voice and words was apparent and painful, but emotion grew too strong for control.

"Augusta, what is the meaning of this? For God's sake do not mislead me! I seem on the threshold of Heaven or madness. Is it possible that I, plain Jabez Clegg, can be 'dear' to you?"

"Dearer than life!"

Clear, full, and earnest came the words from her soul, clear and truthful were the eyes that now sought his.

"Thank God!"

He held her in his arms with a straining clasp, which told how long they had quivered to embrace her so. His eyes lit up with an intensity of love she knew not he could feel, and never had his lips met woman's in such fond kisses as he pressed on hers.

The concentrated love of years seemed gathered to a focus then. "Life of my life!" he called her, and she knew and felt it was so.

If the shade of the departed Ellen could have looked upon them there, remembering how she had rushed to his embrace in that very spot, and how different had been the kiss imprinted on her wifely brow, would she have reproached him? I wis not.

Is it needful to add that, before the summer waned, the Manchester Man, rapidly rising into public note and favour, entered into another partnership; or that Jabez Clegg, in right of Augusta his wife, took possession of the mansion at Ardwick, to the satisfaction of Mrs. Ashton, who said, "Better late than never!" Or to tell how the trade of Ashton, Chadwick, Clegg and Co. continued to extend? Or that Travis remained Co. to the end of the chapter—the children's Co. never taking a wife unto himself.

THE END.

Mrs. G. L. Banks (1821-1897)

Author of the book 'The Manchester Man' which captures so much of Manchester's history.

Mrs. G. Linnaeus Banks was born Isabella Varley on Sunday, March 25th, 1821 at 10 Oldham Street, Manchester. Her father was James Varley, a chemist of Marriott's Court who was a very political man. His wife, Amelia, and his daughter would have helped him in his campaigning and distribution of leaflets.

She always claimed that she was baptised by the Rev. Joshua Brookes who she thrust into the limelight with her 'Manchester Man' novel, but close scrutiny shows that our Isabella was baptised on August 22nd, 1821. She is number 2053 on the rolls of the Collegiate Church, but the signature is that of Cannon Wray, Brookes' assistant. Joshua may have been there just looking on, we will never know, but her mother told her she was baptised by 'Jossie' and that was good enough for Isabella and good enough for us. He was an old man at the time so maybe he just assisted at the August baptisms. On Nov 11th the same year, he died.

At 16 years of age she had a poem accepted for publication, in the Manchester Guardian, and by 22, a book of poetry called 'Ivy Leaves' had been published. She joined the Ladies Committee of the Anti-Corn Law League as their youngest member and was a useful and active contributor to the cause.

She was introduced to a young reporter, George Linnaeus Banks, and they married on December 12th 1845. Almost immediately they set off round the country as George accepted various posts on newspapers, working his way up to editor over a period of 15 years.

Isabella was able to write articles for her husband's newspapers and developed her writing style. She gave birth to 8 children, but lost 5 of them, one of whom was a well-grown boy. To come to terms with her grief it was suggested she write a full length novel, and at the age of 44 she produced 'God's Providence House'. This book centres upon the plague in Chester, describing how a single house was spared whilst every other house lost at least one member of the family.

She was never robust physically, and after her second book her doctors told her that 'she must not expect too much of life'. She wrote to a friend in 1870 saying that she was "starting to write the book she had always wanted" to produce, centred on Manchester but said that she did not know if she would have the strength to complete it. Happily, she did complete it, and although her doctors gave her 6 months to live during a serious illness in 1868, she survived for a further 19 years.

"The Manchester Man" first appeared as a serial in Cassell's 'Monthly Magazine', during 1874 and did not appear in complete, book form until 1876. It is undoubtedly the work for which Mrs Linnaeus Banks is remembered, despite her other work. It is the book into which she poured all of her memories and knowledge of Manchester to weave a tale that includes an account of the Peterloo Massacre amongst many other scenes from the city's history.

She loved Manchester, and wrote with real warmth of the small streets, the Collegiate Church and of the rich social life of the times. Despite the factual basis of the book it remains a novel, however, and her characters are freely introduced into historical situations in order to expand and improve the narrative.

Linnaeus himself died on May 3rd, 1881 and Isabella had sixteen years of widowhood in very poor circumstances. Manchester friends rallied often and there were collections for her among members of Manchester's Literary and Philosophical Society as well as a "Testimonial Performance on behalf of Mrs Linnaeus Banks," at the Comedy Theatre, Manchester, on Saturday, September 21, 1895.

She was a good letter writer and it's from these letters that we get an insight into her life of illness and pain and her struggles to make ends meet. It's also in these letters that we learn of her intention to produce a large version of her best-loved novel "The Manchester Man", complete with illustrations. For some years she had been asking friends and people in the book trade in Manchester for portraits and illustrations to go in the illustrated edition. It was the last thing she did, and she wrote and told friends of her joy when it appeared, published by Abel Heywood from Manchester in 1896, just a few months before she died.

It is that very special edition that we have reproduced here and we hope the book will become as special to you as it was to her.

Isabella died on 4th May 1897 and was buried alongside her husband in Abney Park Cemetery, London.